CALM
Before
THE STORM

Crossings of Promise

Historical fiction with a touch of romance

Janice L. Dick
Calm Before the Storm

Hugh Alan Smith
When Lightning Strikes

CALM
Before
THE STORM

JANICE L. DICK

Herald
Press

Waterloo, Ontario
Scottdale, Pennsylvania

National Library of Canada Cataloguing in Publication Data
Dick, Janice L., 1954-
    Calm before the storm

(Crossings of promise)
Includes bibliographical references.
ISBN 0-8361-9201-X

    1. Mennonites—Russia—History—20th Century—Fiction.
    I. Title II. Series
PS9557.I2543C3 2002   C813'.6   C2001-904060-1
PR9199.4.D53C3 2002

The paper used in this publication is recycled and meets the minimum requirements of American National Standard for Information Sciences—Permanence of Paper for Printed Library Materials, ANSI Z39.48-1984.

CALM BEFORE THE STORM
Copyright © 2002 by Herald Press, Waterloo, Ont. N2L 6H7
    Published simultaneously in USA by Herald Press, Scottdale, Pa.
    15683. All rights reserved
Canadiana Entry Number: C2001-904060-1
Library of Congress Catalog Control Number: 2001098021
International Standard Book Number: 0-8361-9201-X
Printed in the United States of America
Cover art by Barbara Kiwak
Cover design by Sans Serif Design, Inc.
Inside design by Gwen M. Stamm

10 09 08 07 06 05 04 03 02 01 10 9 8 7 6 5 4 3 2 1

To order or request information, please call 1-800-759-4447 (individuals); 1-800-245-7894 (trade). Website: www.mph.org

Preface

Calm *Before the Storm* is a work of fiction, but it is based on truth. My father was born in the Molotschna village of Fuerstenverder in 1918 (see map of Molotschna Colony, p. 9), and my mother's birthplace was Orenburg. My husband's great-grandfather, who inspired the character of Heinrich Hildebrandt, owned three estates in South Russia. The beauty of the "Golden Years" and the devastation brought by World War I and the Revolution are well documented.

My parents' birthplaces are gone, but I hope someday to walk along Nevsky Prospekt, watch the Neva flow, and stand in the shadow of St. Isaac's. Until then, we will have to imagine together.

I give thanks to God for his love and guidance in this project; to my husband and best friend, Wayne, for his love and support; to our children, Christiaan and Lorraine Mau, John and Wendy Hiebert, and Dennis Dick, for believing in me and praying for me; to my mom and greatest fan, Margaret Enns, and to the memory of my dad, John Enns—I think he would have been proud; to Wayne's parents, Walter and Edna Dick, for many prayers; to the Carlton Trail Writers for their encouragement; to Wayne Schmidt for rescuing my work when my ancient computer crashed; to Martin and Janice Whitbread of Living Books for ideas, contacts, and publicity; and to Mary Meyer, my editor, for polishing my work and bringing the project to completion.

—Janice L. Dick

This book is dedicated to my Lord Jesus,
and to you, the reader.
My prayer is that you will meet him
in these pages.

Main Characters

Heinrich Hildebrandt . . . . .wealthy estate owner
Elizabeth Peters Hildebrandt . . . . .his deceased wife
Katarina (Katya) Hildebrandt . . . . .his eldest daughter
Maria (Mika) Hildebrandt . . . . .his second daughter
Peter Hildebrandt . . . . .his adolescent son
Nicholai (Kolya) Hildebrandt . . . . .his younger son
Anna (Anya) Hildebrandt . . . . .his youngest daughter
Johann (Hans) Sudermann . . . . .teacher from Kleefeld,
Molotschna
Paul Gregorovich Tekanin . . . . . . .Russian peasant, Johann's
lifelong friend
Susannah Loewen . . . . .nurse at Bethany Institute
Gerhard Warkentin . . . . .administrator at the Institute

Glossary

Anabaptist—lit. "rebaptizer"; one who is baptized as an adult, upon confession of faith

bolshevik—lit. "majority"; original communist party believing in socialism by revolution

bourgeoisie—middle class

Cossacks—historically nomadic horsemen; troops loyal to the tsar

dessiatine—measurement of land area; 2.7 acres

droschka—Russian, a buggy for traveling

Duma—Russian parliament, "elected" but virtually powerless because of lack of cooperation by the tsar

hansom—a two-wheeled covered carriage with the driver's seat above and behind

liebchen—German, for "sweetheart"

malodushni—Russian, for "coward"

zweibach—German, for a sweetened bread that is sliced and toasted until dry and crisp

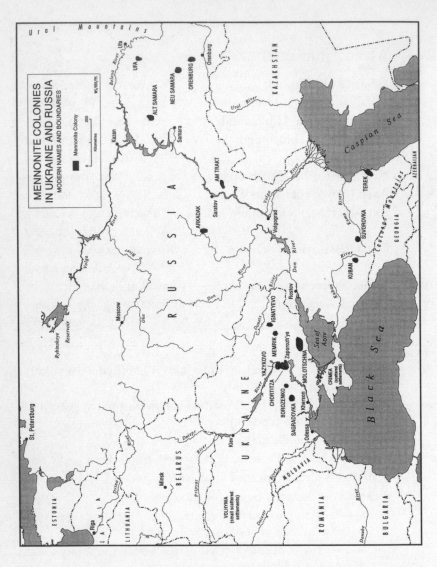

Map credits:

"Mennonite Colonies in Ukraine and Russia," reprinted from *Mennonite Historical Atlas*, William Schroeder and Helmut T. Huebert, p. 14. Springfield Publishers, Winnipeg, Man.: 1996. Used by permission.

"Crimea," reprinted from *Mennonite Historical Atlas*, p. 28.

"Molotschna Colony," reprinted from *Mennonite Historical Atlas*, p. 34.

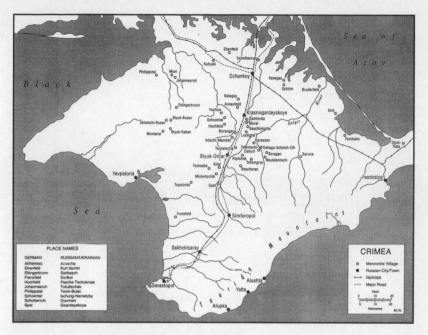

CRIMEA

PLACE NAMES

GERMAN	RUSSIAN/UKRAINIAN
Annenfeld	Annenka
Ebenfeld	Kurt Itschki
Ettingerbrunn	Saribasch
Franzfeld	Dortkul
Hochfeld	Pascha-Tschokmak
Johannesruh	Tokultschak
Philippstal	Temir-Bulat
Schoental	Ischung-Nemetzky
Schottenruh	Dyurmen
Spat	Gwardeyskoye

Legend:
○ Mennonite Village
● Russian City/Town
Railroad
Major Road

Verst
0 10 20
Kilometres
0 10 20
WS/76

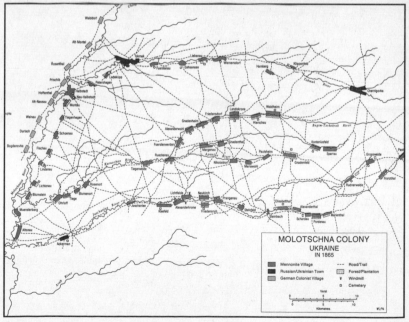

MOLOTSCHNA COLONY
UKRAINE
IN 1865

Legend:
▨ Mennonite Village
▨ Russian/Ukrainian Town
▨ German Colonist Village
--- Road/Trail
▨ Forest/Plantation
▼ Windmill
□ Cemetery

Verst
0 5 10
Kilometres
0 5 10
WS/76

9

When you eat and are satisfied, be careful that
you do not forget the LORD.
Deuteronomy 6:11b, 12

Prologue
Near Asperen, The Netherlands, 1569

The rough stone of the castle wall scraped Dirk's skin as he lowered himself hand over hand to the frozen moat below.

He tried to stand, his knees buckling, and forced himself to relax for a moment. He shivered as the cold North Sea air cut through his thin prison rags. The palace-turned-prison stood staunchly behind him, boasting of power and pride, of control and cruelty.

Almost one year since I last walked outside these walls, Dirk thought to himself. *Almost a year since I've seen my Magda and the little ones.*

The scene replayed itself in his mind as if it were yesterday: "Do not go to the meeting," Magda begged him. "You know the duke has tightened up his search for Anabaptists. Phillip and Stephan can lead service tonight."

"Magda, what has come over you?" he asked, taking his wife gently by the shoulders and turning her to face him. "We are not to fear, but to be courageous and continue to serve our Lord day by day. It's not like you to shrink from danger."

She studied his face, as if to memorize it, then finally spoke. "Dirk, it is different this time. I have a bad feeling about tonight. Perhaps the Lord would have you stay at home and take care of your family instead of tempting the Spaniards to capture you. Oh, Dirk, I just know that if you step out that door tonight, you will never enter it again."

Magda broke into quiet sobs and Dirk pulled her close. "Now, now, my dear. Do not speak such nonsense. I shall be fine. And if anything does happen, the Lord will care for you and the children."

His last comment did not prove to be the comfort he had hoped, rather bringing with it more sobs. Dirk insisted, as firmly and gently as possible, that Magda calm down lest the children awaken. "No need to upset them," he added. "Now dry your tears and let us have a word of prayer together before I leave."

They knelt on the dirt floor of their tiny home and approached the throne of the Father, beseeching him for protection and courage, but above all for his will to be done. That was a year ago.

The scene faded as Dirk slipped on the ice and nearly sat down. Somehow he managed to regain his balance. "I am coming home, Magda," he whispered.

Doggedly he trudged over frozen fields in the direction of his home in Asperen, willing his legs to keep moving. A year on bread and water had weakened him considerably and time was not on his side; the sun prepared to rise above the late winter landscape and give him away.

And so it did. Just as the rays shone out to warm the land, a guard back at the prison palace discovered the rope of rags tied together, anchored to a stout iron hook beside the open window. "Guards, guards!" he yelled. "Prisoner has escaped. After him!"

His shouts were followed by running feet as two men joined him. They clattered across the drawbridge in pursuit, and one pointed and hollered, "There! Near the pond. He must not cross the pond."

Dirk turned at the sound, and to his terror he saw the men running in his direction. "Lord, grant me strength," he gasped. "And courage."

He ran for the pond as fast as his bony legs would carry him. If he could but cross it, he would be safe, out of the Anabaptist hunters' territory. The Hondegat lay before him, iced over still, but the ice was thinning.

Panting now, Dirk skated onto the pond, moving smoothly so as not to cause cracks. *Just a few more strides,* he thought. The forward shore welcomed him to freedom, as behind him the guards reached the Hondegat.

One of them slid out onto the pond while the other two watched from the bank. "I have you now, heretic!" he yelled. "You will burn for this."

Without a pause, Dirk closed the distance to the shore. Suddenly a whip cracked behind him and he winced, anticipating pain. Instead, he heard the anguished cry of the guard. The ice had snapped, giving way under the man's heavier frame.

"Help me!" he cried, slipping into the ice cold water. Dirk turned to see the man clawing desperately for handholds as the edges of the hole continued to break away.

For a moment, time stood still. There was no prisoner versus guard, no Anabaptist versus Mother Church, no right versus wrong. Dirk saw only a man in need, a man loved by Christ. And Dirk, as one of Christ's ambassadors, knew he had made his choice when he became a believer: to love as Christ loved.

Without a second thought, he slid back across the ice to where the guard floundered. "Give me your hand," he commanded, lying flat on the frozen pond and reaching out to his pursuer.

The desperate guard clasped the offered hand and hung on as Dirk pulled him to safety. The man lay panting, then stared up at Dirk. He squinted into the morning sun at the fugitive who had voluntarily become his savior.

"Hold him, Felipe!" ordered the two men on shore. The guard got to his feet and stared at Dirk. Finally, shaking his head, he took hold of him. He led Dirk back across the Hondegat, back to prison—this time a small room with barred windows, at the top of a tall church tower. His legs locked in wooden stocks, Dirk awaited his inevitable fate. It was only a matter of weeks in coming.

> " . . .Whereas Dirk Willems, born at Asperen, at present a prisoner, has confessed that at age fifteen he was rebaptized in Rotterdam, at the house of one Pieter Willems, and that he further, in Asperen, at his house, at diverse hours permitted several persons to be rebaptized, therefore, we the aforesaid judges do condemn the aforesaid Dirk Willems that he shall be executed by fire, until death ensues."

"Heretic! Traitor! To the stake!" The townspeople raised the cry. The guard, Felipe, watched as the dangerous criminal of church and state, the one who had saved his life, was led past and chained to the stake. Felipe's fellow guard set his torch to the wood piled high at the foot of the stake until it caught and crackled.

Felipe, unable to tear his eyes away, stared up at Dirk. The man returned his gaze with a look of such love that it cut to the marrow of his bones. From the prisoner's parched lips came a song, drifting out across the watchers—a song of generations of martyrs, a song to be sung until the end of time:

> "Dear Jesus, Thou Eternal God
> For me Thy blood was shed, On
> Calvary's cross didst Thou die alone,
> Thorns crowned Thy hallowed head.
> All this Thou didst to save my soul,
> Should I not then drink from this bowl
> of wrath? I come . . . to Thee . . ."

The voice grew raspy and finally died, as did the body, but Felipe could have sworn the man lived on. Even after the ashes cooled, the presence of Dirk Willems and his Savior remained.

And they remain today.

Chapter 1

21 March 1914
Succoth Estate
Crimea

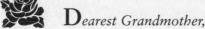

*D*earest Grandmother,

I wish you were sitting here with me on the bench in the olive grove. The nightingales have returned, so I know it is spring. The sun makes lazy shadows on my page and the lilacs are in full glorious bloom now; their perfume wafts across the park and into every window, filling the house with a rich and generous aroma.

Mika, although she is two years younger than I, already turns all the young men's heads. She looks so much like Mama did—dark and beautiful and graceful. She doesn't have Mama's cheery, playful spirit, though, or her gentle ways. Mika has Papa's practical business mind and tries to keep us all under her control.

I miss Mama terribly and wonder why God took her from us so soon. But I'm sure you miss your own daughter more than I know. God comfort you, dear Oma.

Papa is preparing to travel soon to Alexanderkrone for a church conference. Of course, he plans to ride over to Ruekenau to see you, too, which is why I am writing this letter to send along with him. He is taking the train from Boranger, then will rent a horse and buggy at the Molotschna colony. We miss him much when he is gone; one feels like an orphan with neither mother nor father nearby.

Papa purchased a new buggy and a fine trotting horse for

me, for my sixteenth birthday. I love the freedom it gives me to trot down the lanes and through the park and orchard, out past our little estate church to the woods beyond.

I lead such a charmed life here, Oma. The estate is like a paradise, as you well remember. Sometimes I'm afraid the charm will be broken. There is a vague apprehension deep in my soul that I can't explain.

I suppose I must finish this letter now and check on Anna and Kolya. Mika and I are in charge of their studies until we are able to find a private teacher for them. The children send their love, as does our brother Peter, although he can't express it in words. Pray for him; he feels Mama's death more deeply than any of us.

Mika says she will write you soon herself, but I wouldn't hold my breath if I were you! With all my love and many prayers, I bid you farewell.

Katarina Hildebrandt

The breeze teased the pages of her letter as Katarina smoothed and folded them. She stood with a sigh, gathered her writing materials, and walked down Magnolia Lane in the direction of the mansion. Her practical, black shoes crunched on the wide path, making a crisp, friendly sound as she passed the apple and cherry orchards.

She cut across the south lawn to the rose garden, stopping to caress a velvety maroon flower. Roses had been Mama's favorite; she had searched continually for new varieties and colors to enhance the already luxuriant gardens. They shared a great deal, Mama and the roses—both beautiful and fragile, with a scent that lasted long after the flower was dead—a sad, dusky smell that haunted one's soul.

A child's shrill scream cut through Katarina's reverie and involuntarily she snapped the rose from its stem. Petals fluttered to her feet, and she stared at them for a moment.

Another exasperated shriek set her in motion. She picked up her skirts, ran through the gate in the red limestone wall, and hurried up the south courtyard steps.

The Juschanlee River wandered westward over the Russian steppes, collecting little villages on its meandering way, only four to six *versts* apart on either side of the river. In each village, two perfectly straight rows of houses faced each other across a long main street, which became a road continuing on to the next village. Each house, with its attached barn, was backed by a garden and a small orchard. The forest lay further from the river. The church was the center of the village, both physically and spiritually, with the schoolhouse close by. One village looked like the next, a total of fifty or sixty of them making up the Molotschna Colony, named for the Molotschnaya River that formed its western border.

In the little village of Lichtfelde, a Russian Mennonite wedding was in full swing. The Loewens' big barn had been thoroughly cleaned, aired, and garlanded with fresh green branches and grapevines. They had swept the yard and sprinkled sparkling white sand on the paths.

Susannah Loewen was happy for her sister Helena, so elegant in a long white gown, her veil attached to a myrtle wreath that encircled her head. Her Jakob was dashing in his crisp white shirt, black cravat, and long black topcoat. Suse would miss Lena, but she would be only four versts away in Neukirch.

Susannah checked the platters of *zweibach* and filled the coffee urns. There was still plenty of cold, sliced ham and tangy, homemade mustard. The cool plum soup smelled sweet and fruity. She brought in a few more bottles of wine; the wedding guests' merriment had increased in relation to the number of empty bottles on the tables.

Susannah could hear the young people tuning guitars and

violins at the back of the barn. Someone began to play a lively folk song, and her foot began tapping to the rhythm. She picked a tidbit of ham from a platter and popped it into her mouth. Turning from the serving table, she found herself looking into a pair of soft brown eyes, slightly magnified by round, wire-rimmed glasses.

"Johann!" Susannah smoothed back a few stray wisps of honey gold hair and smiled. "You surprised me." She swallowed the ham. "You know what they say, 'The cooks and the cat are never hungry.' "

Johann Sudermann's smile lifted the ends of his carefully groomed moustache. Susannah always thought his smile lit up his whole face.

"Are you on zweibach duty, or would you be free to take a walk with me?"

"I'd love a walk," she said, pulling off her apron. "I can't be gone long, though. I want to be here to say good-bye to Lena."

"She doesn't look like she's in a hurry to go anywhere yet," assured Johann. "They won't have the black bow ceremony until later tonight. Let's head down to the river."

Little bridges spanned the various branches of the river, connecting the villages. Johann and Susannah crossed the south bridge, in the direction of Alexanderkrone, and strolled along the opposite shore under the shade of the oaks.

"I love weddings," Susannah sighed. "Someday, when I get married, I shall celebrate for three whole days."

"I think I would rather everyone shook my hand and went home at once," teased Johann.

Susannah's round, wholesome face turned pink. Johann smiled and looked at the rippling reflection of the oaks in the water. His smile faded, and he said nothing for a time. She glanced at him from the corner of her eye.

"You seem solemn, Hans."

"I'm sorry," he answered, looking into her eyes. "I've been

rather preoccupied lately. Restless, I suppose."

She stopped to consider. "What do you mean?"

"Well, I wonder why I was born in this place and at this time in history." He dusted off a flat rock and sat down, patting a place beside him for her to sit. "Do you ever wonder if there's more to life than going to school, joining the church, getting married, and farming or keeping house?"

She shrugged. "I guess I don't think of it that often. I've always known what my life would be like, just as my mother and her mother before her. What else would I want?"

"It's so simple for you, isn't it? Just do what's expected."

"It's comfortable and secure."

"But is that enough, comfort and security? Does it satisfy your soul, the place inside you that thinks, feels, dreams, and hopes?"

"I think with my head, Hans," laughed Susannah, "or didn't you learn that in school?"

He smiled. "There is a place inside me that seems rather empty. I suppose it's partly because I'm young, with my whole life ahead of me. But how do I fill this emptiness?"

"Perhaps I can help," Susannah offered shyly. "We've always been good friends, and I care very much about you."

"Dear Suse." He hugged her with one arm as they sat on the rock, in the shade of the oak. "You are a sweet girl."

Susannah melted into the embrace, but it didn't last long. Johann stood abruptly, almost upsetting her, and ran his hand through his blond, wavy hair. Unconsciously, he adjusted his eyeglasses before he spoke.

"I don't think you alone can help me, Suse. There's a restlessness in me that maybe only time will fill, but I have to find out. I need to do something with my life."

"You're a fine teacher," Susannah encouraged. "Your students adore you, and you keep them well disciplined."

"Thank you, my friend. But I couldn't do the same thing in the same place, day after day, for the rest of my life. What I came to tell you is that I will be going away for awhile. I need to see other places, meet other people, experience life more fully." He turned toward her. "Can you understand at all?"

"I'm trying," she whispered, blinking back the surprised tears that threatened to spill from her blue eyes. "Are you asking for your freedom?"

He sighed. "I'm sorry. I didn't want to hurt you, but I couldn't go away, leaving you with false hopes." He looked out across the stream, his face taut.

Susannah remained silent for several moments, then looked up at him through eyes blurred with tears. "Thank you for telling me, Hans," she whispered. "I truly hope you find what you're searching for."

"I'd better get you back to the wedding, or Lena will think you've been kidnapped." He took her hand and they followed the path through the trees, back to the music that had sounded so joyful before.

"The black bow ceremony," said Johann, as they returned to the yard. "You almost missed it." They stood together for a long moment, then he said, "I'll stop to say good-bye before I leave."

Susannah smiled a sad smile and squeezed his hand. She let him go, then, and made her way toward the gathering alone. It was nearly midnight. The games and folk dances were done, and the bride and groom sat on one of the benches, surrounded by friends.

The girls began to sing to Helena, accompanied by a violin:

> "The bridal wreath you need no more
> For the duties weight you by the score . . ."

During the third verse, the bridesmaids led Helena to the center of the gathering, removed her veil, and blindfolded her. Twirling her around several times, they backed away, laughing.

Helena chose a direction and moved forward to hand her veil to one of the girls. Everyone cheered as the receiver became the "next bride." Susannah moved away. She had no wish to be here now.

The fun and teasing quieted as the girls resumed their song and fastened a black bow at the back of Helena's head.

> "Bow down thy head, thou lovely bride,
> Thy crown of beauty lay aside.
> Now may this bow adorn your hair
> God keep you happy in His care."

Susannah moved forward again to join in the gaiety, but all the while her heart felt like a stone. One of her dreams had just slipped away, and she was forced to wonder how practical and secure her other dreams were in this changeable world.

With sounds of singing and celebration in his ears, Johann made his way to the stable and saddled his horse. "Come on, Midnight, let's go home. Tomorrow we will make a visit to Paul Gregorovich Tekanin."

He sprang effortlessly into the saddle and headed west, along the river. The weather was fine and the breeze seemed to carry away some of his tensions, if not his resolve.

Midnight trotted swiftly along the road, his ears pointed forward, aware of every butterfly and bee. He was glad for a good stretch. The versts melted away like frost in the morning sun, and soon Johann spotted the Russian village of Ackerman. It was nestled along the Juschanlee, just before it joined the Molotschnaya to flow south to the sea.

He slowed his horse to a walk and followed one of the narrow, twisting streets to a tiny house near the blacksmith's shop.

"Hello the house!" he called, stopping to dismount. Midnight pricked his ears forward as the rickety, wooden door cracked open. Eyes peered at Johann through the narrow opening, then disappeared. All was silent. Johann scuffed his boots on the road and patted the horse's neck, waiting. The door creaked again, and a tall, muscular young man with dark curls stepped outside. He blinked in the sunlight.

"Sudermann! Welcome!" He grasped Johann firmly by the shoulders in greeting, then took the reins and wrapped them around the pole fence. Johann loosened the cinch and pulled off the saddle, setting it on end near a small shed.

"We will walk," suggested the young Russian, and they started off down the road, out of town.

"What brings you here today, my friend? You are having girl troubles, or is it a new horse you want? This one looks pretty good yet."

"Always trying to second guess me, Paul Gregorovich. I've simply come to visit a friend."

"Of course!" He grinned. "What can Paul do for you today?"

"First, I have a question for you: what happened back at your house? Someone acted like I had the plague."

Paul hesitated. "Oh, Sonya, she is just shy." He looked away and began to whistle a cheerful tune.

"Paul, what's the matter with you? Tell me the truth."

Again the slight pause. "You speak the Russian pretty good. You may need it sometime."

Johann sighed. "I thought so. Just because I am of German descent, you don't consider me Russian. Paul, you know me better than that. We Mennonites have lived in this country for over a hundred years. Since 1786, to be exact. We were invited by your empress, Catherine II."

"Of course. Paul knows, but those who don't know you do not care. You are still foreigners. Your people are a little like oil in water," he continued. "They do not mix well with the Russian people."

"The *Privilegium* granted my people sixty-five *dessiatines* of land per family, as well as religious and civic freedom and exemption from military service. We had no wish nor reason to assimilate, but that doesn't mean we don't consider Mother Russia our homeland."

"And she granted her own people nothing!" Paul spat out the words. "You are naive. You do not always know what is outside your gate. Be careful, Sudermann; things change."

They walked on past the edge of town, allowing their sharp exchange to fade into silence, and took the trail to a stand of poplars.

"I have to go away somewhere," Johann said abruptly. "I'm going crazy doing the same old thing every day."

Paul chuckled with his usual lightheartedness. "The wanderlust. I know it, too."

"You do?"

"Of course; I am alive!" They settled down in the long grass, each leaning against a solid tree trunk. "Always I care for my sisters and my mother," Paul continued, "but now I hear the call. Because you have taught me so many things, I have a need to learn more, to use what I know, to make my horizon wider, as you say."

Their thoughts drifted back to the hours when Johann had tutored his Russian peasant friend, teaching him what he himself was learning at the village school. After a long day in the fields or barns, working for Johann's father and uncle, Paul would come inside for the evening meal and a teaching session.

"You are the one who awoke in me the love of teaching," said Johann to his childhood friend. They talked on about politics, about the economy, about old times spent here in the poplar thicket and in the town of Ackerman while Johann's father haggled for horses. Too soon it was time to start back to the village.

Johann looked directly at Paul as they rose. "So where are

you going, and how soon? Do you know?"

"I think perhaps when the leaves fall, I will go. Maybe to Moscow, maybe to St. Petersburg. You?"

"I wish I knew. I'm committed to completing the school year, but after that I'm free to go. No one knows yet except Suse."

"And she is not full from joy?" A knowing smile touched Paul's lips.

"Not really. But she will be fine. We will write to each other."

Paul merely looked at him. Johann raised his eyebrows and said, "What?"

"You make the promise, the wanderlust breaks it."

Johann did not reply. Paul slapped him on the back. "Sudermann! A smile would not hurt your face. If it should be, it will be."

Johann walked in silence for a distance, then said, almost to himself, "I can't but wonder what is missing from my life. And I don't mean a woman," he added, glancing at his friend. "I've followed all the church rules and yet I can't find peace." He shrugged his shoulders. "Yes, well, I should be heading back before it gets dark. I had hoped someday we would go off and seek our fortunes together, but that doesn't seem to be the way of it."

"Not today, and I think not tomorrow. My heart tells me we will be friends far apart."

When the two friends arrived back at the Tekanin *izba*, Johann saddled his horse and untied the reins. "Take care of yourself, Paul Gregorovich. I hope to see you a couple of times yet, before we go off in different directions."

"And you, Sudermann. Follow the wanderlust for a time, then marry the girl that makes your heart beat like galloping hooves. Watch out! Keep the Russian in your pocket, eh?"

With a last salute, they parted, one to re-enter the hovel that was his home, the other to trot off into the evening, destiny unknown. The clouds were gathering, hastening the darkness.

Chapter 2

Katarina opened the large, oak-paneled door to the south wing of the house and heard her sister, Maria, attempting to bring order and discipline to her younger siblings. Her harsh tone had brought tears to little Anna's eyes and a smirk to young Nicholai's face.

"Nicholai, wipe that smirk off your face," Maria remonstrated, "and, Anna, stop your blubbering. You are as much at fault as Nicholai."

When Katarina appeared, Anna sniffled and ran to her. "Katya, Katya! Kolya is so mean, and it is not my fault. I did nothing." She buried her face in Katarina's apron.

"Well," spoke Maria, her perfectly manicured hands on her slim hips, "I see I am not needed here any longer. You waltz in the door and destroy everything I've already accomplished." She turned and regally walked away, head held high.

"Mika!" Katarina called. "Mika, I just came to see what the screeching was about. I didn't even know you were here."

But Maria didn't respond, and suddenly it was as if the battle lines had been redrawn, with Mika against the three of them: Katarina, Nicholai, and Anna.

"Oh, dear," whispered Katarina to herself. "I seem to have set her off again. I'm getting quite adept at that." She turned her attention to the children. "Now, let's all three go sit on the porch steps outside and talk this through."

"Must I?" Nicholai asked, making a face.

"Absolutely! Now come with me, both of you."

They sat on the steps outside, in the shade of the honeysuckle vines, and Katarina listened to each story. Nicholai, eager to run off and play instead of wasting his day sitting in negotiations, readily admitted that he had indeed teased Anna and pulled her braids and showed her his collection of frogs, worms, and assorted insects and reptiles. Anna's sniffling ceased.

"Kolya, you will not bother Anna any more with things that you know she dislikes," pronounced Katarina. "And to make up for some of the distress you have caused her, you will spend two hours after lunch today playing whatever Anna wants."

"No, Katya, please. She'll want to play house and dolls, and I'll have to pretend to be the papa again."

"Better than being the mama, don't you think?" Katarina countered with a smile.

Little Anna giggled and dried her tears. "Maybe we could pretend to be gypsies and take our pony and cart for a ride through the park. "

Nicholai pulled another face, but he knew he was cornered.

"Now," said Katarina, cheerfully, "let's all go and have a nice lunch. Cook will be upset if we don't appear on time. And please," she added softly, "be nice to Mika."

As the children walked down the long, wide hallway toward the dining room, Anna clasped her elder sister's hand and looked up at her. *She's nearly an angel,* the little girl decided.

If the clouds had not blocked out the last rays of the setting sun, he would have seen the rut in the road. As it was, Heinrich Hildebrandt now found himself alone in the darkness, still about six versts away from Alexanderkrone, with a broken buggy wheel. The air was warm enough. A night outside would do him no serious damage, but it definitely didn't fit into his well-planned schedule. His mother-in-law would be expecting him in Ruekenau tomorrow, and he still had business in Alexanderkrone.

Katarina and Maria and the younger children needed him home as soon as possible. But here he sat in the twilight, in the middle of nowhere. Heinrich climbed down from his seat, took the horse's reins, and with one hand on the bridle, urged the horse to pull the buggy off the road. Then he unhitched the horse and looked for a place to tie it. There was always the option of jumping onto the animal and riding it bareback to the first town, but that would mean leaving all his goods and gifts unattended, fair game for anyone who happened by before morning.

As Heinrich searched in the dark for a tree or fence post, the horse pricked up his ears and whinnied softly. Then he snorted, stamped his front foot, and whinnied again, louder this time. An answering whinny sounded in the distance, and soon Heinrich heard the distant clip-clop of approaching hooves. "Thank you, dear Lord!" he said fervently.

Leading his horse onto the road, he waited as the sounds drew nearer. As soon as he judged wise, he called out, "Hello, friend." Since he was near the villages, he used the German language, but perhaps Russian would have been a better idea. "Hello, I am in need of help."

The steady rhythm of hoofbeats stopped, and then a voice, also in German, drifted through the darkening day. "I hear you. I am coming." The hoofbeats resumed and in a matter of moments, a horse and rider stopped directly in front of Heinrich.

Heinrich spoke first. "Heinrich Hildebrandt is my name. I was on my way to Alexanderkrone when my buggy hit a hole in the road and broke a wheel. I'm afraid the darkness overtook me sooner than I had expected."

"The clouds have prematurely darkened the evening,"

answered the voice. "I myself had thought to be home by now." The rider dismounted and approached Heinrich. "Johann Sudermann, from Kleefeld. I'm glad I came when I did. There won't be much traffic by here until morning."

"I am indeed thankful you came this way. I haven't yet decided what I am to do with this wheel."

"Why don't I ride home, fetch a lantern, and return in our buggy?" Johann suggested. "You can spend the night in our house, and we will have this buggy wheel fixed first thing in the morning."

"That sounds wonderful, my young friend. Although I don't like to put you out, I see no other option at present. Thank you. I await your return."

Johann jumped into the saddle and turned to go. "Climb into the buggy and rest, sir," he said. "I will return as soon as possible." With that, he rode off toward Kleefeld.

Heinrich spent the next hour sitting in the buggy, careful not to rock the frame and break something else. He alternately hummed his favorite hymns and folk songs and quoted Scripture from memory:

> When I consider the heavens,
> the work of thy fingers,
> the moon and the stars which thou hast set in place,
> what is man that thou art mindful of him,
> the son of man that thou visitest him?

He looked at the overcast sky and chuckled. "I suppose I should be considering the clouds, Lord; I cannot see any stars. Even the moon hides tonight." At that moment, a break in the clouds revealed a thin slice of moon and a peppering of twinkling stars. One more moment and another cloud denied that the moon had been there at all. Heinrich sat completely still in wonder, and finished the psalm with a whispered reverence:

> Oh Lord, our Lord,
> How excellent is thy name in all the earth!

Hoofbeats and the creaking of buggy wheels nudged Heinrich from his worship. Carefully, he climbed out of the buggy and watched the bobbing light of a lantern approaching. He began to whistle a hymn of praise as Johann hopped nimbly out of his wagon and came forward, lantern in hand. The light reflected cheerfully from his eyeglasses.

"Your taxi has arrived, Mr. Hildebrandt. I'll transfer your goods to my wagon and remove the wheel from your buggy as well."

"Yes, thank you, son. Let us work together."

"This night air is certainly fresh." Johann made conversation as he lifted various packages and boxes from one vehicle to the other. While Heinrich held the lantern, Johann removed the damaged wheel and together they levered it onto the back of the wagon. They tied Heinrich's rented horse to the side of the wagon, and set off for Kleefeld.

Next morning, Heinrich awoke to the sound of a horse and buggy entering the Sudermann yard. Dressing quickly, he stepped to the window in time to see Johann driving the rented buggy, with the wheel repaired and replaced. "Fine young man," Heinrich said to himself.

Johann came to the house after unhitching and caring for the horse. "Good morning, Mr. Hildebrandt. I hope you slept well."

"Oh, indeed I did. And long, apparently! I see you have already been on the road for a time."

"Yes, sir. Your buggy is ready to go. But I believe Mother will not let you leave without breakfast."

They entered the kitchen and smelled the aroma of fresh biscuits, and sausage and eggs frying.

"A bit of porridge to start you off, and you'll be ready for biscuits," stated Mrs. Sudermann. Her plump figure attested to the fact that she was an excellent cook. She called to the rest of the family, and soon all were seated around the large, oak table. Heinrich sat on the end as guest of honor, Mr. Sudermann beside him on the right, and Johann on the left. The younger boys and girls sat on the sides, with Mrs. Sudermann at the far end. When all were seated, Mr. Sudermann bowed his head and mumbled a mealtime prayer. The children sat quietly until he was finished, which was not long, and waited almost patiently for their turn at the plates and bowls of steaming food.

Mrs. Sudermann spent almost the entire meal jumping up to fill serving dishes and coffee cups. "Some more cream in your coffee, Mr. Hildebrandt?" she said, and "Have some more fried eggs, they're fresh this morning." Her cheerful energy reminded him of his Elizabeth, but that was the only similarity. While Elizabeth had been petite and dark and beautiful, Mrs. Sudermann was tall and broad, her straight brown hair parted strictly down the middle of her head and pulled into a tight, no-nonsense knot at the nape of her neck. She lacked the poise and grace of his dear wife. *I'm not being very gracious in my judgment,* thought Heinrich, *but no one compares to my Liesbet.*

"A fine son you have, Mr. Sudermann," he said aloud. "You have done a good job raising him."

"A man is known by the company he keeps, Mr. Hildebrandt."

"A man's character can also be apparent in his actions and his attitude," rejoined Heinrich. "And I have been impressed." Then to Johann he said, "I very much appreciate your help in my need. I will not forget your kindness."

"You are welcome, sir. Perhaps someday I'll be the one in need and someone will do for me as I have done for you."

"Ah, the Golden Rule. A rule to live by." Heinrich enjoyed more eggs and sausage. "So tell me, Johann, are you planning to continue farming once your father gets older? Is the land in your blood?"

Mr. and Mrs. Sudermann exchanged glances. He snorted, and she said, "He's a bit above farming, you see. Our eldest son is a teacher in the local school."

Johann's father nodded and continued, "Yes. Johann does not want to farm. Have you ever heard anything like it? The future on a silver plate, and he chooses to lock himself indoors with a flock of prattling children. I, for one, do not understand."

Heinrich glanced at Johann, who was obviously embarrassed by his humiliation before a guest. Once his parents had voiced their opinions, Johann turned to Heinrich and said calmly, "I teach the primary school here in Kleefeld, Mr. Hildebrandt. It is a profession of some reward, as far as molding young lives and inspiring them to enjoy learning."

"And will you continue here for some time?" Heinrich spoke to Johann, politely excluding the others.

"I've promised this year," replied Johann. With a glance at his father, he continued, "I've decided to broaden my horizons. I don't have any definite plans as yet, but the world is larger than Kleefeld—than the Molotschna—and I intend to see at least some of it." He took a few bites of his food, bracing himself for the onslaught. It was not long in coming.

"You are *leaving*?" came the cry from his mother. "Johann, my son, what are you thinking? Kleefeld is your home; your future is sure here. What nonsense you speak."

"Be quiet, woman!" interrupted her husband. Then to his son he said, "There will be no more talk of this."

The bright morning sun, smiling through the crisp, white curtains, belied the coolness of the group gathered in the kitchen. They ate and scraped their plates in silence. Then the girls and their mother cleared off the food and the boys ran outside to escape the tension.

"Let us have a smoke in the parlor," Mr. Sudermann invited.

"I'll be glad to join you for a short time, but I do not smoke, thank you."

The elder Sudermann looked at Heinrich from under bushy brows and huffed his way into the parlor.

The ensuing visit was short and shallow. Heinrich felt he must endure it, considering the generosity of his hosts, but he did not enjoy it. As he rose to leave, he shook hands with Mr. Sudermann, nodded politely to his wife, and included them both in a gracious thank-you. He clapped his hat on his head and said, "Johann will see me off. God bless you all for your hospitality."

Heinrich shut the solid door behind him and prayed that he would find Johann out in the barn. As if to affirm his assessment of the young man, he found him hitching the horse to the rented buggy just outside the barn.

"Johann, I was hoping to have a word with you before I left."

"I apologize for what happened at the house," interjected Johann. "I should not have spoken my mind so abruptly. My parents have every right to be upset."

"I'll not worry about that, son. I believe that all things work together for good to them that love the Lord and are called according to his purposes. This meeting was definitely fore-ordained."

"I'm not sure I follow what you're saying, Mr. Hildebrandt."

"Well, you see, Johann, you are a teacher, you are young and want a bit of a change. You are a dependable and trustworthy young person, in my estimation. Do you follow me thus far?" A small smile played at his mouth.

Johann answered Heinrich's smile with a grin. "I must not allow such flattery to go to my head. You haven't known me for more than twelve hours yet."

Heinrich chuckled. "Ah yes, but I am a fair judge of character. Now to continue, I have another need which you may be able to meet, and in so doing, you may also meet a need of your own. 'Kill two birds with one stone,' so to speak."

Johann wound the reins around the hitching post and invited Heinrich into the coolness of the large, white barn. "You have my full attention, sir."

"My need, Johann, is for a teacher for my younger children. Down at Succoth Estate, in the Crimea, we are too isolated for the children to travel to a village school. Therefore, I employ a tutor for them. My wife preferred to teach the children herself when she was with us, but the Lord took her home two years ago this summer. Since then, my eldest daughters, Katarina and Maria, have been overseeing the schoolwork. It weighs heavily on them, and discipline is at times difficult to enforce in siblings."

"I am sorry about your wife." Compassion softened Johann's words. "Was she ill or was there an accident?"

"Burst appendix, the doctor said. By the time he arrived, it was too late. Infection had set in. She suffered for five days before she left us." Heinrich ran a hand over his beard and blinked away tears. "She was my best friend." He took a deep breath and blew it out, as if to blow the melancholy from his spirit. He looked out a barn window and saw nothing but Elizabeth's face.

"She must have been a special person," offered Johann.

"Oh yes, that she was." Heinrich turned from the window and looked back at Johann. "What I wanted to ask is, would you be at all interested in coming to the Crimea to teach my children? I do not expect an answer immediately, of course, but I ask you to consider it."

Johann was silent for a time. Then he said, "I will consider it, Mr. Hildebrandt. Would you tell me the ages of your children, please?"

"Of course." He concentrated. "My wife was always better at this than I am. Let's see, Katya is the eldest at sixteen, then Maria—we call her Mika—is fourteen. They have completed their formal education under their mother's teaching. Then Peter is twelve, Nicholai is nine, and Anna, five—no, six."

"Fine. Good ages to work with. Do they enjoy learning?"

Heinrich hesitated. "Well, Anna loves school and people and being busy. She is a happy one. Nicholai—we call him Kolya—is an intelligent boy. The challenge is to keep him still long enough to transfer some facts from book to brain."

"And Peter?"

Heinrich let out a slow breath and pursed his lips in search of words. "Peter was his mother's sweetheart. She understood him and spent many hours with him. You see, Johann, Peter is . . . different. . . . I just don't know how to . . ." His words drifted off, and he shrugged his shoulders helplessly.

Johann said nothing. He did not know what to say.

Finally, Heinrich reached out his right hand, grasped Johann's hand, and shook it firmly. "I have a card here with my name and address. Please keep in contact with me as to my offer." Johann nodded, as he accepted the square of paper. "And here is a little something for your trouble."

Heinrich handed Johann a ten-ruble note. The young man backed away and refused it. "I only did what anyone would have done."

"Yes, but there was no one else. I'll tell you, young Sudermann, God has blessed me richly with material things. I own many dessiatines of land and manage many people. I do not wish to hoard this blessing. I cannot take it with me to the next world, and so I share it where I can. Consider the note a gift from the Lord, or, if you wish, an advance on your fees, should you accept my offer. Oh, by the way, your travel costs would be reimbursed."

"But I . . ." Johann stopped before he stuttered.

"I insist, and I am your elder."

"Then I gratefully accept," smiled Johann. "But not that I expected anything."

"Of course not. I am on my way. I expect to hear from you soon."

"Yes. Godspeed."

So Heinrich Hildebrandt praised God for what he took to be another divine intervention in his life. The horse started off at a quick trot at the snap of the reins; Heinrich knew Mother would be waiting in Ruekenau.

Fallen leaves crunched beneath their shoes as Johann and Susannah strolled along the river. It had always been their favorite place to walk and talk, a natural cathedral. Now it was especially beautiful, adorned with myriad shades of green, red, and yellow, and set off by the clear blue sky and cool, rippling river.

"I remember playing here as a child," said Susannah. "We were so young and carefree then, no troubles or worries greater than getting home in time for supper." She sighed. "Sometimes I wish I could go back."

"I know what you mean," replied Johann, taking her hand as they walked. "In our youth, we wish to be older than we are, and suddenly we're there, and it's not all we thought it would be."

He stooped to pick up an unusually large oak leaf. "Kind of like this leaf, I guess." He handed it to Susannah and smiled. "We want to be free of the tree, of the traditions and expectations of our elders and our society, but once we're on our own, difficult decisions come our way. Life is not always easy or pleasant."

"I never really wanted to be free of the tree, but now it seems I'm being shaken loose."

They walked in silence for a time, basking in the ethereal beauty of the place, a solace for their troubled hearts.

Johann spoke again. "Paul's gone off to St. Petersburg to see what he can see."

Susannah looked up, waiting for him to go on.

"He actually rode over last week to say good-bye. His future is uncertain, but he is determined to go north."

The only sound was the crunch of dead leaves beneath their shoes. Then Susannah asked, "Are your father and mother reconciled yet to your leaving?"

Johann's mouth tightened. "I suppose they are as reconciled as they will ever be, Suse. They don't understand and probably never will. Now they see me as a bad example for the younger children."

"Oh, Hans, that's ridiculous! As if you could ever be a bad example for anyone."

"Thank you for your support. I think they actually expected me to relent and stay."

"And there is no chance of that, is there?" Susannah asked, a trace of hope in her voice.

Johann stopped walking and looked at her. "Suse, would you want me to stay here just to make life smoother and more predictable, and watch me die of boredom and suffocation of spirit?"

"You make it sound as if this is a terrible place to be. I guess I secretly hoped you would change your mind and consider all the good things you have here: family, friends, occupation."

"Ah, Suse, I can't explain how I feel, just that I must try my wings."

"Still friends, though?"

"Still friends."

"You won't forget me?" she asked quietly.

"I couldn't forget you. We've been friends for years, and I highly value that friendship."

"Will you write?"

"Yes, of course." Johann remembered Paul's raised eyebrows at his reference to letter writing. He continued, "I will need a confidante, I'm sure, in a strange place with people I don't know."

All was still in the leafy cathedral. The breeze did not penetrate the thick stand of trees, and even the cuckoo's calls were muted.

"I'm leaving tomorrow. Thank you for being a true friend. May life be good to you."

Susannah wiped tears from her cheeks and held her shawl more tightly around her. Her tears unnerved Johann. He cleared his throat. "Don't cry, Suse." His words of comfort only brought more tears, and he held her close until the sobs ceased.

She pulled away, wiped her eyes with her handkerchief, and took a deep breath. She smiled a sad, little smile and looked up at him. "Forgive me. I know I can't keep you here. Follow your heart, Johann. Experience new things, new ideas. Thank you for a wonderful friendship. I shall treasure it always."

"As will I." He leaned down and kissed her forehead. Turning, they wound their way through the tranquil forest and stepped out into the brilliant, summer sunlight.

"Good-bye, Hans."

"Farewell, my friend." He mounted his black mare, turned for a last smile, and trotted away from her, down the road to Kleefeld.

Chapter 3

Johann noticed the changing climate as the train crossed the salt flats at Chongar Bridge. Although it was only 180 by 240 versts at its longest and widest, the Crimean peninsula offered a wide geographical spectrum. Rocky, saline soils made farming difficult in the north, while the east-central area, where Johann was headed, produced lush crops and boasted fine grazing land.

The Taurida Mountains, ridged along the southeast of the Crimea, made a splendid backdrop for the warm, sandy beaches of Yalta and Alushta. It was known as the Russian Riviera, a natural location for Livadia, the private palace retreat for generations of tsars and aristocrats. The Mediterranean-like climate wafting in from the Black Sea had encouraged an assortment of resorts and spas.

Johann's train clattered along the track, forging its way the length of the peninsula—south from the salt flats in the north, then branching off to the east at Dzhankoi, and continuing to Sevastopol, at the southern tip of Crimea. The coach road that crossed between South Russia and Crimea met the rail line at Dzhankoi, then continued south, side by side with the rails, to Sevastopol. Russian and German villages attached themselves to the coach road and rail line.

The train slowed as it approached Dzhankoi, preparing to refuel and let off passengers. Some, like Johann, would board an eastbound train for the rest of their journey. As the locomotive screeched into the station, billowing black smoke,

Johann stood and made his way to the exit. He was looking forward to a bit of fresh air and firm earth beneath his feet.

As he strode along the plank platform of the station, he stared at the acacia trees around him, and the blue, blue sky, so wide and clear. The breeze blew in gently from the Azov Sea, filling his mind with dreams for the future. "Don't forget to get your hands dirty once in a while and do a little honest work," Paul had jokingly told him. "And stand up for yourself when you need to. I won't be there to save your skin."

The conductor's call interrupted Johann's thoughts, and the huge iron machine began to digest another load of coal. The eastbound train passed a few small villages and several large estates. It was to such an estate that Johann was bound. To Succoth, to be exact, the home of Heinrich Hildebrandt and his family.

Johann had decided to accept Hildebrandt's invitation to become his children's private tutor. Not so great an adventure as Paul Gregorovich would have, journeying to the capital city of St. Petersburg on the frigid North Sea, but an adventure nonetheless.

"Oh, Mika, you are so vain," scolded Katarina, as she swept past her sister toward the dining room, carrying an enormous bouquet of freshly cut flowers. "Mr. Sudermann is a *tutor*, not a suitor."

"Suitor, tutor," Maria replied flippantly. "It doesn't make much difference. I'm just glad for some company." She gave her glistening, gold comb an extra pat and turned reluctantly from her reflection in the ornate, rectangular mirror above the sideboard.

Katarina rolled her eyes and placed her bouquet on the crocheted doily in the center of the long, cherrywood table.

Its glossy surface reflected her face, plain, freckled, and sensible, with a strong mouth. Her hair curled out in sandy brown tendrils, escaping the pins, looking anything but sensible.

"I do hope you'll tame that mane of yours before our Mr. Sudermann arrives," commented Maria.

"Dear sister," began Katarina, in a controlled voice, "he is not *our* Mr. Sudermann, and furthermore, I am not out to impress him. He is here to teach the children. And you would do best to allow him to concentrate on the job he has been hired to do." She gave her younger sister a meaningful glance and left the room.

Maria leaned over to inhale the fragrance of the assorted blooms, pulled out a peach-colored rose, and fastened it in her hair. Her smile widened as she heard the rumble of carriage wheels on the cobblestones. She arranged a cool expression on her lovely face, lifted her chin, and walked regally toward the entry hall.

Johann stepped from the carriage and turned to retrieve his bags, but a young Russian in a black serge suit had already done so. Another man, somewhat older but wearing a similar suit of clothes, strode purposefully toward him and bowed slightly.

"Mr. Sudermann, I presume?" He continued without waiting for an answer, "Please follow me."

Johann stared at the huge mansion before him. It stretched as far as five or six houses in Kleefeld, and that was only the wing he could see from the cobbled yard, the whole of it bordered by a low, red limestone fence. The windows, neatly shuttered in white, were crowned with red brick arches, like a little eyebrow over each one. Ten or fifteen wide steps rose to the main entrance at the front of the house, and a veranda, with round white pillars and a white railing, skirted the entire house, as far as Johann could see. Potted flowers stood on the veranda, hung from the sides of pillars, and leaned out of window boxes. Great vines almost covered the veranda, climbing the walls of the house to the second and third stories, breaking out in large purple flowers here and there on their journey.

"Mr. Sudermann?" It was Black Suit again. Johann realized he had been standing and staring, and that the servants were waiting for him at the top of the stairs.

"I'm sorry," he said, with a little embarrassment. "I'm sure I'll have time to look around later."

Black Suit said nothing, but turned on his heel and made his way to the door, holding it open for Johann.

The large entry hall was cool, and sweet with the smell of spring flowers—massive bouquets of them gracing small tables. Johann was about to follow Black Suit down the hall when a rustle and splash of color arrested him. From the opposite direction, a woman approached. Black Suit waited. Johann stopped and stared again.

The Vision, for such she was to Johann, had long dark hair caught up in curls and combs, and a peach-colored rose fastened above her left ear. Johann took in the pale green silk, high-waisted dress, the slim, dainty figure, and the tiny white slippers. Then his gaze locked on the creature's deep brown eyes, and he was unable to look away. Or to speak.

Black Suit, standing behind him, administered a gentle nudge in the ribs, and said, "Good afternoon, Miss Maria. I was about to show Mr. Sudermann to his room."

"Thank you, Yuri." Her youthful voice sounded like distant bells. "Good afternoon, Mr. Sudermann. Are you not feeling well after your long train ride?" Her lips smiled, but the expression in her wondrous eyes was unreadable.

"Oh, I . . . I'm sorry, I . . . P . . . Pleased to meet you, Miss Maria. Yes, I . . . no, I'm fine. Thank you."

"Good. Then we will give you a chance to change and rest before supper. We will wait until then to discuss matters of business. Yuri . . ."

This last was a command to Black Suit and a dismissal to Johann. Miss Maria turned with a rustle of silk and floated away from them, down the green carpeted hallway. After another gentle tap on the shoulder, Johann turned to follow Yuri in the opposite direction. He was appalled at himself for his lack of control. Maria appeared to be a good deal younger than he, in spite of her grown-up ways. After several minutes of maneuvering through hallways and up stairs bordered by sturdy oak banisters, the two men stopped before a wide, green door. Yuri turned the handle, pushed it open, and stood back for Johann to enter.

"Ai, yai, yai!" he croaked, as he stepped into what was obviously to be his room. His bags stood neatly on the floor at the foot of a massive, four-poster bed. Dark, cherrywood tables and chests of drawers graced the carpeted floor, and two cozy armchairs by a fireplace invited the weary traveler. "My whole family could live in a room like this!"

He glanced at Yuri, who had developed a slight twitch in his moustache. Yuri bowed and said, "I trust you will be comfortable here. Supper will be served at seven. I will send Fyodor to show you to the dining room. The water closet is down the hall, to your right and just around the corner."

The man withdrew, leaving Johann to stare at the closed door. He turned, dazed, to look around him, then made his way to the window. Drawing aside the dark blue, muslin drapes, he peered out at the view to the south, the back of the house. Apparently, his room was in the central part of the house. There was a wing on each side, forming a courtyard beneath his windows. Vast lawns stretched across his view, seamed here and there by wide walkways and circled and intersected by trees, shrubs, and flowers. He pushed open the casement and was greeted by birdsong, a fresh breeze, and the sound of children's laughter.

"This is paradise," he whispered, in awe. He sank down into the cushions of one of the blue armchairs and grinned to himself. "I have discovered the garden of Eden." His grin widened. "And I think I have seen an angel!"

A short time later, Johann decided to inspect the water closet. To turn a tap and watch clear water pour into an enamel basin was amazing. Equally amazing, and amusing, was the automatic flush when he pulled a chain hanging from a ceramic box on the wall, just above his head. These people had truly discovered a life of ease and luxury. Such inventions suited the vision of loveliness he had seen in the entry hall.

Thoughts and imaginings filled Johann's head as he left the WC and walked back to his room to change for supper. Turning the corner, he collided with a young woman carrying an armful of fresh flowers. She must have been as lost in thought as Johann was. The collision, though not serious, was enough to send the girl's flowers flying in all directions. Johann caught her arm to steady her. "I'm so sorry," he blurted out. "I was preoccupied and not looking where I was going."

The young woman seemed greatly embarrassed. "Oh, it's my fault. Mika is always telling me to keep my head up when I walk and not to hurry so."

They stood in silence for an awkward moment before Johann offered to help her pick up her scattered flowers. They both bent over at once and bumped heads in the process.

"Oh, I'm sorry!" cried the young woman, one flower-stained hand reaching up to a reddening blotch on her forehead. Her eyes were brimming with tears, but she valiantly blinked them back, self-consciously pushing her rather frizzy hair back from an unremarkable face.

Johann was mortified. "This was my fault entirely." He patted her arm. "Are you all right?"

Suddenly, a few tears spilled down the girl's cheeks and she hiccuped, then giggled, then tried to suppress the mixture of laughter and tears by putting both hands over her mouth.

At first, Johann didn't know what to make of her. Then he stepped back a pace, bowed, and said, "Good afternoon. I am Johann Sudermann, newly arrived from the colonies." His eyes twinkled. "I have come to help you pick flowers."

She giggled again, dried her tears, and said, "I thank you, sir, and accept your offer of help. Let's pick these, here." Bending carefully, so as not to collide again, they got down on hands and knees to retrieve the fallen blooms. As soon as all were rescued, the girl smiled, repeated her thank-you, and turned quickly to deliver the bouquets where they were needed.

She looked tall and sturdy as she hurried away, her brown hair escaping from its braid in fuzzy bits all over her head.

"You didn't tell me your name," Johann called after her. She turned slightly and murmured something into the flowers that he could not quite hear, then turned again, her durable black boots well visible beneath the practical, brown skirt. A pale linen shirtwaist completed her dress. This strong, young woman with large, capable hands and a frizzy braid could prove to be his first real friend here, mused Johann. He continued on to his room, remembering to keep his head up.

At precisely five minutes before seven, Fyodor tapped at the door to show Johann to the dining room. The family had gathered and was being seated. The Vision, Miss Maria, sat next to her father, who took his place at the end of the long cherrywood table.

Mr. Hildebrandt rose as Johann approached. "Well, well, it seems the time has come at last for your arrival. Welcome to our home, Mr. Sudermann. Sit here, on my other side tonight. Katarina won't mind."

"Thank you for inviting me here," replied Johann, taking his place opposite Miss Maria and next to Heinrich. "I have been welcomed, and am already glad I've come." He shot a quick glance toward Maria, who gave him a polite smile.

Two younger children entered. "Children, come and meet your new teacher," said Mr. Hildebrandt. The little girl stepped forward somewhat hesitantly, the boy boldly and with a bounce in his step. "This is Anna," said her father, "and she is six years of age." The little blonde girl, with dancing eyes, gave a small curtsey and said, "Welcome here, Mr. Sudermann, sir." Then she stepped back, her face flaming. *She reminds me of the servant woman I ran into upstairs,* thought Johann.

"And I am Kolya!" The boy, a couple of years older than his sister, reached out an eager hand to shake Johann's.

"His name is Nicholai," corrected Maria.

"Welcome here, sir," said the boy, ignoring his sister's remark. He grinned, and an endearing dimple appeared beside the wide smile. Kolya's dark hair was slicked back carefully. Johann noticed his brown corduroy knee pants, smart white shirt with matching knee socks, and brown lace-up boots.

"I'm pleased to meet both of you," answered Johann. "Perhaps after supper we can visit a bit." He assumed they would be expected to remain silent during the meal.

The children both smiled and took their places, Anna beside Maria, and Kolya next to Johann, with one empty chair between them.

Maria spoke to her father. "Peter is not feeling well today and will take his supper in his room."

"I'll look in on him after supper," answered Heinrich. "Where is your other sister today?"

"Oh, who knows for sure?" Maria remarked. "No doubt visiting the Russian workers or else lost in the gardens somewhere."

At that moment, the awaited sister tripped in through the door, immediately slowing her pace to suit the occasion. Johann turned to look just as Heinrich introduced her.

"My eldest daughter, Katarina. Katarina, this is Mr. Sudermann."

Johann rose from his chair, then stopped still. "You!" he blurted, with a surprised smile. "I thought . . ."

Katarina's hand went to the slight bruise on her forehead. She smiled and gave a small curtsey, murmuring, "Pleased to meet you." Johann held her chair. She had tidied the braid, though it threatened to fuzz again at the slightest provocation, and changed into a dark skirt and pale green, silk blouse. An oval-shaped, jeweled gold brooch gleamed at the collar. She sat next to Johann, cheeks burning and eyes downcast.

"You have already met?" asked Maria in surprise.

"In a manner of speaking." Johann came to the rescue, as he sensed the tension between the sisters. "We passed in the upstairs hall before supper."

"What were you doing up there?" demanded Maria of her sister.

"Just bringing flowers."

"Children, please," interrupted their father. "Let's not bother Mr. Sudermann with trivialities. Shall we pray?"

After saying grace, Heinrich turned to his guest and said, "Now, Johann, tell us about your train ride from the Molotschna."

Johann described the gradual changes in climate in such a way that the two younger children listened with interest. He encouraged their questions. Though the setting was formal, the entire family seemed free to engage in conversation.

"You would love the train ride, Miss Maria. It is so grand," Johann said, trying to include her in the conversation.

"I have ridden on trains before, Mr. Sudermann. We visit our grandmother in Ruekenau from time to time."

"Oh, of course. I should have known." Johann was confused. First she had given him smiles, now coolness.

"The younger children haven't been north for quite some time, though," volunteered Katarina. "I'm sure they don't remember much about it."

Johann sent her a grateful look.

He enjoyed the pleasant meal of roast chicken and bubbat, with lots of raisins mixed into the cake like stuffing. Potatoes and gravy, fresh tomatoes, and warm rye bread filled their plates, followed by cold, juicy watermelon and cantaloupe. Kolya's hands were thoroughly sticky by the end of the meal.

"You will no doubt be rather weary by now," said Heinrich, when everyone was done. "We'll meet tomorrow in the schoolroom on the second floor of the east wing—to discuss the children's curriculum."

"That will be fine, sir," answered Johann. "I look forward to it." With smiles all around, he and the family rose from the table and went their separate ways.

Chapter 4

The meeting with Heinrich and his daughters was set for nine o'clock on Tuesday morning. Johann wanted to be prepared, to ask questions and to present his own plans. He rose early, while the dew still glimmered on the grass, and stood looking out his bedroom window. In the new morning sun, the paths through Eden were golden, shining like the streets of heaven itself. Quickly, so as not to lose the moment, Johann descended the carpeted stairs to the back garden entrance.

A walkway led south, then branched off in several directions —right to the vegetable gardens, straight ahead to the fruit orchards, and on to the brook, with its little bridge to the chapel. Johann proceeded straight ahead, intent on physical exercise as well as exploring the myriad paths crossing and winding through Eden.

His boots sounded on the path with a strange crunch and, bending to the ground, he discovered the reason for the golden streets. He scooped up a handful of earth and inspected it: seashells, crushed and mixed with fine stones. Frequent rains would make the paths impassable if not for the shells, he realized. The delicate curve and iridescence of the shells reflected the gold of the sunlight and, at night, the silver of the moon.

"Fascinating!" Johann declared, letting the earthy gems sift through his fingers. He rose and set off down the path, identified by a quaint, hand-scrolled sign as Magnolia Lane. As he walked briskly along, the sun rose, full and sure, overhead. Day had arrived and his stomach rumbled with emptiness.

Reluctantly, he returned to the house. A small, tidy kitchen garden to the right of the single door greeted him with a heady mix of thyme, basil, summer savory, dill, and anise. He couldn't identify the plants, but the combined aroma tantalized his senses.

Striding through the door and down the hall, with a smile on his face, Johann poked his head into the large, sunny kitchen, already buzzing with activity. A robust woman with an air of command noticed him at once.

"What can we for you do?" she asked politely. "You are lost?"

"No, no," he smiled. "I am merely searching out a bit of breakfast. My stomach is rumbling like thunder."

The stout woman, already red-faced with punching bread, blushed more and said, "The people from the house, they are served in the dining room at eight o'clock. You not can wait?"

"I can if I must. But I would much prefer to sit in a sunny corner and eat a few crusts of bread with butter, than be faced with all that formality. You see, at my home, we have only one table, and that is where we eat, talk, laugh, and argue. It would make me feel at home if I could eat here." He tilted his head slightly to the side and grinned disarmingly at the older woman.

"Well," she said gruffly, the pleasure on her face belying the sharpness of her voice, "I suppose we could let you sit over there by the window." With a slight smile, she added, "But you cannot bother us. We've much work to do."

Before Johann had settled himself in the leather-seated straightback chair by the window, she had set before him a steaming bowl of porridge, topped with molasses sugar and splashed with fresh cream, and a plate of zweibach and jelly.

"Tomorrow, you come sooner and you get cracklings with potatoes and brown bread." She turned away abruptly and marched back to her post, surreptitiously casting glances at him now and then, to see that he was well satisfied.

The sweet, warm, filling porridge soothed Johann's stomach and energized his brain. When he was finished, he gave a sincere thank-you, to the head cook's obvious pleasure, and with a new friend to his credit, ran lightly up the stairs to the schoolroom.

Young Fyodor had already deposited Johann's books and notes there the evening before. He chose a spot on the opposite side of the table, where he could lay out his material and meet the eyes of all who came in the door. Reviewing his plans, he became lost in thought. How different would this venture be from the large schoolhouse at Kleefeld with its fifty students of all ages and capabilities? He was so wrapped up in the excitement of his new project that he did not notice the arrival of one of his associates.

She watched him silently from the doorway, studying his intensity, his excitement, and his pleasant eyes behind the round glasses. She was about to withdraw to await the arrival of the others, when Johann glanced up and saw her. Immediately, he rose from his chair and reached out a hand to her.

"Good morning to you, Miss Katarina. A lovely morning, isn't it?"

"Yes, it is. Good morning to you, too," she answered, advancing shyly toward him.

Sensing her hesitation, Johann tried to lighten the mood. "I'm sure we are safe from collision with the table between us."

She smiled, but her face turned crimson and her hands came up to cover her burning cheeks. Scolding himself inwardly, Johann picked up one of his books and held it out to her.

"*Botany: A Study of Native Russian Plants and Flowers,*" he read, as he handed it to her. Katarina took the volume with interest, giving Johann a slight smile and sinking into a chair. She leafed through the pages, which were filled with sketches, photographs, and diagrams. Pleased that he had put her at ease at last, Johann also resumed his seat. As she relaxed, he ventured a question. "Katarina, does your forehead hurt where I bumped you with this hard head of mine?"

"Oh, no, it's quite fine by now," she answered quietly. "A bit of ice and the swelling disappeared." Her curls, never quite tamed by combs and pins, nicely covered the purple bruise.

"You like botany?" he asked conversationally.

"Yes, I do." After a slight pause, she continued. "My mother showed me much about growing things. We worked together often in the gardens."

"Your mother must have been a wonderful gardener and a superb teacher."

"That she was." Katarina smiled as she remembered. "She often told stories as we worked, about the tiny people who used the flowers of the ladies slipper as shoes, about the frogs who were actually princes of the amphibian world, and about the crickets who played their music for wee folk's parties."

Johann was amazed at Katarina's transformation as she spoke. Her shyness melted away like dew in the sun, her green eyes sparkled, and her smile warmed her whole expression. She ceased fidgeting with the buttons of her skirt and leaned back in the chair, in complete contentment.

"You must have had a wonderful childhood," Johann encouraged her to continue.

"It was wonderful. A fairy tale really," she said, glancing up at him. Almost imperceptibly, her face took on a sad look. "It is unfortunate that Kolya and Anna do not have this same legacy."

"How old were they when your mother passed away?"

"She's been gone for two, almost three years now. Anna was three and Kolya, five. Too young to lose a mother." Katarina looked directly into Johann's eyes. "I try to keep her memory alive for them, but sometimes I wonder if she is real to them any more." Her eyes searched for understanding, but at the same time, the depths were guarded and unreadable. Perhaps, with time, she would allow him into her life.

"I'm glad you told me of your concern, Katarina," he said. "I'll try to include your mother in conversation as we learn together."

Her eyebrows rose in surprise at his sensitivity. "I . . . it would be . . . thank you," she said, finally. Then, in an un-guarded moment of openness she added, "And please call me Katya. I prefer it."

"I will gladly do that, Katya," he said, "if you agree to call me Johann." They exchanged pleasant smiles.

Maria and her father entered the schoolroom just as the Kroeger wall clock chimed nine times. "Johann!" boomed Mr. Hildebrandt, filling the doorway and bringing his energy in to the room. "What a day this is."

"Yes, sir," answered Johann, shaking his hand. "Beautiful." His eyes strayed to Mika as he said the word.

Maria followed her father, her charm and beauty matching his energy. The plain skirt and blouse she wore only accentu-ated her carefully arranged curls, rich brown and soft, and her large dark eyes.

"Good morning, Mr. Sudermann," she said, offering her tiny hand with a gracious smile. "We must get right down to business, as Father has important things to attend to."

Today he had received a smile. So the tone for the meeting was set. They took their seats around the table, and Johann was about to open his notebook when Mr. Hildebrandt's voice interrupted his thoughts.

"Dear Father," he prayed, "we beg of you to give us wisdom and guidance as we discuss the children's studies. Grant patience to Johann and the will to learn to Anna and Nicholai. Amen."

Johann, somewhat unsettled at Heinrich's familiarity with God, offered a quick smile and cleared his throat.

"Yes. Thank you, sir. Now, we need to come to an agreement as to which areas of study are important for the children. I have a few suggestions, which I will present to you, and then I welcome your ideas."

He proceeded, and the final outcome of the meeting seemed to satisfy everyone: reading, grammar, composition and dictation, all in the German language; mathematics, politics and geography, botany, music, and art; and the practical teaching of agriculture and homemaking, for Kolya and Anna respectively. Katarina and Maria would help where they could and supervise study times. One of the Russian teachers from a nearby village would come once each week to instruct the children in the Russian language. "We must be sure to spend time with the Russian language," stated Johann, "as our tsar has decreed."

Johann reviewed the list after the others had gone. He would spend the afternoon preparing some lesson plans and begin with Anna and Kolya in the morning.

Just as he was beginning to feel an emptiness in his stomach again, a light knock on the schoolroom door startled him. He opened the door to the curtsey of a maid with a tray of food.

"Your dinner, sir," she said, walking briskly into the schoolroom and depositing the tray on the table. "Just leave the tray outside the door when you're done, and I will pick it up later."

"Please, one moment," Johann stopped her as she prepared to leave. "What name does the head cook go by? What do you call her?"

The girl looked at him strangely. "Cook," she answered. "We all call her Cook." With another curtsey, she retreated down the hall.

"So," thought Johann. "This is where I will take my noon meals." He sighed. "Later on, I will take a walk and breathe some fresh air."

He scribbled ideas in his book as he ate the steaming cabbage borscht and fresh, brown bread spread generously with rich butter. When he had finished the food and his coffee, he closed his books and carried the tray down to the kitchen. As soon as Cook saw him with the tray, she started in on the maid.

"Hilda, why did you not tell Mr. Sudermann to leave the tray up the stairs? Now he has interrupted his work your job to do."

Quickly, Johann set the tray on the counter and held up both hands imploringly. "Please, please, Cook. She did tell me to leave it by the door, but I disobeyed her. I needed a bit of a walk outdoors to clear my head, and I also wanted another chance to spend time with you."

Cook blushed thoroughly and pushed him out the garden door. "Out with you, you young charmer," she scolded, good-naturedly. "You do need to clear that head of yours." She slammed the screen door as he chuckled on his way to the orchard.

Next day, after a hearty breakfast in the kitchen, Johann hurried up to the classroom to await the children's arrival. He had met both Kolya and Anna several times the previous day, and their excitement to begin their learning experience matched his own. Apparently, Peter was still ill.

As nine o'clock approached, Johann felt prepared. He had set out scribblers, with pencils and the children's readers. Both children appeared at the same moment, escorted by a servant, most likely to assure that Kolya actually reached the schoolroom on time.

"Good morning, Anna. Good morning, Nicholai," said Johann, as they entered the room. "I am happy to see you both

and eager to begin. Anna, please sit here," he said, motioning
to one of the chairs opposite him, "and Nicholai, here."

"I'd rather sit by the window, if you don't mind, sir," said
Kolya, innocently. "It inspires me to see the beauty of nature
as I work." He grinned at his teacher, and his dimple appeared.

"Perhaps we will work our way to the window, Master
Nicholai!" Johann laughed. "I will observe your work habits
and we shall see what we shall see." Then he added, "I'll
leave a chair open for Peter, should he feel well enough to join
us later." A strange look he could not define passed between
the children as he spoke of Peter. *No matter*, he thought, *I
will find out in time.*

Reading and composition classes went well, but the gram-
matical drills proved to be Kolya's undoing.

"What for do we have to repeat all those silly rules?" he
asked in disgust, as they turned to the final drill exercise. "As
long as I can understand you, and you can understand me,
what's the reason to waste time on such details?"

"Oh, Kolya," fretted little Anna. "You must not speak so
to the teacher. You know Papa and Mika would not like it."

"Don't worry, Anna," Johann said immediately, to dispel
her anxiety. "I require respect in my classroom, but I also
allow for honest questioning. I believe that rebellious atti-
tudes often spring from unanswered questions. So," he turned
to Kolya, who eyed him with new interest, "we will discuss
your question further."

Anna smiled in relief, as she realized there would be no
struggle for power.

"Now children," said Johann, "time for botany. We will
march quietly down the stairs and out to the gardens, where
Katarina will meet us. On the way, we'll discuss the pros and
cons of proper grammar and learning by repetition. Now," he
clapped his hands, "let's go."

The botany lesson was a pleasure for both teachers and

students, as they strolled from place to place in the park south of the mansion. The small herb garden that grew near the kitchen proved fascinating, as Katya pointed out the various herbs and their uses in treating illness and injury. She rubbed a peppermint leaf between her thumb and forefinger, releasing its sharp aroma. "Peppermint is wonderful," she said. "It is good for stomachache, sore throat, and toothache. White lilac blossoms can help draw out a fever, and orange juice and vinegar can stop a nosebleed."

"Where did you learn all this, Katya?" asked Johann, as the group wandered back toward the house.

She smiled. "A lot of it Mama taught me, of course, and her mama taught her, and so it has been passed on, from generation to generation. But some of the treatments came from Russian peasants. The people who work for my father have their own history of herbal medicine."

"So you acquired all this wisdom right here on the estate! I'm impressed with your knowledge and memory."

"Well, there are many places to pick up knowledge, if you're attentive. The estate has its store, and other ideas come from other sources," Katya added, somewhat evasively.

"Other sources? Like books and papers?"

"Some." Again, she did not offer to tell him anything more.

"You're not about to tell me your secret sources, are you?" Johann asked, with a smile. "I will respect that, but just so you know, I do not tell tales. I can keep a secret, if you ever need to confide in someone."

She looked at him steadily for a long moment and nodded. "I believe you can be trusted. One of these days I may show you."

Supper was a pleasant affair that evening. Maria was in a charming mood and shared her grace and beauty with them all. Johann noticed that as she gained control of the conversation, she smiled more. *Too bad*, he thought, *that her sister Katya remains so quiet. She really has a lovely personality.*

But Johann's eyes rested mostly on Maria. She had a magnetism that kept him attentive to her words, and he did not fight the power. He saw little of her during the day, as she did not take an active role in teaching her siblings, other than supervising Anna's embroidery. "I really am quite busy managing the household," she said, when he asked her about it. "I am not a teacher."

She said the word with distaste, as if it were a lowly job, one belonging to a servant. Johann learned to keep his place, to respond to her when she decided to notice him, and to not bother her when she didn't. Those were her terms, and he accepted them as if he had no choice. He wondered sometimes if there shouldn't be more to a relationship, but he never answered the question completely. He was not willing to give up even the little that Mika offered him.

The third day after Johann's arrival dawned bright and clear, the sky an inverted bowl of blue capping the greening earth. Spring had sent out its roots in search of summer, and they had taken hold in the rich soil.

After a brisk walk through the park, Johann took the back stairs two at a time to his second-story schoolroom. The children arrived, reflecting the beauty of the day, and engaged themselves in their assigned studies, with Johann guiding, assisting, and suggesting.

Then from a distance, they heard the sound of awkwardly running feet, becoming louder as they approached. Suddenly, the door of the classroom burst open with a crash, and a thin, wild-looking boy of twelve or thirteen stared in confusion at Johann and the children. Muttering unintelligible words, he searched the room, then called out loudly and desperately.

Kolya and Anna had sat rooted to their chairs, but at this outburst, both jumped into action. "Mama's not here, Peter. She's gone. I'll go get Katya." Kolya ran from the room in search of help, while Anna touched Johann's hand and whispered, "It's Peter. We must calm him."

She advanced slowly toward Peter, speaking soft, soothing words to disarm whatever demon had invaded him. "It's all right, dear Peter," she said. "Katya's coming and she will help you find Mama."

"Ma! Ma! Ma!" rasped the boy, not looking at Anna, but seeming to respond to her words. He stepped forward and grabbed a pencil from the desk. "Give me the pencil, Peter. I need it," Anna commanded gently. Then to Johann, "Please take it from him quickly, Mr. Sudermann, before he hurts himself."

Johann, still in a state of shock, stepped forward to reach the potential weapon clutched in Peter's bony hand. As he drew near, Peter became more agitated and began to jab himself with the pencil.

Just then Kolya arrived with Katya, who held her brother in a firm hug from behind, commanding Johann to take the pencil now. At Katya's presence, Peter melted. She literally carried him to a chair, where he slumped as she supported him.

"Hello, Peter," she said, in a pleasant voice. "How are you today?"

"Ma, Ma, Ma," he insisted, more quietly now.

"Yes, Mama's in the churchyard. Katya will take care of you. Mama is happy and Peter should be happy too."

"Ma, Ma." The syllables came softly now. The boy looked exhausted.

Anna looked up into Johann's wide eyes and smiled weakly, patting his hand. "It's okay now, Teacher. Katya is here."

Abruptly, Peter stood and began to walk about the room, picking things up, dropping them, touching, tasting, while

Katya policed him. After a few minutes, she asked Kolya to help her lead him back downstairs.

Johann cleared his throat and straightened his shoulders. "I'll help." But as soon as he stepped toward Peter, the agitation took hold again.

"All right, then," conceded Johann, his hands up in resignation. "You go." After Katya left with Peter, he saw Mika in the hallway just outside the classroom.

"What is it?" she asked. "What's all the noise in here?"

"Your brother Peter found his way up here," he answered, still shaken. "He was quite disturbed."

"My brother Peter." She turned and entered the schoolroom, walking over to the window and gazing out on the park, not really seeing it.

"Don't worry, Maria. We will get over it. I was just shocked, since no one had told me anything about Peter's condition." His tone was mildly admonishing.

Mika turned to him and stared coolly into his eyes. "We do not enjoy discussing his condition, whatever it is," she waved her small hand vaguely in the air. "I would appreciate if you would forget the incident and carry on with your work."

"But it's nothing to be ashamed of. You didn't cause it."

"We are not ashamed. We just don't speak of it. There is nothing to be done about it. Do you understand me?" Her voice was condescending.

Rather than argue or confront, Johann simply gave a slight nod that could be translated as a bow if she wished, and returned to his desk. She walked regally from the room.

Life had changed for Susannah more than she ever thought it could. The change began with Johann's good-bye and was followed by much soul-searching.

First, she was no longer a girl with a male admirer. Perhaps someone would come along soon, her friends told her, comfortingly, but she didn't like to think about it. She had really cared for Johann Sudermann.

And now her sister Helena was in Neukirch with Jakob, setting up her own household. Lena was always willing to listen to Susannah, but it wasn't the same as in the girls' room at home, whispering secret hopes and fears late into the night. Besides, now Lena's typical response to problems was, "Just give it time, Suse. Everything will work out."

Maybe it won't, thought Susannah, as she helped her mother gather cantaloupe and watermelons for fresh eating and pickling. As she snapped beans and picked up the large red potatoes, the foundation of her dreams was being shaken, and she hesitated to build again on that place.

Her family and friends commented on her solemnity and "wool-gathering," but in truth she was thinking deep thoughts, a pastime unfamiliar to her and startling in its results. "Why am I here and not in a Russian village or an English country house or even in America?" She began to ask Johann's questions, trying to find answers for her own peace of mind. "What makes my soul so restless now? It's as if I've awakened in another world, without the securities I clung to in the old one."

She paid closer attention in church, while the other girls blushed and blinked at a covert wink from one of the boys. Could the minister find comfort for her before the service ended and the visiting began?

In the last she was ever disappointed. Keep the commandments, he said, especially obedience to parents and respect for elders. Use discretion in business affairs and handle material possessions responsibly. Beware of entanglement with the world.

"The world," she knew, meant anything or anyone beyond

the villages, beyond the control of the bishop and the *Schulze*, the religious and civic leaders.

For the first time in her life, Susannah Loewen experienced the twinges of questioning, the claustrophobic pangs of uncertainty. These new patterns of thought pinched and cramped as she attempted to carry out the routine that had always been enough for her before.

She straightened her shoulders and smoothed a hand over the thick, blond braid curled neatly around her head. The root of these new thoughts was still hidden to her, but she would continue to search for their source. Unknown to her, the Source stood by, waiting to be found.

Chapter 5

The sun was just past its zenith as Katya emerged from behind the yew hedge and arrived at the barns. She greeted the stable manager in Russian. "Good morning, Misha. Would you please help me hitch Sunny to my wagon?"

"Where you ride today, or will you even tell me?" asked the old man with a smile, laying aside the harness he had been oiling.

She returned the smile and wrinkled her nose. "I'm off to the land beyond the sea, where I shall find gold and jewels and bring them back for you. And I promise to return by suppertime."

"I thought as much. You just watch where you drive and stay to the main roads. There are gypsies about, and they are without conscience."

She made no reply, and he stopped to look in her eyes. "Katarina," he said sternly, "*djipsaya* are not to be trusted. They would fill your hands with trinkets and then stab you in the back to regain them. Promise me you will stay clear of them."

"I'll be careful," Katya answered, evasively.

"Somehow this does not comfort me." He turned to retrieve a light buggy harness from the rack on the wall. "If you are not here by supper, we will start to search immediately."

"I appreciate your concern, Misha, but I will be fine. I'm almost seventeen now and able to take care of myself."

He watched her scramble up to the loft to retrieve her baskets, then shook his head at her lack of fear.

Katya and Sunny set off at a brisk trot down the cobbled yard that led to the brook and over the bridge to the estate chapel. She whispered a quiet "Hello, Mama" as she passed the large tomb in the cemetery. After that, the lane degenerated into a dirt trail, winding through the fields past groves of trees and clearings of wild flowers. Cattle and sheep grazed in some areas, watched by shepherds and dogs. The sun cast familiar warmth over the countryside, as Katya leaned back and enjoyed the sweet breeze.

Several versts farther down the road, she rounded a large grove of trees and came upon gypsy wagons. There were at least a dozen, brightly painted and decorated in bright blue, green, red, and yellow. The wagons formed a lopsided circle, enclosing a grassy center. Olive-skinned children chased each other and laughed in the clearing, their long, dark hair wild and free.

Djipsaya were the untamed wanderers of the steppes and grasslands. Their horses were sleek, their women pretty, and their tempers volatile. There were many stories of jealous fights and injury within the caravans. The gypsies traded with peasant farmers and even colonists and settlers who cared to deal with them. They came near the towns from time to time, to set up their makeshift tin smithies, but preferred their own company.

Katya's mind flew back easily to the day several years ago when she had been out riding her pony. The day was cool, the horse frisky, and she'd lost her balance and taken a tumble as they jumped a creek. When she hit the creek bank, everything went black.

When she awoke, she didn't know where she was, except that it was dim and smelled odd. As her eyes grew accustomed to the lack of light, she became aware of someone at her side. Looking up, she stared into the blackest eyes she had ever seen, shining at her from a smiling, dark face, framed by an abundance of ebony hair.

The face belonged to a woman named Natalya, and in response to her kindness and care that day, Katya had kept in touch from year to year as the caravans moved through the backcountry. She had told no one. She valued her freedom too much to reveal her secret, and she and Natalya had developed a strange but trusting friendship.

'Djipsaya' dangerous? It all depends, thought Katya, *on how you treat them* . . .

This day, as she rode out in the buggy, she was searching for adventure. Katarina did not usually take unnecessary risks, but at the center of her being was a wistfulness that sometimes grew into restlessness. She needed to feel the wind in her face, to leave the confines, however idyllic, of the mansion and its park, to roam free and wild over the grassy plains and in the wooded thickets. It was the wildness that called her, she supposed, so in contrast to her usual quiet contentment. She watched a hawk swoop overhead, screeching its disgust as a ground squirrel disappeared down a hole hidden in the grass. She envied him his freedom and wildness.

Passing the stand of poplars, she saw Natalya's wagon, second from the far end, its bright sun-yellow door gleaming in the summer heat. An eerie feeling came over her, without warning, without reason. She tried to shrug it off, but it persisted, affecting Sunny as well. He nickered nervously, his ears pointing sharply forward, then pivoting to detect the direction of the distraction.

On impulse, Katya whirled around on the buggy seat, and found herself under the steely stare of a dark, wild-looking young man. She sat frozen, eyes staring, her breathing shallow. *Hawk!* she thought, as she came to herself. He resembled the hawk she had seen a few moments before.

Gradually, courage and resolve filled her and she spoke. "Good day to you," she said quietly, in the local Russian dialect. "I'm sorry to intrude, but I've come to find Natalya."

The young man, disarmed by her quiet control, blinked and stepped back. Without a word, he disappeared into the trees. Katya sat waiting. She spoke softly to her horse, and he gradually relaxed and began nosing around for a clump of grass.

Several minutes later, the man came riding from the wagons, and motioned for her to proceed. Rolling up to the wagons, she jumped out of the buggy and handed him the lines. He pointed in the direction of the second last wagon and said, "Natalya," in a voice like distant thunder.

Katya reached into her buggy to retrieve a rather large satchel, but the young man stopped her with a word and demanded the bag. *May as well comply,* she thought. *If I leave it in the buggy, he will go through it anyway.*

He inspected the contents—a few jars with seeds in them, a roll of bright yellow cloth, and a book. Satisfied that there was nothing inappropriate within, he held the bag out to her and nodded his head toward the wagon with the yellow door.

Katya was aware of many eyes watching her as she walked across the grass, but she felt no fear. Now that the initial shock was over, she was confident and trusting. Her time with the dark-eyed woman passed quickly. They shared, without many language barriers, the gifts of seeds and cloth and written word.

"Bible," said Katya clearly, as she held out the book to her friend.

"Bible?" questioned Natalya.

"God's words to us," Katya explained. "For you to read and to keep."

Natalya eyed the book suspiciously. Strangely enough, she could read, more for survival than her own wishes, but reference to God seemed to put her on guard. She pushed the book away. "You keep. I no read."

"But I'd like you to know what God says to you."

"Your God, not mine," Natalya insisted.

With a sigh, Katya put the book back in her bag, along with a small collection of dried herbs and a brilliant green and red sash with long tassels. She wished she could wear the sash, but such an action would bring her secret into the open, to be stomped on and curtailed immediately by her well-meaning family. Best to keep the sash hidden in her wardrobe, under the baby clothes from her infancy.

Katya thanked Natalya for her time and gifts, gave her a quick hug, and climbed down from the wagon. Natalya walked with her to the place where Sunny and the buggy waited, then said something in dialect, definitely a command. The young man appeared, and was directed to escort Katya partway home. She began to say she would be fine alone, but Natalya waved her on. Katya knew it would do no good to argue. She would pretend to be a queen and ride regally home along the prairie path with the Hawk prancing beside her on his sleek, chestnut mare.

On Sunday, the Hildebrandt family and its servants gathered at the main entrance of the estate house, then walked together through the park and down Magnolia Lane to the chapel.

Heinrich marched ahead like an ambassador, with Anna holding one hand and Kolya walking on his other side. Maria and Katarina walked behind them, with Johann between them. The rest of the household followed quietly, except for the few who needed to mind the kitchen and stay with Peter. Johann was acutely aware of Mika, her fine clothes rustling, and her tiny hands protected from the summer sun by white lace gloves. Her wide-brimmed hat sported an enormous ostrich feather, no doubt from a milliner in the colonies, where these things were more readily available.

Katarina dressed more simply, but with an honesty that gave her a fresh, welcoming appearance. She wore a small hat that allowed the breeze to play with her curls.

"What a perfect day," commented Johann. "The air is so clean and clear, like it's been washed and left to dry in the sun."

Mika glanced at him from beneath her hat, with an uplifted eyebrow. "It will be too hot by the time we walk home again," she said, putting his remark into her perspective.

Katya spoke quietly. "Well, I would agree that this is a treasure of a day, something God unwrapped for us as the sun rose. It's a blessing to be grateful for." Johann smiled at her and she smiled back. Maria made no comment, but raised her chin and tucked her hand into Johann's arm.

"I agree with you, daughter." Heinrich's strong voice echoed down the sunny lane. "This day is a gift from the Lord and we must cherish it. Even the brook is happy today. Do you hear it laughing, Anya?" The little girl grinned up at her papa as they crossed the bridge.

Succoth Chapel stood white and serene in the morning sun. Blackbirds chirped in the oaks and maples, which leaned over the building and the adjoining cemetery. Johann almost felt a blessing as he stepped aside to allow the ladies to enter, then followed them in. They seated themselves in the small room and bowed their heads in reverence for some minutes.

Maria did not fidget, but Johann sensed her uneasiness, because he felt it too. Katya sat perfectly still, wrapped in reverence. *What is her secret?* Johann wondered. He had already sensed her peace, her inner composure. Oh, Mika had composure, too, but it was practiced and controlled—not innocent like Katya's.

After a time, Katarina rose quietly and stepped up to the

front pew, where her father sat alone. She took up a guitar and tuned it to the first string, then began to strum softly.

The holy presence in Succoth Chapel held an identity all its own. Johann and even Maria were eventually swept along in the tide of its loveliness. Katya softly sang a hymn of the Reformation, still strumming her instrument, and Heinrich's rich voice sustained hers:

> "Dear Jesus, thou Eternal God,
> For me thy blood was shed . . ."

Maria and the children joined in, and the servants in the back pews added heavenly harmonies. Johann hummed along, not sure of all the words until Anna lifted a thin hymnal from the bench pocket ahead of her, turned to page twelve, and handed it to him. He followed the numbers on the page and read the accompanying words.

A few more songs and Heinrich stepped up behind the small, hand carved pulpit. Katarina laid the guitar carefully on the front bench, wrapped in its protective blanket, and returned to her seat beside Johann. Anticipation shone in her green eyes as she looked up at her father.

"For our meditation this morning," he began, "we will read the word of the Lord as taken from the prophet Micah, chapter six and verse eight." Johann marveled again at the man's sense of self and dignity.

Heinrich paused as his tiny congregation flipped through the thin onionskin pages of their Bibles to locate Micah. "Johann, would you please come forward and read the Scripture for us?" Johann's head snapped up in surprise, but as he met Heinrich's eyes, he knew it was safe to comply. With a quick glance at Mika, who had put up her handkerchief to hide her smile, he walked to the front of the church and took his place beside Heinrich. The older man put one hand on his shoulder and with the other, pointed out the verse in his Bible.

Johann cleared his throat and read, " 'He has showed thee, O man, what is good. And what does the Lord require of thee? To act justly and to love mercy and to walk humbly with thy God.' Thus far the reading of God's word."

Before returning to his place between Mika and Katarina, Johann looked out at the room and noted the differences from his own church in Kleefeld. His home church boasted a large congregation, with ministers trained to preach, a sizable youth choir and other important figures who assumed seats at the front for the duration of the service. The mood was formal in the extreme, and sober, too. *An act of tradition, of form,* thought Johann.

But this, this was a family, gathered to worship their Creator and Lord. The difference was in the hearts of the worshipers.

Johann resumed his seat and sat ready to listen to Heinrich Hildebrandt. In the end, it was not Heinrich's words that spoke to his heart, but the word of God.

"Why do we keep wondering what God's will is for us?" Heinrich looked at the faces before him. "He has shown us what is good. It is all in this book, in his example of sending his only Son to die for our sins. Is it because we don't like what he says, because it would cause us discomfort to obey?" He paused to allow the words to sink in.

"The writer of Proverbs says it again, in chapter one and verse three: 'doing what is right and just and fair,' and again in the prophet Zechariah, chapter seven, verse nine: 'This is what the Lord Almighty says: Administer true justice; show mercy and compassion to one another.'

"Are we showing fairness? Are we being just with our thoughts, words, and actions? Are we doing what we know is right?"

Maria's hands moved slightly, picking at the lace on her gloved fingers. Otherwise, she sat still as a stone. Katya lifted her handkerchief to her eyes as she took her father's message to heart. *As if she were doing anything other than what is right,* thought Johann.

Heinrich continued. "First Chronicles eighteen, verse fourteen states that 'David reigned over all Israel, doing what was just and right.' Can that be said of us, my family and friends?"

As by some unspoken permission, Johann's mind gave in to self-examination and found him wanting. "You could never be a bad example to anyone," Susannah's words came back to him, but he knew he was capable of living as a hypocrite. Still, the key evaded his grasp. The door to understanding remained closed. But he had begun to search, and a path was laid out to follow.

Hosts and servants mingled after the service and walked home with much chatter and freedom. It was the one day of the week that they all ate together at the long, cherrywood table. They all helped themselves to juicy roast beef and lightly browned roast potatoes, steaming carrots and beans, this year's pickles, and a beautifully iced chocolate cake with coffee for dessert.

Cook was ushered to a place of honor at the foot of the table and not allowed into the kitchen for cleanup. Her troops had been well trained, and they did her bidding completely and efficiently.

"A lovely day of rest," said Johann to Heinrich later, as they lounged in wicker chairs on the veranda.

"Such it was meant to be," smiled Heinrich, then leaned his head back and closed his eyes. Soon his snores drowned out the song of birds and the croak of frogs, and Johann quietly left for more tranquil surroundings.

Chapter 6

 Heinrich was agitated as he came down for supper that evening. Tucked under his arm was the July 2, 1914 edition of *Friedensstimme*, a German-language newspaper printed at the Raduga Print Shop in Neu Halbstadt, Molotschna.

"It's ironic," he stated after supper, that the 'Voice of Peace' carries such an announcement."

"What announcement, Papa?" asked Katya.

Heinrich cleared his throat. "Archduke Franz Ferdinand of Austria has been assassinated. I fear this incident is not isolated," he continued. "Something is amiss, and we, in a world of our own, have not been aware of it."

"Who engineered the assassination, sir?" asked Johann.

Heinrich nodded at the sheet in his hand. "According to this paper, the shots were fired by a young Bosnian student, presently living in Serbia." He continued to scan the write-up.

"Where is Serbia, Papa?" asked Kolya.

"Johann?" prompted Heinrich, with the hint of a twinkle in his eye. "I believe this is your area of expertise."

Johann smiled. "Serbia is a small, European country just south of Austria-Hungary. Bosnia is a province in Austria-Hungary. We'll locate it on the classroom map tomorrow."

"Why did they shoot that man?" asked Anna, with a troubled look on her face. "Was he bad?"

Heinrich took over again. "That man was Archduke Franz Ferdinand, the heir to the throne of Austria-Hungary, my

Anya, and no, he was not necessarily bad."

"Why are people so cruel?" questioned Katya. Her question was rhetorical, but Heinrich could not refrain from answering. "Liebchen," he began, "it seems that in political crises people cease to view others as people, and instead consider them merely a means toward an end or, in this case, an obstacle to a desired end."

"So termination is the simplest way," finished Katarina, with a sigh. "This world is indeed a sad place when we forget the importance of an individual soul."

Johann had been watching Mika, as was his unconscious habit, but became absorbed in what Katya was saying. He hadn't known a woman could be interested in political discussion, never mind offer her opinion. He was aware, though, that in this motherless household, family discussions were open forum, allowing for equality, unity, and a sense of belonging.

Suddenly Mika, who had been fidgeting impatiently with her coffee cup, blurted out, "I don't know what's so important about some man being shot, somewhere far from here, for reasons we don't understand. People die every day. What has that incident to do with us?"

Heinrich spoke to her gently, knowing there was fear behind her anger. "My dear Maria, I know political talk bores you, but we must stay aware of world happenings. It only takes a spark to start a forest fire, and if what editor Kroeker records is true, this incident may be the igniting spark in the ongoing dispute between Austria-Hungary and Serbia. It may yet have an effect on us."

The kitchen staff came then to clear the table, and Johann joined Heinrich in the parlor. Johann, his curiosity piqued, was looking for details. "When did the assassination take place?" he asked.

"On Sunday last, June 28, just before noon in Sarajevo.

Both the archduke and his wife were killed. The assassin simply broke away from the crowd, jumped up on the running board of the touring car, and fired several shots. Austria-Hungary is angry, as can be expected. I don't know what their next move will be, but I expect retaliation of some kind."

Johann considered this. "But surely this is not far-reaching enough to affect us here. I tend to agree with Mika. What have we to do with the European power struggle?"

"Well, my dear Mr. Sudermann, Russia has not been overly friendly with Germany lately, and as you know, Germany and Austria-Hungary are allied at the present time. They joined with Italy as the Triple Alliance back in '82. I don't profess to understand all the intricacies of political scheming," continued Heinrich, "but there are some things that apparently cannot be overlooked, and ties and alliances will be tested."

"Yes," agreed Johann. "I begin to see your concern." They sat in silence for a few minutes, each occupied with his own thoughts.

Johann broke the silence with a new subject. "Is there any help for Peter? I have not been able to reach him at all. In fact, he seems to be afraid of me. I hope I'm not stepping out of line. Maria instructed me never to speak of the problem."

A ghost of a smile touched Heinrich's face and he said, "Don't mind Maria. She is a proud young woman. She has a need to control."

He sighed and rubbed a hand over his whiskered face. "Would that there were some way to reach Peter," he finally said, rising and staring out the window into the darkness. "No one seems able to find the place where his mind dwells. Elizabeth came close, with a mother's love. She would sing to him when he became agitated—sing and rock him and pray."

"I imagine he was smaller then and easier to control."

"Oh, yes. Although the strength of a disturbed mind can lend great power to even a weak body. But now he is growing into a young man, and what is to become of him, God only knows. All we can do is what we have been doing: keep praying."

"If you allow me to speak my mind, sir, perhaps there is something we can do. There are various hospitals and institutions in the colonies. I could write for information on his condition and the methods being used for such cases. I have a friend back home named Susannah. I'm sure she could look into it as well."

"Whatever you like," answered Heinrich, hopelessly. He lifted weary eyes and looked at Johann. "Thank you for caring. It is a tremendous burden for us to bear. If only Peter could be strong of mind and body like you, young Hans." He sighed. "But God's ways are best."

Johann stiffened. "Excuse my abruptness, sir, but how can you say that? Surely you don't believe that God wants Peter to be so."

Heinrich smiled a sad smile as he contemplated his answer. "You have much to learn about God, my friend. If we could understand him, we wouldn't need him. He is far beyond our comprehension. But let me tell you one thing about this God of ours, Johann. He knows your heart and appreciates your honesty, something like the way you deal with your students."

"Sir?"

"Oh yes, Teacher. I hear many reports of your methods, of your being the best teacher ever." He smiled. "Just don't let it go to your head. But to continue, I encourage you to talk to God of your doubts and allow him to teach you. Only God can answer your questions to your satisfaction."

Johann stood and bowed slightly. "Thank you for the advice, sir. Because I respect you, I will consider it. But God will have to do some explaining to me about Peter." With that, he bade his host goodnight and proceeded upstairs.

A cool breeze played with the drapes in his room and calmed him with the gentle perfume of hundreds of flowers from the park, as he sat thinking in one of the blue chairs by the dark, cold fireplace.

He puzzled for some time over the confusion in his soul. Never before had he actually wondered who God was. In his experience, religion had to do with church, with read sermons, recited prayers, and the long-preserved traditions of his people. But a personal God? This was something new, rather disconcerting to one who preferred to wrap his life in nice, neat packages to be stored on shelves in his mind. Peter, the unrest in Europe, God. These thoughts and more swirled unrelentingly in his head. Johann stood and prepared for bed, not sure whether or not he would sleep.

Heinrich kept abreast of the political situation through the German publications *Friedensstimme* and *Der Botschafter*, as well as occasional copies of *PRAVDA*, a national paper launched a few years back by a young man named Iosef Djugashvili. Some news was sketchy, but Heinrich understood the general feeling that Germany was angry with Russia, which had apparently been meddling in the Balkans, particularly Serbia.

The family set aside politics for a time, as summer smiled on the land. "Are the preachers all scheduled for the conference, Father?" asked Maria, one day in early July.

"Of course, child. They're due here in a little over two weeks." He smiled at the excitement in his daughter's eyes at the opportunity of planning another faith conference at Succoth. It was important to stay in touch with the people of God, and to expose his children to spiritual teaching. "Some of them were confirmed at last summer's meeting already. One man is coming out from Germany especially for the gathering, while others, like young Hengstein, will stop in on his preaching circuit."

Mika took a pencil and paper from her skirt pocket and

scribbled a few notes. "The servants are preparing the upstairs rooms, as well as those on the main floor which we can
spare." She placed a checkmark beside another item on her
list. "Cook has planned the meals and is working out a list of
needed supplies and jobs to be done." She looked at her father
as they walked across the wide expanse of lawn near the rose
gardens. "What other details need to be looked after, Father?"

"Well, my dear, we'll set up the main tent there, near the
gazebo, as usual," he said, pointing to the southeast corner of
the park.

"Yes, of course. Are the tents in good order, no tears or
holes?"

"All in good order, Madame General," her father teased.
"And in what way may I be of service to you?"

She eyed him uncertainly and he laughed, grasping her
hand. "My dear girl," he said fondly, "you do such a fine job
of organizing the convention. Your mother would be so
proud of you. She always loved hosting events, especially
anything spiritual in nature." He looked at her again.

"Mother and I are alike in some ways more than in others,"
Mika stated, matter-of-factly. "I will be much too busy to actually attend the services."

Heinrich sighed. "I hoped you might try, at least, to listen
to some of the preaching. It's encouraging and edifying, something we redeemed sinners can use." They walked in thoughtful
silence for a while, until Katarina joined them from the vegetable garden, where she had been weeding.

"What on earth were you doing in the vegetable garden,
Katarina?" questioned Maria in disgust. "We have servants
for tasks like that."

Katya simply smiled and said, "I enjoy it. Dunia and I have
such lovely visits as we work together." She fell into step beside them, rubbing the dirt from her hands. "What were you
two discussing so seriously, or need I ask?"

Mika managed a smile. "I am planning and organizing to my heart's content."

"Good," answered her sister. "That way I am spared the bother. I'd rather just sit and listen to the preachers—most of them, that is. Who's coming this year, Papa?"

"I was just telling Maria." He related the information to her. "There's always such an interesting blend of pietism, Blankenburg ideology, and Mennonite traditionalism. Lots of food for thought."

"What exactly does each group stand for?" asked Katya.

Heinrich pondered a moment, to pull together a summary of the various schools of thought. "Pietism, of course, involves holiness, living a quiet and godly life in this world. The outward trappings of this group are quite austere. Many religious groups in Germany and elsewhere have adopted its ideas and taken them to heart. The Blankenburg Conference also clings to these beliefs, to a life of love and forgiveness in the light of what Christ has done for us, but without the extreme outward asceticism. They prefer to center on inner purity."

Mika focused on her notepaper, but Katya listened intently and posed another question to her father.

"Isn't that what we Mennonites believe as well?"

"Yes, theoretically," answered Heinrich. "But many of us have become bogged down in our traditions, the outward form, devoid of commitment."

"Like the Pharisees?"

"Like the Pharisees. Some seem to think that since the Jews rejected Jesus, we are now God's chosen people." Heinrich said this tongue in cheek, but continued to illustrate his statement. "There's a lot of pride and arrogance among us which threatens the work of God's Spirit in our lives. I am sure that topic will be addressed at the conference."

Maria seemed in excellent spirits as she and Johann set off in the open buggy for Karassan. The annual Succoth Conference was mere days away, and the two young people were to purchase some more lumber for benches, additional hymnals from the bookstore, and a few odds and ends at the large general store. Misha accompanied them as a matter of propriety, but Maria totally ignored him.

"You look happy and lovely, my dear," commented Johann to Maria.

She acknowledged his comment with a graceful nod of her head. Johann was amazed that her hat, with its enormous brim, remained pinned to her hair. It definitely kept her face from the sun.

"It's a lovely day," she said, "and I thrive on the busyness of conference time. Organizing events is my forte. Since Mama is no longer with us, I must also assume her share of the planning, but I really don't mind. At least it's something to do."

Johann considered her words. "Are you saying you don't have enough to occupy your time at Succoth?" he asked, pushing up his glasses and squinting at her against the sun.

"Oh, not really. I mean, there are always things to do, what with a large household and the children and so on, but some of the tasks are so mundane. Sometimes I get sick to death of the daily drudgery of it all. Surely you must feel that way, just teaching facts day after day."

"Oh, I know what restlessness is about," he answered. "That's what brought me here. But I love my occupation and the children, and we learn much more than mere facts. I must say," he looked over at his beautiful companion, "Anna and Nicholai teach me as much as I teach them. Life is a constant learning."

Maria raised her neatly curved eyebrows and remained silent. Then she said, "Well, I suppose you have a more contented personality than I. I long for new people, new places, new experiences. The serenity of Succoth drives me mad sometimes. I'm so glad you came, Johann." She graced him with a smile.

Lost in her smile, he spoke words he hadn't planned to say aloud. "A pleasant diversion, am I? A temporary amusement to pass the time?"

She looked sharply at him. "You needn't be rude, Johann. It spoils the day. Besides, I did request your company."

With that, she dismissed the subject. She chattered lightly as they rolled into Karassan, as she anticipated seeing various acquaintances and impressing them with her new hat.

Johann managed to swallow his pride, and by the time they returned to Succoth, had almost convinced himself he had misunderstood Mika. Of course she cared for him. He had seen it in so many ways: looks, words, smiles, shared confidences. Sometimes life was extremely confusing.

Time flew by with the many preparations for the conference, and soon Katya was seated with a large group of people, listening to the visiting preachers expound God's word.

"This one obviously loves history," commented Johann to Katya, as they sat comfortably on a large quilt near the back of the gathering.

" . . . having a common bond with the Hebrews of old, a people without a homeland, displaced and wandering. From the beauty of Bavaria, Moravia, and the Netherlands to the insect-infested marshes of Prussia, our forefathers came, with determination in their stride and on their countenances. They fled for their lives from their human oppressors, the angry state church, to the ravages of a hostile climate. But in time, they drained the swamps of the Vistula Delta with a series of dykes and dams to create a vast fertile farm and dairy land."

The speaker, a small man with a large voice, stopped to mop his brow with a snow-white handkerchief and to sip water from the cup handed to him.

He continued. "Then again, like the Israelites, they were forced to leave, having become a threat to the people of the land because of their financial, social, and religious progress." The gentleman cleared his throat to signify that he had come to an important juncture in his historical revelation. Several among the crowd jerked awake and looked around self-consciously.

"It was at this time that the providential invitation was extended by Catherine II, Empress of All the Russias, for the Mennonites to farm the vast steppes of South Russia and the Ukraine. This our forefathers accepted as from God, settling in the colonies from 1798 to 1806, and later sending out daughter colonies in various areas of this new homeland.

"And here we are today, a well-developed society with beautiful and locally governed villages and highly organized industry, commerce, and social policies. Through all the years, we have brought with us our belief in God, brought him along as a prized possession."

The man stopped speaking and looked from face to face at his audience. He clasped his small hands before him and looked up at the clear blue of the summer sky as if beseeching help from above. Bees buzzed among the abundance of flowers and butterflies fluttered softly in the shade of the hedges. The congregation waited, wondering at his lengthy pause.

"Beloved, while I commend the preservation of the faith of our fathers and of a pure and honest lifestyle, I believe we have lost something on our many journeys. Do we still retain the commitment and devotion of men like Menno Simons and Dirk Willems?

"God is not something to be possessed, a feeling, a tradition, a religion. God is Supreme Ruler of the universe and Creator of all. Yes, he was with us in all of our trials and travels, but only because he seeks our companionship and the opportunity to show us his compassion. Friends, this great God of ours loves us and has tremendous plans for us. He calls us to approach him, but there is only one gate by which we may enter the fold. That is through Jesus Christ the crucified."

The preacher's small stature was forgotten in the power of his words. "If we do not know Christ within our hearts, if we have not accepted his sacrifice on our account and asked for the forgiveness it brings, then we cannot know God. People, only through the blood of Christ can we boldly approach the throne of the King of kings and Lord of lords."

He continued in gentler tones, the pitch of his voice rising and falling in soft cadence, but the words whirled around in Johann's head, trying to fit into one of the boxes on the shelves of his mind. He was religious. He attended the services, sang in the choir, read prayers. He had been baptized into membership in the congregation and the community at age eighteen, like the rest of the young people. It was the prescribed way. Now he wondered, *prescribed by whom?*

He knew he wasn't perfect, but who was? Even that little fellow with the big voice on the steps of the gazebo wasn't perfect. *But*, he reasoned, *my life has been more good than bad.* He wondered how it all evened out, but that thought led to other thoughts about death and eternity, and these he did not wish to consider now.

With immense relief, he saw Mika approaching from the house, walking gracefully across the grass, regal as ever, her eyes on him. His inner turmoil gave itself up to the pleasant stirring that always accompanied Maria's attention. He rose quietly to meet her.

"Johann," she whispered, "I would appreciate your help.

Faspa is ready and we need to stand by the tables and talk with the guests. Would you join me, please?"

Without waiting for an answer, she turned in the direction of the mansion, where long tables had been set outside with white bread and zweibach, fruit breads, cheeses, cold meats, various pickles and preserves, and early yellow cherries, peaches, and summer apples. Johann followed obediently, anxious to please his lovely young friend. *Lord and lady of the manor,* he mused. *I could become accustomed to that . . .*

"Good afternoon to you," he said later, as people filed by to fill their plates. Looking into the eyes of the man as he spoke, Johann was momentarily stunned. It was the small German preacher. He set down his coffee cup to shake Johann's hand warmly and to smile, but his gentle gaze was at the same time piercing. Hazel eyes, denying any particular color, looked into Johann's as if they could see into his soul. Johann blinked self-consciously and looked away for a moment, but when he looked back, the eyes were still reading him.

"Pleased to meet you," said the German, after what seemed like an eternity. "Fritz Hengstein is my name. I hope we are able to visit later."

That would not be my choice, thought Johann, but he said, "Perhaps. Enjoy your lunch," and walked away to converse with others.

Tents dotted the park like Arabian dwellings at an oasis. As many rooms as possible had been made available in the house for guests, especially for the speakers, families, and elderly people. Extra servants had come from neighboring estates and Russian youth from surrounding villages had been employed temporarily to work in the stables, the kitchen, and the laundry. Mika thrived on keeping everything running smoothly.

"You could be a bit more gentle with the employees, Mika," Katya had suggested that morning. "Reducing them to tears is not efficient and it makes my job more difficult."

"Your job?" Maria raised her eyebrows.

"They come to me, sister, with their grievances, and I must keep the peace. They really are doing their best."

"Good heavens, Katie, why do you worry about how they feel? They are here to do a job. Let them do it."

Kátya shook her head as Maria hurried away to attend to her duties.

As the fifth and final day of the conference drew to a close, Katarina hurried down the stairs from her second floor room and ran lightly out the garden door and across the lawn. She did not want to miss evening devotions and singing. All those voices raised in praise to God sounded like angels in chorus. It stirred her soul to hear it, and even more to take part. The music soothed and comforted her, and once it was done, and coffee and sweets offered to anyone who wished, she knew she would sleep soundly.

As she hurried across the lawns, she met Johann going the opposite direction.

"You're going the wrong way, Teacher," she said good-naturedly.

"Now that depends on your perspective," he answered with a smile. "I was just going to see if Mika needed help with anything."

Katya's smile faded slightly. "Oh, I'm sure she has everyone . . . I mean everything . . . under control." She turned and proceeded to the meeting at the other side of the park.

Johann stood for a moment, deep in thought. As he watched Katya run lightly toward the gazebo, something inside him yearned for the peace and joy she displayed in her life. He envied her the deep faith that strengthened her and that she embraced with such commitment. Pushing the wonderings to the back of his mind, he returned to the house to look for Mika.

When the final meeting was over, Johann checked on horses and carriages and mingled with guests, making sure their needs were met. Tents were dismantled and folded to be stored until next year. Johann felt quite satisfied that he had managed to avoid Herr Hengstein after their first conversation.

As if fate had spoken in his ear, he felt a hand on his shoulder. Turning, he knew he would be looking into Hengstein's fathomless eyes.

"My friend, it's almost time to leave, and we have yet to talk together."

"Ah, yes. Time goes quickly when one is busy. And now it seems everyone is leaving."

Hengstein held his eye. "This place is a wonder, is it not?" He looked around appreciatively. "Shall we sit there in the shade of the magnolia tree?"

Johann hesitated. "Well I . . . Perhaps I could spare a few moments." *Now you've done it. How are you going to get yourself out of this one?* he thought.

They moved together into the cool shade and sat down on a bench. Hengstein wasted no time in trivialities. "How goes it with you, brother? Earlier when I was speaking to the assembled group, I sensed in you a reticence, almost an aversion to my message."

He tried to go on, but Johann interrupted. "No offense, please, Herr Hengstein. Just a wandering mind and a hungry stomach."

Hengstein raised a hand to stop the apology or the excuse, whichever it was meant to be. "First of all, my name is Fritz, or just Hengstein, if you wish." He smiled. "I am not offended. I am an instrument through which the Lord may speak if he so chooses; I don't take such responses personally. But if my message causes discomfort or anger, I try to locate the root of the problem. Which is what brings me back to my question: how goes it with you?"

Johann was perplexed. Subconsciously still avoiding the issue he said, "My name is Johann Sudermann. Call me whatever you wish."

The preacher's eyes continued to dissect Johann's soul and wait for a real answer to the question he had now raised twice.

Johann took a deep breath, blew it out in frustration, and looked away. After a moment to collect his thoughts, he turned back to his inquisitor. "I've been trying to answer that question myself, and I'm still not sure. I thought everything was fine."

He went on to list his religious qualifications, finishing with a shrug of helplessness. "Aside from an unnamed restlessness, which I took for youthful wanderlust, I believed I was very well, thank you. When you spoke of a personal relationship with Christ, it didn't fit into any of the boxes in my life. It rather upset the balance I try to maintain. I'm at a loss as to how to respond."

The preacher smiled broadly. "Dear brother, you have just half solved your dilemma. In admitting to a problem, you are well on the way to the solution." With that, he reached inside his suit jacket, removing from the inner pocket a thin, well-worn black book. "May I read something for you?"

Johann nodded his assent. *Now it begins. Why are you playing into his hand?* he asked himself. He pushed the question into the back of his mind, freeing himself to listen. Hengstein turned the onionskin pages to a particular passage, followed the text down with his forefinger, and found what he was looking for. "Here we are. The letter of the apostle Paul to the church at Philippi, chapter three and verses four through six: 'If anyone else thinks he has reasons to put confidence in the flesh, I have more: circumcised on the eighth day, of the people of Israel, of the tribe of Benjamin, a Hebrew of Hebrews; in regard to the law, a Pharisee; as for zeal, persecuting the church; as for legalistic righteousness, faultless.' An impressive list, yes?"

He looked up to find Johann watching him intently. "So if that wasn't enough," the young man asked, "what more could he add? What do I need to do?"

Preacher Hengstein shook his head. "You add nothing. It's rather the opposite that is required. Here, let me read the next verse. 'But whatever was to my profit I now consider loss for the sake of Christ. . . . I consider everything a loss compared to the surpassing greatness of knowing Christ Jesus my Lord.'

"You see, my friend, you can do nothing to please God on your own. No talent, no gift, no sorrow or sacrifice is enough to put you in a place of acceptability before almighty God."

"Then what is the key? Help me here, Fritz. Let's see this thing through."

"Give it to Jesus, brother. Give it all up, the good and the bad. Accept his forgiveness and be born into his kingdom. He calls you now."

Tears came unbidden to Johann's eyes. "That's all?" he asked, his voice thick with emotion. "Just ask?"

"Yes. Ask and receive. And then you will live in the light."

"I don't know. I . . ." He looked at Hengstein as a drowning man looks to his rescuer. The inner voice warning him against change faded away unheard as he said, "I want that. I've seen it here, in the lives of Heinrich Hildebrandt and his daughter Katarina. I've seen it shine from the eyes of the visitors. I just never knew what it was. But now I know: it's Jesus."

"Let's pray," responded Fritz. Together, they came before almighty God to acknowledge and accept Jesus' sacrifice, made once for all sin. And the sweet Spirit of peace settled in young Johann Sudermann's soul. Both men wiped their eyes as Heinrich approached from the house.

"I sense something significant has happened here," he said. "Tell me if I am correct."

"You are," confirmed Johann, rising from the bench. "This friend, whom I did not know previously," he put a hand on Fritz's shoulder, "took the time to show me what I was missing. I have come to truth in Christ, sir."

Without hesitation, the big man clasped Johann in a firm embrace. "Praise the Lord," he said reverently. "Welcome to the fold, son. Now we are family. Anytime you have questions, please feel free to come to me. I may not have the answers, but my ears and my heart are always open."

Hengstein took his leave with a joyous heart. All the traveling had been worth it.

Chapter 7

Dear Hans,

    *Thank you for your letter. I read over and over
again your description of Succoth Estate, and it does
indeed sound like paradise. However, my own Lichtfelde
is so beautiful at this time of year that I have no yearning
to be elsewhere. The grape arbor is hanging heavy with
fruit, though it is still quite green. The yellow cherries
and peaches are sweet and juicy, and the melons in the
garden grow bigger each day. I can hardly wait to slice
them open and enjoy the sticky coolness inside.*

    *Summer is busy as usual. I help Mama a lot now, since
Helena has her own household. Sometimes I go over to
Lena's and help her, too. She and Jakob are happy in their
new life together.*

    *I've thought a lot about what you said, about restless-
ness of the soul. A traveling evangelist came through here
not long ago, in fact I believe he was even at your conference at Succoth. Hans, I made some basic changes in
my life after listening to him. I have made a personal
commitment to Jesus Christ, and I feel such inner joy and
freedom. I wish you could know the joy I know; it would
still the uneasiness you feel. I will pray for you.*

    *I think God may have other plans for me than what I
always expected, but I don't know yet what they are. I
plan to go with Father to Halbstadt next week, as he has*

*business there. I will see what I can find out about a hos-
pital or institution that would accommodate Peter.*

*Thank you for introducing me to your family. Anna
and Kolya sound delightful; Heinrich seems like a good,
strong man. I would love to meet Katya, and Mika must
indeed be pretty, according to your many words of praise.
Good-bye for now.*

*Your friend,
Susannah*

"It has begun." Heinrich stated in measured tones, as Johann
joined him in the library.

"Sir?"

"War. Only a few days ago, Austria-Hungary declared war
on Serbia because of the assassination of the archduke. Now
Germany, as a loyal ally, has declared war on Russia." He
began to pace, hands clasped behind his back.

"What now?" asked Johann, staying seated in the soft,
leather chair near the desk.

"I'm not certain," Heinrich answered. "I did not expect
this to blow up so quickly."

"I suppose each country has to defend its rights against
meddlers and usurpers," offered Johann. "It seems Russia has
offended."

Heinrich stopped and stood before Johann. "And what
good will this do? What happened to negotiations, or weren't
there any? What is solved by our soldiers killing theirs? Does
it change any values? Adjust any beliefs? No!"

He continued loudly, venting his opinions with frustration.
"Each side becomes more stubborn in its own views, and the
armies continue to take lives day after day. For the life of me,
Johann, I can't believe in war, in its effectiveness or its ac-

ceptability. It is simply a gigantic, colossal waste of men and resources."

"Perhaps it will be a short fight." Johann had given little thought to the political situation to this point. Now he had no choice.

"Hmph," Heinrich scoffed. "Short or not, it is a mistake—a bad decision for all concerned." He thought for a moment, stroking his chin. "Perhaps," he began, thinking as he spoke, "perhaps we can make a difference."

Abruptly, he excused himself and strode purposefully from the room.

Johann didn't have to wait long for an explanation. After supper that evening, Heinrich Hildebrandt stood at his place and called the family to silence.

"Children," he addressed them, "we have been reminded lately that life is full of trials and difficulties that we do not expect or wish." He leaned on the tabletop, resting on his fingertips.

"Our Russian neighbors will soon be leaving to fight this war, with which we are associated against our will. They leave behind fields ready for harvest, with little manpower to take it in—families that without the harvest will be hungry this winter. Now tell me, children, how would Jesus respond to this tragedy? How shall we respond in his name?" He looked from face to face around his table, holding each pair of eyes for a moment. Waiting.

Anna was the first to speak. Shyly, she smiled at her beloved papa and said quietly, "We can pray for them, Papa. Jesus would pray for them."

Heinrich smiled and nodded. "A little child shall lead them," he murmured. "Anyone else?"

"We might rally several other estates and help the local farmers take in their crops." Johann spoke of the only need he perceived.

"Thank you, Johann. Certainly we shall help them. Perhaps you would be willing to spread the word tomorrow?"

"Of course, sir. We could possibly complete our studies in the morning so that the afternoon would be free."

Katya spoke then, clearly caught up in the spirit of the thing, suggesting bundles of clothing and warm blankets. "Mika and I will begin tomorrow morning," she decided, turning to her sister, who fixed her with an icy stare.

"Kolya, my boy, what have you to say?" asked his father, watching the boy's face as he turned the dilemma over in his mind. "What is your suggestion?"

"We should take our guns and shoot all the bad men, and then there wouldn't be any war." A stunned silence followed his statement.

"Nicholai!" Heinrich's sharp tone caused the boy's face to redden. He continued, more quietly, "It does no good to hate. Did Jesus hate and destroy?" The boy shook his head and met his father's gaze.

"No. But maybe he should have, and then we wouldn't have bad people around anymore."

Heinrich sighed and scratched his head. "Well, son, if that were the case, there wouldn't be *any* people left. Not one of us is 'good' on our own."

Katya broke in with her gentle voice, a hand on her brother's arm. "It's all right, Kolya. Sometimes I feel angry at all the evil in the world too, but then I remember that my anger makes me just like them." She paused, letting the words sink in. "Always remember, dear little brother, that God hates sin, but he loves sinners."

"Kolya, would you like to join Johann and me in the library?" asked his father. "Perhaps we can discuss this further."

"Oh, yes, Papa," he agreed. To be included with the men was a bonus he had not counted on. He jumped from his chair and began to leave, but caught himself and stopped abruptly before his father. "Thank you for the supper, Papa," he said in such a grown-up way that his father had to hide his smile.

Summer greens blended into autumn golds and browns as the leaves fell and crops were taken into the barns. The Hildebrandts worked both at home and on the neighboring farms and fields. The girls kept busy, gathering clothing for the needy and delivering fresh baking and meals to families whose crops were being harvested. Katya was happy with the simple joy of giving, but something disturbed her—disturbed all of them, in fact. Anna voiced it innocently, as she and her sisters walked through the rustling leaves along Magnolia Lane.

"Why don't the Russian people like us when we take them food and clothes and help with their crops?"

"It's a simple lack of manners," stated Mika. "They don't know any better."

Katarina challenged her immediately. "For shame, Mika. They may have different customs than we do, but their lack of gratitude has other reasons. I just don't know what they are."

"Do they hate us, Katya?" asked Anna sadly.

"I don't know, dear. It almost seems that when we give them things, they feel we are simply giving them what was theirs in the first place. As if we've been usurpers these last one hundred years."

Mika spoke up. "Well, we aren't usurpers. We came here with nothing and built up a social system that runs as smoothly as a finely tuned clock. They just haven't tried."

"I agree that it takes hard work, Mika, but somehow my heart goes out to them as they struggle to survive. They've struggled like this for centuries, without recognition. Sometimes I think the tsar has totally forgotten them, until it comes to needing soldiers. Then the emperor remembers his subjects. At least we don't have to fight."

"Papa," began Kolya at supper that night, "Why do we not fight in the war like the Russians? We're Russian too, aren't we?"

"Of course we are Russian. Generations of our people have been born here on this soil." Heinrich paused to sip his coffee. "Why do we not fight? Well, son, we are a people of peace. We embrace the teachings of Jesus, as set forth in God's word, and he says, 'Thou shalt not kill,' and 'Vengeance is mine, I will repay, says the Lord.' In the end, justice will be done and evil punished, but for now, we must trust that God is in control, and concentrate on obeying him."

"But why does God let all these bad things happen?"

"I wish I knew, Nicholai. His timing is different than ours. His ways are not our ways, and they are beyond our understanding."

"People reject God over and over again," said Katya, who had been listening quietly. "And then when things go wrong, they blame it all on him." She shook her head sadly. "I don't know how God puts up with us sometimes."

As the people of the German colonies worked to lessen the sufferings of their neighbors, the Empress Alexandra and her elder daughters converted the elaborate Catharine Palace near St. Petersburg into a military hospital to ease the pain of the wounded.

Paul Gregorovich Tekanin repeatedly covered the twenty-three versts between the capital and the imperial residence at

Tsarskoye Selo, following news stories. After several months of living by his wits, Paul had landed a job as junior reporter at *PRAVDA*. He had been in the right place at the right time. Djugashvili took to him and, with encouragement, Paul developed into a fearless, first-class reporter. He still lived by his wits, his sixth sense of danger and opportunity. The editor prized this—this and his ability to adhere to strict confidentiality.

As Paul's horse loped along the roadway, he worked through the latest news in his head. The tsar himself had gone by rail to the war front in an attempt to encourage the soldiers. In truth, Paul knew, it was not just the men at the front who needed motivation, but those in later troops—the ones without proper uniforms or decent boots and weapons. "Assigned to pick up the weapons of fallen comrades," Paul wrote in his notebook. He had soon learned that facts were not as important as the slant one gave to them or the perspective the editor chose to use. He did not wish to arouse unnecessary anger; he just did his job. He listened much, spoke sparingly, and always looked over his shoulder.

When he arrived at his flat that evening, he dressed carefully in clothes borrowed and bought with precious rubles from his job at *PRAVDA*. Nothing must be left to chance. To be admitted to an exclusive party in St. Petersburg—which some of the elite still insisted on calling it, in spite of the official change to Petrograd—was a rare opportunity. He looked in the cracked mirror of his tiny attic room. In the lamplight, his high cheekbones and broad brow gave him an aristocratic appearance, framed by curling black hair, glistening with pomade.

The starched collar of his white shirt stood stiff against his neck, making him seem even taller than he was. He learned it was extremely uncomfortable to slouch when condemned to a starched, upright collar. "You're no *muzhik* tonight, Paul Gregorovich," he said to his reflection.

Tucking a small notebook and pencils into an inner pocket of his black, tailed coat, Paul turned down the lampwick, hoping the rumors motivating him this evening would prove true. Would the *starets* really be in attendance?

It was a long trek down the dark streets of Petrograd. It was not the best place to be at this hour, Paul knew, but he was loath to spend money on a taxi after all his clothing expenses. With common sense and his quick wits, he would arrive safely.

Cool, damp air blew in from the Gulf of Finland upon this great city, as terrible and beautiful as its founder, Peter the Great. "Human beings were never meant to live in this place," a friend had commented one day. Paul knew what he meant. Rain fell almost constantly here. There were only about thirty days in the entire year when the sun came out of hiding, and in winter, daylight only lasted a few short hours.

Tsar Peter had chosen this place because of its harbor to build and float his beloved ships, but he had also used his ingenuity and love for Western influence to create a breathtakingly glorious city on the Neva River delta. Untold numbers of trees and rocks had been sunk into the marsh, along with the bodies of thousands who did not survive the harsh labor, to form a firm foundation.

Enormous and extravagant palaces and cathedrals built by Italian and French architects reflected Peter's vision of glory in their gold, marble, jasper, and pearl. The Italian baroque-style St. Peter and Paul Cathedral pointed its proud spire 407 feet into the sky.

The inhospitable climate of the city, however, dispensed an aura of bleakness. Paul never failed to be amazed at the extremes: fantastic wealth, degradation, and hopelessness. It was a great, ravishing, pathetic metropolis of misery.

St. Petersburg society, made up of aristocrats, government officials, and their respective servants, seemed preoccupied by an undefined, but real, dread. Their response was to seize upon unrestrained living. Morality had, for the most part, been tossed into the marsh and trampled.

Paul asked himself why he stayed. Sometimes he wasn't sure, except that it held more hope than a hovel in Ackerman or a place on the front lines without a firearm.

He smiled at the lucky bit of information that had led to his present mission. Was the man he intended to see as much of an enigma as people believed? "Hypnotic," "compelling," "fascinating," "lascivious"—these were some of the words used to describe him. Starets, holy man, personal friend of the imperial family, especially of the Empress.

Paul flashed his invitation at the door and stepped into the immense hall. The place was bustling with bluebloods. Silks, satins, and pearls blended with black tuxedos, and wine and vodka flowed freely.

He made his way as unobtrusively as possible around the outside of the large ballroom. Several of the ladies, mostly older women trussed up like turkeys for a feast, smiled invitingly at him. More than one of the gentlemen, if he could call them that, did the same. Paul moved away in disgust, feeling a sense of shame for these people.

Finally he located the object of his interest. "Our Friend," as the tsarina had dubbed him, sat on a couch in a dim corner of the room, surrounded by women of all ages and the odd male admirer. He joked and laughed and drank as he toyed with his listeners. Paul edged closer to hear the conversation.

"God is good, my dear," said the starets, holding in his large paw the hand of a fine-boned young woman who sat at his feet. "He loves you."

"Oh, Father, what is to become of our country?" asked another devotee.

A painful expression passed over the holy man's face as he answered. "Ah, yes. Our poor fatherland will suffer greatly.

We should never have gone to war. But look to me, my dear. I will save your soul, hmm?"

Without warning, the holy man, Grigory Rasputin, lifted his riveting gray eyes and looked directly at Paul. The starets' long, greasy hair fell away from his fleshy face, revealing a large nose and sagging jowls. There was a bald spot on the top of his head, which Paul knew was the result of an attack some years earlier.

But his eyes mesmerized Paul, gray-blue daggers piercing into his private soul. Unable to break eye contact, Paul was filled with such fear and revulsion he felt he would suffocate. Someone jostled him from behind, and he was finally able to turn away and seek fresh air. But an evil presence seemed to follow him. Who was this man, this so-called holy man, masquerading as a savior?

Paul had never experienced such a vile spirit. He wanted to go home—not just to his attic room, but to the steppes of his homeland, to the wide-open spaces, and away from this absurd, evil parody of holiness played night after night.

But he knew that doing so would sacrifice his freedom. He would be sent off to the war that he feared they could not win. For now, the cold sea air from a nearby window revived him so he could think. He needed a friend he could trust; he needed Johann. Sudermann always had a stabilizing effect on him. They respected each other as people, apart from nationality and language, culture and religion. How he missed him! He would go back to his attic room and compose a letter to his friend. He would pour out his soul, tell of the evil here, of the holy devil, of the imperial family who were seldom seen in public, of the state of the army as they fought against East Prussia in the north and Austria-Hungary in the south.

A shrill scream ripped the air, pulling Paul from his thoughts. A tall woman with a resolute face knelt before the holy man, both her hands grasping a knife embedded in

Rasputin's abdomen. His demon eyes stared into hers as she slowly released the weapon and stood to her full height. As if shaken from a trance, several men descended on the woman, caught her by the arms, and led her away. The serene gathering had been transformed into a melee of panic, men calling for silence and control, women fainting and sobbing. The starets slumped forward, supported by those nearest him.

The journalist in Paul took over. "What did you see?" he asked a young man next to him.

"Stabbed him," he said, coldly. "She stabbed him in front of everyone."

"Who stabbed whom?"

"Some woman. Stabbed the starets. There's a doctor now."

Later that night, the event blurred in Paul's mind as he tried to remember details. He had almost run off like a spooked child, but now he had a story to write. *JEALOUS WOMAN STABS STARETS.* The jealous woman part would surprise no one. It was well known that the holy man believed in salvation through sin. Rasputin had been associated with the Khlysty cult, which practiced flagellation and unrestrained orgies.

Many would welcome the news of the stabbing; the reasons were endless. Many of the aristocracy hated Rasputin because he was closer to the imperial family than they were. The *Duma*, Russia's "elected" parliament, detested him, because he was a prop of the aristocracy they wished to destroy. Rasputin had aroused the ire of the army by spouting pacifism, and the envy and contempt of the state church for his power over the people. Doctors either coveted or doubted his miraculous healing power over Crown Prince Alexis. The list went on.

The only reason the dirty peasant from Pokrovskoye had remained in Petrograd was because the empress demanded it. She believed in him and in his miracles; she obeyed his instructions in detail, even persuading Tsar Nicholas II to do so, to the horror of his advisors. In the eyes of the empress, Paul knew, Rasputin constituted the only hope for her young son should he suffer another hemophilic attack.

From pub to palace, people whispered a question: Will the starets succumb?

Chapter 8

 Anna's cries could be heard from a long way off as she ran sobbing toward the house. Mika hurried to meet her.

"What happened, baby?" she asked, taking the child in her arms.

"Sh, sh-h. Quiet down now, and tell me what happened." With a bit of comforting, the sobs decreased until Anna could speak.

"Mitya pushed me and threw rocks at me," she whimpered, and the sobs came again. Maria shushed her sister impatiently and asked, "Why did he push you? What were you doing?"

"Nothing!" the little girl cried. "We were just having fun at the playhouse, and when I said something he called me a dirty German and pushed me out of the house and threw rocks at me." Anna hiccuped and heaved a huge sigh. "He said the Germans should go back home where they belong or the Russians would kill them all."

"That boy will be punished," Mika said angrily. "He's nothing but a servant. He has no right to hurt you."

"But he was my friend. Why do people hate each other, Mika?"

The older girl looked away from Anna's innocent, questioning eyes. She had no answer, but she knew it was true. Right now she hated Dmitri, and the family that had planted such irrational thinking in his head. "Come to the house, dear, and we'll find a treat for you."

A few minutes later, Katarina came up to talk to Mika, but her words died on her lips as she noted her sister's angry face.

"Mika, what is it?"

Mika wasted no time or tact in telling the story. "The boy must be severely punished, and perhaps his family should be sent away. I am going to talk to Father about it."

"Oh, my!" Katya's quick tears spilled over and ran down her cheeks. "I'll come with you. Is Anna all right now?"

"Yes, she's in the kitchen helping Cook make tarts."

At supper that evening, the air was charged with accusations and pleas.

"But he apologized," burst out Katya, to Maria's consternation. "We need to forgive as we have been forgiven."

"That's all well and good," countered Mika, "but people must also face the consequences of rash words and actions, and Dmitri must be punished as an example to others who might have similar fits of anger."

Heinrich had remained silent throughout his daughters' exchange. Now he spoke. " 'Dear children, let us love one another, for love is of God.' Yes, we need to deal with Dmitri, but Mika, we do not own him. He is not a slave, but an employee. This kind of action cannot be tolerated, but we will work it out in a fair and honorable way."

He called Anna to him and lifted her onto his lap. "How are you, little one?"

"I'm fine, Papa," she smiled up at him. "I forgive Mitya. He must be very afraid to be so angry."

"You are probably right, Anna. Fear and uncertainty cause people to act against what they know is best." He tipped her chin up to look into her eyes and said, "It is good to forgive, Anna, as you have done. Now I must ask you also to take care. Don't be afraid, but stay nearer your sisters or Nicholai when you play. Can you do that for your papa?"

She nodded her head and snuggled against his broad chest.

Heinrich's strong arms moved protectively around his child, and he rested his chin on her soft, blond hair. *Oh, to be able to protect them all from life's pain. Father God, we are in your capable hands. Please strengthen our faith.*

Peter's illness came suddenly. By afternoon, he was in bed with a raging fever. Katarina sat with him, singing softly and cooling his head with a wet cloth. In the morning he had fidgeted and mumbled; now he was silent and still. Too still. After classes, Johann came down to see him.

"Is he any better, Katya?"

"Worse?"

"I don't know."

"Shall I sit with him for a while so you can stretch your legs and get some fresh air?"

"Oh, thank you, Johann." Katarina stifled a sob, her hand over her mouth.

"Katya, what is it?"

She struggled for control. "I can't help him, Johann. He wants Mama. He needs his mama."

With a tortured glance at her brother, Katya fled from the room, from the house, running away from what was now, and crying for what used to be. When she tired of running, she trudged on through the park and the orchards, and over the bridge that led across the stream.

She stopped at the church and stared up at the steeple, pointing heavenward. Grasping the stair railing, she climbed the steps to the door, stopping at the top with her hand on the doorknob.

"I can't talk to you now, God. I am so angry. So helpless. Where are you?"

She turned, ran down the steps and into the little cemetery

to the large, brick tomb standing at the far end under the shade of the birch trees, built into the ground like a root cellar. She fell to her knees before the structure, her hands on the flat stone in front of the door, on which these words were chiseled:

Elizabeth Peters Hildebrandt
1875-1911
Beloved wife and mother.
"Precious in the sight of the LORD
is the death of his saints."
Psalm 116:15

Katarina read the words, tracing over the letters with her fingers, and lingering on the word "mother."

"We need you, Mama," she cried out. "Why did you have to go? Peter is so lost. I think his heart is broken." She covered her face with both hands and cried out, "I don't know what to do for him."

She wept until all anger was spent; then she lay motionless on the ground beside her mother's grave. Gradually, the sobs became heavy sighs and then deep, even breaths. After a time, Katya opened her eyes, now swollen from her tears. She lay on her back, knees bent, watching the clouds float by, white puffs in the vast, smooth, washed blue of the endless sky. "Precious in the sight of the Lord," the words ran over and over in her mind. *He sees me, he knows me, he loves me.*

Thoughts of timelessness and goodness flitted through her mind like the sparrows that flew from tree to tree, chirping busily. "Life goes on, and so must we," she prayed. "I cannot depend upon myself, Lord, because I am empty. But when I am weak, you have promised to be strong. I'm ready now. Ready for you to take over. Thank you for waiting for me."

With the prayer still on her lips, Katarina rose, brushed the grass from her dress and hair, and headed home. She stopped at the stream to splash some cool water on her face and walked confidently down the wide lane between the eglantine hedges. She could not explain what had happened within her in the little graveyard, but she knew that now she possessed the peace she needed to face her problems. "Yesterday is gone," she said to herself, "and tomorrow is in God's hands. No regrets, no worries. I can put all my energies into this day."

"How's Peter?" she asked softly, as she entered his room.

"Sleeping now, I think," replied Johann, rising and stretching. He looked at Katya with concern, noticing her red, swollen eyes. "He was quite restless again, and then, about half an hour ago, his fever seemed to break and he settled down." He stared at her as she broke into a smile. "Are you all right, Katarina?"

"Oh, yes, I'm fine now, thank you. Quite fine. I just needed a renewed perspective on life."

He studied her clear, honest face. "And the Lord obliged you?"

"He did. God's patience is amazing."

"You're an angel, Katya. I don't know what we'd do without you." He smiled and rested his hands on her shoulders. "I'll check back later."

Johann left encouraged in spirit, with only a small question at the shadow in Katarina's eyes when he called her an angel. He was beginning to realize there was much more to her than he had thought. Her unremarkable looks concealed extraordinary courage and deep compassion.

He climbed the steps two at a time, intent on writing to Susannah before supper. He wanted to keep her informed of Peter's situation and ask if she had any more suggestions for him. *The only such institution is Bethany Home,* she had written last. *It's a distance of perhaps sixty five versts from Halbstadt, where I am now studying nursing. I have always found learning a challenge,* she added, *but this, this is what I was meant to do: to help people and to have the knowledge to do so. It is so exciting . . .*

On his way down to supper, Johann met Heinrich coming out of the library.

"Good evening, Johann."

"Sir."

"Have you heard the latest on the war?" Without waiting for an answer, he escorted Johann back into the comfortable book-lined room. He picked up a newspaper from the desk and read:

"Although Russia suffered many losses in the Masurian Lakes battles in East Prussia, they have been victorious against Austria/Hungary at Lemburg, and have advanced a good distance into enemy territory."

Heinrich shook out a fold in the paper and continued to read. "However, a new threat hangs over South Russia, particularly Crimea, as Turkey has now entered the war on the side of the enemy and is known to be advancing from the Black Sea, possibly hoping to take over the rail line from Sevastopol to the Mainland . . ."

"It continues with the details," reported Heinrich. "I'm just glad we don't live any nearer to the rails."

"Will it involve us personally, do you think?" asked Johann, as the two men walked down the carpeted hallway toward the dining room.

"It may well, and we should be prepared as to what our response will be." He looked at his companion. "We will not speak of this at supper. Katya has had a difficult day with Peter, and we need rather to encourage. "

Johann wondered if the man realized his daughter's strength of character.

Autumn days passed in a vague blur of work and play. Thoughts of war hovered over each household, and the Mennonite community added to the work they were doing among their neighbors. At the government's insistence on the participation of young Mennonite men in the military, the Mennonites had come up with a plan to satisfy the government without compromising their commitment to nonresistance. The Forestry Service, set up in 1880, was an alternate form of serving the country. It required most young Mennonite men over the age of eighteen to spend several months in forestry camps set up in South Russia, building roads and bridges, clearing brush, logging, working as medics—whatever was needed most.

"So far, Johann has not been called," said Maria, one day in late October. "Perhaps he will be able to serve his time in a nearby camp, and every other week, instead of continuously."

"Perhaps," answered Katarina, busy with her handwork. She had thought many times of Johann leaving them, serving his country in a camp set up nearer to his home, nearer to Susannah. Every time the thought arose, she squelched it. They needed him here, as teacher, part-time companion for Peter, and friend for Papa. She could no longer imagine Succoth without Johann.

Mika was fuming about the ingratitude of local Russians when Johann joined them in the sitting room. He tried to calm Mika's ruffled temper with sensible words. "As I see it, there are only two options. Either we help them or we ignore them. I can only consider helping. Their response is their decision."

"Besides," said Katya, attempting to change the subject, "we need to discuss the annual leaf festival. It should take place this next week before the winter rains begin."

Mika was immediately drawn to the details of the project. "I will talk to Cook this afternoon about the potato roast, and we will also need to check on the number of rakes in the equipment shed." She glanced toward Johann. "Would you mind doing that, please? We will need quite a few for those who don't bring their own."

The weather cooperated with a crisp, dry day for the leaf festival. Schoolchildren and their families arrived at Succoth immediately after lunch, many carrying rakes over their shoulders. The leaves had fallen in colorful abandon, and were now being relegated to huge mounds on the walkways. Mika loved being in charge. She marched around the park, barking orders like an army commander, and received good results.

All work was finished by four in the afternoon, in time for a tea with fresh baked goods and fall fruit, served on tables set up on the lawn. The children delighted in the sweet lemonade offered in little cups. In the meantime, Heinrich and Johann joined the other Succoth men in burying freshly dug potatoes and ears of corn under the piles of leaves. At the signal, a shrill whistle, the leaves were set ablaze.

The crowd sat on blankets or benches with their tea and sweets, and talked as they watched the fires. Using Mika's skill and Katya's gentle coaxing, the sisters organized the children into groups for games and races. When the fires burned down, there were hot baked potatoes and roasted corn for everyone, with plenty of butter and salt.

Usually, the annual celebration built positive relationships and friendliness between the German family and their Russian neighbors. As everyone headed home, there was a sense of the season being complete, of things being cleaned up and put away, ready for winter.

This year, though, landlord and tenants seemed reluctant to mingle. Tempers lay barely disguised beneath a veil of civility and came almost as close to exploding as some of the potatoes in the fire.

A soft snow fell in huge flakes that settled on bushes and trees. Katya stepped lightly along the beautifully decorated hallway toward the parlor, her arms full of freshly cut evergreen boughs.

Johann emerged from the library just as she passed and flattened himself against the wall. "If there's one thing I've learned," he said with a grin, "it's to stay out of Katarina's way when she's on a mission."

Katya laughed and waved a branch at him threateningly. The rosy glow in her freckled cheeks, her sparkling eyes, and wildly curling, snow-frosted hair gave her a wholesome look.

"Better not let Mika catch you tracking in snow," he warned, raising his eyebrows conspiratorially.

"Not even Mika can dampen my spirits today," she countered. "It's almost Christmas."

Just then the object of their conversation floated into view, like a queen in her palace. Katya shot a glance at Johann and continued on her way. He retreated into the library to hide his smile.

"What were you two talking about?" demanded Maria. "You look like you've been caught with your hands in the cookie jar."

Johann cleared his throat and took Maria's elbow. "Come sit, my dear. The fire is warm and the room smells of pine and spices. It's almost Christmas."

"Yes, it is," she said, allowing him to lead her into the library. "But that means I have a lot to do before the 25th. We'll be having quite a lot of company, so rooms need to be aired and made up and food planned and prepared." She looked at Johann thoughtfully. "As a matter of fact," she said, "I have some things for you to do, too. Come on." And she led the way from the warm, comfortable room to wherever she was going.

"Yes, sir," replied Johann as he followed meekly.

"What was that?"

"Yes, dear," he corrected himself. It seemed to satisfy her.

"Papa, Papa, did the *Weinachtsmann* come?" Anna whirled into the library like a tiny spinning top. Still in her ruffled flannel nightgown, her blond hair loose and tangled like clean straw, she dived at her father and climbed into his lap. She threw her arms around his neck and, nose to nose, repeated her question in a stage whisper. "Papa, did the Weinachtsmann come?"

"Well, if this giggling, wriggling little girl will be still for a moment, I will tell her."

She stifled more giggles by pressing her two small hands against her mouth. "All right, Papa," she mumbled, her eyes large and shining.

He sat back in his chair, not to be rushed. "Perhaps we should wait for the others, so I can tell all of you together."

"No, please, Papa," she pleaded.

Oh, Liesbet, he said in his heart, *she has your eyes. You know I could never resist those eyes.* Holding Anna close, he whispered in her ear, "If I tell you, will you promise to be very quiet?"

"Yes, Papa," she whispered, wriggling again.

"He came."

With a screech of joy, Anna flew off his lap to run laughing around the room, her arms spread wide like a bird in flight.

"What's all the noise in here?" Johann peeked in, dressed for the day and faking a yawn.

"It's Christmas, it's Christmas!" sang the flying bird.

"Ah! Shall we all run about the room with our arms flailing?"

Anna collapsed in a laughing heap on the great Turkish rug

before the roaring fire. "You would look so funny." Then she asked, "Where are the girls and Kolya? Who's bringing Peter? The Weinachtsmann has come."

"Haven't heard from Kolya yet, but I imagine the girls and Peter will be down shortly."

They were, without their youngest brother. Katarina escorted Peter into the library and settled him in a plush chair near the fire. She sat beside him on the arm, her hand on his shoulder. Peter sat stiffly, wringing his hands and kicking his feet. His eyes wandered continually around the room, never quite focusing on anything. He had lost weight since his illness and was excessively thin.

Mika entered the room, a puzzled expression on her face. "I can't find Nicholai. He's not in his room, in the hallways, or here." She caught Katya's eye. "He'd better not be outside yet." A dark look came over her porcelain features, warning everyone of the outcome of defying her.

"Relax, Maria," said Heinrich gently. "I have a suspicion where he might be. Everyone bundle up, and we will meet at the garden door in ten minutes."

Anna was the first to be ready. She pranced around the doorway like a colt on the end of a tether. In a few moments, Heinrich and Kolya arrived.

"Where were you, Kolya?" she asked, grabbing his arm as she jumped up and down.

He shook her off. "Why do you want to know?"

She appealed to her father, "Papa, I want to know."

Heinrich stood with his hands on his hips and said sternly, "Enough. It's Christmas morning and we need to show love toward one another. This day we remember God's gift to us, the Lord Jesus, born in Bethlehem. Consider what gift you may give to him."

Anna stopped jumping, and Nicholai creased his forehead

in concentration. The little girl slipped her hand into her brother's and looked up at him sweetly. It was impossible not to melt at that smile. Nicholai returned it and looked up at his father, as if weighing something in his mind.

Finally, he reached into his coat pocket and pulled out a handful of little button-shaped cookies, spicy and still warm, and held them out to her. Anna's eyes grew round as she reached for some and popped them into her mouth one by one.

"Pfeffernuesse!" she mumbled as she looked up at Kolya. "I know. You were in the kitchen." He smiled at her and put a finger to his lips. He was surprised that Anna did not blurt out his secret as the others joined them.

Heinrich looked around at them all. "Let's go," he said, opening the garden door. The sun reflected off the delicate blanket of snow insulating the park, generously sequined with sparkling diamonds of frost. The younger children ran off, following a path made in the snow by large boots. They yelled and laughed as they discovered sweet and tasty treasures dropped in the snow by the elusive Weinachtsmann.

"Come, Peter," encouraged Katya, taking his hand. "Let's go find some candy too." Johann appeared ready to join them, but Mika put her hand on his arm.

"Let the children play. I need to talk to Cook. Come." She turned regally and re-entered the house. Johann stood for a moment, caught between desire and instinct. He looked at Heinrich for help, but the older man simply shrugged his shoulders and moved off into the snow. With a longing look after him, Johann sighed and turned to the house. Heinrich, with a glance back, smiled and shook his head. *Ah, the way of a man with a maid.*

Chapter 9

January 1, 1915. Katya penned the date at the top of the first page in her new journal, a Christmas gift from Johann. *He has no idea,* thought Katya, *how appropriate his gift is or how often his name will appear on its pages.* To Katya, this was a timely release for her often-confused emotions. Putting pen to paper was a gift she did not take for granted. She thanked the good Lord for it daily.

On this clean sheet, she set about writing her feelings, her fears, her beliefs, and her goals. *A new year, like a fresh start in my life's journey. So far I've been given seventeen fresh starts.* She glanced out the window and was at once enchanted by the beauty of the scene outside.

It was as though angels of the snow were dusting the earth, sprinkling liberally, like Cook sprinkled powdered sugar on her amazing creations. Peacefully, gently, snowflakes descended to settle gracefully on branch and earth, on hedge and roadway, flake upon lazy flake, until it lay thickly everywhere.

Katya sat musing, pen in hand, her journal forgotten. "Just like God's love," she said quietly to herself. "He keeps sending it down on us, making us lovely if we allow him to, covering our faults and inadequacies."

She started from her reverie at the sound of bells and laughter. Suddenly smiling, Katarina grabbed her heavy cloak and the mittens from Oma Peters and ran in the direction of Peter's room.

"Peter! We're going for a sleigh ride!" She entered the

room to find her brother huddled in a corner on the floor. Rocking back and forth, he hummed tunelessly as he cradled a black-and-white kitten. The kitten had succumbed to Peter's fierce affection. It was quite dead.

At that moment, Johann appeared at the door of Peter's room. "Just looking for you, Katya. The sleigh's out . . ." He stopped talking mid-sentence, winced, and walked toward Peter. The boy did not shrink from him or become nervous in his presence as he had in the past. The turning point had come about the time of Johann's conversion at the conference that past summer.

Katya, shaken at the sight of the dead cat, watched as Johann eased the limp animal from the boy's grasp. "Let's go for a ride in the snow, Peter. I'll take kitty outside."

Together, Katya and one of the maids helped Peter into his winter clothes. He was altogether meek and passive, his eyes dull and listless, his cheeks sunken and sallow. *Perhaps some fresh air will help,* thought Katarina as she ushered him to the front entrance. Johann appeared again to help her get Peter down the steps and into the sleigh. The boy stopped as the horses turned their heads to look back.

"Bells," he said in a raspy voice, then proceeded to climb up onto the seat. "Bells." Katarina and Johann stared at each other in amazement.

Heinrich appeared in another jingling sleigh, Anna beside him and Kolya at the reins. "We're going for a drive," the boy yelled, "but Papa says I can't race you. Too bad." His horse pranced and snorted at the tickling snowflakes.

Katya and Johann settled themselves on either side of Peter. "Where's Maria?" asked Katya.

"She's not interested in coming," answered Johann. He spoke with a finality that discouraged further questioning. Katya simply met his eyes above Peter's head and then looked forward. Johann snapped the reins, and off they flew in a flurry of snow and bell music. Their laughter floated with them as they disappeared from view, while an angry Maria watched from her upstairs window.

In another place, many versts to the north, a lone *salazki* flew through the snow and bitter cold, heading east from Petrograd, east to the edge of civilization, the edge of the world. A middle-aged socialist, named Iosef Djugashvili, more widely known as Josef Stalin, was pulled from the sleigh and escorted roughly onto an eastbound car belonging to the Trans Siberian Railway. It was his fifth or sixth exile. What did it matter? He raised his fist in the icy air and hollered, "You've not heard the last of me!" His cry echoed across the frigid Siberian wasteland, a voice that would one day cause the world to shudder.

The late winter sky was a cool blue, remembering snow but promising spring. A warming sun had melted the snow, and icy, clear water rushed in gushing rivulets to swell the creek and connecting pond.

Kolya was enjoying himself immensely, stalking through the woods at the edge of the creek, pretending to be a Russian soldier sneaking up on the enemy. He placed himself always on the side of the Allies: Great Britain, France, and Russia— a short Russian soldier with a decidedly German accent.

He could hear the other boys now, their boots snapping twigs on the other side of the trees. *If I can reach the bridge,* Kolya thought, *I might be able to sneak beneath it and hide or even crawl across before they spot me.* It was all such a lark.

As Nicholai sneaked along the bank behind "enemy lines," he spotted someone on the bridge. The thin figure sat down on the edge, almost toppled off, then righted itself again, settling outside of the railing and rocking back and forth. Kolya froze. *Peter!* The water was not deep, but Peter had a way of becoming paralyzed in a crisis, and for him, this was definitely a crisis. He seemed to lack the natural instinct for survival.

"Rudi!" Nicholai called softly, moving toward the other boys. At sight of him, they yelled and came to attack. It was only the uncharacteristic look of fear on Kolya's face that finally persuaded them to listen.

"It's Peter," he said. "On the bridge. We have to keep him from falling in." He thought quickly. "Rudi, take a couple of the boys to the bridge and try not to let him see you. When he gets nervous, he kind of goes crazy."

"He's already crazy," said one of the group.

Kolya glared at him, and the boy turned away.

"All right," continued Kolya. "The rest of you run back to that narrow place where we put planks across. Cross there and come around to the other side of the bridge. Let's go, and don't spook him."

They were about to make their way cautiously to each side of Peter, when they heard a horse and wagon approaching. They knew they must get to Peter before the wagon did.

Kolya sauntered toward the bridge, while the others ran like a pack of hungry wolves, low and fast. "Whatcha doing, Peter?"

His brother jerked and wobbled dangerously on his perch, hands twisting and shoulders moving.

"I bet you can see far from where you're sitting."

Kolya stood as close as he could on the stream bank, while his friends edged in from behind.

"Can I come join you, Peter?" he called, pleasantly. Peter grew more agitated. Kolya glanced at the other boys, almost in position, then Peter noticed them too. At the same time, the wagon appeared near the bridge. Peter became more excited and Kolya motioned to the boys to grab him.

Peter seemed to be going over the edge of the bridge, moving away from the threatening sounds and people. "Oh God, please help us!" Kolya cried in desperation. At that instant, a shadow passed beneath the sun. It was a stork, flying above them in the winter sky.

"Peter, look at the stork!" For once, something clicked in Peter's mind and he looked up at the huge bird sailing low overhead. Peter loved storks.

The boys reached him and held him firmly, as Kolya ran onto the bridge to join them. They managed to steer Peter off the bridge, only to have him go rigid. The man from the wagon stopped his horse and jumped down to lift the terrified boy into his vehicle.

Kolya thanked his friends and vaulted up beside his brother, as they continued on toward the house. He glanced up at the sky; the stork was nowhere to be seen. "Must've landed somewhere in a tree," he said.

"What landed where?" the man asked.

"The stork."

The man laughed. "Too early for storks, boy. Couldn't have been no stork." He snapped the reins on the horse's rump.

"Was too a stork," muttered Kolya to himself. "You saw it didn't you, Peter?" But Peter's eyes were dull and unseeing. Kolya looked up at the sky and said quietly, "I know what I saw." Then an amazed expression lit his face. "You sent it special, didn't you?" he whispered to the sky. "Thank you, God."

As the wagon approached the house, Kolya saw a tall gentleman descend the front steps rapidly and mount his horse. He tipped his hat to them as he galloped off in the direction of Karassan. Heinrich stood at the top of the steps, a newspaper in hand and a frown on his bearded face. Seeing Peter, lying stiffly in the wagon, he threw the paper onto a bench by the door and ran down the steps.

"What happened?" he asked, reaching for his eldest son. "Is he hurt?"

"He's all right, Papa. Just scared I think."

Heinrich relaxed visibly. "We'll take him to his room, Nicholai, and then we'll talk."

"Yes, Papa." Suddenly Kolya felt guilty instead of heroic. *I should have been looking after Peter instead of playing,* he thought. *Katya can't watch him all the time.*

Katya came down the stairs to help settle Peter, and Heinrich sent for the rest of the family. "First, we need to know what happened. Kolya, please."

Nicholai told it to them straight, taking the blame for not watching his brother.

"And had I asked you to watch him today?"

"No, sir."

"Then you are not at fault. You took responsibility at the right time, and we appreciate that. I'm proud of you." Heinrich stared long at Kolya as he haltingly told of the stork. Instead of laughing and shaking his head like the wagoner, he asked, "So how would you explain the stork?" Kolya cleared his throat, self-consciously. "I don't know. Maybe . . . maybe God sent it."

"Maybe?"

"No." Kolya smiled. "I believe for sure God sent it to save Peter because Peter really likes storks."

Heinrich nodded at Nicholai's decisive reply. "Family, come out into the hall with me."

When they had followed him from the room he said, "We need to discuss this problem. Several times Peter has been in danger of his own making. The house is large, and he's often isolated from other family members and house helpers, except for the person assigned to him. It's difficult to find a willing companion for him."

He looked around at them all: Johann, concern showing on his face; Kolya, proud to be included in the discussion; Anna, putting her hand in his and smiling up at him; Mika, stern and distant; and Katya, his strongest support in this seemingly unresolvable area of their family life.

"What are some ideas? How can we better care for Peter?"

"Perhaps we adults can take turns with him, so he is never alone," suggested Katya. "I know it's too much for one person to do it all the time."

"Well, you can't expect me to do it," retorted Mika. "He doesn't like me." She folded her arms defiantly.

Katarina glanced at her sister with pity, but Mika returned her glance with withering look.

Johann, not wanting to interfere in family business, waited while the rest spoke. Heinrich sensed his hesitation, and turned to him. "Johann, you are one of us, but as one who has come in recently, you may have a clearer picture of our dilemma. Please feel free to share your thoughts."

"Thank you, sir." He reached into his shirt pocket and removed a piece of paper. He unfolded it, skimmed over the words, then looked up. "I have a letter here from Susannah, a friend from Molotschna." He avoided Maria's eyes. "She has recently enrolled in the nurses' training course in Halbstadt. She writes, 'I have heard quite a bit about Bethany, the mental institution near Einlage, in the Chortitza Colony, but have not yet seen it for myself. As part of my training involves caring for the mentally disturbed, I anticipate spending some time at the institution.' "

Johann skimmed down a few lines, reading to himself: *Johann, I feel I am a different person than when I knew you . . . such freedom even in this frightening, new adventure . . . a whole new world opened up for me. . . . Although our parting was painful, I want to thank you for setting me free. Now God can use me where he wishes and I am not tied to any one person or place. I look forward to my future . . .*

He read on aloud. " 'I think of Peter every time I hear about Bethany. They have adequate staff there to give each patient constant supervision and care, as well as develop new treatments to help these people and make them more at ease.

" 'The present chairman of the executive committee is Jakob J. Sudermann, of Apanlee. I have included his address so you can write for further information. Let me know if I can help. I wish the best for Peter.' "

Johann raised his head and refolded the letter.

"Hmph," said Heinrich, stroking his beard. Katarina stood hugging herself, a stricken look in her green eyes.

"Dear Lord," Heinrich's deep voice boomed as if volume alone would carry his prayer to the portals of heaven, "we bring this matter before you and ask for wisdom and guidance. You know we want only the best for our Peter. Amen."

"He's asleep now," commented Maria, upon peeking into Peter's room. She sniffed and raised her chin before meeting her father's eyes. "I'll sit with him a bit if you want me to."

Heinrich smiled and put his arm around her. "My dearest Mika, that would be fine."

It wasn't until supper that the topic of the specially delivered newspaper came up.

"Papa, who was that man on the black horse, and why was he here?" Kolya said, between bites of chicken and mashed potatoes.

Heinrich glanced around at the others, then wiped his mouth and folded his napkin beside his plate. "That man was from Karassan. He brought me the latest copy of *Der Botschafter*. He wanted to make sure every German-speaking settlement had a copy." Heinrich leaned his elbows on the table and clasped his hands above his plate. "It seems we have come into disfavor with the tsar."

"We?" questioned Johann.

"We of German descent: Mennonites, Lutherans, Catholics. We are all under suspicion since Russia is fighting against Germany in this despicable war."

Katarina glanced from one to the other. "What did the newspaper say, Papa?"

Heinrich took a deep breath and blew it out. "Our emperor, Nicholas II, has issued an edict that all lands held by Germans are to be confiscated by the government to be redistributed to the Russian people. As far as we know, there is not yet a plan or date for enforcement of the act."

"But we are *Russians*." Johann pounded his fist on the table, startling Anna. "I'm sorry, little one," he apologized, then he addressed the others. "Even the empress is German born and raised. How can they do this?"

"Easily, it seems," answered Heinrich. "By divine right, to be exact. Forgive me, but I don't believe that man has what it takes to rule. He never wanted the position, and his father didn't prepare him for it. Alexander III must have presumed he would live forever. Now *there* was a strong ruler."

"They can't just come and take our land away," declared Mika. "What would we do?"

Her father answered quietly. "I don't believe they're worried about what we would do. Perhaps they hope we will just disappear, or go to Germany—and in the middle of a war! This country is too vast to maintain from far-off Petrograd."

An idea began to form in his mind and he caught Johann's eye. "Have you ever been to Petrograd, Hans?" he asked.

The entire estate was in an uproar as the family finalized plans and packed their trunks.

"To be gone in spring is a great sadness," sighed Katarina as she helped Mika finish her packing. "I shall miss my special solitude here."

Mika snapped her brocade valise shut. "I am quite excited about visiting the Molotschna." She fixed a gold comb in her carefully arranged hair. "I just wish Johann and Father would be with us."

Katya turned away, pretending to straighten the cushions on the window seat. Why did she resent Mika's references to Johann as if she owned him? Why did they irk her so? She had no special feelings for Johann, besides friendship. Or was she deceiving herself?

"Oma is overjoyed that we will be staying so near," she said, to change the subject. "Alexanderkrone is within walking distance or at least a short buggy ride." She turned back to her sister. "Excuse me. I need to see to Peter."

The one bitter pill in the plan was parting with Peter. As a family, they had decided to take Peter to Bethany Home, the institution for the mentally disturbed Johann's friend, Susannah Loewen, had written about. Katarina wasn't sure how she could leave her dear brother with strangers, but it seemed to be for the best. *Oh God, please take him under your sheltering wing. He is so helpless.* Katya continued to pray quietly as she descended the stairs.

"This certainly is a long drive," Katarina commented wearily, as they neared Einlage. She was glad the children had stayed behind in Alexanderkrone with Mika. She peered at Peter, who sat between them, holding tightly to his carved stork figurine. It was a parting gift from one of the boys at Succoth. In the distance, Katya could see a cluster of buildings surrounded by trees. She tensed. "Is that Bethany, Papa?"

He was staring in the same direction. "It may be, child," he said, reaching for her hand. He could read dread and sorrow in her eyes. "Under the circumstances, Mama would understand," he said, as the horse trotted steadily on.

As they neared the village, Katya's heart settled some, for the view was captivating. Alt Kronsweide, nestled in a shallow draw between low hills, was a tiny oasis in the vast grassland. A sign, "BETHANY: Psychiatric Institution," pointed to the east side of the settlement.

They followed the straight, main street through town to a large estate, totally enclosed by a high, wrought iron fence. People sat on benches in the shade of the large oak trees, while nurses and orderlies in crisp, white uniforms kept watch or interacted with patients. The pastoral scene calmed Katarina. She could picture Peter here, supervised, secure, and calm. As Heinrich tied the horse, she straightened her shoulders and stepped down from the buggy. Her father assisted Peter to the ground.

"This is Bethany, Peter," she said, softly, as she took his hand. Heinrich signaled the young man at the gate to bring the trunk. She was grateful that Susannah would be here. Although Katya felt a niggling bit of jealousy about Susannah's relationship with Johann, she took comfort in the fact that this unknown woman cared about Peter. She trusted that her brother would have help to become accustomed to this place.

In the midst of her musing, Katarina saw a figure approaching. She expected a matron or someone in charge. Instead, she met a short, rather plump young woman with her thick, blond hair braided and coiled around her head. Her pretty face was expectant and friendly. She smiled as Katya looked her way.

"Hello. I'm Susannah Loewen. You must be the Hildebrandts."

Heinrich had also turned to meet her. He reached out his hand to her. "Heinrich Hildebrandt," he said. "My eldest daughter, Katarina, and this is Peter."

Susannah immediately focused on Peter, but made no move to touch him or speak to him. Still looking at the boy, she said to the other two, "I've been waiting to meet Peter for a long time. I feel I almost know him already, from the reports Hans has sent."

She met Heinrich's and Katya's eyes, and continued. "It will take time for him to adjust, longer than it would for you or me. But I believe he will." She paused. "Let me show you to the office so you can fill out the necessary forms."

As they made their way down the sidewalk to the administration building, Susannah spoke to Katya. "It's a pleasure to finally meet you. I've heard so much about you. Hans says you are the heart of Succoth, the mainstay on whom everyone else depends."

Katarina was taken aback by this stranger's warm and outgoing personality. "You'll like Susannah, I think," Johann had said.

"I've heard much good about you too," Katya answered. "It's been a great comfort to me to know the Lord arranged for you to be here when we arrived."

"It's difficult for you to leave your brother here, isn't it?"

Katarina clasped Peter's hand more tightly as she blinked back the tears and nodded. Susannah put a hand on her arm and said nothing, a solace better than words.

While Heinrich filled out the registration forms and saw Peter settled in his room, Susannah showed Katarina around the facility and grounds. As they walked, they talked of Peter, of Succoth, of the Molotschna, and of the war. Inevitably, the conversation turned to Johann.

"We were an item for over a year, you know," Susannah stated matter-of-factly. "When Hans left, I always hoped he would return to me, but something inside told me he wouldn't."

After a short pause, she confessed, "I could tell he needed to be free, so we decided to give up on the romance and just be friends." She sighed in resignation, then smiled. "But now the Lord has opened up a whole world of purpose in my life. Nursing is what I was born to do.

"Hans writes much about Mika in his letters. He seems quite enamored with her." She waited for Katarina to comment. When she made no reply, Susannah sought her eyes. What she saw made her clap her hand over her mouth.

"Oh, my. I'm sorry. I didn't know," she said, dropping her hand to Katya's shoulder. "You have deep feelings for him, don't you?"

"No! I . . . I mean, yes. We are good friends, but that's all."

"Katya, your eyes tell me otherwise."

Katarina glanced at her through tear-filled eyes. It was all the affirmation she needed.

"Does he know?"

"No," choked Katya. Sniffing, she dabbed at her tears with her handkerchief. "I hadn't even admitted it to myself. No one knows."

"Not even Mika?"

"Of course not. She's much too absorbed in herself . . . I'm sorry, that's uncharitable. But you've never met Maria. She's attractive enough to turn any man's head, and she has certainly gained Johann's attention. I admit to feeling jealous, but she's my sister. I couldn't cause strife between us."

"So you suffer in silence while Hans praises your virtues and follows after Mika's beauty." Susannah frowned. "Sometimes men are truly blind." She turned to Katya. "You know something?" Without waiting for an answer, she said, "I think he will come to his senses eventually."

Katya turned her head to look into her eyes. "What do you mean?"

"I mean, my friend, that Hans will notice your loveliness and see your heart." She nodded to emphasize her prophecy.

"As I said," countered Katya, "you've never seen my sister.

I am as plain, compared to her, as a cornstalk is to a magnolia blossom." She said this with conviction and was quite surprised when Susannah laughed outright.

"When is the last time you gave thought to yourself, Katarina Hildebrandt? I've known you but an hour, and already I see a depth of character, a great love for the Lord, whom I understand Hans has also come to know, and a steady beauty that shines from your eyes."

Katarina looked at her in disbelief. "Tell you what," her friend continued. "I will pray that Hans will see the light."

"Oh, Susannah, is that proper?"

Her new friend threw up her hands theatrically. "All right. Suppose we pray that if it is God's will for Hans to discover you, he will. And if the feelings you have are not proper, that God will remove them from your heart. There," she concluded. "Is that more palatable to you?"

Katya grinned and nodded. "I give up with you," she said, in mock frustration. "I have a feeling even God may not be able to withstand your petitions on my behalf."

They walked on, beneath the row of trees along the back fence. Katarina suddenly stopped to face her companion. "Susannah," she said earnestly, "I have never had a friend like you, and we've only just met. Growing up on an estate and being privately tutored didn't give us much chance to socialize. I can't for the life of me be jealous of you for your past relationship with Johann, and I greatly admire your level-headedness in moving on from there. I thank you for your prayers and for your concern for my brother, Peter. God bless you richly."

Susannah smiled warmly, and wrapped Katya in a firm hug. "We shall write letters," she said. "Perhaps this war will be over soon, so we can live normal lives again. Well, we should return to the residence to check on Peter and find your father. I shall not forget you, Katya. I will carry you in my heart."

Katarina smiled at Susannah's extravagant expression of feelings. "And I you," she answered, wholeheartedly.

Katarina and her father left arm in arm, supporting each other, and Katya cried off and on during the long way back to Alexanderkrone.

Chapter 10

Heinrich was deep in thought as the train rattled its way from familiar Taurida District into Kharkov Province. Katarina had looked so bereft at Lichtenau train station, watching the Great Southern carry him and Johann away from her. *To be one parent alone,* he thought, *is not good.* Every time he left his family on church or government business, he left them virtual orphans until his return. He did not wish to hurt them, but neither could he remain home constantly, neglecting his other duties.

A wife was what he needed. A deep frown lined his strong features as he stared out the train window. Fields of green waving wheat, dotted by villages and settlements, went past his window, but he saw only the face of his Elizabeth. He simply could not seriously consider any of the widows or spinsters he knew as replacements for the only true companion he had ever known.

"Would it help to talk about it?" The words came from another realm, another world, breaking into his consciousness. Heinrich felt a hand on his arm and turned to see Johann, regarding him with concern.

"I'm a fairly good listener, if you need to talk," he said. "You look deeply troubled."

The older man grimaced. "I'm sorry to be such poor company," he said. "Leaving my family always causes me to give in to melancholy." He smoothed the plush velvet upholstery of the armrest as he spoke. "We led an idyllic life in the first years of our marriage, with our young family. Then Liesbet left me. I know she would have loved to stay with me and the children, but she belonged first to God, you know, and he called her home. I'm sure heaven is a better place with her there." He turned to Johann. "That sounds like heresy, but I don't mean it so."

Johann shook his head. "It sounds like love. I'm sorry it's so painful for you, sir."

Heinrich looked at him as if surprised by his presence. "Mmm," he answered, then continued. "Now we've taken Peter away. For the better, we say, and I wonder if it really is better for him or for us."

"It is the reason Bethany Home was established," encouraged Johann, "to try to bring peace and contentment to troubled minds."

"Well, whether it's right or not, it's done. No help to brood about it. But sometimes I feel like I'm losing my family, bit by bit. Anna is still my angel." He smiled. "But Kolya is growing into a young man, and I always seem to be expecting more of him than he offers. I love him dearly, but for some reason I have trouble praising and encouraging him. When I do, he always takes it the wrong way—as if I'm not completely satisfied with him."

Johann said nothing, his mind drifting to his own father and their less-than-perfect relationship.

Heinrich continued. "Katya is near to my heart, although she is so solitary sometimes. And Mika . . . "

"Ten minutes to Kharkov station." The conductor's voice shattered his revelation. "Those headed to Moscow and Petrograd will leave us there and join the Great Northern passenger service. I remind you that all seating is subject to the requirements of army personnel."

So far, they had not witnessed much military presence. This was soon to change. As the Great Northern lurched into Tula later that day, a commotion arose on the station platform. Johann had been dozing, his head sagging forward on his chest, glasses tucked into his jacket pocket. Heinrich snored deeply, a pillow between his head and the window, his head back and his mouth open.

Both men jolted awake at the ruckus outside, their eyes bleary from a poor night's rest. Johann's chin bristled with morning growth.

"Soldiers," informed a middle-aged man across the aisle on the platform side. "Scruffy-looking fellows."

Those on the west side of the train hung onto seats for balance as they vied for a view of the station. Several officials appeared to be questioning the soldiers, who seemed uncooperative.

"Deserters, I'll wager," offered a slightly built young man, pushing up his wire-rimmed spectacles. "Lots of deserters these days, coming back home in droves."

"And what would you do without a gun, and only one slice of bread a day for rations?" asked another passenger. "Look at their uniforms. Rags is all that's left of 'em."

Outside, one of the officers drew a gun. The growing crowd intervened and grabbed the soldiers.

"Mob justice," commented the young man.

"Look at that!" whispered Johann to Heinrich in German, adjusting his own glasses as he peered outside. "The people are protecting the soldiers from the police. They're letting them get away."

It was true. The mob had come between the law and the guilty and stood against the law.

"The tsar has overstepped his capabilities in this war," a brave soul voiced his opinion in Russian.

There was a murmur of agreement in the coach as a raspy female voice added, "Certainly isn't the first time, and it's doubtless not the last."

Heinrich glanced at Johann and stepped back to his seat. "The farther north we get, the more anti-government sentiment we hear. Perhaps this was not a wise time to seek an audience with the Duma. They will have their hands full holding things together in the capital."

"We don't have much choice as to timing." Johann's voice was strained. "If we don't do something, we will be homeless, too, as ragged and hungry as those renegades at the station."

"Tula Station, last stop before Moscow!" shouted the conductor. "Hang onto your bags and billfolds. It's not a friendly crowd out there. Reboarding in thirty minutes."

"Anna's having the time of her life, Oma," said Katarina, setting her empty coffee cup on the table. "And I haven't seen Mika this happy in ages."

Her grandmother smiled at her and slurped some well-creamed coffee from her saucer. "She needs people around her," answered the weathered, old woman. "Maria is a socialite; growing up without peers has not been the best for her."

"I liked it fine," commented Katya, "but I'm different from Mika. The wide choice of companions is exciting for Kolya, too. He's always off with a group of boys. And Anna is happy with her little neighbor, Sarah. They play with their dolls and dress up and pretend to travel all over the world." She laughed. "One day last week, they made believe they were sailing across the ocean to visit Mama's brother, Uncle George, in Kansas, America."

Oma smiled, but her eyes lost their sparkle. She sighed. "Yah, yah, that Uncle George. Now he talks of selling out and moving north to Canada. With the time it takes to get mail, he and his family may well have relocated already."

"It's hard to imagine them so far away."

"Yah, child." Oma looked hard at Katarina and reached out to take one of her hands. The old woman's soft, purple-veined hands contrasted sharply with Katya's smooth, firm ones. "Your life will hold many changes, Katie," she said. "I fear nothing will ever be the same again for Mother Russia."

"As long as I can still write to you, Oma, and come visit once in a while." Katya's voice was that of a child, seeking re-assurance.

"Katie dear." Her grandmother's tone cut through the pretense. "Look at me. I am old. I have lived on this earth nearly seventy years. This home, here in Ruekenau, will be my last before heaven, and I'm glad of it. This body is beginning to give out, and I look forward to leaving it behind and taking on a new, eternal one."

Katarina sat, holding her dear grandmother's hands, as tears trickled down both their faces. Oma spoke again. "You, my dear, are young and strong, with the world before you. Live each day thankfully and joyfully. Don't get old and stern before your time. And when the hard times come, as they most certainly will, trust God, who is ultimately in control of all things. He has led our people through many difficult circumstances."

Katya sniffed and smiled through her tears. "I know God is in control, but I don't understand at all why he allows certain things to happen."

"It's right you should wonder. Our minds cannot grasp God's ways. He is too great for us to comprehend. That's where faith comes in."

"But who can have that much faith in God, when so many things seem to contradict his authority?"

"Everyone needs faith to live," Oma answered. "If we don't believe in God, we must put our faith in ourselves, or in others. Tell me whom you would trust more, God or the tsar, God or yourself."

"I see what you mean, Oma. God is the only one worthy of total trust."

"Never forget that, Katie girl. God will see you through."

Spring melted into summer and the world, at least the sheltered world of the Molotschna, was vibrant with life and beauty. Grape arbors hung heavy with fruit, orchards and gardens offered their bounty, and a riot of color lined walks and yards in beds of pansies, petunias, poppies, and asters. Huge sunflowers and tiny bachelor's buttons added to the kaleidoscope. The air was sweet and clean, the sky a carefree blue, with occasional summer clouds to bring refreshing showers.

Katarina relaxed in the hospitable home of the Reimers, in Alexanderkrone. Childless and middle aged, Abram and Cornelia were dear friends of Heinrich. They would have been offended if the four Hildebrandts had not stayed there. Although there was more work to do in a household of six, the workload was lighter and more pleasant with added hands and company. Mrs. Reimer soon became like a mother to the children.

"Katya, are you coming out with us tonight?" Mika asked cheerfully. "We're walking over to Lichtfelde for a youth meeting. About six or eight of us are going."

Katya considered. "I'm not sure. I'll wait and see," she said, finally.

Maria put her hands on her hips in frustration. "Katarina Hildebrandt," she said firmly. "You are becoming an old maid. Remember, you're eighteen years old! Have some fun once." She paused, to let the words take effect. "Now, are you coming or not?"

Katya smiled at her sister's theatrics and held up both

hands in self-defense. "Yes, commander, I'll come. When do we meet?"

"At seven this evening." Maria smiled sincerely at Katarina before turning to leave the house. "I'm off to Tina Rempel's until supper. We're organizing a singing for Saturday evening."

Katarina smiled and shook her head as Mika left the house. She loved her sister, but they were so different that sometimes it was hard to like her. The thought of Mika playing with Johann's heart bothered Katarina more than anything. She thought a lot about her own feelings for Johann and decided that her jealousy of Mika might stem from just that. Mika used Johann for her own means, without thought to his heart, and Katarina didn't want to see Johann hurt.

It gave Katya a sense of peace to finally analyze her feelings and find them acceptable. She still wasn't sure what to do with Susannah's observations, though. *She said she saw it in my eyes. What did she see? Am I hiding something from myself?*

After many days in the coach, Heinrich and Johann felt jostled and dirty. The humid air of Petrograd was a refreshing change from the stale atmosphere of the train. They were more than 1500 versts from home and appreciated the moderate temperature.

"It's such a relief to try my land legs again," remarked Johann, as the pair trudged down the street from the train station at Five Corners. They were searching for the hotel the agent at Great Northern had suggested.

"I still weave as I walk," chuckled Heinrich. "Hope someone doesn't take us for a couple of drunkards and clap us in a cell for the night."

As they walked, Johann wondered aloud about his friend, Paul Gregorovich, whom he had told Heinrich about on the train. "It's been several months since I received a letter. Who knows if he's even in the city anymore?"

"We can inquire at the *PRAVDA* office."

"Yes. I think you would like Paul, and I'm sure he would welcome contact with someone from back home." Johann patted his vest pocket. "I stopped in at Ackerman while we were in Molotschna. Wasn't received too well at first, but when Paul's mother heard we might see him, she dictated a letter. I have it here."

After settling into the plush Hôtel d'Europa, they flagged a hansom cab and directed the driver to take them to the *PRAVDA* office.

"Don't know where it is," he hedged.

"You drive a cab in Petrograd and don't know where the *PRAVDA* office is?"

"Some things it's better not to know."

"But have you really no idea? What's the problem, anyway?" On sudden impulse, Heinrich said, "All we want is to locate Tekanin, Paul Gregorovich. Do you know him perhaps?"

"Paul Gregorovich!" The driver slapped his forehead and beseeched heaven with exasperated mutterings. "Get in!" He indicated his carriage and turned to snap the reins, still mumbling under his breath. Heinrich and Johann jumped up and shrugged their shoulders at each other.

The hansom careened around a corner, sped down a curved avenue, and came to a breathless stop in front of the Astoria Hotel, still within sight of the Hôtel d'Europa.

"You are both hungry. Go eat." At their surprise and hesitation he said again, "Go!"

Obediently, Heinrich and Johann stepped down from the cab, paid the driver, and with several backward glances, mounted the steps of the establishment. The hansom was gone before they reached the entrance doors.

A maitre d' welcomed them into an enormous room full of

tables, some separated from the rest by delicately painted Chinese screens. All tables were set with fine painted china on snow-white linen cloths. Heavy, wine-red velvet draperies framed the tall windows. Paintings by Kandinsky and Chagall graced the walls.

"A table for two?" the gentlemen asked in impeccable French.

"*Oui,*" answered a somewhat bewildered Johann.

The maitre d' seated them at a small table in the middle of the busy room. Waiters bustled here and there, serving demanding parties of two or four-gentlemen in expensive suits, ladies in silks or finely tailored linen suits, all glittering with jewelry. Heinrich and Johann started in surprise as their waiter leaned between them and whispered in Russian, "Please come with me."

He led the way to a table in a dim corner, behind one of the oriental silk screens. Sunshine filtered red through the draped windows and reflected off the chandeliers as a small orchestra played strains of *Scheherezade.*

The men stared at each other, totally bereft of words. Their amazement increased as another waiter, white linen cloth draping his arm, bowed over their table and asked quietly in German, "And what may I order for you, Herr Sudermann?"

Johann's head snapped up and his mouth fell open as he gazed directly into the dark eyes of his friend, Paul Gregorovich. Still Johann's mouth would not work.

"No greetings for an old friend?" Paul asked innocently.

Gasping, Johann stuttered. "Paul! Paul? What . . . how did you . . . would you tell me what's happening?"

"One moment please, Monsieur," he said, and stepped away from the screen to say a few words to the maitre d'. Stepping back, he pulled up a chair and sat between them. He shook Heinrich's hand and introduced himself.

"Heinrich Hildebrandt of Succoth, Crimea," returned

Heinrich. "Pleased to meet you, Paul Gregorovich." Nodding across the table at Johann he said, "and my tongue-tied associate you already know."

The two grinned at Johann, who continued to shake his head and slap his friend on the shoulder. Pointing a finger at Tekanin, Johann finally spoke. "Why did the cabby refuse to take us to the *PRAVDA* office, and how did he know you were here?"

Paul put his finger to his lips and shook his head slightly. "Not now, my friend. Let's just say these walls have ears."

"But what brings you here? I thought you worked as a journalist," said Johann curiously.

"This is a good place to listen, no? Information is a valuable commodity in my business."

Further questioning was squelched with a smile and shake of the head. Johann patted his chest in mock pain saying, "Too much excitement for my heart." As he did so, he patted his pocket, and remembered the letter. Drawing it out, he handed it to Paul. "A letter from your mother," he said.

Paul's previous poise and control vanished, and he turned white. His hand shook as he took the paper. After staring at it for a long moment, he slid it into an inside pocket of his jacket. "Thank you, my friend," he said. His eyes lingered on Johann's, speaking volumes.

"So what are you doing now?" asked Johann.

Paul laughed and waved a hand at the tables around him. "Rich people like to eat."

Johann began again, only to realize he would receive no clear answer. His friend had certainly changed, from an innocent Russian peasant to the image of confidence and savoir-faire.

Paul asked about Johann's family and was introduced to the Hildebrandts. He listened with interest to stories of life at home and the sad tale of Peter.

"And Susannah?" he asked, glancing at Heinrich.

Johann also glanced at Heinrich. "I . . . she . . . we thought it wise to remain casual friends, as time and distance separate us."

"Ah," Paul nodded knowingly. Then, with a twinkle in his eye, he turned to Heinrich. "And I take it your daughters are beautiful young women."

Heinrich grinned and Johann colored. Paul leaned back and laughed. "You rogue!"

Then he asked about his family: his mother and Sophie, and the little ones. Johann found it difficult to relate the depth of need in the Russian villages, but he did his best, pointing out the generosity of Heinrich and other estate owners. Paul barely acknowledged the benevolence and moved on to other topics.

"What great concern has brought you gentlemen so far from home and hearth?" asked Paul. Heinrich explained the tsar's new plan for confiscating land and their hope to gain an audience with the Duma. They would press for rescinding or, at the least, modifying the edict.

Paul masked his emotions and commented politely.

"You're holding out on me, Paul Gregorovich," said Johann knowingly.

Paul toyed with a silver spoon as he carefully measured his words. "This is a vast land," he said, turning the spoon to catch the fiery reflection of the chandeliers. "There are millions of poor and starving people. Perhaps our most exalted emperor," he said, with unmistakable scorn, "feels the need to more evenly distribute the wealth of those more fortunate."

"You sound like a Bolshevik!" exclaimed Johann.

The two men locked eyes. Abruptly, Paul pushed back his chair and rose to his feet. "I must go," he said. Then, with a smile, he added, "I have a job to do. My patrons are waiting."

Johann had risen as well. "Let's meet again. When can we see each other?"

"I'll be in touch," answered Paul. After shaking hands, he was gone, leaving the others deep in thought. Within the minute, another waiter arrived with a meal fit for royalty, compliments of the house. It was a most startling welcome to a strange and startling city.

"I'm concerned about Peter," the matron said to Susannah, as they made their customary rounds on a May morning in 1915.

"Yes, I know," Susannah responded, stopping to smile and speak to a patient in a wheelchair. "He grows ever thinner and seems to be agitated all the time." She turned to the older woman and asked, "Do you have any suggestions, anything I might do to help him?"

Her companion kept walking. "Pray," she said. "We have no answers, but God does, and Peter belongs to God."

"Yes, ma'am," Susannah agreed. "Thank you."

They parted at the door between wards, and Susannah proceeded down the hallway to Peter's room. As always, he sat huddled on the floor beneath the window, wringing his hands and rocking back and forth. He did not look up as she entered, but the rocking and wringing immediately grew more agitated.

With a prayer on her lips, Suse hummed a happy song and went about straightening up the room. She began to talk to Peter as she worked, little comments on the beauty of the gardens outside his window, the smell of the flowers on his table, and anecdotes from her work. She knew better than to approach the boy directly. He shrank from touch as if it burned his skin.

But somehow, she couldn't leave him like this, lonely and forlorn, a sack of bones on the hard floor. Settling herself beside him, Susannah began to pray, first aloud so Peter could hear, then wordlessly. It gave her peace to know that God cared.

"I'll be back later, Peter. It's time for your breakfast." True to her word, Susannah returned several times that day, even stopping after all the patients were in bed to check on Peter and to say a prayer. It was a unique therapy, which continued throughout the summer and fall. She sought to establish a routine for Peter, one bathed in prayer.

Services at the Mennonite Brethren church in Alexanderkrone were sober, strict, and long, but the leaders preached the true word. The Hildebrandt family naturally attended there on Sundays, but more and more time in between was spent with youth from the Allianz congregation in Lichtfelde. These people seemed so joyful and free. Mika liked it better, of course, because it gave her more opportunities for socializing and organizing. She loved nothing better than to attend social functions, and she encouraged her elder sister to attend.

Katya began to enjoy the gatherings herself. "I think I'll come along to Friesens' house to play games tonight," she offered one summer day.

Mika looked shocked, then smiled. "Good for you, sister. Anna and Nicholai are invited tonight, too, as the Friesens have several younger children."

"That Aaron Friesen is a good-looking young man, isn't he?" asked Katarina, innocently.

Mika raised an eyebrow. "Sure."

"You seem to enjoy his company."

"And is there a law against that?"

"No. Just wondering if you'd be as friendly to him if Johann were here."

Maria stared at her, stonily. "Johann isn't here, and life goes on. We're not married, you know."

"I realize that, Mika, but it seems you're being rather unfair to Johann."

"And when I want your opinion, I'll ask for it," Mika answered hotly, flouncing from the room.

Now why did I say that? wondered Katya. *First of all, it's miserable to be at odds with Mika, and second, I should be glad she's interested in someone else.* She sighed and picked up her needlework. *Not that Johann would ever consider me in a special way.*

Chapter 11

 Anti-German sentiment is high," warned Paul as he and Johann sat talking in Tekanin's attic apartment. "Whatever you do, don't speak German. Your Russian is good enough to get you through, and you are also dressed more appropriately. No use asking for trouble."

"But I'm not ashamed of being German or Mennonite," answered Johann in frustration.

"You won't be ashamed if you're dead, either. Things happen all the time, and no one's the wiser. You don't know the ways of the city."

"This is certainly quite the city," Johann commented. "Heinrich and I did a bit of touring the past couple of days, and we're suitably impressed. We walked through the Hermitage and Kazan Cathedral and toured the Emperor Public Library. And every time we visit the Astoria, we see the statue of the Bronze Horseman in the shadow of St. Isaac's Cathedral."

"Did you see Peterhof?"

"Yes! The palace is magnificent and the gardens and parks are amazing. There must be fifty fountains there."

"Sixty-four. An extravagant waste!"

"A what?"

"A waste," repeated Paul. "All that money and materialism for the glory of one man."

"Peter the Great was an amazing tsar. I suppose you're right, Paul, but you can't say it isn't a splendid display of architecture and landscaping."

Paul paced his tiny apartment. Stopping in front of Johann, he said, "While you and your rich friend were touring the capital, did you by chance pass through the southwest section? Did you see the people who have come in from the countryside, the children in rags, the old people with sunken eyes and sallow skin, the tired workers struggling to earn enough to buy bread for their families? All this while the fat aristocrats of Petersburg lounge away their days at fine restaurants and lavish parties!"

Johann stared dumbly at his friend, usually so calm and controlled.

"Come!" ordered Paul. "I will show you the heart of Russia, and it isn't Nevsky Prospekt or the Winter Palace or Peterhof."

He clapped his tweed newsman's cap on his head and pulled the flat brim low on his forehead. They clattered down the rickety flights of stairs, Johann rushing to keep up. It didn't take long to see the things Paul had been talking about, for Tekanin's apartment was near Apraksin Market, where the poor gathered to plead their cause or beg for bread.

"Quite different from Peterhof, isn't it?" asked Paul.

Later, the two arrived at the door of a small, noisy tavern. Young people, mostly students from the universities, gathered here to drain a couple of pints on their way home. Young women mixed freely with their fellow students, discussing country's situation and suggesting solutions. These solutions most often included a socialist ideal and excluded the present head of government. It was a volatile issue in this city of the tsars.

Johann felt out of place among the intellectuals and diplomats. Paul glanced back at him, a smug look on his handsome face. He fit in perfectly, with his open-necked cotton shirt, sleeves rolled up halfway to the elbows, and his hat pushed well back on his head to reveal his snapping black eyes and thick curls.

"Vodka for me, and a strong black coffee for my friend," he ordered, as they sat at a small table in the dim light.

Tekanin leaned his chair on its back legs and looked steadily at Johann. "Welcome to my world," he said.

Their drinks came. Johann welcomed the coffee. "Strong enough to stand a spoon in," he remarked, as he took a sip. "Settles the nerves." He set his cup down and met Paul's eyes. "I came hoping to find Paul Gregorovich Tekanin. For a while I thought I did, but I may have been mistaken."

Paul's expression softened. "I'm sorry," he said. "I'm being rather hard on you. I can't expect you to understand everything at once."

Johann raised his hand to stop him. "No, my friend. I'm the one who's sorry."

Paul cocked his head to one side and frowned, "What do you mean?"

Johann cast about for words to express his discovery. "You've always been passionate and intelligent and perceptive. But you kept it veiled, at least from me and possibly even from yourself. I've only seen you from my perspective, through the filter of my lifestyle. I've not seen you truly as you are."

Paul didn't interrupt, but a look of genuine respect gradually replaced his former smugness.

Johann pushed up his glasses and continued. "To be honest, I'd have to admit I've been arrogant in the face of your impoverished background. I've never admitted it, even to myself, but I've been proud of who I am as a Mennonite, proud of our self-sufficiency."

He paused for a moment, looking around him at the people in the tavern. He took another sip of bitter coffee and looked back at Paul. "I was wrong. No one person is worth any more than another. What we accomplish or don't accomplish is unconnected with our value. We're all equal in God's sight."

"Now I know why we've always been friends," answered Paul, in a subdued voice. "You're always trying to walk in the other person's boots. I appreciate your honesty." Picking up his glass of vodka, he added, "I disagree with you on one point, though. God has nothing to do with it. In fact, I don't believe God exists." With that, he drained his glass and set it down soundly on the table, challenge in his eyes.

Johann had to smile, in spite of himself. "You're a character," he chuckled. "Always ready for a debate. Well, I have to tell you, you're not the only one at this table who's changed." He sat back and folded his hands on his lap. "While you've been discovering that God is dead, I've learned to know him personally."

"You grew up in a tight, religious community," Paul scoffed, "and you didn't know your God?"

"That's right. I had no idea."

"I don't believe you."

"I can't make you believe me, friend, but I must be true to myself and the truth I found. I never knew the Lord at all really, just knew about him. But when someone offered God's friendship to me, I realized I wanted it more than anything I'd ever wanted or needed."

"So now your life is a barrel of blessings. How nice for you."

"Sharp words, to cut my heart or to soothe your own?"

Paul leaned forward, his elbows on the table. "It's a crutch, that's all. Religion is like vodka; it soothes the emotions and dims the brain. And when all's said and done, you don't feel any better for it."

Silence closed in on the pair in the midst of clattering bottles and glasses and scraping chairs. The steady hum of conversation continued around them as the two considered their differences.

The bartender approached and whispered something in Paul's ear. "Excuse me a moment," he said, following the messenger to the back and through a curtained doorway. Johann felt conspicuous and alone, waiting for Paul to return. Then he was back, his cap again pulled snugly down on his head.

"I must go. I'll drop you off at your hotel."

They hailed a cab and rode back in silence. As they neared the hotel, Paul finally spoke.

"I should not have ridiculed your faith. It was wrong of me. There are many schools of thought in the cities these days: Tolstoyan, Rozanov, Ulyanov. Sometimes it's all quite confusing."

"No offense taken, Paul Gregorovich," assured Johann. "We will agree to disagree, but remain friends always."

They shook hands, as Johann stepped from the carriage. "Until next time," he said. Tekanin, too, jumped from the taxi and sprinted off in the opposite direction.

Katarina kept busy throughout the spring, working both in the house and in the garden. She endeared herself to Cornelia Reimer with her gentle and helpful ways and often took time to play with the young children and read to them in the shade of the cherry trees. As she did, her mind often strayed south to her beloved Succoth or north to the Gulf of Finland and the vast city nestled there, on the 60th parallel. Johann had shown her where it was on the map and pointed out the features he knew. She had smiled, looked interested, and pretended she didn't already know these facts. Then she chided herself for not being honest with him.

What she didn't know was how Johann and Papa were faring now. A telegram had arrived, announcing their safe travel and good health. They might have sent letters as well, but mail grew less and less dependable as the war progressed. They had received no further word as yet.

News of the war found its way to the Mennonite settlements via newspapers, telegrams, and people. Everyone knew someone who knew someone else who had an acquaintance who said such and such.

"There's more news of the war!" called Katarina, running through the doorway of the Reimer home.

"Then I'll be leaving," retorted Mika, laying aside her needlepoint and shaking out her skirts. "I'm sure I have better things to occupy my mind."

Katya slipped the paper into her skirt pocket. "Like it or not, sister, there is a war going on and it may be advisable to keep posted."

"Well, dearie, you can tell me when the soldiers come to town. Until then, I choose to ignore it." Mika swished out of the house, her chin high, and her thick, dark hair spread across her shoulders like a shawl.

Katarina shook her head and called out. "Who's home? I have news!" *Mrs. Reimer must have gone out,* she said to herself and followed the path from the kitchen door to the small carpenter shop in the backyard. There she found Abram Reimer carefully fitting spindles into the back of a new chair.

"That's beautiful work," she praised, looking around at the matching pieces. "Have you had any more time to work on the clock?" She wandered over to the far wall and ran her hand over the smooth, oak surface of the seven-foot grandfather clock.

Abram smiled. "Not today, my dear. The chairs have taken priority. Practicality over pleasure, you know."

"That's how life goes, isn't it? We put our plans on hold while life takes over."

"Such a young philosopher," Abram smiled again. "I think the key is to enjoy life as it comes and fit our plans into it. My father used to say, 'If you can't do what you like, then like what you do.' "

Katarina considered this. "So it's all a matter of the mind. Deciding to live in a positive manner."

"A matter of the mind, and a matter of faith. It's far better than moping around like Mrs. Wuest. You don't want to become like her. Remind yourself of that when you are tempted to cynicism."

Instantly, the image of Frau Wuest came to Katarina's mind, a short and stout woman, with thin gray hair painfully pulled back into a bun. Her thin lips drew down at the corners, and thick eyeglasses accented her narrow, beady eyes. She had a hunched back and whiney voice, and she hobbled along the street with her cane, complaining to anyone unfortunate enough to meet her.

"No, Mr. Reimer. I don't want to be like her. I'd rather be like you. Or like Oma Peters in Rueckenau."

"It all starts when you're young," said Abram. "Now, what was it brought you out here?"

"Oh, I almost forgot in the peacefulness of this place." Katarina retrieved the paper from her pocket. "It's the war."

Abram set aside his tools and leaned against the workbench, his arms crossed. "Go ahead," he urged Katarina soberly.

She unfolded the paper. "It's bits of information I gathered from whatever newspapers I could find. It seems there's a deadlock on the western front. And Italy has joined the Allies."

"Ah," was his only response.

"Will Italy's presence help Russia, Uncle?"

Abram rested his chin in his hand and shook his head slightly. "Sit down, girl," he said gently, taking the well-folded paper from her hands. "Perhaps I should not infect your mind with my misgivings, but I believe we need to face reality."

He picked up a chunk of rough wood, as long as his forearm and as thick around and held it before her. "This," he said, "might represent Mother Russia." He took a chisel and began to cut and chip away splinters of wood as he continued his analogy.

"A huge country, strong and capable, rough and violent. But over time, it has eroded without and within from different forces." He had carved out a portion of the wood, leaving a thin neck in the length of it.

"The autocracy has tried to keep it all together, but the knobs and gnarls of Russia's different cultures and political climates have proven difficult." The piece of wood had taken on an almost grotesque look. Another thin "waist" barely held the top and bottom together. Abram reached for a can of varnish and proceeded to brush it onto the wood.

"A long line of tsars has attempted to ignore the weaknesses by adhering to strict and often inhuman rule, but, as you see, it was not able to overcome the difficulties at the heart of our nation—injustice, cruelty, fear, hunger."

"Why do the Russians suddenly hate us, even when we try to help them?"

"It's not sudden at all, Katie. Some of our newspapers, like *Der Botschafter,* have been telling us for years that we are not well liked by the Russian populace. We still live and work and worship in German fashion, and it makes them suspicious, especially now with the war going on.

"But we're on the same side, and we're trying to help them!"

"In our minds, yes, but old suspicions die hard. You see, when our forefathers came to this country, we were poor, but we had hope in a new land and in the protection of Catherine the Great for settlement, self-government, freedom of religion, and freedom from military conscription.

"The peasants had none of that. Most of them were still crawling out from under serfdom. Alexander II had freed them; they called him their Emancipator Tsar. But he expected them to purchase their own land without means or support or special status."

"So when our people came and took over and prospered," Katarina broke in, "it was like a slap in the face."

"And has been ever since. Getting the picture?"

"Much more clearly than I did. Thank you, Mr. Reimer. It helps me understand their hostility."

"Now we have Nicholas II," Abram went on, "a shy, reserved, mild-mannered man with romantic dreams. He has limited world vision and no heart for the throne. He is forced to rule this huge dinosaur of a country and to try to maintain order and economy, which have never existed effectively. He is this weak section of wood here," he said as he dabbed at the thin neck with a sticky brush. "I'm afraid all the varnish of a successful military offensive cannot prevent the inevitable."

Katarina looked at him in shock. "You mean we won't win the war?"

His face was sorrowful. "I'm not a prophet, Katya, but I don't believe we have a chance under heaven to win this war. We have had phenomenal losses, and besides, the war may be the lesser of our worries."

"What do you mean?"

"The problem is internal, Katarina, a cancer that eats away life, like a chisel that chips away the wood." He set the unsightly carving on an old piece of newspaper. "Our country is collapsing from within because of the revolutionary ideas of desperately abused citizens. A timely blow may well bring our total destruction."

He gave the wood a sharp tap at the "waist," and it broke in two, the top end falling to the chip-cluttered floor to break into further fragments.

Katarina gasped involuntarily and exclaimed, "What are we to do? What will become of us?"

"I can't even speculate," admitted Abram. "Our present answer, I believe, is to live according to the law of love and to do what good our hands find to do." He looked at Katya.

"And to trust God with a stronger faith than has been exercised by our people for several generations."

Chapter 12

I miss my family," said Heinrich. "I'm tired of this wretched city with its uneasy atmosphere. It feels as if something is about to explode."

"I sense it, too," agreed Johann. "As if it's a timed explosion, and we hear the faint ticking of the clock." The two were staring out the window of their hotel suite, with a distant view of the Neva River through trees and steeples.

"Do you think our search for justice is futile?" Johann asked.

The older man remained silent, considering. Then he said, "Perhaps not. I think it's time for an all-out justice-seeking campaign. We must attempt to speak to the Duma ourselves; we can wait forever for someone to help us." He paused, then raised a fist in the air and said, "To the Tauride Palace."

"To the Tauride Palace," echoed Johann. Heinrich grabbed his satchel of papers, and they ran down to the lobby to hail a cab.

The streets were busier than usual as the cab made its way down Liteyny Street and onto Nevsky Prospekt. Horsedrawn taxis and cars vied for right of way.

"Where do you want out?" asked their driver.

"At the main entrance, please," answered Heinrich.

The cabby turned to him in exasperation and retorted, "This is a palace, stranger. Lots of doors. Now, which one?"

"I . . . do you know where the Duma meets?"

The driver whipped his ample frame around with amazing agility and stared at the two men through narrowed eyes.

"Now I *know* you are crazy! Why would you want to go there?"

"We need to talk with someone in government."

"Where you from, anyway?"

"The South of Russia. We have a matter of utmost importance to our people that we must discuss with the Parliament."

The man laughed. "So, who doesn't! Listen, my advice to you is to go back where you came from. Things are heating up, and this is no place for innocents. Look," he said, "I like you. Wouldn't want you to get hurt."

"Why would we get hurt?"

"You see those horses coming down the street? Cossacks. From your part of the country, but I doubt they would recognize you. They'd as soon cut you down as look at you. Cold-blooded, those."

Heinrich and Johann looked at each other in alarm.

"Is the situation so grim, then?" Heinrich asked, unwilling to accept defeat.

"Look," assured the cabby, "if the Cossack Regiment is this close, something's in the air. I've seen more activity here lately than usual. If you have anywhere else to be, then get out of here. You'll never get into the Tauride Palace as an ordinary citizen."

"Just let us out here, and thank you for your concern," Johann handed the man his fare, with a healthy tip, and the two men stepped out of the taxi.

"Crazy people!" muttered the cabby as he pulled away.

"We will simply present ourselves as representatives from South Russia," said Heinrich confidently, unaware that the simple plan would end up anything but simple.

Susannah's "ministry of prayer" was in its third month. Each day she stopped several times on her rounds to pray for Peter, aloud or silently. She was so close to the situation that it was difficult to evaluate the effects of her consistent ministry. Perhaps she had merely grown accustomed to Peter's ways and they no longer seemed quite so strange.

Her prayers covered his family as well, so Peter regularly heard the names of his sisters and brother mentioned before God. At least Peter was present in body when Suse prayed. Whether he heard or understood was another matter.

This sunny afternoon in June, the grass was a lush green and the flowers brilliant. Inspired, Susannah had coaxed Peter out into the courtyard.

"Now, I know you prefer the security of your room, Peter dear, but I want you to absorb a bit of this sunshine. It's so beautiful out here today, don't you agree?" She chattered on and on to Peter as he stumbled clumsily along beside her, hand clasped tightly in one of hers.

They stopped to admire a row of larkspur along the fence, and as they turned to find a bench, the boy said, "Peter dear." Susannah stopped in her tracks and stared at him, but his wandering eyes and drooling mouth gave no hint that he had spoken.

Susannah gently put an arm around his bony shoulders and repeated the only words she had ever heard him speak, "Peter dear." And for the first time, Peter did not become rigid or pull away.

"Praise the Lord!" exclaimed Susannah, her heart overflowing with gratitude.

Peter may never be able to function as other people do, thought Susannah, *but maybe we can unearth a tiny corner of his heart and begin to apply the salve of friendship.* She would continue to love him, and of course, to pray.

"Hey you! Get out of the way!" shouted a middle-aged man, swerving his horse to miss Heinrich and Johann. Horns blared and people shouted as the two dodged and darted their way across the wide street toward the palace.

"Let's try those doors there!" shouted Johann, looking for the nearest entrance to escape the chaos of the street. They trotted toward the heavy brass double doors. Suddenly a burly young man appeared from the shadows and blocked the entrance.

"Go home!" he insisted.

"But we have business . . ." Johann attempted to plant himself by the entrance until the young giant moved, but soon they were surrounded by more men of similar build. The strangers grabbed them roughly, in spite of their protests, and threw them bodily into the back of a horsedrawn wagon. "Take them to the Hôtel d' Europa!" commanded the leader. "And don't lose them."

Johann struggled to sit up and managed, just as the wagon rumbled past St. Isaac's Cathedral, to see over the side of the wagon box. What he saw was the burly brute, saluting a handsome young man with a tweed newsman's cap pulled down low over his curly, black hair.

Johann turned to Heinrich, as a troop of Cossacks cantered smartly past them in the direction of the palace.

"It's a telegram from Papa!" called Katarina, as she arrived at the door of the Reimer home. Excitement gave her plain face a definite glow. "Mika, children, come!"

It was nearly suppertime, and the entire family was busy preparing the meal and setting the table.

"What's it say?" shouted Kolya, at the top of his lungs. "Is he all right?" asked Anna, more quietly, a worry line across her forehead.

Katya laughed. "I'll tell you, and, yes. Papa and Johann are coming home!"

A general riot of joy followed among the Hildebrandts. Maria smiled and exclaimed, but held back from the jubilation. "When will they arrive?" she asked.

"I'm not sure. I'll just read it to you:

Dear Children Stop Mission Unsuccessful Stop
Leave P June 10 Stop Love Papa

That's it."

"Hmmm. Now how long did it take them to travel there?" asked Abram, calculating. "Two weeks or so, with all the stops? That means, if all goes well, they could be here by June 24th."

Anna groaned. "Such a long time yet. I miss my papa."

"So do I," agreed Katya. "But we'll keep busy, and the time will fly. You'll see." She wished she believed her own words.

"I'm not lonesome," insisted Kolya. "Men don't get lonesome."

Katya put her hands on her hips and laughed. "I don't believe a word you say, little man," she said. "Besides, I know Papa is lonesome for us."

Not knowing how to respond, Kolya punched Anna in the arm, making her squeal.

"Outside with you," demanded Katarina. "Run around the house and wear off your energy until I call you for supper."

As order again settled on the household, Katya caught Mika's eye. "What is it?" she whispered. "You don't look very excited about the news."

"Of course I am," answered Mika, but she refused to hold her sister's eyes. She began to talk about the picnic planned for the coming Saturday.

June 24 came and went, and soon hot July was upon the colonies, but there was no further word from Heinrich and Johann. In spite of the heat, the villages buzzed with activity.

Gardens were weeded and raked as neat as dirt could be. The roads and streets were kept free of weeds and the front yards swept daily with straw brooms until they were almost as clean as the inside of the houses.

Watermelons were cracking ripe, and watchmen maintained their vigil against vandals and birds to protect the delicious fruit.

Cornelia Reimer enlisted Katya and Mika to help with making watermelon syrup and spiced watermelon pickles. No one seemed to tire of *rollkuchen* and watermelon for supper. The strips of dough, deep-fried to a crispy golden brown, were the traditional companion to cool, juicy melons.

Anna sat with her elbows on the table, a huge slice of melon in her hands, its juice running down her sticky arms. "Honestly, Anna," reprimanded Mika. "Look at you. Have you no manners whatsoever?"

"Don't be too hard on her," said Cornelia. "Watermelon makes fools of us all. Why, last summer when we had our community picnic along the river, we had a melon-eating contest and some of our most prominent citizens were sticky from eyebrow to elbow."

"Well," conceded Maria, "I suppose that's true, but sometimes I wonder if Anna will ever be a lady."

"Oh, I'm sure she will," assured Cornelia.

"I wish I could come on your picnic, Mika," pouted Anna, finishing her meal and running to the pump to wash.

"Well, you can't," Mika called after her. "It's for grownups."

"You're not a grownup," teased Kolya. "You're just my sister. And Katya's older than you."

Mika glared at Nicholai, who smirked and ran off to join Anna at the pump.

"That boy can be so irritating," Mika said, angrily.

"Oh, Maria, leave him alone. He only teases you so you'll

pay some attention to him," comforted her older sister. "You know he loves you."

"Well, maybe he could learn to show it in a more appropriate manner."

"He will, but by then he'll be grown up, too."

"Katya," said Mika, changing the subject, "you must come to the picnic on Saturday. We're having games and singing and, for the *pièce de résistance*, a photographer will capture it all on film. Some of the men are leaving for Forestry Service soon, and some of us will be forced to return home, so we thought we'd preserve the memory on film."

Katarina silently contemplated the statement "some of us will be forced to return home." "What a good idea. I might come, but I don't much like photographs."

"Don't you want your children and grandchildren to remember you as you were when you were young?"

Katya sighed. "Not really. I hope to improve with age." She laughed at herself and said, "Oh, I don't care. My looks may never attract anyone, but I don't think they'll actually scare anyone away, either."

"That's better, Katie," remarked Cornelia, who had come into the kitchen partway through the conversation. "You look lovely, and once people get to know you, they can't help but love you. Now you just plan to attend the outing on Saturday and get to know more of the young people.

"By the way, girls, Abram has a furniture delivery to Fuerstenwerder tomorrow morning. He'll pass directly through Ruekenau on the way, so you can go along and visit your Oma, if you like."

Katarina decided to do so. Knowing that her time in the colonies was short, she wished to spend as much of it as possible with her beloved grandmother. Mika, not surprising anyone, chose to stay at home with some of her friends.

Katarina's visit with Oma Peters was special, as always.

"But," scolded Oma, "you should be with people your own age, making friends and enjoying life, instead of sitting here with an old woman."

"Why, Oma, I love being here with you! Are you afraid I won't find a husband if I don't go on outings with the young people?" teased Katya.

"Oh, you'll find a husband all right. But you need time to get to know people, and with you so shy and shut away at Succoth with hardly any social life, you should enjoy it while the opportunity is here."

At Succoth, Katya thought, *there was only Johann.* And even as her heart beat faster when she was near him, she knew that he had fallen head over heels for Maria. She told Oma as much.

"Strange," answered the old woman. "Whenever I've seen Maria, she is always with some other boy. She's never mentioned Johann to me. But then, she and I are not close like you and me, Katie."

"You're not the only one who's noticed that, Grandma. Maria flirts with all the boys and especially with that Aaron Friesen. I asked her once what happened to Johann, and she told me to mind my own business."

Oma chuckled. "You have a lot of nerve!"

"Well, what she is doing is unfair to him. I don't know what I should do about it."

Oma placed a wrinkled hand on Katarina's shoulder as they sat side by side in the shade of the honeysuckle hedge. "You, my dear Katie, will do nothing. You just sit back and let things fall into place as they should. Besides, why would you be so concerned about Johann? Can he not look after himself?"

Katarina did not reply. She walked over to the peach tree in the corner of the yard and pulled off a ripe fruit, one of the few left on the tree. As she brought it back to the bench where her grandmother sat, the old lady spoke: "Look at me, Katie." She searched her face and found what she suspected.

"Yah, yah," she said, shaking her head. "It's rivals you are, you and Maria. You both want the same man."

"But, Oma, she doesn't even care about him, and they're not right for each other. She understands nothing of the deep things of the soul. It's all frills and lace to her, games to be played with people."

"Now, now, child. Have you ever considered that she needs friends too? Sometimes popular people are really very lonely."

"Oh, Oma, I've tried not to be jealous. I've prayed that my feelings for Johann would remain with friendship, but the unwelcome feelings won't go away. I don't know what to do about it."

"Same advice as before, my dear. Wait and trust the Lord. Your time will come, and when you are old like me, you'll wonder how it could all pass so quickly. My goodness, I remember being your age. Such fun we had, singing and dancing. Course, nowadays, the dancing is frowned upon. I understand their reasoning, but it sure was fun."

She giggled and Katya joined her. "Oh, Oma. You are always so honest with life."

"I may as well be," Oma shot back. "It's certainly been honest with me!"

Johann couldn't remember being so tired and dirty in his life. Poor Heinrich was curled up uncomfortably on his bedroll in the corner of Tula Station. Johann was sure he wasn't resting well, either. *Why Tula?* he asked himself. *Why couldn't they put us off in Moscow? Then we could at least tour the Kremlin and the universities. What is there to see in Tula besides smoking factories and deserting soldiers?*

A year of fighting had resulted in more than four million dead or missing Russian soldiers. They had no supplies, no ammunition, and no food. And then the tsar had the audacity to depose his uncle, Grand Duke Nicholai Nicholaiovich, commander-in-chief of the army, at the whim of the empress. The grand duke didn't care much for the empress' friend, Rasputin. The so-called holy man, in spite of poor health after the attempt on his life, had offered to come to the front to pray for the troops.

"Yes, do come," the grand duke had replied. "I will hang you." And so the tall, feisty old soldier, the only one with any hope of leading a successful Russian army, had been ousted for spite, and replaced by the weak-willed tsar himself.

Heinrich stirred and sat up, rubbing his bearded face with both hands to wake up. Seeing the many soldiers around, he commented, "Looks like half the tsar's army has left him."

"Can't say I blame them for deserting," said Johann. "They have no hope of victory, and our exalted leader can offer no sort of reward back home, only more hunger and poverty. I'm beginning to understand why Paul is so passionate about his beliefs."

Johann recalled his last meeting with Paul, two days before they left Petrograd. Johann had accused him of turning on their friendship, referring to the fiasco at the Tauride Palace when he and Heinrich had attempted to gain an audience with the Duma. Instead, they had been unwillingly escorted back to their hotel in a wagon box.

"Turned on you!" Paul shouted with Russian vehemence. "I saved your life! You *kulaks* have no idea what could have happened to you, with all those Cossacks and revolutionaries milling about."

"What do you mean?" asked Johann. "We merely wanted to get in to see someone in the Duma, and you had us thrown into a wagon like two sacks of potatoes. I saw you as we were leaving."

"Listen to me, Sudermann," hissed Paul Gregorovich. The two men stood eye to eye, the air charged with emotion. "This government has never paid any allegiance to the Duma. The tsar believes he has control over it, but mark my words, the present order is doomed. Russia as you know it no longer exists, and you may as well accept it and move out of the way. You could've been hurt or worse; I simply removed you from harm's way. We have plans for this country. It is time for change."

"Who's we?" Johann had demanded. "You speak as though you yourself were going to change this nation."

"You aren't very bright for a schoolteacher. If you were a teacher here in Petrograd you'd be on the front lines for change." Paul's voice became a whisper. "There's going to be a revolution, Sudermann. The proletariat has had enough. The working classes are ready to throw off the yoke of their oppressors."

"And there are enough of you to make it happen?"

"We are *Bolshevik*, 'the majority,' " boasted Tekanin. They had been speaking a mixture of German and peasant Russian, but now he spoke the word in its modern Russian translation.

"Aren't you afraid of what may happen to you if you're caught as a Bolshevik?"

"I'm no *malodushni*. If I am caught, I will hang. But we will change Russia and then the world."

Johann sighed and backed off. "No, you're no coward— never have been. But I fear for you. You've lost your identity in the masses. I've just discovered my identity in Christ, and I see you drowning in your cause. Where will you end up, my friend?"

Paul had brushed away his concern as if sweeping a fly off his arm. "Don't speak to me of religion. It has nothing to do with me. The Revolution needs strong men and women, willing to give their lives for the cause. Many will die, but we must sacrifice in order for the plan to work."

"Are you sure your plan is worthy of the ultimate sacrifice? Will you be able to carry it through and really change Russia for the better?"

"Anything worthwhile involves risk. As to carrying through, we already have an amazing commitment to the cause. *PRAVDA* has been forced underground, but there seems to be more interest than ever in the revolution. There's no turning back now. We're on the verge of great change. The fruit is ripe for picking."

Johann smiled sadly. "Reminds me of another story of fruit ripe for picking. All humankind paid for that one."

Paul wasn't listening. He paced his tiny room again, deep in thought. Johann tried to get his attention.

"Paul, Heinrich and I are going back home. I wanted to see you again and ask you if I can relay any message to your family. I would gladly ride to Ackerman for you."

Paul looked bewildered. Then his face took on the hard edge he wore of late. "My family is dead to me," he said. "This is the life I have chosen. Everything I am is tied up in the cause, and I dare not, no, I will not be distracted by outside influences."

Johann was shocked by the hardness that had crept into his old friend's character, but he also detected a sense of desperation. Paul had gambled all he had and, as he said, there was no turning back now.

Johann rose and reached out his hand to his lifelong friend. "I must take my leave now. I will keep the memory of our friendship in my heart. I will always consider us friends."

For a fleeting moment, Johann glimpsed in Paul's dark eyes the young man he had known and loved, and they embraced. "I will pray to God for you, Paul Gregorovich, even though you don't believe in him. May he keep you safe."

Tekanin drew his sleeve across his eyes, as if to clear his vision. "Thank you," he mumbled, as Johann turned to leave.

"Sudermann!" he called after him. "Tell my mother . . ." He struggled against the sob rising in his throat. "Tell her I love her, and I will make her proud of me someday."

"I will tell her." Johann walked back and put a hand on his friend's shoulder, looking at him with great love. Then he had turned to descend the rickety stairs to the streets of Petrograd, where change was definitely in the air.

"I'm sorry your last meeting with Tekanin didn't go better," offered Heinrich now. "I know how much you care about him."

"He's always been there for me. I guess I took him for granted." Johann was silent for a moment. "I think I take a lot of people for granted."

He looked directly at Heinrich. "Sir, I appreciate all you have done for me, as well as your friendship. As it stands, I haven't many friends. Now that I've become a true believer, I have so little in common with my peers back in Kleefeld."

Heinrich smiled and clapped the young man on the shoulder. "Your friendship has done me good, too, you know. We all need someone to talk to."

"I must talk to Maria as soon as we return to the colonies. I fear I've also taken her for granted."

Heinrich said nothing, as the two hunkered down on their bedrolls.

Chapter 13

 The day of the picnic dawned bright and clear. Maria was up early, to pack the picnic lunch with Cornelia's help, and to fix her hair properly.

"I haven't seen you in such a good mood since the last picnic," quipped Katarina, joining them in the kitchen. "Is there anything left for me to pack into my basket?"

"I'm so glad you're coming," said Mika. "It's going to be a perfect day."

A dozen young adults from Alexanderkrone, Lichtfelde, and Kleefeld traveled in buggies packed with food, games, and musical instruments wrapped carefully in blankets. They made a charming picture, rolling along the tree-lined roadway to a wood near the Juschanlee River.

They stopped and unpacked in the shadow of the windmill at the southeast edge of Alexanderkrone. The group found a clearing with low grass on one side and large rocks suitable for climbing and for seats. The overhanging willows made a shady spot, where the girls spread out the blankets and lunch items.

"Set the samovar over at that corner so it won't be in the way," directed Mika in her take-charge voice. "And be careful with the bottles of wine. They should go over there, too. Now, where are the dishes?"

Before long, all was ready for lunch. "What a leisurely way to spend an afternoon," one of the girls said. When the picnic was ready, the young men climbed down from the rocks, where they had perched to keep out of the way.

"These meat rolls are so light," commented Katya, searching for something to say.

"Oh, thank you. My mother and I made them," Martha Friesen said, pleased with the compliment. "I brought a fresh cheese as well. Mmm. And how are we going to eat watermelon without getting sticky from head to toe?" They laughed as they cut the melon into bite-sized pieces.

They lingered over tea and wine. "How about some music?" suggested Mika. "Let's tune the guitars."

Everyone clapped and cheered as guitars, mandolins, and a *balalaika* appeared. Mika sat up on a rock, her dress arranged charmingly around her. It was a finely crafted garment of creamy, white linen. Intricate flower and leaf cutouts on the bodice and hem showed glimpses of a sea-green silk underdress. The sleeves ended just past her elbow, lending a casual touch.

That's our Mika, thought Katya. *Simple elegance. Inviting, but untouchable.*

"Maria always looks so regal," noted Martha, stopping beside Katya with a basket of foodstuffs to load into the wagons. "Even at a picnic, not a hair out of place."

Katya unconsciously tucked a strand of wayward hair behind her ear.

Aaron Friesen had settled on a rock near Maria and studiously tuned his mandolin. He strummed a few chords, got the pitch, and announced a popular folk song. Everyone joined in and sang merrily. Katya shifted out of the warm sun to find a shadier spot. The young man with the balalaika winked at her and patted a place on the rock beside him. Katya ignored the invitation and looked away, her face red.

Martha leaned in close to her and whispered, "Daniel is just being friendly, Katie."

"Well, he's certainly much friendlier than he was before he drank all that wine. I'm staying right here." She had felt more and more out of place as the afternoon went on, and a too-relaxed attitude spread through the group of young adults.

As the songs continued, Daniel managed to move close to Katya, a pleasant smile on his tanned face. A blond curl escaped his hat. "Have you ever played one of these?" he asked, indicating his instrument.

"No, actually," answered Katarina, shyly. "I do play the guitar some."

"Well," he said, assuming the role of teacher, "a guitar has six strings, a mandolin has four, and my balalaika has only three. So, you see, it's the easiest to play."

Katarina smiled. Daniel took it as encouragement, and continued. "Here, you take it and see what you can do."

"Oh, no, I don't know how," she said, embarrassed, and pushed it away.

"You know, Katie, the first time I picked up a balalaika, I didn't know how to play it either. Imagine that!"

She giggled, and he offered her the instrument again. A quick glance at his face made her blush again, and she immediately looked down at the triangular instrument. Taking it in her hands, she plucked one string, then another. She experimented with the frets on the neck of the instrument to get an idea of how the notes were laid out.

"I like the sound of it," she admitted.

"You're a natural."

"Oh, no, I just like music."

"Perhaps I could offer you instruction."

Katya looked at him in shock. What was happening here? He misinterpreted her once again and suggested, "Why not Saturday? I could come by after supper and show you what I know."

"But I . . . we . . ." She looked around helplessly, while Martha smiled at her from her place near the wagon. "Papa's coming, and we'll all be leaving for the Crimea again. I'm afraid I won't be able to take lessons from you." She managed to swallow her shyness and add, "But thank you for the offer. It's kind of you."

Now it was Daniel's turn to look shocked. "When are you leaving?" he asked.

"Probably within the week," she answered.

"All of you?" he asked, his eyes straying to the goddess seated on the rock. Katya caught the look and realized he was using her.

She knew she wasn't beautiful, not eye-catching like Mika. But it hurt every time someone compared the two and found her wanting. Not that she was seeking a suitor—her heart was secretly committed to Johann—but it still bruised her soul to realize the shallowness of some males. Was beauty really all that mattered to them, and if so, then why had God created her plain?

With a look of reproach, Katya handed the balalaika back to Daniel and stood to leave. "Katie, what is it? What have I said?" he asked innocently.

"You've been most kind," she said, "but I decline your offer. Perhaps my sister would be interested in lessons."

Daniel stared at her, then looked at Mika. "Do you think so?"

Katarina escaped as quickly as she could and hid her tears at the far side of the windmill. "God, help me to endure," she prayed. "Please don't tempt me with what I cannot have. Clear my head and heart of Johann, and allow me to be content with who I am." She wiped her eyes with her handkerchief and muttered, "But it's going to take a miracle."

"I wonder where that photographer is?" Mika checked her pendant watch and called out to a boy at the top of the rocks. "Can you see anyone coming from there?"

"Yes, there's a buggy traveling very slowly," he answered. "He must be worried about breaking his precious equipment."

As the photographer set up his camera and tripod, the young people arranged themselves on the rocks and grass in an informal grouping. The men grew impatient, and the women fidgeted with their dresses and their hair. Except for Mika. She seemed to know exactly how she looked and was pleased with it.

The photographer snapped the picture, then ducked out from under the black cape designed to keep excess light away from the camera.

"Let's have one of just the ladies," he suggested, arranging the young women to his liking.

Maria, of course, sat at the center, serene and straight-backed. Elizabeth leaned her head against Mika's shoulder, a pensive look on her sweet, dimpled face. Martha leaned against Katya like a lifelong friend. It made Katya feel uncomfortable. Although she liked Martha, they had never been close. The two other girls, in dark skirts and crisp, white blouses, sat on the grass at their feet. One wore a black silk scarf, tied loosely below her collar, the other a beautiful brooch.

Katya unconsciously straightened her simple, dark dress. It was cotton, a cool, loose-fitting sailor dress, with a large white collar and six brass buttons. Her hair refused to stay pinned, and she gave up trying to fix it. *I am who I am,* she said to herself, *and I am definitely not Mika.*

"What's that deep sigh for?" asked Martha. "You look fine." She glanced over at Mika. "Maria, on the other hand, looks divine."

Katya glared at her, but Martha, not realizing the effect of her words, remained beside her with sisterly closeness.

"Almost ready," the photographer mumbled from under the cloth. "Serious, now." They held as still as they could, except for sweet Elizabeth, who couldn't keep her dimples from forming.

The shutter flashed, and the image of six young women

was imprinted on the photographic paper to be developed and cherished long after they were gone.

Johann carefully aimed his new box camera and pressed the button, capturing the chaotic scene at Kharkov Station. People collected their belongings and jostled in line as the long-awaited train appeared on the horizon, snorting black smoke and whistling shrilly.

"They've promised us room on this one," said Heinrich, clutching his satchel with one hand and hefting his bedroll onto his shoulder with the other.

"Not many soldiers around here right now," agreed Johann. "Just weary travelers like us."

"It's been a long month on the road," said Heinrich, "far longer than I ever dreamed it would be."

"Sometimes I think we may have gotten farther on foot, but for robbers and bandits."

"And the elements. Train stations may be dirty and crowded, but at least they have four walls and a roof."

"I can hardly wait to get home," said Johann, stepping aside to allow Heinrich to enter the coach. "I need familiar surroundings."

Heinrich climbed aboard, located a double seat, and tossed his bedroll underneath. He collapsed onto the wooden seat, covered by a remnant of leather, and leaned his head back. "Yes, I imagine Kleefeld will be a welcome sight to you, son."

Johann sat down next to him. "Oh, I wasn't thinking of Kleefeld. I mean I'm anxious to return to Succoth. It seems to have become my refuge, as well."

Heinrich looked at him and said, "That warms my heart. It was meant to be a refuge. Do you know why it's called Succoth?"

"I know I've heard the name before, in the Bible I believe. What does it mean?"

"The word actually means 'booths,' " Heinrich answered. "It refers to the place where Jacob built booths for his cattle and a house for himself, after separating from his brother, Esau. To me it means home, my refuge." He smiled. "I never return without seeing, in my mind's eye, my dear Liesbet running down the steps to greet me. She was my beacon in many a storm."

He was quiet for a while. Johann kept silent as well, allowing memories to flood and gradually seep away.

"Now I must be the beacon for my family," Heinrich said, finally. "You know," he added, looking over at Johann, "a woman makes a better beacon than a man. She seems to have a natural ability to wait and to welcome. A woman is 'home.' "

"Do you feel homeless, then?"

"Not really," returned Heinrich. "I was married to a wonderful woman, and that gives a sense of completeness that never quite leaves me. But there are times when I must confess I feel somewhat like a ship without an anchor."

"Adrift?"

"A stronger word than I might use, but I suppose it's the right idea. Let me explain. It's difficult to draw a straight line between two points, but when you put an extra dot between them, it becomes easier. Elizabeth was that reference point in my life. Now that she's gone, my course sometimes loses its exactness, if not its direction."

"I think I understand," replied Johann, "although I've never lost a love like you have. Suse and I were good friends, not soul mates."

"We must cling to the Lord for our confidence and fulfillment," offered Heinrich. "God is faithful and has promised never to leave us. Only God can carry through such a promise."

After a companionable silence, Heinrich asked, "So what of my Maria?"

Johann met his eyes, then looked ahead, as the train lurched away from Kharkov Station and picked up speed. "Maria. She is an enigma—at once beautiful and formidable, a dream and a nightmare. I think of her constantly and live my days as though she can see each move I make. She has literally pierced my heart."

Heinrich leaned his head back and chuckled. "Welcome to the world of love." He patted Johann's knee. "I'm sorry for laughing. It's just that no man will ever be able to explain the workings of a woman's mind, and no woman will ever divulge the secret."

"An unwritten law to be kept hidden forever?" asked Johann, with the hint of a smile.

"Ah, yes. Even my Elizabeth continued to be a puzzle to me, and we were, as you say, soul mates."

"So how does a man cope?"

"One of two ways, young man, one of two ways." Heinrich turned in his seat to face Johann, and put his finger on his chest. "Either you find a deep, dark cave and hide away there, until you are blind and deaf, or," he tapped Johann with his finger, "you simply accept your particular woman and love her. The perplexity remains. There is no cure."

"No cure?"

"None!"

"Papa's coming, Papa's coming!" screeched Anna, erupting through the Reimers' kitchen door, her braids flying behind her and a piece of paper clutched in her hand.

"What is it?" called Katya, from the sitting room, where she sat with a book of short stories.

Anna waved the paper in her sister's face and stood panting before her. Katarina grabbed the paper and read it. "Oh, oh. Today, this very afternoon! Mika, where are you?" She stood to her feet. "She's gone to Friesens' again." She sat down. "Kolya!" She jumped up. "He'll be back for dinner. Oh, Anna, isn't this wonderful?"

The two sisters hugged and giggled and danced around the room, not noticing Abram, who had walked in from his carpenter shop. He stood watching them, a huge smile on his kind face.

"Good news, I take it?" he asked, laughing.

Katya felt her cheeks grow hot with embarrassment, but Anna ran to the man who had become a second father to her. She wrapped her arms around him. "My papa's coming home. Today! And Teacher, too. The train arrives at three o'clock this afternoon."

Abram smoothed Anna's hair and the smile lines at his eyes deepened, even as a silent sadness crept in. "Such a wonderful surprise!" he said. "And I have another for you. Would you like to see it?"

The little girl's eyes grew larger than ever, and she bounced up and down in excitement. "Please, yes," she blurted out.

Katya wanted to tell her to calm down and act like a lady, but under the circumstances, she would feel like a hypocrite.

"Come, Katie." Anna reached for her hand and drew her along as they headed for the workshop.

Chapter 14

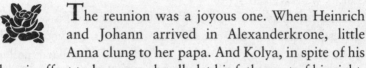The reunion was a joyous one. When Heinrich and Johann arrived in Alexanderkrone, little Anna clung to her papa. And Kolya, in spite of his heroic effort to be a man, hardly let his father out of his sight.

The children were overjoyed to see their beloved Teacher as well. Johann told them of his recent adventures and seemed genuinely glad to see Katya. His eyes, though, kept straying back to Mika. She steered clear of him as much as possible, but she maintained her poise when she couldn't avoid speaking to him.

Johann's eyes revealed a mixture of perplexity and desire—the little boy and the man striving for balance and understanding. He found no opportunity to speak alone with Maria, though he tried diligently, until the next day. When Heinrich, Katya, Kolya, and Anna drove off toward Bethany for a visit with Peter, he seized the chance.

"Maria, it is so good to see you again. You're as lovely as ever. I thought of you almost constantly while I was away." Johann could not hold back his heart as he sat down beside Mika on the brocade settee in the parlor. He took her hand in his.

Mika pulled free and stood. "You shouldn't have," she said, in a subdued voice.

Johann was taken aback. "But I couldn't help thinking of you. I'm sure you did the same . . ."

"No!" Maria stopped him with her exclamation. She hesitated, then lifted her chin, and forged ahead. "I was quite pleasantly occupied while you were gone, thank you."

"Maria." He said her name almost as a reprimand. "What are you saying?"

She stamped her foot. "What did you expect from me? We made no promises. Our friendship was merely a convenience, since there were no other young people at Succoth. You knew that as well as I did."

Mika's words took Johann's breath away. She couldn't have surprised him more if she had thrown a bucket of cold water in his face. He sputtered, stared, and blinked. Finally, as her words sank in, he cursed himself silently for his foolishness.

He had misread all the signs, interpreting them to mean what he wanted them to mean. No, Maria had not given him any promises. She had been friendly, then cool, then coy, but never loyal or even interested in him. He should have known. Subconsciously, he had known, but the thrill of attention from a beautiful woman had blinded him.

Johann and Maria told no one about their conversation, but the result was obvious. Johann was crushed, Maria haughty and irritable. Johann borrowed a horse from a neighbor and rode off to his home in Kleefeld, to spend the remaining time before leaving for Succoth.

Anna sat on the buggy seat beside her father, playing with the toy Abram had crafted for her as a special surprise. It was a dog, made of wood dowels about two centimeters in diameter, strung together with strong thread. It was connected to a small, wooden platform by strings attached through holes in the platform. At the ends of the string were brass rings Anna could manipulate to make the dog jump, wiggle, and wag its tail. The little puppet dog amused her for hours as the Hildebrandts bumped along the roads toward Bethany.

"Papa, what happened with your mission to Petrograd? Were you able to make any progress at all with the officials?" Katya asked quietly. She had changed places with Anna at their last stop and now sat in the front seat with Heinrich. The younger children were occupied with their guessing game, so it was safe to talk.

"No one seemed the least bit interested in our predicament."

"So what's going to happen to our land and our friends' and neighbors' land? What about all the German Lutheran and Catholic colonies on the outskirts of our settlements?"

Heinrich shook his head. "I don't know, daughter. Our only hope is for this great European war to distract the tsar and his government enough that they won't enforce it. But that is little comfort. The effects of the war are so devastating that our lives may be changed drastically anyway."

Katya sighed. "What an unsettled time to be alive." She pulled a newspaper from the bag at her feet and skimmed through it. "I've been trying to keep up with war developments, and it looks bleak," she told her father. "Millions of soldiers dead, low morale in the army, and major desertions, in many cases full retreats. And no one seems to have any faith in the tsar."

"It's a fact. There's no love lost there, anymore." Heinrich paused, then spoke from a sense of duty. "He may not be as capable a ruler as his father, but he is still our tsar. Nicholas II deserves the respect due his position."

"But, Papa," Katya broke in, "the Russian people are starving, and he has done nothing but push them deeper into poverty. No wonder they are rebelling."

Heinrich's silence confirmed his agreement, in spite of his sense of loyalty. "They hate the empress," he said. " 'The German woman,' they call her. She seems to be under the spell of that devil Rasputin, recovered from his brush with death, and she influences her husband with the staret's wild ideas. You wouldn't believe the bunch of simpleminded men and reprobates who now pretend to run this country!

"The people of Petrograd are fed up with the Romanovs, and I think there will be great upheaval in our land before things improve."

"Did you see much violence?" Katya asked, her eyes large with apprehension.

"Not out and out violence, no, but a strong undercurrent of discontent, anger, and volatility. Things are falling apart, and when they do, I believe we will see more violence than we could ever prepare for."

He glanced at her stricken face and squeezed her hand. "You forget something, my child. Our Father in heaven knows what is happening here. People have rejected him without reservation, and, although he could stop the evil, he chooses to let us have our own way in this world.

"We are God's children, and he loves us more than we can imagine. No matter what comes our way, God will be with us. I promise to do all I can to protect my family from the coming storm, but I am not master of our fate. We must place ourselves daily in God's care."

Katya bowed her head as she clasped his hand, and he realized she was praying. *My angel,* he thought. *Liesbet, you would love her so. She has your heart.*

Susannah greeted the Hildebrandts when they arrived at Bethany Home, where the scene from the gate was as pastoral as they remembered it. Susannah's sunny smile and serene expression exuded love and warmth. Everyone felt immediately at ease with her. She gave Katya a warm hug and Heinrich a smile and a firm handshake.

"And you must be Anna and Nicholai. Was the buggy ride very long?" Soon she had the children chattering and laughing, as she tried to make Anna's little wooden dog wag his tail.

Susannah led the family to the administration office and offered them refreshments. As they relaxed, she spoke of Peter and his improvement.

A knock on the door interrupted their discussion, and a tall, blond man joined them.

"This is Gerhard Warkentin," said Susannah. The young man smiled warmly as he shook hands all around. Katya didn't miss the wink he gave Susannah as he straddled a chair, resting his arms on its back.

"What a pleasure to meet you all," he said. "You must be anxious to see Peter." He paused for a moment, searching for just the right words. "Would you mind if I asked you to observe him first, without his seeing you? It would give you a chance to adjust before your actual meeting."

"Peter seems to thrive on tranquility and routine," added Susannah, with another warm smile. "We don't want to throw him off too much. He's a fragile person."

"What exactly is his condition?" asked Heinrich. "Is there a name for it or a cure?"

Susannah's pleasant blue eyes filled with tears that threatened to spill over. "Peter's mind and emotions are confused," she said. "We don't have a name for it. What we do know is that he is easily upset and agitated, but you already knew that. There is no physical cure, *but* . . . I have been experimenting with a spiritual treatment."

She explained to them her "prayer care" and its apparent benefits. "He has even spoken a few times when I'm with him. I call him 'Peter dear' and he repeats the name. The other word he says is 'Mama.' " She looked at Heinrich with compassion.

"Ah, yes," he said, his voice tight with emotion. "His mama loved him dearly. I'm afraid none of us has ever been able to take her place with him."

"Was Peter as troubled when your wife was alive, sir?" asked Gerhard.

Heinrich pondered the question. "Yes, he was," he answered, "but he was younger and smaller, and his main solace in life had not yet been taken away."

They sat in silence for a few minutes, then Katya managed to voice what was on her heart. "I would like very much to see my brother," she said, "but if it will upset him too much, perhaps we should not let him see us." She looked at Susannah and Gerhard. "What do you think?"

Heinrich reached for his daughter's hand and stoically nodded his assent. "We do not wish to create any more confusion for him."

"Your love and concern are overwhelming," Gerhard said quietly. "We appreciate your perception, but the decision is entirely up to you, his family." He paused, then added, "If you do decide not to meet with him, I want you to know that Peter has bonded closely with Susannah and receives great comfort from her visits and prayers. She's an excellent nurse."

It was a difficult experience for the Hildebrandts, seeing Peter but not actually meeting with him. "See how he holds Susannah's hand and allows her to put her arm around him," said Katya, as they watched through the thin curtain on the common room window. "He'd never have done that with us."

"Hmm." Heinrich had noticed as well, and it hurt him deeply that a stranger could do what he and his family could not been able to do for Peter.

Katrina saw her father's pain; she felt it too. "This is a special place, Papa. They don't expect more of Peter than he can give. Their whole attention is spent in calming his mind so he can function more normally."

"Why can't we go to him?" asked Anna. "We're his family."

To Katya's surprise, it was Nicholai who answered. "Because he'd get all mixed up again. We need to leave him alone. We're stronger than he is, you know."

Now Susannah was showing Peter pictures from the album Katya had made for him. "This is Papa. Remember Papa? And Katarina . . ." Peter looked at each one, but his concentration wandered, and he rose to look out the window facing the yard. His thin hand picked at the draperies.

"He certainly looks healthy," said Heinrich to Susannah, as she left the common room to talk with them. "I do believe he's put on a some weight since coming here."

Katarina knew her father was making a supreme effort to be positive. She felt grateful indeed for all Susannah and the other staff were doing for her brother.

Before they left, the family knelt with Susannah and Gerhard in the administration room and prayed for this child with whom they could not communicate.

Anna and Nicholai slept as much as the rough roads allowed, and it was late in the night by the time the family arrived at Alexanderkrone, exhausted in body and spirit.

The next morning, Mika asked about Peter. "How is he? Does he still become so uncontrollable? Is he content where he is?" The questions poured out of her. Even she was surprised at how much she missed her brother.

"He's as content as he's been since Mama died," said Katarina. "We saw him and watched him, but decided not to let him see us." At Maria's shocked expression, she went on to explain.

"I'm glad I didn't come," Mika said, finally. "I couldn't have endured it. To go all that way without even a word or a hug."

"You know how Peter is when we try to hug him," Katya reminded her. "Besides, we received a warm welcome from

Susannah and Gerhard. Those two seem to have hit it off quite well, too."

"Well," interrupted Heinrich, "we must pack today. My heart longs for home. I will spend the afternoon with Mother Peters and tomorrow we leave."

Mika tensed and rose from her chair. Her hands clasped and unclasped as she looked directly at her father and said, "I don't want to go."

Heinrich was taken aback. "You've been here almost four months, child. Postponing it by a day or two won't make much difference for you."

"That's not what I mean, Father," she said, with determination in her voice and on her face. "I don't want to leave. I wish to remain here."

Katya stared at her in shock.

Heinrich's face was pale beneath his beard. Finally, he spoke. "Do you not want to go home with the rest of your family?" he asked, pain evident in his voice.

Maria's eyes grew misty, but she persevered. "There's nothing to do at Succoth, and no one to spend time with. It's lonely and isolated, and I hate it. All my friends are here now, and I don't want to leave."

"What about Johann?" Katya asked. "He won't be here."

"Oh, what about Johann!" Mika snapped. "He's just as tiresome as the rest . . . " She stopped abruptly, realizing she had said more than she'd planned. "I'm sorry, I didn't mean that. I love you all very much, but I just can't bear the isolation any more."

Heinrich rose from his chair like an old man. He started toward the door, then turned back to face Mika. "I need to consider and pray," he said simply and left the house.

Katarina gave her sister a look of hurt and anger and walked out the back door toward the orchard. She needed air and time to pull herself together. *First we lost Mama,* she thought, shuffling blindly along the garden path, oblivious to the brilliant red geraniums and blue delphiniums. *Then we took Peter away . . . and now Mika wants to live apart from us.* Katya felt too numb even to cry.

That evening, a subdued group sat around the Reimers' kitchen table. "I've spoken to Mr. and Mrs. Reimer," stated Heinrich, his voice gruff with emotion. He looked across the polished oak surface at Mika. "They say you are more than welcome to live here with them for as long as you wish. You will need to thank them."

"Of course," murmured Mika, turning to the Reimers at the end of the table. "I appreciate your willingness to allow me to stay. I will help with the daily chores and anything else you require of me. Thank you."

A heavy silence descended, broken finally by Katarina, whose eyes were wet with tears. She fumbled for her handkerchief. "Mika, are you absolutely certain this is what you want? We will miss you so much."

Anna cried quietly, leaning into Katya's arm.

"She's made up her mind. Why don't you leave her alone?" Nicholai spoke bluntly, sending a shock through the room.

"Kolya, where are your manners?" Katarina chided him. "You were not asked for your opinion."

Heinrich reached over to pat Katya's hand. "Let him be, daughter. He's right, you know." He turned his attention again to Mika. "Although we would prefer to have you home with us, we will try to understand your feelings." With as much sincerity as he could muster he continued. "We give you our blessing and admonish you to live pleasing to the Lord and to your family, and to abide by the guidelines set forth by Abram and Cornelia. They have my permission to hold you accountable. Agreed?"

"Yes, Papa." Maria wiped her eyes and attempted a smile.

"Now then," said Heinrich, as he rose. "Time to finish packing."

With great courage, Mika rode along to Lichtenau Station with her family and the Reimers. She had slept poorly the night before, but in spite of her red and slightly puffy eyes, she carried herself with her usual dignity.

"I shall miss you," whispered Anna, clinging to her sister's arm and leaning her head against her. Mika blinked rapidly and raised her chin, even as she put her arm around the child and held her close. When she had composed herself she said, "I shall miss you too, Anya. You must be cheerful, and help Katie and Papa to be so also, and don't fight so much with Nicholai."

"That will be hard, I think," the little girl sighed. "Not fighting, I mean. He always starts it, you know."

Mika smiled in spite of her heavy heart. *It's not the end of the world,* she told herself. *I'm almost sixteen years old. Many girls are already married and live away from home at sixteen.* So she consoled herself as they rattled along through Kleefeld and Juschanlee Village, then turned northwest to follow the Lindenau road to the rail line.

Meanwhile, Johann had cantered his horse into Ackerman, where he pulled up before the Tekanin izba and dismounted to deliver his short but poignant message.

Paul's mother peeked suspiciously out of the door. Then, recognizing Johann, she motioned him inside. The tiny house let in little light, and it took a minute or two for his eyes to adjust to the dimness. A wooden table, warped by many rains leaking through the thatch roof, stood near a small window. Two broken chairs perched beside it, along with a couple of overturned baskets. The only other furniture was an old bed frame in the corner, covered with a straw tick that seemed to have a life of its own. Johann felt the urge to scratch.

The children were no doubt toiling in some nearby field, to earn enough to eat while their mother cooked something over the fire.

"Tell me what you know," she rasped in Russian, pushing her thin, gray hair back into its untidy bun. "Is he dead? What?" She steeled herself for the grief that seemed to have become her lot in life.

She might have been an attractive woman once, Johann thought. It was clear, though, that she had spent her youth and spirit on endless work far too difficult for a woman in order to feed and clothe her family.

"*What?*" she repeated, taking hold of Johann's lapel with one hand. Realizing her apprehension, he shook his head.

"No, no, Mother Tekanin. Paul is fine. At least the last time I saw him he was." Johann had rehearsed his speech many times and, he told himself, it was true. Even so, there was much truth he would not divulge to this work- and worry-worn soul.

"He has many friends in Petrograd. He lives in a small, comfortable room in a tenement building near Apraksin Market."

"And what does he do?" she asked, eager for details.

"He works for a newspaper and also serves at a fine restaurant called the Astoria."

"A newspaperman. My Paul." Mother Tekanin released her hold on Johann's coat and looked beyond him to a memory. "Has he changed since he left?" She seemed aware that Johann was holding back.

"He's as tall and handsome as ever and full of energy," he replied.

The little wisp of a woman looked Johann directly in the eye. "And has he changed?" she repeated.

Johann ran a finger under his collar, which felt suddenly

too tight, and searched for words. The demanding gray eyes waited with impatience, and he was forced to answer.

"Yes, he has changed some," he conceded. "Become more worldly-wise, I suppose, more self assured."

"Is he a Bolshevik?"

Johann blanched. "He, ah, he might lean in that direction."

She considered. "Good," she said.

"Good?"

"He's going to help us. If somebody would just get rid of those Romanovs, the people could make things work."

Surprised by her knowledge of the situation and her vehemence for the cause, Johann felt sorry for this lonely woman.

"He sends his love," he said in compassionate tones, "and says he will make you proud someday."

She acknowledged the message with a nod of her head. "This is not a time for sentiment. He must put his hand to the plow and not look back."

She opened the door for Johann and said, "I thank you for your concern. I will not see my son again." With that, she turned back to her pot of thin soup.

Johann was left to mount his horse and follow the trail toward Lichtenau.

A large crowd milled about at Lichtenau Station on the Great Southern trunkline. Johann recognized many as soldiers or former soldiers by the bits and pieces of uniforms that made up the rags they wore.

He tied his horse, then went in search of the Hildebrandts. He dreaded the thought of seeing Maria, wondering how he would endure the trip south and living in the same household, now that things had changed between them.

His heart was raw with the shock of her rejection, so unexpected. He chided himself over and over for dreaming she could be content with the likes of him, a boring, bespectacled schoolmaster.

They had enjoyed some good times, but she had dismissed them with a wave of her slim hand. *Crushed.* That's how he'd heard it described, this agony of the soul. He felt more as if he'd been run over by a train, with a general ache and recurring twinges of distress.

His wounded spirit was sinking again into dismay when he felt a tug on his coat sleeve. "Teacher!" It was Kolya, looking cheerful and full of energy. "We're over there in the shade of the oak trees. Come."

Johann followed in a trance, and Kolya looked up at him in concern. "Are you sick, Teacher? You look awful."

Johann grimaced. "A little under the weather, I suppose. When's the train due?"

"Not for an hour or so. It's late again." Nicholai kicked a rock ahead of him until a scowl from a tired-looking woman made him stop. "People are sure grouchy today," he commented.

"Yes, well it's crowded and hot out here. Did the Reimers come to the station too?"

"Oh, yes, and Mika too, even though she isn't coming back home with us."

"Even though . . . what did you say?"

"She's not coming back. She's tired of living at Succoth, and she's staying here at Reimers'. They said she could, and Papa said so too." Kolya paused, and his face became thoughtful. "It makes Papa awful sad."

"I can imagine," said Johann, trying to sort out a jumble of emotions, ranging from relief to sorrow. Shaking his head to clear it, he followed Nicholai and prepared to meet the inevitable.

The breeze that had earlier brought relief from the sun's

heat and insects had now fled, and the crowd at Lichtenau Station sweltered in the heat.

Several well-dressed, aristocratic families had cleared a place to sit in the shade near the Hildebrandt clan. To do so, they had deftly displaced a number of ragtag soldiers and some Russian peasants, carrying their belongings in small bundles on their backs.

Johann saw the problems coming, but too late. The peasants only frowned and complained at the self-important aristocrats, but the soldiers displayed their anger strongly.

"What gives you the right to push us out of our spot?" demanded one rough-looking deserter. "We've got as much right here as you."

The dignified families chose to ignore the remark, and the women deflected the rough words with a swish of their elegant fans. It was not a wise choice.

"Hey, old man, I'm talking to you," the burly man said loudly. "I was here first. Get out of my way!"

The patriarch looked down his nose at the troublemaker. "Would you mind?" he said. "You are upsetting my family. Move along now."

This proved too much for the soldier. With a vulgar remark, he put his hand on the old man's chest and shoved. "We'll see who moves," he shouted. His cronies joined in, menacingly.

Johann grabbed Kolya by the shoulder and tried to steer him away from the confrontation, but another deserter behind him hollered, "You running away, coward? Are you all talk and no backbone?"

"No. I'm not with them. I don't intend to get in your way."

The surly man snarled at him and pushed him aside, with more nasty words. Johann and Nicholai hurriedly left the area and beckoned to the rest of the family and the Reimers. Heinrich immediately understood the situation and moved his family far from the scene.

The confrontation grew in intensity. More rough characters joined the mob as insults flew back and forth, and fistfights and brawls followed. The scene turned ugly as several town officials rode up on their horses, clubs in hand.

"What's the problem here?" shouted the constable above the racket. But things had gone too far for words. The officials wielded their clubs, hitting those within reach, only soldiers and peasants. The wealthy family managed to scramble away, unharmed and only slightly ruffled.

Katya watched, her hands clenched into fists of anger, and tears running down her cheeks. "Katya, come away," insisted Johann, taking her by the shoulders and steering her toward the corner of the station platform and the rest of her family.

"Didn't you see what the constables did?" she cried. "They punished the poor, while the rich went away unscathed. It's not right!"

Johann kept her walking in the direction of the platform as he spoke. "I know, Katya. Your father and I witnessed this several times in our travels. I also concluded there is little justice in this land. But there is not much we can do in the face of clubs and fists and possibly hidden weapons."

"Then what will we do? Nothing? Sit and watch?" Katya was angry now. Johann had never seen her eyes so fiery or her expression so troubled. In fact, he couldn't remember noticing much about her at all in the past year. She was always there, a friend to talk to, a saint to lean on. But he had never realized her vulnerability. Katya gave much and asked for little in return. Now she was asking from her heart what could be done about the injustice in their world, and Johann had nothing to offer.

The train whistle shrieked like an angry mother coming upon a family fight, and the rioters fell back as if reprimanded. The constables, giving one last glare at those involved, wheeled their horses to keep track of the hot, restless crowd that was now pushing and shoving to get to the train.

"I should have bought a buggy," muttered Heinrich to Johann, as they surveyed the scene. "Now we will just have to make the best of it."

The Hildebrandts said tearful farewells to the Reimers, and to their sister and daughter. Mika simply nodded to Johann and offered her small hand. They brushed fingers formally, and he turned away to help Katya and the children to the train.

Boarding the train was a long, drawn-out process, made worse by the recent altercation.

"There will be no fighting or bullying on this train," the conductor said, with as much authority as he could muster.

No one listened. The people pushed and snarled as they made their way onto the train. After what seemed like hours, the Hildebrandts and Johann Sudermann collapsed into rickety wooden seats in the seventh car, content to be out of the direct sun with a place to sit.

As the Great Southern chugged steadily down the line from Lichtenau to Melitopol and on to Crimea, the course of Russian history spiraled steadily downward into revolution. The tsar had now lost support from the nobility as well as the bourgeoisie and was called his own worst enemy. In the meantime, following Empress Alexandra's superstitious intuitions, Rasputin filled the imperial cabinet with indecent and incapable appointments.

Paul's busy life became hectic as he organized workers' groups, hassled the establishment, and wrote illegal literature to incite the working classes. He continued to wait on tables at the Astoria, doing his job efficiently and with style as he gathered more useful information than his patrons would have believed possible.

"The Big Man is coming back" was the word in the Petrograd underground. Revolutionary writings by Vladimir Ulyanov, known by the people as Lenin, filtered down from Norway where he lived in self-exile, to his loyal followers in the Russian cities.

Paul devoured these writings and reprinted and adapted them in his publications. With Josef Stalin absent, *PRAVDA* had become Lenin's mouthpiece to the people. Paul had no time to think of home or family or friends, and he hardly remembered the old times with Johann Sudermann, so involved was he in the cause to which he had committed his life.

Chapter 15

As the train crossed Chongar Bridge and headed for the east branch line at Dzhankoi, the Hildebrandts relaxed and slept. Most of the deserting soldiers and hotheads had disembarked at Melitopol, and the train was now calm and quiet. Sleep evaded Johann as he relived his earlier trip down this same track over a year ago. Back then, he'd had pleasant memories of Susannah and no idea he was about to fall for Maria Hildebrandt the moment he arrived at Succoth.

At that time, the war with Germany and Austria/Hungary had not yet begun, and although hostilities existed, he had known nothing of them.

Now, at the end of August 1915, all of Europe was at war. His own country was in turmoil, and his heart devastated. It seemed the war had affected him personally, invading his spirit. The opinions and prophecies of Paul Gregorovich Tekanin distressed him during the day and haunted his dreams at night.

He felt, lately, as if he were caught in a swiftly flowing river and being borne steadily toward a powerful waterfall that cascaded into deep, roiling waters.

Johann helped Heinrich and Katya secure their luggage and keep track of Nicholai and Anna as they changed trains in Dzhankoi. Now they would head east for the last leg of their journey.

"It surely is calm here, compared to the colonies," commented Heinrich. His furrowed brow showed he was not calm within. "I don't like to think of Mika living away from us, and Peter, but there's nothing to be done about it, I suppose."

Katya slipped her strong hand into his arm. "Papa, only days ago you told me we're in God's care and although everything seems to be going wrong, he is still in control."

Heinrich put his other hand over hers and squeezed it. "Thank you for the reminder, my child. Someday when you are a parent, remember your words then, too."

Katarina clasped her hands and sighed as the buggy turned off the main road and onto Magnolia Lane. The magnolia, cherry, and peach trees, still green and lush with summer beauty, waved a welcome in the warm breeze. Clipped sweetbrier hedges bowed from either side of the lane with formal and aromatic elegance, and bees buzzed in the late summer sun.

Succoth. "We're home!" Katya said joyously. As they turned off the lane onto the cobbled yard, the mansion came into view, stately and inviting. It offered warmth, security, and a deep sense of well-being.

Servants lined up along the steps outside, smiles on their faces and welcome in their eyes. "Good to see you, sir," offered Yuri, as Heinrich jumped from the buggy.

"Good to be home, Yuri," he answered, pumping the man's hand.

"Ma'am." One of the maids curtsied as Katarina stepped down.

"Dunia, I've missed you," she said, clasping the girl's hands. Cook received hugs all around, and everyone chuckled as Nicholai turned handsprings on the grass.

"Where's Maria?' asked Cook, looking at the carriage expectantly.

"She's not coming home," said Anna, in a soft voice. "She likes it better in Alexanderkrone."

Cook raised her eyebrows and the servants exchanged subtle looks. "I wonder how we shall ever manage," one muttered quietly, sarcasm tingeing her words.

Johann heard, and for the first time honestly considered how these people must view Mika and her condescending attitude. He watched as Katya put her arm around Dunia and talked with her as they entered the house. *How different the sisters are,* he thought. *I hadn't noticed it before. I wonder what else I missed while I was wandering about in the fog of infatuation.* He had been enamored with Maria and blind to her true character. She wasn't a bad person, he knew, just proud and controlling.

Reaching for some of the luggage, Johann squared his shoulders, smiled at young Fyodor, and started up the steps. He was home. He would heal. He would reevaluate his life and be the best friend and teacher to the Hildebrandts that he could be.

Supper that first evening was a celebration. The servers vied for the chance to bring in food, all joining in the jokes and telling the family what had transpired over the past several months.

Mika's chair, across from Johann's, sat empty. His heart tugged at memories of her beauty. But with God's help, he would adjust and carry on.

A week later, sitting at the same table, Johann believed he was on his way to a comfortable routine again. He had spent time in Bible study and prayer, in personal evaluation, and in setting up a school curriculum for Anna and Kolya. He planned to add French and Latin to their studies this fall. *It's certainly easier this time,* he thought, *knowing the children and what they can do.*

When the servants had loaded the table with roast lamb and creamed potatoes, a fat loaf of rye bread, and a crystal bowl of mixed fruit, Fyodor placed a long, white envelope beside Johann's plate.

The postmark was Halbstadt, and the script looked official. Curious, Johann slit the envelope with his pocketknife and unfolded the crisp white stationery. Nervously clearing his throat and glancing around the table, he silently read the contents.

"What is it, Johann?" asked Heinrich, noticing his pale face. "Bad news? You know we stand by you whatever it is."

Johann slowly raised his eyes until his gaze settled on Heinrich. "I am to report to Lichtenau for Forestry Service duty in one week. My name has been drawn."

He looked from face to face and was surprised to see tears in Katya's eyes. *She is such a gentle spirit,* he thought.

"I wish I could go," said Nicholai. "I would plant trees and build roads and serve in the medical corp. You're so lucky, Teacher."

Suddenly, Johann was ashamed. Here was a boy of ten years willing to serve his people and his homeland, while Johann preferred to hide behind his books and his students. So far, he had done nothing to support his country in this time of war. It was time he joined the ranks of young Mennonite men in alternative service. Perhaps it would even be a good diversion for his mending heart.

"How long will you be gone?" asked Katarina, her voice a mere whisper.

Johann checked the letter. "Four months, for now. I'll be home for Christmas, if all goes well."

Katya said nothing. The family paused to pray and ask protection for Johann in this new experience. Katya pushed her dessert back and forth on her plate, unable to eat more than a few bites. As soon as etiquette allowed, she excused herself and left the room.

Johann himself needed fresh air and a chance to deal with this news. He walked down the green carpeted hallway toward the kitchen, stepped out the garden door and followed the seashell path to the grape arbor.

Deep in thought, he reached the bench in the olive grove and was surprised to see Katarina there. She had not heard him approach, as she sobbed into her handkerchief.

"Oh, I'm sorry," he said, awkwardly. "I didn't see you, I was so distracted." Katya, who had been dabbing at her eyes in embarrassment, again buried her face in her handkerchief and cried.

"I . . . oh . . . what can I do?" stuttered Johann. He pulled up the lawn chair that sat in the shade of the cherry trees and wait out the storm. He would rather hurry back the way he'd come, but he couldn't leave his friend alone in such a state.

Eventually, Katya's sobs subsided. She blew her nose and looked up to find her friend patiently waiting to listen. At the sight of his compassionate hazel eyes looking earnestly through the thick lenses of his glasses, she began to weep again.

Johann reached out to her and pleaded, "Please stop, Katya. Don't cry anymore. It breaks my heart . . . There, now tell me what's bothering you."

Katya looked away, mortified. She searched for an escape, but realizing there was none, met Johann's gaze. She took a deep breath and said, "I don't want you to go."

"Well, if it's any comfort to you, Katya, I don't really want to go either. However, I need to do my part at this crucial time, so I will set my mind to it."

Seeing no change in her wounded expression, he added, "If it's the teaching that has you worried, I will leave all my notes and plans for you to follow." Again she looked ready to cry. "If you want them, that is," he went on. "I'm sure you would do fine on your own." He felt as if he were dodging arrows.

Katarina's head drooped, her lower lip quivering, and she twisted her handkerchief tightly. "I don't know how to help you if you won't talk to me, Katya," he said finally, with a sigh. "We've always been able to talk."

Trying another tack, he said, "It's so beautiful here. It's really become home to me. When I'm honest with myself, I realize that it wasn't just Mika who made me want to return. I'm content here without her. I can't put my finger on it, the claim this place has on me. It's partly the beauty, and the fact that it's the place of my spiritual rebirth, and, of course, my friendships with all of you."

He turned to face her. "Katya, I value your friendship highly. It is a refuge for me, as Succoth is a refuge to us all. I seem to be able to adjust my mind to your sister's absence, but I don't know what I'd do without your friendship . . . Have I done something to hurt you?"

With uncharacteristic forthrightness, Katarina stood, her handkerchief clenched in her fist, her face red with tears and anger. "If you can't work it out for yourself, I'll certainly not tell you, either!"

She slipped past him and ran toward the churchyard, seashells crushing with each footfall. Johann stared after her, his mouth hanging open stupidly, his hands out in a gesture of bewilderment.

It was nearly dark and Katya had not yet returned. "I wonder what's keeping her?" Johann wondered aloud as he sat on the front patio, his eyes fixed on the lane.

Anna was playing with her cat on the wide steps. She looked up thoughtfully at Johann and said, "I think my sister likes you, Teacher."

Johann returned her gaze. "I don't think Maria even thinks of me anymore. That is all past."

"No, Teacher," the little girl explained patiently. "I mean Katarina. I think she likes you very much."

"Oh," his face relaxed. "Yes, we are good friends. We rely on each other quite a lot." With another glance down the lane he added, "But I don't always understand her."

Anna let out a frustrated sigh and shook her head. She put the cat down and walked up to Johann's chair. "Cook was right," she said with innocent honesty. "You wouldn't know it if it stared you in the face!"

Now she had Johann's full attention. "What wouldn't I know? You and Katya and Cook all seem to think I should know something. What is it, pray tell?"

"Katya," she answered simply and marched into the house.

Johann threw up his hands in despair and said, "Would someone please interpret for me? I need to talk to a man!" He charged into the house in search of Heinrich, whom he found in the library, engrossed in a favorite volume from the hundreds that surrounded him.

Heinrich looked up at Johann's abrupt entry and nodded for him to come ahead. "You look like a man with a mission, or perhaps in desperate search of one," he said, laying aside his volume. "Sit down."

Johann sat, then ran his hands through his hair and adjusted his glasses. "I need your help, sir. The females in this place have conspired against me, and I don't understand any of them. I am blind, they say, and then they walk smugly away or run off in tears."

Heinrich's face showed concern at first, then humor, and then empathy. He listened patiently as Johann told of his confusion, then asked, "Who walked away and who ran?"

"Sir?"

"Who walked away from you and who ran?"

"Katya ran. Anna walked. Cook, I didn't see."

"And what did you say before Katya ran?"

"I told her I appreciated her friendship. That's it."

"And Anna? What did she say?"

"That little pixie told me Katya liked me and that I should see the answer if I looked at her. I don't . . ." He paused as realization dawned on him. "Surely not! Can this be?"

He looked at Heinrich, who leaned back in his plush leather chair, a compassionate smile on his face.

"Am I right, that Katarina feels more for me than I thought she did? Have I misread her all along?"

"Well, I don't know how long she may have hidden these feelings for you, if that's truly what 'it' is, but I think you may be on the right track—speaking from experience."

"Oh, my!" Johann stood and paced about the room, muttering and arguing with himself. "What a dunce. I am so blind. Do you think she really feels that way? I could have saved us both a lot of uncertainty and heartache if I'd caught on sooner."

Heinrich sat quietly, his face sober, but his eyes dancing with humor. "I hate to give advice in a situation like this, but perhaps you need some time to ponder and to pray before you meet with Katarina. In my experience with females," he said sagely, "I've discovered that approaching these things unprepared often makes the problem worse."

"Oh, absolutely, yes," muttered Johann. "I'll go up to my room and consider this . . . this revelation. I'll go now," and he marched out the door without another word.

Heinrich covered his eyes with his hands, his shoulders shaking with laughter. "Poor boy," he said, wiping the tears from his face. "I hope he can remember where his room is." He shook his head as he picked up his book to resume reading.

Next morning, Johann was in a quandary about where to take his breakfast. If he went to the kitchen, Cook would glare at him. If he went to the dining room, he would meet Katya, and he wasn't ready for that. Morning light had made him doubt last night's assumption, and he wondered if he'd merely jumped to conclusions about Katarina's outburst.

Anna solved his present problem by intercepting him in the hallway and inviting him to breakfast with her. "Katya isn't coming down, and I need company."

"What about your father and Nicholai?"

"Nicholai isn't company—he's my brother," she said. "And Papa's just Papa."

"Oh," he said in an understanding way. "I'd be glad to keep you company then. I'm rather hungry."

She looked up at Johann and slipped her small hand into his. In a loud whisper she asked, "Are you going to talk to Katya today?"

He looked down at her and smiled at the knowing look in her eyes, his puzzlement growing again. "Do you think I should?"

"You'll have to decide that for yourself," she said, skipping into the dining room ahead of him. He stared after her, recalling Heinrich's words, "Don't try to understand a woman; just love her!" *They certainly learn young,* he thought.

"Mika has been so quiet since her family left," Cornelia Reimer commented to her husband at breakfast that same morning. "Do you think she regrets her decision to stay with us?"

Abram considered her words. "I don't think she's sorry to be staying here," he said, "or sorry that she didn't go back. Maybe there's something else. Why don't you ask her, Nellie?"

Mrs. Reimer stood and reached for the coffeepot on the back of the stove. "Another cup, Abram?" She poured without waiting for an answer. "It's a tricky thing, looking after Maria. She is a haughty, high-class young woman and at the same time an insecure child. If I should ask the wrong questions of her, she might well be angry."

"Not like Katie," her husband said. "With her, you can speak freely and reason, and if there's something she doesn't want to say, she just doesn't say it."

"Now don't go comparing the two again. My mother always said that's the worst thing parents can do to their children. Besides," she said, as she began clearing the breakfast things, "I know whom you favor. But we love them both and need to understand and support Mika as much as possible."

Abram rose and gave his wife a peck on the cheek. "I'm going out to my shop," he said, then mumbled something about finishing a gift for his Katie.

The day arrived for Johann's departure to Lichtenau and he had still not spoken alone with Katya. They both seemed to be avoiding it. The whole situation struck him as bizarre. Two weeks ago, he had assumed he was courting Maria Hildebrandt and that they would both be at Succoth, where their relationship would deepen.

A bit of a Joseph, he said to himself. *Always dreaming of things far beyond my reach.* Now Mika was in Alexanderkrone, without a care for him or his feelings for her.

He missed his friendly talks with Katarina. They shared so many interests and opinions. Somehow he couldn't imagine her being in love with him and hiding it all the while. Surely there would have been some sign, he told himself. But perhaps there *had* been signs, and he had been blind to them.

Perhaps that was the reason for her shyness at times or her covert glances. He felt sorry for her, but not in a pitying way. Katarina was not a person to be pitied. She showed a strong, consistent character and great spiritual reserves, disregarding her outburst in the garden a few days ago.

Johann strapped up his suitcase and checked the room again, in case he had forgotten to include an item. He recalled vividly the first time he had entered this room, so large, so elegant yet masculine—how the fireplace and the windows to the park had appealed to him. He considered the sort of lodging he would be experiencing in the near future, and it contrasted sharply with this room.

Probably a tent, he thought. *At least the weather will be cooler now that summer is over.* Remembering the approaching winter, he added a scarf and woolen cap to his luggage.

Fyodor knocked and, seeing the door open, came in to carry the bags down. Johann gave him a wry smile. "This is silly," he said. "In a couple of days I will be doing constant physical labor, and I can't even carry my own bags."

"It's my job, sir," replied the valet.

"I know," Johann answered, "but I think, in view of the future, I should carry them myself."

"As you wish." Fyodor set the bags down and stepped out with a slight bow.

Johann carried them to the front entrance and retraced his steps down the green hall, past the kitchen and out through the garden door.

September. The most beautiful month of the year, he thought. Some of the trees still flaunted their greenery, while others wore a mature blend of russet and gold. The trees kept their leaves longer here than back home, at least two or three weeks longer.

This was a paradise of a place. It was no wonder the tsars had vacationed on Crimea's southern coast for centuries.

As he strolled along Magnolia Lane between the hedges, Johann soaked in the beauty, sunshine, and peace. He needed to collect his thoughts, to prepare himself for what lay ahead. He would miss this place and these people. He wished that things were different between him and Katya because he really needed to talk. She was such an encouragement to him, able to listen and sort out what he was saying.

Crossing the bridge over the stream, he glanced up at the little family church and was startled to see someone sitting on the steps. It was Katya. He couldn't turn back now—she had already seen him. *Oh Lord,* he pleaded, *give me the words to say. I don't want to hurt her again.*

He stopped, one foot on the bottom step, and rested his arm on the handrail. "Good morning, Katarina," he said. "I hope I'm not intruding on you, but I just needed to walk through the park once more before I left. It seems we come to the same places for solace."

He stopped speaking and studied her. The breeze played with her abundance of curls, teasing them around her broad face. She looked the picture of health—clear green eyes, her face sprinkled with freckles. Self-consciously, she tucked her hands behind her back.

"I haven't seen you much this past week, Katya. I miss our friendly talks."

She reddened, but remained silent.

"I'm confused about where I stand with you. I'm afraid I've hurt your feelings badly." He climbed the stairs to where she sat. "May I?" She moved over for him.

"Katarina, you are special to me. Right from the start you welcomed me, accepted me. Why, you prayed for me to find God, and the Lord answered your request. For that alone I am eternally grateful."

She acknowledged this with a slight smile but remained silent. *I'm certainly bungling this,* he thought.

He turned to face her and reached for her hand. "Why do you always hide your hands?" he asked gently.

Katya looked up at him. "They're so big," she said, reluctantly pulling them from behind her and placing them on her knees. "My hands and feet are big like Papa's, not small and delicate like Mama's and . . . Mika's."

He reached again for her hand, and her heart raced. "I think they are strong and capable. After all, what's a hand for but to do things? Write, dig, comfort. And feet—they balance much better when they're bigger." He stuck his large, black boots out in front of him and they laughed.

Johann pushed his glasses up onto the bridge of his nose. "Katya, I've played the fool with Maria. She doesn't realize what powers she has."

"Oh, yes, she does."

"Anyway, I feel ridiculous now that I didn't catch on sooner. She did me a favor by remaining in Alexanderkrone. I've had a chance to analyze my heart."

"And what did you find?" Katya asked, something akin to fear in her voice.

"Well, I realized it was infatuation on my part and nothing but a game on hers. You could have told me that before, right?"

She sat with elbows on knees, her chin in her hand, and said nothing.

"Katya, I received another letter from Susannah." Katarina stiffened. "She writes to tell me about Peter, of course, and what she writes is encouraging. I believe you have made an excellent decision in sending him to Bethany." He shifted his position to look at her more directly. "But what I really wanted to tell you is that she speaks highly of you. I didn't realize you two had become so close. I seem to have taken you for granted. Your friendship really means the world to me."

She looked at him and smiled, her heart relaxing. A strange

peace seeped through her. Susannah had promised to pray, and God would take care of the timing. "Your friendship means a great deal to me too, Johann. I wish you all the best in the service."

Katya was immensely relieved that her friend hadn't told him their secret. But then, Susannah wouldn't do that. And it was obvious that Johann wasn't at the same place as Katya in their relationship. Such things could not be pushed. They had to come from both hearts of their own accord.

"Could we make peace and renew our friendship before I leave? It would certainly ease my mind."

Katarina swallowed her hopes and sent up a prayer for grace. Love demanded was not love at all. "Of course, Johann. Have you come to terms with joining the Forstei?" She would bide her time and trust in God. *After all,* she thought, *God knows best.*

They walked back to the house together, Johann sharing his heart about leaving and the exciting but frightening future ahead of him, Katya thanking God for her newfound peace. She knew this war of the heart was not over, but at least the present battle was won.

The buggy sat ready with Fyodor at the reins, baggage loaded. The Hildebrandts and several of the servants gathered to bid farewell.

"Well," said Johann. He put out his hand to shake Heinrich's.

"All the best. We will pray for you daily."

"Good-bye, Teacher," chorused Anna and Kolya. Johann patted Anna on her golden head and gave Nicholai a jesting punch on the arm. "Take care of your sisters, young man."

"Farewell," said Katarina, reaching out her hand.

"Until Christmas," he said, surprising himself and the others by embracing her. He turned to go. *What is ahead for me?* he wondered. *Where will I be stationed? What will my duties include?*

"God go with you," called Heinrich, as the buggy rolled away down Magnolia Lane, out to the main road and the rail line north. Katarina stood hugging herself to stop the quaking of her hands and her heart.

Chapter 16

Autumn days flew by for Katarina. The memory of Johann's parting embrace, although given in friendship, still caused her to close her eyes and sigh. In spite of the emptiness she felt at his absence, Succoth covered a multitude of yearnings.

Katya loved the freedom of the wide-open grasslands beyond the stream, the beauty of the yard and park, the solitude of life here. Let the world go mad—this was her place of refuge.

The annual potato roast had been canceled for political and practical reasons, but the potatoes had still been dug and distributed to the neighbors. Katarina enlisted the help of Anna and Kolya to work alongside the field hands, which the children did not find particularly rewarding. She promised them an excursion to Spat if they helped without complaining or arguing.

Lessons were challenging. Katya relied much on Johann's notes and plans for guidance, but she also felt free to modify them to her own liking.

She became more acquainted with Johann through his notes, which were meticulous, thoughtful, and resourceful.

Anna must possess a firm knowledge of her arithmetic before she proceeds to the next level. Extra problems may be beneficial. . . . Insure that Nicholai's history lessons are interesting; he will absorb and remember if I make the stories live for him. . . . Make use of the gardens and barns in horticulture, botany, agriculture. Allow Nicholai to take part in calving, training horses, planting and harvesting crops. . . . Remind Anna that her mother ordered many of the trees from a distance and decided where they should be planted.

Katya especially appreciated the mention of Mama. Johann had remembered to do his part in maintaining the memory of a woman he had never met. She also loved his humor and easygoing nature that smiled out between the lines of "proper teaching":

> Allow the children to hunt frogs, to get dirty, to lie on the grass and watch the clouds. Avoid kidnapping by gypsies, falling through ice, tumbling from trees, etc.

She laughed as she noted the next day's plans. It was not the season for tadpoles, but they could certainly watch clouds and teach science under that guise.

The jostling train ride back to Lichtenau proved to be a quiet one—no engine problems, no deserters, just the steady clatter of iron on iron. Upon arriving, Johann joined the young men who gathered in the church to be divided into groups and sent to various camps scattered around the south.

"Sudermann, Johann, son of Heinz Sudermann of Kleefeld, Molotschna, Taurida Province . . ."

Johann stepped forward to await his designation. "Schwarzwald Camp." He accepted his information packet and joined a dozen or so others in the Schwarzwald group.

As soon as the assignments were completed, individual leaders took over to give further orders. Three of the units headed back the way Johann had come, a mere twenty to fifty versts south of the Molotschna Colony. Two units took the Tokmak line across the northern edge of the Molotschna settlement, followed by a one-hundred-verst ride to their posts. Three more groups headed west by wagon to Kherson Province, across the Dnieper River. Johann's unit took the Great Southern from Lichtenau north, then were transferred to wagons for several hours of travel to their barracks.

Schwarzwald, Johann read in his pamphlet, was built about 1909. Also known as Chornole, it was located near the Dnieper River in the general area of the Chortitza Colony where Peter lived at Bethany, and two or three hundred versts northeast of the other three Dnieper camps. The area surrounding the camp was flat grassland that offered grazing for cattle and shade in cottonwood thickets along the ravines.

The barracks, Johann decided, were tolerable, being only about seven or eight years old. Each man had a bunk, mattress and pillow, and space in a closet. He had brought his own bedroll, as requested. Since the forestry camps were solely supported and managed by the Mennonite colonies, the men were expected to decrease costs by supplying their own clothing and personal needs.

The first evening, after a short orientation, the new recruits were allowed to turn in. Most were exhausted by the trip and the new experience. The veterans of the camp looked them over and decided which ones would have a hard time. Johann felt their stares and heard their loud whispers. He decided he didn't care what they thought and fell asleep.

Though all the chosen men were Mennonite, they descended on Schwarzwald from many villages and several denominations. Johann knew no one at all in his unit, but he supposed that would soon change.

Mika knew she really shouldn't go to Prischib with Aaron Friesen, even if his sister Martha and her friend Daniel Esau

did go along. It was at least twenty-five versts from Alexanderkrone, all the way up to Halbstadt and across the river.

The German Lutheran village of Prischib was a cultural
center, with a population of about two thousand. Of course
Halbstadt was larger, with its school of commerce, mills, tile
factory, and motor factory. It had many stores, the nurses'
training school, and an electric power plant. But Halbstadt
was familiar. It was Mennonite, and sometimes Mika just
wanted to see something new and exciting.

The whole atmosphere in Prischib felt different, freer. And
there was the fair! They could try out exciting rides for a few
kopecks each, and the midway offered the mysteries of the
strange and bizarre for mere kopecks.

The German Lutherans sold a variety of homemade pies
and pastries, sausages, and fresh-baked breads. The four
young people enjoyed their day to the fullest and left for
home later than they had planned.

On the drive home, Aaron and Daniel pulled out a stash of
alcohol they had hidden in the back of the *droschka*, and the
homeward journey became more and more lively. Mika and
Martha had only a taste, but the young men indulged freely.

"Do you think we should travel so fast over this bumpy
part of the road?" Martha hinted to her brother as he
snapped the reins. Mika held on to the side of the open-air
buggy for balance.

"Too fasht for you, li'l Martha?" he slurred.

Mika decided it was time to take over. "Slow this rig down
immediately, Aaron," she ordered. "I don't intend to be
thrown out onto the road because you've had too much to
drink."

A sly grin came over Aaron's face, and he hauled on the
reins. "Whoa, Blackie, whoa." He slowed the buggy down
and pulled over to the side of the road. Wrapping the reins
clumsily around the front piece, he turned to Mika.

"Shlow enough for you?" His breath reeked of spirits as he threw his arm boldly around her shoulders.

"Aaron Friesen! Get away from me."

Aaron tipped his head back to laugh and was momentarily distracted by the starry sky above him. "Wouldya look at that? Sure ish pretty." He looked back at Mika. "But not ash pretty ash you." He leaned toward her again.

A sharp slap from Mika revived his brain, but also his temper. "I'd say it's time to get you home, pretty Maria." Grabbing the reins, he snapped them hard and urged the horse into a trot, then a canter. He didn't let up until poor Blackie was running for all she was worth, fancy droschka careening down the road behind her, its occupants holding on for their lives.

"Have you lost your mind?" shouted Maria, trying to grab the reins. They were on the last stretch toward home, between Tiegerweide and Alexanderkrone, and the road was deserted. Martha screamed and begged, but her brother kept driving, anger and alcohol in full control now. Daniel had passed the point of fear. He had slithered to the floor of the buggy, moaning about his stomach.

Suddenly, Blackie veered to the left and Aaron fought desperately to keep the buggy from turning over. "What's come over you, you crazy horse?" he hollered.

Mika felt the presence before she saw it—a large figure on a dark horse, silhouetted against the sky. Out of the night, from behind a stand of poplars, three or four more horses trotted up to the buggy.

The dark figure grabbed the terrified Blackie by the bridle and called out in raw Russian, "Where do you go in such a hurry? I don't see fire."

Aaron appeared quite sober now. "We're just heading home, if you'll move out of the way."

The leader laughed. "He wants us to move," he announced sarcastically to the other riders. They laughed with him.

"A little late for a nice boy and girls to be out, eh? How come you got two girls? You bring one for us?" There was laughter again, and Mika heard crude comments.

Martha began to cry. "Shut up, Martha," hissed Mika.

"Oh, we have a pretty one here, boys." The strangers rode closer to appraise Mika. She edged back against Aaron, but he didn't seem happy for her nearness now.

Just then Daniel groaned from the back of the buggy. "Hey, we got us a nice, drunk Mennonite! Does your mama know where you are, sonny?" One of the riders pulled Daniel from the wagon, and he tumbled onto the road.

"You better get that boy home," the man mocked. "He needs his mama."

Aaron drew a ragged breath and asked, "What do you want? We need to get on our way."

"What do we want? Well, that one, for sure." The leader grabbed Mika's arm. She wrenched away from him, crowding against Aaron, but she did not scream or beg, while Martha sobbed enough for all of them. Mika's mind was whirling, searching for a distraction.

"How about some vodka?" she asked, and reached back for it. "Martha, give me what's left." Sobbing in terror, Martha found a couple more bottles, which she gave to Mika.

"Here, from us to you," said Maria, "if you let us go. I'll give you some money, too." She reached for her satchel, and before she knew it, the bag was whisked away.

"That's all?" they complained. "A few rubles? You have more. Give us the money or we take the girls." Feverishly, the frightened trio checked their pockets and billfolds, which the bandits immediately confiscated. They also relieved Daniel of his possessions.

The leader walked his horse around beside Mika and took her arm again. "Come on, pretty one. Let's go." She tried again to pull free, but he held her firmly. All reserve gone now, she screamed and kicked at him, determined not to go without a fight.

The men's laughter was drowned out by shouts. "It's the constable! Let's get out of here." And with a wicked swipe of his arm, the leader cuffed Mika across the side of the head, sending her into Aaron's lap. She clung dizzily to the edge of the wagon, her blood dripping down the side and onto the ground.

Fast-approaching hoofbeats rang louder and louder, and a uniformed constable, astride a tall horse, pulled up to the droschka. "What's going on?" he barked.

Aaron finally found his voice as he pointed toward the trees. "Robbers!" he croaked. "Stopped us in the road." He looked down at Mika, who was trembling, and pulled her up gently. As the constable dismounted, Aaron found his handkerchief and began wiping the blood from Mika's face. She cried quietly, tears running down her cheeks, and was overcome with shaking.

Martha continued to sob hysterically, and Daniel crawled to the side of the road and lost his supper. The wind picked up as dark clouds scudded across the navy blue sky, blotting out the stars.

Susannah moved swiftly from room to room in her ward, closing windows and pulling blinds. A storm threatened, and she knew many of the patients at Bethany would respond in terror. It was going to be a long shift. *But that's what I'm here for, isn't it, Lord?* she prayed as she worked. *To calm and to comfort. And to show your love by word and deed. I ask, as always, that you meet my needs and the needs of these residents from your unlimited resources.*

As she entered Peter's room, Susannah saw him silhouetted against the open window, the wind playing with his hair, his face turned to the darkening sky. She hummed a happy tune so her presence wouldn't catch him off guard.

"Good evening, Peter dear," she sang in her sweet voice. Peter didn't move, he was so captivated by the breaking storm. She walked to Peter's side to observe his face. His wide eyes watched the sky, his mouth hanging slack.

All at once, he turned to look at her. Susannah reached out to wipe the corner of his mouth with a handkerchief, but he pushed her hand away. "Storm," he said clearly. "Mama." He turned back to the window.

Susannah allowed him to watch for a while longer, then gently guided him to his chair. He looked up at her expectantly, his clear eyes showing that at this particular moment he was completely lucid. "Mama," he repeated. She knelt before him and took his hands. "Mama's gone, Peter. I'm Susannah."

"Mama. Storm." He began to rock back and forth in his chair as she prayed for wisdom. A flash of light split the night, and in her mind she was a small child again, finding solace from the storm in her mother's arms.

With sudden insight, she pulled a chair close beside his and wrapped him in her arms. "Did your mama hold you when it stormed, Peter dear? Did she sing to you?" The bewildered child in the body of a young man calmed in her arms. His head rested against her shoulder and, as the storm unleashed its fury, Susannah sang lullabies and Peter slept.

A storm of another nature brewed off the Gulf of Finland. Paul Gregorovich Tekanin walked quickly along a side street, heading from the Astoria to the latest hiding place of the illegal printing press. They had been forced to move several times during the past few months, and Paul had learned to be alert at all times and trust no one.

He took several sharp turns, walked through a few dark alleys and doubled back, arriving at an abandoned warehouse near the waterfront. He rapped sharply four times on a basement window, crept around the side of the building, ducked behind a fir tree, and climbed into the window that his co-worker, Grisha, opened for him.

"How goes it?" he asked the stocky man in his thirties as they descended a set of stairs to the basement. A door at the bottom opened for them when they produced the password. "It's as hectic as ever," Grisha replied, running ink-stained fingers through his reddish hair.

The clicking and clacking of presses filled the large room, and the smell of printer's ink was heady. Paul picked up a pamphlet from a pile on a desk.

WHILE THE EMPEROR SITS AT THE FRONT IN A GILDED TRAIN, WE STARVE IN THE CAPITAL, he read. The article went on to decry the folly of feeding more hapless Russians to the German war machine.

"I have another prepared," said Paul. Not willing to implicate himself or the others in this dangerous game, he carried no papers with him, only well-organized thoughts in his head. These thoughts he now transcribed to paper as Grisha and the rest bustled about their work.

Vera Guseyva worked behind a small desk in the far corner of the basement, editing and checking copy for errors. She glanced up and caught Paul's eye as he entered the room, but no other communication occurred between them.

Guseyva was efficient and thorough. And angry. Her younger siblings were starving, and her parents simply could not find enough food for them on their tiny plot of land outside the city. In the summer, her seventeenth summer, she had left their tumbledown shack to seek her own way. Through a string of circumstances, both fortunate and otherwise, she had found her way into the underground movement.

It was not an easy life, with its constant secrecy and deception. And it required its own brand of self-sacrifice. But the revolution depended on people like Vera, committed to the core. She would allow nothing to come between her and the cause. She would sooner cut off her right arm than betray the process of change that had been set in motion.

Only on completion of her present project did she allow herself to glance again at Tekanin. She didn't know much at all about him, but she did know where he stayed, and that was enough. The less one knew of another these days, the better off everyone was.

Paul stood and pulled his hat down onto his forehead. Making his way around the various desks and machines, he dropped the paper on Vera's desk. "This is for release tomorrow. Can you get it done?"

"Of course," she replied, flipping her straight brown hair back over her shoulder.

Paul bent close, as if to point out a word or phrase on his paper. "I must work at the restaurant tonight," he whispered, and she understood. Times were dangerous, and one did not set one's heart on anyone or anything. This she told herself as she swallowed her disappointment.

It was the nature of life, Guseyva concluded. Loneliness, uncertainty, and danger in a never-ending circle. Sometimes she wished . . .

Vera began working on the copy with renewed vigor, and soon her mind was again under the influence of the revolutionary fervor that pervaded the capital.

Chapter 17

The field trip to Spat was set for November 1, and the day dawned clear and warm. Katya bustled about, checking on food baskets and games, making sure everything was in order.

Mika would have had it all organized in her head, she thought, and a longing for her sister tugged at her heart. *I hope you're happy, Mika.*

They had heard of the bandit attack in the Molotschna, and it caused great worry for the family. But this was a special day, not to be spoiled by such thoughts. Katarina determined to keep it so.

"Come, Anna," she called. "Let's go out to the buggy." Fyodor held the reins, with Kolya beside him, helping when his begging became too much to endure.

Heinrich decided at the last minute that he would accompany them as well. "I need to speak to Brother Janzen about a new plow," he explained, but Katarina knew the real reason.

The wide coach road from Perekop in the north of Crimea down to Sevastopol in the south had become a high traffic route for military personnel since the second year of the war. This created little problem besides the unpleasantness of overcrowding and longer waiting periods for public transportation, but Heinrich knew to be cautious of the soldiers. The Black Sea fleet had a nasty reputation. He was not about to leave his children, the only ones remaining with him, to some unknown fate.

So the family and Fyodor set off for Spat in cheerful spirits. They crossed the rail line when they reached the village and drove their wagon to the waterfall near the windmill. It was a favorite picnic spot, but since it was a weekday, there were not many people there.

The beauty of the trees, the softness of the lush grass, the waterfall's music, all combined to wrap Katya in a cloak of peace and relaxation. Later, she planned on stopping at Franz Goosen's bookstore. He carried a variety of authors: Goethe, Schiller, Pushkin, Lermontov, as well as novels by the Mennonite preacher writer with the pen name Ernst Schrill. For now, she was content to watch the children run to the river while Heinrich stretched out on a blanket. Katya began to set out the lunch.

Heinrich turned on his side and propped himself up on one elbow. "This is a good thing you are doing, Katie."

She smiled. "I promised, and it seemed time for a change."

Heinrich made no further comment, retreating into a world of his own. Katya had noticed his silence more and more lately, but so far she had let it go. She knew the importance of private contemplation. Today however, since the two were alone, she ventured to speak. "You've been so quiet lately, Papa," she began. "Is there some concern that could become lighter by sharing it with me?"

Heinrich looked at his eldest daughter with eyes of love. "Such a big heart you have, my dear," he said. Then, after a minute or two of soul searching, he continued. "I don't wish to upset you, or worry you unnecessarily, but . . . " He stopped, at a loss for words.

Katya picked up where he left off. "But our days of picnics and carefree hours in the sun are numbered. Is that what you're trying to say?"

"Now you're a prophet."

Katarina smiled sadly. "Not a prophet, Papa—an observer."

She looked off to the train station east of town. "All those soldiers are not out for a field trip. The war is going badly for us, and unrest in the country escalates daily."

"When Johann and I were in Petersburg—excuse me, Petrograd," said Heinrich, sitting up, "Paul Gregorovich made a statement to Johann that sits at the front of my mind like a banner of doom. He said, 'Russia as you know it no longer exists. Everything's going to change.' I fear he is correct. Most of our people in the colonies are unaware of the impending changes or else in denial of them."

Katya glanced again at the station and the steady stream of traffic moving from it to the town. Then her eyes rested on Anna and Nicholai as they played at the edge of the water and chased leaf boats along the shore to watch them catapult over the falls. "Why must our lives, which yearn for sweetness and peace, be so often tainted with bitter experiences? Why is it so, Papa?"

She spoke as a child, her innocence of character and purity of heart shining through her expressive green eyes. At that moment, Heinrich would have given anything in the world to take his child in his arms and assure her that everything would turn out all right, that she had no need to worry.

He did not believe this, however, and it would be a great disservice to tell her so. She was too wise to be fooled, anyway. He prayed that in spite of the difficulties he saw coming, his Katie could maintain her innocence and purity. So he spoke what was on his heart. "My dear Katya," he began, "the Lord never promised us that life would be all sweetness and peace. In fact, he said, 'In this world you shall have trouble.' He also said, 'Take heart, for I have overcome the world.' "

He waved a hand toward the station and the busy bridge, with their bustle of humanity. "God has set life in motion, and he continues to oversee it and to control it. But God refuses to force himself on people. And so, it is as the ancient prophet

Samuel said to Israel, 'You have rejected the Lord as your king. Now you will see what it is to do things your own way.' "

"I know, Papa," interrupted Katarina quietly. "We have no right to expect a life of ease because we live in a world that has rejected the Creator and King."

"But take heart, Katya," Heinrich repeated, with a soft smile. "God has overcome the world. He gives us all we need to endure, and afterward . . . afterward we have an eternity of peace, sweetness, and righteousness in God's presence forevermore."

Katya leaned over and kissed his forehead. "Thank you, Papa," she whispered. "I needed to be reminded."

Johann was wakened at sunrise by the sharp call of a barracks supervisor. "Everyone roll out! Morning devotions in ten minutes."

Dutifully he dressed and splashed cold water on his face. Smoothing his hair back with a comb, he hurried out to the mess hall. The chaplain, a middle-aged man from Halbstadt, read a Bible passage and a prepared sermonette, then a prayer from his prayer book, and the day began.

The food was good enough, Johann thought. Some of the young men complained, but they had obviously never been far from their mothers' kitchens. Johann recalled one of his father's favorite sayings: "Unless you are starving, don't complain." So he kept his peace and ate what was set before him.

The man in charge, the Boss, as veterans referred to him, stood in the mess hall and addressed the men. "So far, most of our men have been occupied with improving the roads in this area. We have accomplished much.

"However, a greater need has arisen and we will answer the call. The war continues to inflict heavy casualties, and the need for medics is increasing. Therefore, we begin today, with the call-up of new men, an intensive training program that will enable you to deal with wounded soldiers. We meet immediately in the open area just south of the barracks, where you will receive instruction. You will proceed there now."

Johann filed out with the others and headed to the exercise area. By evening, his head was swimming with facts and procedures. Thankfully, there would be reviews and practice sessions before they saw any real casualties.

"I guess we'll finally see some action," said recruit Isaac Neumann, on the way back to their barracks. "Better than building roads."

Johann pushed up his glasses and glanced at the tall, well-built man beside him. "I will go where duty calls and do what I must," he replied, "but I do not look forward to 'the action,' as you call it."

Neumann returned his gaze and said, a little more loudly than necessary, "Whatsa matter, Four Eyes? Scared of the sight of blood?"

"Yes," answered Johann, matter-of-factly. "It turns my stomach to think that wounds have been purposely inflicted by another human being." He continued toward his building, talking as he went. "And I believe anyone who is honest with himself would agree."

Reaching his barracks, John dug his Bible out of his knapsack and headed off to a nearby stand of water poplars. He had no idea where the medical corps would be sent, but he imagined long, hard hours of difficult and unpleasant work in the days ahead as autumn turned into winter.

"Did you ever wonder what we would do if the war came to us here in Bethany?" asked Susannah, as she and Gerhard strolled through fallen leaves on the grounds of the institution.

"That's certainly a dismal topic for such a gem of a day," Gerhard responded, a slight smile touching his clean-shaven face. "I would think you'd be thinking of Christmas or visits with friends and family."

Susannah did not smile. "I may not be the most intelligent person," she said, "but I do have serious thoughts from time to time."

The smile left Gerhard's face, replaced by remorse at the effect of his words. "Suse, I'm sorry. I meant no discredit to you. I know you're capable of deep and significant thought, and I had no intention to imply otherwise."

"Oh, I know. I just overreacted," she said, glancing up at the tall, business-like young man. He was so decisive, yet careful of the feelings of others.

"What I meant to say is, you're usually concerned with the present. You do your work with a compassion that doesn't worry about what tomorrow may bring or about things we can't control."

Susannah considered his words. "You're right, to a degree," she replied. "When I'm meeting a need, it is with all of me. But when present needs are met, I sometimes imagine needs which may arise in the future."

"It's not like you to worry."

"I don't think I'd call it worry. A better word would be realism. Word is all around, Gerhard, of what's happening to our country. I lived my childhood in a secure and predictable village. It was a fairytale life. Now I exist in another protected environment. But I hear about the war and the unrest, and I feel it in my heart, in my bones. This idyll cannot last, and then what shall we do with the residents here?"

She looked to Gerhard for answers, and he feared he had none. "I can't tell you what you want to hear, Suse."

"I know. I don't expect you to solve the problems of humankind single-handedly. I guess I just needed an outlet for my wonderings."

"You can always talk to me, Susannah. I am pleased to listen. . . . Susannah?"

"Yes?"

For a moment, it seemed he would dismiss the thought that had stopped him. Then he reached for her hands and looked into her eyes, as blue and clear as the November sky.

"Susannah," he said again, "I don't know what the future holds. I expect it will bring many challenges our way. But I'd like to propose that we face them together."

She stared up at him, her golden hair shining in the autumn sun. Her eyes were wide and questioning. "What are you saying, Gerhard?"

He blew out his breath and looked at the sky for guidance. No words appeared there, so he looked back into her eyes and saw what he was searching for.

"My little angel of mercy," he spoke, from his heart. "I can't imagine life without you, and I know I could face any obstacle with you by my side."

Still she stared, speechless. He led her over to a bench and nodded for her to sit. Then, kneeling before her, he looked up at her.

"Susannah, I love you and want you with me always. I want you for my wife."

Susannah gasped, her blue eyes filling with tears.

"I realize times are unstable, but I promise that as God gives me strength and ability, I will protect you and care for you. Will you have me?"

She smiled, then, as the tears slipped down her cheeks. Tenderly, she touched his face. "Oh, yes, dear Gerhard. I will have you. We will face our tomorrows together."

It was one of those days that gets under one's skin. Katya tried to concentrate on reading, but Goethe seemed stilted. She took up some handwork to make Christmas gifts for her sisters, but soon became frustrated with her mistakes.

Outside, the air was crisp and clear. There were no rain clouds in the sky, but its color was a winter blue, a darker, stronger shade with a hint of gray. In exasperation, she threw down her handwork and ran upstairs for warmer clothing.

With only a fleeting second thought, she pulled on the heavy woolen trousers she had taken from Peter's closet, donned a warm sweater, and ran down the backstairs and out to the stables.

A chilly breeze tugged at the leaves that still clung tenaciously to mostly bare branches, and played with Katarina's scarf. She tied the ends more tightly under her chin and ducked into the calm of the stable.

"Hello, Misha!" she called, relaxing at the smell of clean straw, fresh hay, and horses. The elderly stableman peeked out from behind a large chestnut mare and stared at her. He came forward, currycomb in hand, and began to chuckle deep in his throat.

"Hah! You had me fooled. Who is this half man-half woman creature who comes to my barn? Hah!"

Katya turned red. She had completely forgotten how silly she looked. Laughing with him she said, "I need to ride. The wind and the fields call me. The woods are preparing for winter, and I need to say farewell."

Misha had know her since she was a child, and understood perfectly what she was saying. "I've been expecting you one of these fine days," he said. "It looks to me like you want to ride in a saddle, not a buggy?"

She smiled her answer and reached for a bridle as the old man hefted her saddle and blanket off the rack. "Beautiful day today," he noted, "but there's a storm coming. Rain for sure, maybe even snow."

"Snow at the beginning of December?" Katarina asked.

"Oh, yah. It happens often. Of course it won't last long, but winter comes creeping."

Katarina spoke softly to her mare as she slipped the bit into her mouth and the leather over her ears. Misha cinched up the saddle and adjusted the stirrups. Katya didn't often ride astride, and she was a tall young woman.

The mare, Sunny, felt the weather too, and pranced as soon as her young mistress climbed into the saddle. For Misha's sake, and to warm up the horse, Katya walked her out of the yard and onto the dirt lane. Then she leaned forward over Sunny's neck and whispered, "Okay girl, let's go." Back at the barn, Misha smiled and shook his head as the sound of galloping hooves faded into the distance.

As she rode, the wind teased Katya's scarf off her head, releasing her thick curls to fly in all directions. She felt like a newly escaped prisoner and let out a triumphant shout of freedom. "Wouldn't Johann be shocked at my behavior?" she laughed, as she reined in her mount and relaxed in the saddle. "I'm going to be stiff tomorrow, girl," she said. "But it's worth it. Just feel that wind. Taste the air. Something's coming all right."

They stopped just beyond the large grove of trees, where her gypsy friends usually camped when they traveled through. But today no brightly-painted wagons or laughing dark-eyed children greeted her. She came to the place and saw evidence that they were there recently.

"I've missed them!" she cried, dismounting to study the signs—campfire circles, a large circle of flattened grass, paths leading in and out of the trees. Suddenly her eyes caught sight of brilliant color. Walking closer, she recognized a shawl on a tree branch. It whipped back and forth in the wind, and Sunny nearly bolted with fright.

"Whoa, Sunny girl." Katya patted the horse's neck. "It's just a shawl. But it doesn't look like it blew here. It was tied on carefully." Inspecting it more closely, she realized the shawl exactly matched the sash Natalya had given her at their last meeting.

Carefully, almost reverently, she untied the brilliant red and green shawl. She threw it over her shoulders with a smile, and tied it in front. "See, Sunny, I'm a gypsy!" She bowed and twirled while the horse's ears pointed straight forward at the sight.

"Thank you, Natalya!" she cried out in Russian to the wind. "Now winter can come. I am prepared."

Winter had already descended on Petrograd. Hard, wet snow pelted the ground, the buildings, and the people who struggled against the cold wind. Every year it was the same; the icy blasts came from the north, across the strait.

People bundled themselves in whatever clothing they could find and continued with everyday affairs, which were as diverse as they themselves. Burly Piotr cursed the cold wind as he rounded the corner of Liteyny on his way to the nearest livery. Schoolchildren ran wildly against the storm, while old Anna stood, ragged and shivering, in a lineup for bread. Svetlana rode by in her enclosed carriage to purchase sweets and goat cheese for her little soirée that evening.

The sturdy Russians continued with their plans, undaunted by any sort of weather. They did, after all, descend from the same stock as Peter the Great, that giant tsar who had built this city over two hundred years ago.

Armed Cossacks, mounted on handsome horses, patrolled the main streets, keeping disturbances at a minimum.

Inside the attic room, Vera watched as Paul Gregorovich straightened his stiffly starched collar, preparing for his job at the Astoria. "Some of your colleagues would throttle you if they caught you dressed like that. You look like a regular aristocrat."

Paul flashed an incredibly handsome smile at her in the mirror and pulled his woolen coat and hat from the closet. "They would not recognize me."

She laughed. "Oh, yes, they would. Who could mistake a handsome face like yours?" She stopped abruptly and changed the subject. "Do you like to dress up in rich men's clothes?"

"Necessity," he answered, reaching for the doorknob. Looking back at her, he said gently, "Wait a while before you leave and walk out the back way. I'll see you at the meeting later."

Then he was gone. With a sigh, Vera rose and walked to the window. Peering through a tiny gap between the curtains and the window frame, she watched Paul stride down the street. "He's already forgotten me," she whispered to herself. "What have I become?"

Turning from the window, she repeated Paul's excuse, "Necessity," and dressed herself for another day at the presses. *It's high time I got there,* she thought, as she descended the stairs and pushed open the front door of the apartment building. Starting down the street, in a world of her own, she suddenly remembered, *Take the back way out. Too late now,* she thought, and began walking faster.

Turning left at the end of the street, Vera glanced behind her. There had been someone there—she felt more than saw him, but no one was there now. What should she do? Heart pounding, she crossed to the other side of the street and headed into an alley that led in the direction of the secret presses.

Glancing back again, she distinctly saw a man in a long gray coat and fur hat cross the street toward the alley. Behind him, a sleek, black motorcar turned the corner in her direction.

Vera's mind raced, and her mouth went dry. She must not lead him to the press. Neither did she wish to expose any of her people. Where should she go? Walking quickly along the alley, trying not to run, she spotted a narrow space between two buildings and ducked into it. She pressed herself against the brick wall and held her breath. Sweat poured down her back, in spite of the cold wind that whistled through her hiding place. Her heart beat so loudly she was sure it would give her away.

A few moments later, the gray-coated man trotted past. She waited cautiously until his steps receded, then crept to the alley and peered out. Before she knew what was happening, a gloved hand clapped over her face, and she was dragged further down the alley and pitched headfirst into the car that waited on the next street. Her side hurt fiercely where she lay on the floor of the car. Someone got in beside her and pushed her head down as the car lurched away from the curb. Fear seeped into her being as the cold from the floorboards penetrated her body. Her mind whirled in terror.

Paul's day at the hotel progressed more or less as expected. Just before noon, one of the other waiters entered the kitchen with a tray in his hand and caught his eye. "Trouble!" he mouthed and jerked his head in the direction of the dining room.

Immediately, Paul slipped past the chefs and dodged out a back door into the alley. Seeing a black car pull into the back street, he returned to the hotel. He used a secondary staircase, jumping three steps at a time, escaping just as two gray-coated men burst into the kitchen from the back door, and another entered from the dining room.

"What you want in my kitchen?" cried Henri, the chef, in disgust. "Get out of here immediately."

"Shut up, you!" yelled one of the intruders. "Where's Tekanin?"

"I don't know any Tekanin."

The fussy French chef suddenly found himself plastered against the back wall, feet dangling just above the floor. "Where did he go?" hissed the man. "I know he was here."

"If you mean the waiter, he went out the back," squeaked Henri. The intruder let go, and the little chef slipped to the floor like a deflated soufflé. He had happily fainted by the time the two toughs returned from a quick search of the alley. After looking around the kitchen, one of them headed up the staircase. The other returned to the dining room.

Meanwhile, a tall, robust, darkly handsome woman wearing a long, silk dress and veiled hat descended the front steps of the Astoria and hailed a motor cab. She did not wait for the driver to open the door, but opened it herself and climbed in, somewhat clumsily, inadvertently showing enough leg to cause the driver to shudder with revulsion.

Vera huddled on the floor of the tiny room where she had been thrown. Outwardly sullen, she tried to hide the terror she felt, but the shaking would not stop. She had no idea who these men were or why they had brought her here, unless they had somehow found out about her association with *PRAVDA* and its revolutionary propaganda. She'd sat for hours on the cold, stone floor while the chill crept into her bones and wondered hopelessly when anyone would miss her.

In her fear and isolation, she tried to console herself that her condition was not so different from any other day. "I'm often cold, lonely, and afraid. But at least I can usually keep busy to bury the fears and feelings. Now I must sit and wait . . . wait for what?" She began to tremble violently, recalling what the revolutionaries had done to other opponents of the revolution. She wished she didn't know those details now. The fear inside her became a monster from which she could not hide, and she cried out in anguish, "Please! Someone help me!"

"All here, except Guseyva," reported Grisha. "She didn't show up for work today."

Paul was alarmed. People had been arriving at various

times from different places and by different entrances. The room at the back of a busy Jewish grocery now contained five men and three women. It was past time to begin, and Paul knew he could not stall any longer.

"Couldn't we wait a minute longer for Vera?" asked one of the women, as Paul called the meeting to order. "She must have run into trouble. She's never late."

Paul knew this, but as their leader, he must carry on. "We all know the risks, including Guseyva," he stated, suppressing the worry rising in his mind. "We will begin our meeting and afterward do what we can to find out what happened to her. But we will at no time endanger our cause because of it."

They had recently received direct communication from Lenin via the underground. They were to step up revolutionary propaganda to prepare for Lenin's return. Now working with a Jew by the name of Trotsky, the Big Man had great plans for Russia and the world.

"Thankfully," he wrote, "Rasputin and the empress are saving us much trouble by creating the means by which the imperialistic government is rotting from the inside out, leaving nothing but an empty shell. We simply crush that shell, and the power is ours."

After much discussion on policy and plan, the gathered revolutionaries began to disperse as stealthily as they had come. Paul cautiously returned to his apartment, checking it first from the street, then climbing up the half-broken fire escape in the back. All seemed quiet.

Once inside, he searched everywhere for clues as to what had happened, but true to form, Vera had left nothing behind, no clue that anyone besides him had ever been there.

Had she used the front entrance and been seen by the wrong people or had someone picked her up in the alley behind his apartment? After his brush with danger this morning at the Astoria, he knew something was afoot. If indeed someone had taken Vera, what was their reasoning?

You know the reason for it, Tekanin, he told himself. *You get to a person through someone they care about.* The revolutionaries had used this method countless times. He also knew the policy: if you make a mistake, you're on your own. The cause of the revolution was not to be jeopardized for the sake of an individual. Vera knew this, too.

But something made Paul sneak out again to make covert inquiries about Vera. Had anyone seen her? When? Where? Unbidden, Johann's compassionate blue eyes came to mind, but he shook off the thought. "Must concentrate on the matter at hand," he said.

Finally, Paul did the only thing he could do. He walked back to his apartment to wait. Obviously, whoever had Vera would contact him, sooner or later—unless she had fallen to a worse fate. "Can't think about that," he told himself.

He fully expected it was the same people who had come for him in the restaurant, but he had not actually seen them. At this moment an elegant silk dress and veiled hat smoldered in a garbage bin behind his apartment. It paid to know people in high places, but right now even they could not help him.

Chapter 18

 With another Christmas just days away, the estate house at Succoth bustled with activity. In spite of only four Hildebrandts being present instead of the original seven, excitement was up for visits from Mika and the Reimers as well as Johann's return from Schwarzwald Camp.

Johann had written several letters to the family, as well as a number addressed specifically to Katarina. He had accepted and adjusted to this major interruption in his life and had, in fact, begun to sound quite patriotic. While he hated the war, he found consolation in helping those who had been wounded. Katya cherished his letters. He wrote to her of thoughts and experiences he may not have wanted read aloud at supper, and Katarina was willing to wait for him to feel the same for her as she did for him. Often it was only Susannah's promised prayers and words of encouragement that kept her believing it would happen.

Mika and the Reimers arrived three days before Christmas, but Johann had not returned. The joy of reunion surrounded the family like a warm cloak.

"It's so good to have you home," smiled Katya to Mika, as they relaxed in the small parlor. "You've changed."

"I hope you mean that in a good way," her sister said, with uncharacteristic uncertainty.

"Of course. I've missed you. Sometimes absence makes us realize what our relationships are worth." Both sisters sat in silence as each considered their own particular friendships.

"Are you still spending time with Aaron Friesen?" ventured Katarina.

Maria turned a shocked expression Katya's way. "Not on your life!" she said. "Not after his rude and shameless treatment of me. I won't speak to him."

"I'm sorry. What keeps you occupied, then?"

Mika leaned back against the sofa cushions and unconsciously smoothed her hair. "There are a good number of young men and women in the area who meet for singings, poetry readings, concerts, lots of things. They're going Christmas caroling while I'm gone. I hate to miss it, but I thought it was time to come home for a visit."

"Would you ever come back here to live?"

Maria met her sister's eyes and shook her head. "I couldn't bear it—the isolation and all." She stopped, at a loss for words. Finally she continued, her voice low. "I don't belong here. I never did. I need people, and living with Mr. and Mrs. Reimer is an excellent arrangement, giving them my help in exchange for room and board."

"Room and board! Is that what you call it?" questioned Katya. "To me, they are like family."

"Oh, you know what I mean. They're very good to live with but I can't actually confide in them."

"Why not?"

"Because they don't understand me. They expect me to be like them, and I'm not."

At Katarina's puzzled look she said, "You know. They expect me to go to all those stuffy church meetings and Bible studies, and it's all just too tiring. You should come back with me for a while after Christmas, Katya," she continued. "Get a little socializing into your life. How do you stand it here?"

Katarina smiled and shook her head. "We're so different, you and I. People make me tired. I like them, but it's such a chore to think of things to say. Then all I want to do is come back here and enjoy the peace and quiet. Being alone doesn't necessarily mean being lonely."

"I suppose to be alone without being lonely, one must be comfortable with oneself." Maria rose gracefully and then turned back to Katarina. "I'm glad you are who you are, Katie. You've always been the strong one. Please don't change." She planted a kiss on top of Katya's head and left the room.

Katya sat staring after her, amazed that Mika had, if only for a moment, lowered her mask of poise and confidence. "I will be strong for you then, dear Mika," she said, as the swish of skirts faded down the hallway.

"Telegram for you, Miss Katarina." Yuri stood tall and serious at the parlor door, a white envelope in his hand. He gave it to her, bowed, and left as quietly as he had come.

"Thank you, Yuri," Katya said absentmindedly, opening the envelope and pulling out a small sheet of paper. For some reason, her hands trembled, and her heart began to pound. She forced her eyes to scan the words printed on the page, then read them again. Her hands dropped to her sides as tears sprang into her eyes.

Mika re-entered the room with a rustle of silk. "I've come to escort you to supper, Katya. It will be a celebra . . . Katarina, what's wrong?" She stooped to pick up the sheet that had fallen to the floor. ". . . *not coming home*," she read. ". . . *sent to the front with medical corps immediately. So sorry to miss . . . Merry Christmas to all. Johann.*"

She reached down to take Katya's hand in hers. "I'm sorry, Katie. I know you two are good friends, and you were looking forward to his visit. This old war spoils everyone's plans." She took her sister's arm and led her from the room. "We'll have a good Christmas anyway, you just wait and see. I have some wonderful plans . . ."

Katya walked dejectedly beside her sister as she chattered on cheerfully. "Could be worse," said Mika. "At least he's still alive." Katya's troubled eyes finally silenced her, and they continued on to the dining room.

"But he promised to come!" chorused Nicholai and Anna, when they heard the news. Heinrich raised his hand for silence. "He did not promise. He planned to come. He did not decide to go away—he was sent. Consider his disappointment. Now, let's pull ourselves together and pray for his safety. This assignment is a dangerous one."

The presence of Abram and Cornelia Reimer brought life to the festivities, in spite of Johann's absence. Heinrich relished their company. He and Abram spent many hours in discussion, and Cornelia added a motherly touch, even though she had never had children of her own.

"Maria just can't seem to relax, can she?" Nellie commented to Katya one morning. "She's a bundle of plans and organization, never calm enough to consider the true meaning of the Christmas season."

Katya smiled. "She's always been like that."

"Well, that's a bit of a comfort. I thought perhaps she was unhappy with us or our arrangement with her."

"Perhaps she is just running from herself," said Katya. Not wishing to betray her sister's confidence, she didn't mention their recent conversation. Instead she said, "I think it's a spiritual problem. She's not willing to let God take charge of her life, so she keeps the reins tightly grasped in her own hands."

"Yes, I see. And the celebration of Christ's birth is just another reminder of that struggle for control. Well, I suppose what she needs is prayer and love."

"You're right, Aunt Nellie." Katarina smiled warmly at her and said, "I'm glad you're here. It's almost like having a mother again."

Cornelia placed her arm around Katarina's shoulders. "The Lord is filling a void in both of our lives. I love you as my own, and I'm thankful that I can also bring some joy to you."

After a companionable silence, Cornelia spoke again. "This place is wondrous—so spacious and comforting and peaceful."

Katarina smiled. "Our refuge."

"Your *earthly* refuge," corrected Mrs. Reimer. "We must remember that our only true refuge is Christ Jesus himself."

Snow began to fall in huge, wet flakes as the Forstei trucks bumped and swayed over frozen roads. It was so sudden, this assignment. It seemed like yesterday that Johann had arrived at Schwarzwald Camp and medical training had begun. He had anticipated using his newly acquired skills as soon as the course was completed.

That was when he was introduced to one of the first rules of life in the service: the only thing you know for sure is that you know nothing for sure! Consistent inconsistency, they called it. Instead of heading to where casualties were heaviest, Johann found himself clearing brush for a field hospital. From there, his unit worked on road repair west of the Dnieper River, in company with the Razyn Camp.

The Razyn commando was greatly different from the Schwarzwald group. Johann had grown accustomed to strict discipline, hard work, and spiritual input through the chaplain. This new camp, however, contained a wider variety of young men and offered little spiritual encouragement. The administration lacked the skills to motivate and control the men, and gradually a sense of purposelessness permeated the group.

Johann was greatly frustrated, but the slackness of the program seemed to appeal to his fellow forester, Isaac Neumann.

"Care for a smoke, Four Eyes?" he asked. He knew Johann hated the nickname.

Johann ignored the offer. He was tired of Neumann's insolent attitude. "Heard any word of our next assignment?" he asked instead.

"Nope. Can't say as I care, either. I'll serve my time and get back to my life. By the way, Sudermann, you should join us for cards tonight. You could win yourself a train ticket home to your sweetheart for Christmas."

"Thanks," replied Johann dryly, "but I think I'd do better to hang onto what I have."

"So what's your girl's name, heh?" Johann had tried to deflect this type of annoying banter since the first day at Schwarzwald, but it wasn't getting any easier. "Don't have one, Isaac, as I've told you before." Once, he had said his girl's name was Anna and she was seven years old. That had opened up a whole new vein of teasing, however, so he mostly kept quiet and took the jabs.

Lately, there had been talk of a move for the unit, but no one knew any details. The uncertainty was harder on some men than others. Johann prayed daily for grace to accept and cooperate.

The one positive result of his experience at Razyn Camp was discovering Philipp Wieler. Philipp was a quiet, unassuming young man, with a pleasant countenance. He good-naturedly accepted more than his share of abuse.

"How do you put up with it?" Johann had asked him one day during their first week at Razyn. Early December snow dusted the grounds and the barracks roof as they walked toward the mess tent. Philipp stamped the snow from his boots and stepped aside for Johann to enter the tent first.

"Hey, it's little Philipp Wieler. How's mama's boy today?" taunted Isaac Neumann, self-proclaimed ringleader.

"Fine, thank you," said Wieler, with a smile. "And how are you?"

"Fine, thank you, and how are you?" imitated Neumann, to the delight of the rest of the group. Wieler simply smiled and moved toward the food line.

"Don't let them do this to you," said Johann quietly. "You play into their hands." Philipp smiled up at him. "A good friend of mine taught me to turn the other cheek—to offer my cloak, as it were. I try to follow his advice."

"And who might that friend be?" asked Johann, anticipating the answer.

"His name is Jesus. I've known him for years and he's never let me down."

"Hey, Sudermann, watch out!" yelled Isaac. "He's gonna preach at you. The little Jesus boy will get you saved if you don't be careful." Raucous laughter spread over the eating area, and Johann's stomach knotted. He knew he should say something, but the words stuck in his throat. Philipp was a fellow believer in Christ, a true spiritual brother, but Johann lacked the courage to admit it publicly.

Snatching a zweibach from the serving tray, he left his plate and marched out of the mess tent without a word. His disgust with his own lack of courage gave him a headache, and he walked on until he found himself at the river.

Standing on the bank, he watched the icy water slip past, splashing against partly submerged boulders and continuing on its way. He began to notice the obvious: the rocks, perpetually tormented by the ever-flowing river, stood firm. No amount of trouble moved them, though the water seemed to overwhelm them.

"I am slow to learn and slow to trust, Lord," he prayed. "Forgive me. I need to be a rock, to stand true like Philipp, to allow you to take care of the problems."

Returning to the barracks, he found Philipp sitting quietly, his Bible open on his lap, while a group of servicemen played a loud game of cards over in the corner.

Johann approached him. "Excuse me, Philipp. I hate to interrupt, but I need to speak with you."

"Of course." Philipp looked up with his innocent green eyes and smiled.

Johann took a seat beside him and cleared his throat. "I'm sorry."

"For what?" Johann saw more than innocence in his eyes then. Wisdom and integrity also dwelt there.

"For walking out on you. I'm sorry that I denied God by my silence back there in the mess tent."

"And have you told that to God?"

"Yes."

"And has God forgiven you?"

"Absolutely." A hint of a smile eased Johann's strained expression.

"Then I can do nothing but forgive you also." Philipp reached out his right hand to Johann and they shook on it, smiles lighting both their faces.

It was the beginning of a strong friendship, with shared Bible studies and prayer times. Johann realized how childish his faith had been before, and how much he had needed spiritual nourishment. He wouldn't have been at all surprised if he learned one day that Philipp Wieler had disappeared from this earth to report to God for his next assignment.

As it was, however, Johann would discover that Philipp had feet of clay, just as he did.

The announcement shocked them all. On a brilliant Friday morning in mid-December, the units assembled for what many expected to be notice of a Christmas recess—or even better, completion of service. Most of the men were in good spirits, in spite of having spent a late night at cards.

They took no hint from the commander's stonelike expression. "Attention, men!" he barked, his voice carrying to the back of the crowd. "As of tomorrow morning, we will be transferred west, as far as the fighting will allow."

Exclamations of disbelief broke out. "Quiet!" he shouted. "Many wounded await you. Pack your things and review medical procedures. A general review will take place in the mess tent after supper tonight."

The commander stepped back and men began to complain. "Silence!" he roared. A tall, thin, middle-aged man stepped forward and spoke above the hostile stillness. "Scripture reading and prayer will follow the review. All are expected to be present."

In spite of the commander's efforts to control the situation, things degenerated into a state of mayhem. Everything from pleas to threats erupted from the surprised and angry gathering. Johann stood silent, astounded at the news. Less than one week until Christmas and he was going west. To the front. To the war zone.

Nervously he tried to recall medical training and what he had learned there. It was easy to forget about blood pressure and bullet wounds while picking rocks and splitting logs.

"How are you faring?" The voice belonged to Philipp Wieler. He seemed as calm as ever and as selfless.

"Not great, but no worse than you, I'm sure."

Wieler smiled. "You'll make it," he said.

Yes, thought Johann. *I'll make it. But what of Katya and the others? They've been looking forward to Christmas and a return to normal life.*

As if reading Johann's mind, Wieler added, "I don't want to be pessimistic, but I don't think our lives will ever be the way they were before."

"Why do you say that?" asked Johann. "Perhaps the war will end, and we will all be free to return home."

A sad smile touched Philipp's gentle face. He looked up at Johann as they moved away from the knots of angry foresters to the edge of the open area. "Hans," he said, as if to a child, "you apparently haven't heard the rumors, and although I don't usually deal in rumors, these seem to ring true.

"There is much disquiet in the cities, especially Petrograd and Moscow. Even if this war should end, and it's not likely to for a long while, we have our own problems."

"You mean revolution." It was a statement more than a question.

"That's exactly what I mean. Our golden years of existence in Mother Russia are ended. She no longer loves us or wants us."

"It sounds bleak," said Johann, though he knew as well as anyone the state of the government. Paul had told him plainly in almost identical words. "I need hope, not despair."

"I'm sure we all do," answered Philipp.

"What about those who are left behind, the ones counting on us, waiting for us? What about them?"

When Philipp didn't answer, Johann glanced at him and was startled to see tears in the soft, green eyes. "Philipp," he asked gently, "who did you leave behind?"

"Agnetha," he replied in a barely audible voice. Fighting for control he continued, "We were married one year ago tomorrow. Our first child was to be born at Christmas, but she . . . I received word in October that the child was born prematurely and passed away within twenty-four hours."

"I'm so sorry," Johann said. "I had no idea you were married. What about your parents?"

"Gone. Deceased. It's just Agnetha and me, and now she's alone, without anyone to look after her. I . . . she insisted I serve my time."

This revelation calmed Johann's heart enough to let him look around and notice how others were handling the shock. Neumann's loud voice covered a multitude of hurts, Johann was sure. His brashness was a mask for insecurity, as was his abusive treatment of others. *Insecurity and fear. No excuse,* thought Johann, *but a reason for bitterness.*

Just then his attention was drawn to the center of the open area, where a knot of men were shouting with raised fists at the commander's hut.

One of the men had collapsed, but instead of helping him to a quiet place, Neumann and the others merely kicked him out of the way and continued their tirade.

Stunned by their cruelty, Johann pushed his way through the crowd to where the man lay gasping for air. He was greatly agitated as Johann loosened his collar and checked his vital signs.

"Hey, Four Eyes!" Johann knew the voice without looking up. "Let him be. It's none of your affair."

Johann's lips pressed together and a nerve in his jaw twitched as he continued caring for the fallen man.

"I said, leave him alone!"

Johann stood to his full height and, by force of habit, pushed up his glasses. All fear and uncertainty left him as he stood eye to eye with Isaac. After what seemed an eternity, Neumann flinched and finally turned away with a confused look.

Johann turned back to the now quiet group. "Get a stretcher, quickly, and take him to the infirmary."

More than enough men stepped up to transfer the patient to the sick room, and others offered water and words of comfort. When the crowd cleared, Johann discovered Philipp Wieler on his knees at the edge of the clearing, head bowed in silent prayer to God for a miracle. Slipping to his knees beside him, Johann joined in thanks for answered prayer.

The eve of 1916 found Paul Gregorovich caught between success and failure. His efforts for the revolutionary cause seemed to be spreading slowly but surely—not a forest fire, but definitely an unquenchable flame. Continued frustration over the "war to end all wars" was causing many Russians to transfer their allegiance to something that might actually benefit them. As Lenin said in his manifestos, the power needed to be in the hands of the people.

The failure facing Paul was that he still had no contact with Vera. He didn't know where she was being held or even if she was still alive. He and his associates kept their eyes and ears open, but so far nothing had materialized.

In desperation, Paul had approached one of Lenin's top aides when he stopped by the *PRAVDA* press to personally inspect its operation. Inviting the lanky fellow into his tiny office, Paul offered him coffee and used his journalistic skills to extract any information he could about Vera.

"So you are saying you have no idea where Guseyva is or who is holding her." Paul turned his question into a statement.

Kamenev, Lenin's agent, answered coolly, "I did not say that. We highly suspect the tsar's henchmen of involvement, but I don't believe they were the ones who seized her."

"Then who?"

Kamenev sent him a level look, detecting Paul's desperation. "Hmmm," he said under his breath, as if adding the impression to his mental files, then continued. "Sometimes, Tekanin, we are our own worst enemies. Sometimes people like you and me get caught in the trap of subjective decisions. We lose the ideals of the revolution in favor of a more pragmatic approach."

"You mean," interrupted Paul, "that some of our own have decided to cooperate with the government to try to achieve our goals without revolution? And have sacrificed Guseyva to get to me in order to get to those higher up?"

Kamenev chuckled, but there was no warmth in his humor.

"You are so very proletarian," he quipped. "Everything must be spelled out in black and white."

"And you, sir, are amazingly evasive."

Kamenev straightened and the smile left his face. "Remember your place, Tekanin."

"My *place!*" Paul leaned forward until the two men were eye to eye. "The whole basis of the revolution is to put the power into the hands of the people where it belongs, to erase the lateral divisions of society. If I am not mistaken, that makes us equals."

Kamenev rose to his feet, contempt in his eyes. "You obviously don't realize that someone must be in control."

Paul stood to face him. "You mean some will always be more equal than others."

Kamenev, his eyes hard, turned to leave. "A bit of diplomacy would do wonders for you, Tekanin. Anger seldom uncovers information."

With that, he left Tekanin seething, his hands clenched in angry fists, his mind reeling with questions and doubts. Would he have had more success if he'd kept his tongue, if he'd played along like the two-faced colleagues Kamenev had called pragmatists? Opportunists was more what they were.

Now, sitting in his corner, hunched over his battered desk, Paul's mind would not concentrate on his editorial. Every time he raised his eyes to the room beyond, he saw Vera's desk. In his mind she still sat there, so diligent, so committed . . . so alone.

Grisha had assumed the empty chair, endeavoring to handle both his job and hers, becoming increasingly weary with the effort. Paul shoved his papers aside and gave in to his worries. Why had they picked Vera Guseyva? History had shown women's loyalties were often stronger than men's. He believed she could withstand interrogation, but cringed when he thought of what they might do to her.

Why hadn't they simply skipped a step and taken him? Heaven knew he was vulnerable at times. Did they think what he and Vera had was strong enough, important enough, to override their political persuasion? Well, they were on the wrong track. He and Vera were workers committed to the same cause, merely comforting each other from time to time in the most basic way known to humankind.

That's why you can't sleep nights or focus during the day. His conscience kicked him for his self-directed lies. He was young and impressionable, though he considered himself to be worldly wise. His relationship with Vera had affected him deeply. They had crossed a sacred line, and he was beginning to see there was no possible return.

He knew what Johann would say. He would tell him that people were vastly different from animals, which relied on instinct alone. He would say that human beings have the responsibility and privilege of caring for each other on a much higher level, of respecting each other and putting the other person first.

Paul dropped his weary head in his hands. His last meeting with Johann had been less than ideal, but he knew Johann would always remain loyal to him, even though they had strongly opposing views. It was a comfort to have an ally like that. Maybe someday . . .

Paul's fist came down so hard on the desk that Grisha jumped. Their eyes locked, and Paul detected pity in his coworker's gaze. He didn't want pity. What he wanted, what he had not allowed himself to think of, was a normal life.

But again he had crossed a line. He knew too much, knew too many people, knew too many plans. If he backed out now, it would mean his death. He had no options; the only way was to forge ahead. With his mind in its present disturbed state, that could also be perilous. He felt absolutely trapped, like a caged Siberian tiger he'd once seen at a circus.

Grabbing his jacket, he rushed outside into the biting Gulf wind. He walked and walked until, numb with cold, he returned to collapse onto his bed in the attic apartment and fell into a sleep of exhaustion.

Chapter 19

 Johann shivered as he and Philipp erected the tent that would shelter them again tonight. Pellets of snow whipped them in the darkening twilight.

"Not a moment to lose if we want protection from the elements." Philipp attempted a light tone to encourage them as they worked.

He's always doing that, thought Johann, *supporting and cheering his fellow medics.* Johann admired him for it. He himself was just keeping despair at bay.

Due to the storm, the air was free of bombs and bullets. Just snow. A colder, slower death. Johann shook his head to clear away distracting thoughts. *Concentrate. Fasten the ropes to the stakes. Tighten. Tie.* Soon there would be food or at least some questionable nourishment to keep them alive till morning.

The next day broke clear and bright, offering a fresh horizon not yet corrupted by boots and blood.

"Today's the day," Johann said as they disassembled the tent and bundled it up for transport.

Philipp eyed him. "The day for what?"

Johann felt ruthless and hadn't the strength to control it. "Today we face the enemy and practice our amateur art on some poor soldier who probably won't go home again. Today we see the demon up close and try to undo some of the damage."

"This is the day that the Lord hath made," quoted Philipp. "Let us rejoice and be glad in it."

Johann stopped mid-stride and glared. "Be glad!" he repeated. "Philipp, as much as I respect you, that's going too far."

Philipp, who made gentle answers a habit, dropped the rope he was carrying and walked briskly up to Johann. Hands on his hips, he looked up into his surprised eyes and spoke firmly.

"You, brother Sudermann, are becoming a cynic. You want your faith to grow, but you don't want hardship. How else does one learn? Where else does one face tests? Life is not a vacation or a well-ordered classroom. We must accept each day as from the Lord, who gives it and oversees it. We will face nothing that God has not first filtered especially for us, and he has promised us sufficient grace to bear it.

"At this present moment I have fresh air to breathe and a job to do. For that I am grateful. What comes after we will deal with at that time. You and I, Hans, are possibly the only representatives of the Master in this camp. Let us reflect him appropriately." Philipp picked up his coil of rope and began lugging it to the transport wagon.

Johann stood shocked and humbled. Philipp was right, of course. This is where his life was today so he would not look back. There was only one way to go and that was forward. The choice was in how he would proceed, and he thanked his friend for his caring rebuke. It would make all the difference in the days ahead.

The enormous house at Succoth nearly echoed with emptiness. Abram and Nellie Reimer and Mika had stayed for a month, but their departure left a huge void in the lives of those who remained.

"Why don't you go along with them, Katya, and stay in Alexanderkrone for a while? It would do you good." Heinrich's words, given with a brave smile, had struck Katarina like the cold wind outside. She was glad they were alone in the library for she had trouble voicing her answer.

"Papa." She shook her head and walked into his embrace. "Don't even think about it. I'm not going." She stepped back and read the relief in his eyes.

"Who would take care of you and the children?" she asked, though her mind was firmly made up.

"I'd be fine here. The children could go along."

Katya smiled at his attempt to sound enthusiastic. Again she shook her head. "Dear Papa, I'm not going anywhere without you, and you and I both know we need to be here. This is our home. So you can save your breath."

She rested her face against the rough wool of his vest. She loved her papa as honestly and completely as she had when she was a child. His strong gentleness and integrity made him her solace in the storm. Now she would be here for him, and it would be no sacrifice.

"Ah, my Katie," he said simply, as she stood in the circle of his arms. Katarina resolved in her heart to bring joy and completeness to the halls of Succoth again. *I may not be able to do anything about this floundering country or the Great War,* she thought, *but I can influence my family and those who live among us here.*

"How were classes today?" Heinrich asked Anna one February evening, as the four of them relaxed in the small parlor. "What did you learn?"

"Nothing!" interrupted Kolya with a twinkle and a grin.

Heinrich silenced him with a look and turned back to Anna. "Oh, yes, we did learn something, Papa," she said excitedly. "We learned all about the Russian tsars—all the Romanovs, from Michael to Nicholas II, three hundred years of them."

"And who was the greatest, do you think?"

"Peter the Great," exclaimed Kolya. "But he was also the most different."

"*Decadent*," corrected Katarina with a smile.

"Yes," agreed Anna. "He was intelligent and also very wicked. I think I would be afraid of him."

"When Johann and I traveled to Petrograd last year," said Heinrich, "we saw the city Peter the Great established and the palaces and the shipyards. He had an amazing mind."

"Nicholas II isn't nearly as smart or as . . . decadent," commented Kolya, with disappointment in his voice.

"And what makes you think that?" asked his father.

"Well," he said, screwing up his face in concentration, "He doesn't listen to the people. He doesn't know what's happening to them. Our neighbors are poor and hungry, but he doesn't even know."

"And if he did know, what would he do about it?" Heinrich recognized the spark that had come to life in the boy's mind and sought to fan it to flame.

"He would help them," offered Anna.

"Of course he would, my dear."

"Maybe," said Kolya doubtfully. "He's so busy with the war that he might not have time. Or maybe he doesn't have enough money to buy them all food."

"We have money," said Anna. "If the tsar's too busy, why don't we help Russia?"

Katarina smiled at her sister's innocence. "We don't have enough money to help everyone, Anya." She pulled the little girl onto her lap. "Remember when the war broke out and some of our Russian neighbors had to go away to fight?"

Anna nodded.

"Many of them didn't come back," commented Nicholai.

"No, they didn't. And what did we do to help?"

"I know. We took clothes and food." Anna's smile faded as

she remembered. "And they didn't like us. Why didn't they?" She turned a sorrowful face to Katya.

"Because they were jealous that we were rich and they were poor." Nicholai wasted no words.

"But why?" persisted Anna.

Katarina looked to her father for support and he set out to answer Anna's questions. "To them, we are newcomers to this country," he began, his hand pulling at his beard. "We've been here scarce more than one hundred years, while our neighbor families have lived here for thousands of years. They resent the fact that we have prospered so quickly and they remain in their poverty. But for most of those thousands of years, most of the Russian people have lived as serfs . . . "

"What are serfs?" Anna asked Katarina, in a loud whisper.

"Slaves—servants who don't get paid," she answered.

Heinrich continued with his history. "The law forbade them to own property or to keep what they earned. They had no way out of their misery."

"The Mennonites came here when Catherine II invited them." Katarina took up the explanation, and Anna and Kolya listened as if it were the first time they'd heard it. "She allowed them to rule themselves."

"That was Catherine the Great," Anna added. "She was German too."

"So we were able to prosper while the poor peasants continued living much as they had in the Middle Ages."

There was silence as the family considered the benefits that had brought them to their present prosperity.

"We should give as much money away as we can," Anna suggested then. "Do we give money to people who are poor, Papa?"

He smiled. "Yes, little one," he assured her. "We give a large amount in taxes to the Forestry Service to help build roads and hospitals and buy medicines. The colonies are in charge of all the finances for the Forestry. We also help support Bethany Home, where Peter is, so he and the other residents have food and care. There are also many hospitals and schools in the Molotschna to which we send money regularly. And, of course, the Home for the Aged in Ruekenau, where Oma Peters lives."

Anna smiled. "I'm glad we help Oma," she said happily.

"But what do we give to the Russians?" Kolya wanted the facts. "All this money is for our own kind of people. How do we help our neighbors?"

Heinrich hesitated before he spoke. "The Russian peasants may be poor in material things, but they are rich in pride. They do not accept charity easily. But I have found a way to contribute that they know nothing about." He pulled at his beard, as if wondering whether or not he should say these things. "There is an Orthodox priest in Karassan, a wise and humble man, who accepts my anonymous donations for a fund to help his parish."

"That's wonderful, Papa!" exclaimed Katya. "Why haven't you told us before?"

"Because, my child, we are not to dwell on our own generosity or it becomes pride. 'Let not the right hand know what the left hand is doing . . . ' What I have told you tonight is not to be spoken of beyond these walls. It is enough to know we are doing something for our neighbors. Agreed?"

"Yes, Papa," they chorused quietly, admiration on their faces.

"Now," he said, "we will read a psalm and kneel for evening prayers. Let us thank the Lord for blessing us and for allowing us to share our bounty with those in need."

Gerhard and Susannah were married on a cold, crisp January day in Lichtfelde, Molotschna. They had wanted the wedding sooner—"an engagement should never last more than two weeks," her father had insisted. But it was difficult to arrange for both of them to be away from Bethany at the same time, especially at Christmas. "Perhaps we should get married in shifts," Gerhard had quipped.

But it was arranged and the other staff at the home gladly stepped in to give the happy couple a few days away. "Don't you worry about anything here," instructed Mrs. Schroeder, the head nurse. "We will keep things running smoothly, you'll see. We'll take extra good care of Peter too."

She knew she shouldn't have mentioned Peter, for Susannah's face fell immediately. "Poor Peter. He will be so lonely. I don't want him to regress now that he's come this far."

Gerhard put his hand on her arm as they sat in the covered buggy, ready for the ride to Molotschna. "You've said your farewells, dear one, and you've explained why you're leaving and when you'll be back. Peter might not understand you, although personally I think he does, but he will be fine while we're gone. Or are you having second thoughts about getting married?"

Susannah calmed down quickly. "Absolutely not," she declared. "I will be Mrs. Warkentin tomorrow and I can hardly wait. And you're right, Peter will be fine. *I* will be fine." She settled herself again on the fur-covered seat and tucked the heavy woolen blankets around her knees. "Shall we?"

Smiling, Gerhard pulled the door shut and they were off to Lichtfelde. The trip took most of the day, with a stopover at Halbstadt to warm up with a hot meal and hearty conversation. They arrived in Lichtfelde for supper and an evening wedding shower.

"Such a retreat from tradition, this one-day celebration," laughed Gerhard. "Everyone else has to endure at least three days of ceremony." He and his new wife were relaxing in the parlor of her sister's home in Neukirch the day after the wedding ceremony.

"Yes," agreed Susannah. "It was so good of Jakob and Helena to offer us their house while they visited Mother and Father. I guess they know a couple needs time to themselves. They've only been married two years."

"And tomorrow we make a wedding trip."

Susannah laughed. "It will be lovely, even if it is a trip back to work."

Gerhard grabbed her hand and pulled her into his lap. "Do you mind so much?" he asked, his face suddenly serious. "Going right back to work, I mean? Would you rather stay at home? We could find another nurse, I'm sure, although no one could match you."

"Stop your worrying, husband," she answered, and kissed him until they momentarily forgot what they'd been talking about.

Then, catching her hands and holding her tightly, he tried again to understand. "Not many married women go off to work every day, Suse. Is it going to be too much for you? Will you be happy?"

She looked deeply into his kind eyes and saw the love and concern. "Gerhard, my dear man," she said softly, stroking his face as she spoke, "as long as you are by my side, I shall be happy. I've been a traditional girl with small dreams and easy contentments. I took life for granted and assumed it would continue in the same way.

"Then God took hold of my life and led me to nurse's training in Halbstadt, and I've never looked back. It's in God's hands, all of it. I will continue to do what I'm doing until he tells me otherwise."

"And how will you know?"

"I'll know." She smiled. "God has ways of getting my attention." Then she grew sober, her mind drifting to the one person for whom she felt special concern.

Gerhard watched her face and played with her thick golden braid as she sat lost in thought. "Suse?"

She pulled her thoughts back and sighed. "No matter what I tell myself, I still worry about Peter," she said. "What will happen to him if the time comes for me to stop working at the Home?"

"Now you listen to me, Susannah." Gerhard lifted her chin till their eyes met. "You've just been preaching to me about how the Lord will take care of everything. Now you talk as if Peter is your own private worry and God has left you alone to care for him.

"Think about it, my dear. God will make a way. And if the time comes that we or Peter must leave, we will keep him ourselves—unless, of course, his family takes him."

Susannah's blue eyes brightened and her usual smile lit up her face. She looked gratefully at her new husband. "Really, Gerhard? You would do that for me?"

"Of course. For you, and for Peter. I care too, you know. We will do whatever is called for. Now, will you leave this worry behind?"

"Yes, dear."

"And will you come with me?" he asked, taking her hand.

"Yes, dear," she said again, with a shy smile.

Paul Gregorovich couldn't believe his luck. The youth in Piotr's Pub obviously had not known what important information he possessed, and as Paul cunningly persuaded him with flattery and a few ruble notes, he spilled all the facts.

It was the first stroke of luck in a long series of dead ends. Paul's mind raced as he hurried to the pressrooms. Grisha would be ecstatic over the news, for practical as well as personal reasons. Paul knew Grisha felt a brotherly protectiveness for Vera, and her disappearance had hit him hard.

They all pretended, in public at least, that Guseyva's kidnapping was an unavoidable consequence of their Bolshevik extremism. "Those who live by the sword . . ." Theoretically, it was not surprising so the Petrograd movement feigned a matter-of-fact attitude. But each in his heart felt devastated about this flesh-and-blood comrade who had sacrificed her freedom.

But not yet her life, Paul comforted himself. Vera remained alive and so there was hope. It was a great piece of luck that the boy happened to deliver goods to the St. Peter and Paul Fortress on its tiny island in the Neva River Delta, and that he had spotted a thin young woman there one day who matched Vera's description. Vera shared the same fate as many who had been imprisoned in Peter and Paul since it became a political prison in 1703, a fact that made Tekanin shudder. He knew Lenin's brother, Alexander, had spent time there until his execution for his attempt on the tsar's life.

Plans coursed ceaselessly through the pathways of his mind, and methodically he discarded or filed them. Finally he arrived at a strategy which even to his mind was daring. But it was not impossible.

"But how do we get past the Cossack guard?" asked Grisha, from behind Guseyva's desk. "You know how dedicated they are to the imperialist arrangement."

"*Were*," corrected Paul. "For a lot of them it's habit, this dedication. People are beginning to question the effectiveness of the present government. But that's merely an observation. We cannot count on widening the chink in their armor before the end of next week."

"Well, I'm relieved to see some realism here. It's a formidable obstacle to consider." Grisha dabbed sweat from his face with his handkerchief, even though the damp cold penetrated the walls of their warehouse office. He continued to pursue his responsibility of tearing holes in Tekanin's plan.

"How do you know the procession of prisoners will take

the prescribed course? What if they choose another route?"

"They won't." Paul's confidence was strong. "The only reason for a 'parade' is to gain publicity, and where else would there be more people? They will drive through Apraksin Market and along Nevsky Prospekt."

"And where shall we be?"

"Just as the carts turn onto Nevsky on their way to the Winter Palace, we will cause a distraction that cannot be ignored . . . "

"You're talking about explosives."

Paul narrowed his eyes at the hesitation he felt in his comrade. "It's the only way."

"Sounds like the assassination of Alexander II, only we have to do it right the first time."

"It's not an assassination attempt, but there may well be loss of life. All the better for distraction." Paul glanced over at Grisha, who shrugged his shoulders apologetically.

"I'll never get used to the violence," Grisha said softly, "even though I know it's the only way. I'm not a hateful person. I wish there was another option." He looked at Paul, but saw a hint of anger instead of understanding.

"This is no time for weak stomachs, Grisha. The stakes are enormous. We aren't speaking just of Russia, but of the entire world." Paul rose and began pacing his small office, gesturing to promote his point. "We must rid the world of class distinctions and put power in the hands of the people. Yes, we begin here, but as soon as the world sees our success, the Utopia created by a classless society living and working for the common good, nations will follow our lead."

He stopped in front of Grisha and added, "And then the violence needed to topple the old regime and establish the new will be worthwhile, like a woman giving birth in pain is blessed by the child she brings forth. But at this point, the individual is unimportant. It is the ultimate goal for which we must strive."

Grisha could almost hear a band accompanying Tekanin's

oratory, and it irritated him. "So why are we spending so much energy and risking so much for Guseyva? She is but one person. Perhaps she is merely *hors d'oeuvres* for the growing socialist ideal."

He knew he had spoken out of turn—against his own beliefs as well as those of Paul Gregorovich—but sometimes the air needed to be cleared.

Tekanin stood stock-still, as if rooted to the floor. His mouth worked, but no sound came out. Grisha had pointed out his double standard and held it up for him to see. Paul hated to face his own inadequacy. Doubts like great, dark clouds thundered through his mind, and he tried to fight them off with his adopted ideas.

Why had he embraced this bolshevism? What made him think he could make a difference or that the ideal itself would change people? What had Johann told him on one of their Petrograd visits? "Change must come from within the heart. It cannot be legislated. Outward changes are only that, unless the heart is first convinced." *Is that true?* Paul asked himself. *Do all of my actions amount to nothing if they are based on a faulty premise? How am I to know?*

Again Johann's words stood out in his memory: "You will know the truth and the truth will set you free. There is only one foundation worthy to build on, and that is Jesus Christ."

The last two words came from Paul's lips now, as a curse. As he spoke, the blackness of his dilemma descended heavily on him. Grisha saw it, and it frightened him. The fury of desperation was about to be unleashed.

Grisha felt he had helped nurture the beast that was now consuming Paul Gregorovich, but they were both up to their necks in it. They would have to see it through and bear the consequences.

"Sit down, Tekanin," he said. "Tell me the rest of the plan. I'm listening and I'm in."

Paul sat, shook his head as if to clear it, and spoke as if nothing had interrupted. "And so after the explosion, we will take her to the place where she will meet the agent who will instruct her further. Follow?"

"Follow. When?"

"Thursday next. We will need a munitions man."

"I know of one. I'll contact him tonight."

"Good." Paul stood to leave, then paused. "We must succeed." Grisha sensed he meant in more than the present plan. He hoped for success. He had staked his life on it.

Chapter 20

Thursday, February 20, 1916, dawned cold and cloudy. A storm brewed off the coast of Finland, dancing nearer to Petrograd in frenzied twirls and capers. Paul awoke early, not sure if he had really slept or just dozed fitfully. His nerves were taut, waiting for the outcome of his scheme. His part was already done. He had orchestrated every detail, but his colleagues would not allow him near the scene.

"You're too recognizable," they said. "We'll create your diversion and escort Vera to the meeting place. You can speak with her there before she leaves again."

"Is everyone in place? Do they know their jobs?"

Grisha grimaced. "Thanks to your belief in repetition, we could carry it off with our eyes closed."

"I dreamed of it all night long," joked another man. "I only wish the weather would settle some. A blizzard will not help us. Too bad we can't postpone it until another day."

"This is the day the prisoners are being transported to trial at the Winter Palace. If we don't act today, it will be too late," said Grisha, voicing what they all knew.

"Well, the time for talking and dreaming is done," announced Paul. "I will meet you later. Good luck." He grasped Grisha's shoulders, then clapped him on the back.

"Waiting will be the most difficult part," warned Grisha. "But under no circumstances are you to come. Above all, if something goes wrong, disappear as fast as you can. We will find each other again . . ."

"Go then," said Paul with a salute. He backed off as the others filed out into the back street, on their way to their assigned positions. Paul threw a knapsack on his back and left by another door.

He walked by side streets and alleys to a coffee shop, across the street from where his people would bring Vera. They had chosen this waiting place for Paul to watch for them, for their signal. Time would be short, and he was determined to speak with Vera before she moved on. It was the least he could do since he felt responsible for her capture. He wanted a few moments to tell her he cared and that he was sorry she had unwittingly become his scapegoat.

He also wanted to offer her hope, to give her a promise of better times, of a deeper commitment, of all the things he knew were right and good, but he could offer her none of these. If tomorrow continued like today, their life situation would only deteriorate.

This is not a time, he thought, *for personal commitments and involvements, but for sacrifice and hard work, risk and loneliness. And to try to believe it is worth giving your life to what you're doing.*

Thoughts as dark as the sky nagged him, threatening to overwhelm and obliterate the agenda, to interfere in the project they had put in motion.

Then the snow began to fall—first large, feathery flakes of wetness that brushed the café windows and slid melting to the ground, then larger blobs flung haphazardly through the frigid air. They gathered in white mounds on streets and buildings. Soon he could see nothing but a wall of white, the very thing that could ruin all his best-laid plans. Of course, the procession would be ruined, as no one would be able to see it, but the rescue effort had only one chance to act, and it must act, whatever the weather.

Grisha was right—the waiting was a killer. Paul thought he

had sat an hour at the chilly window, but his timepiece only verified ten minutes. Grabbing his tote, he left the shelter of the quiet café and jogged out into the street. Traffic had come to a complete halt, leaving him virtually alone in this white world.

Keeping close to the buildings, he felt his way back in the direction of Apraksin and Nevsky. There was slim chance of being recognized in this storm—anyone venturing out looked like a walking snowman, bundled up and huddled against the elements.

Paul had his doubts about the munitions man, though he trusted Grisha implicitly. The plan allowed no room for error, and already the weather altered things. Was the man capable of pulling it off? Did he care enough to put his life on the line?

My life has become a bundle of questions, he thought. *I am a doubter leading others, a blind guide!* His mood darkened as he fought his way through the thickening snow.

The muffled clatter of hooves and clinking of swords jolted him from his musings. He stood in the shelter of the buildings and tried to get his bearings. The procession was late. It should have passed this place already.

Fear rose up to choke him as he struggled through drifts and wind to run ahead. Where were Grisha and the others? The mission should be at the crucial stage, but white silence surrounded him instead of the blast of explosives. Should he check it out himself? It seemed impossible to sit back and wait.

Paul fought his way to the place where Grisha's expert was to be, and there he was, looking cold and unhappy. His face registered alarm when he saw Paul. He immediately began to defend himself with words of excuse.

"It's too blamed stormy—I can't see where they are. How do you expect me to be accurate?"

"I don't care if you're accurate," hissed Paul. "Just do your job so we can do ours."

"I thought you weren't supposed to be near here."

"Well, I am, and it's a good thing. Listen, I hear the horse guard coming. Are you ready?"

"Ready? I can't see who I'm blowing up!"

A crazed look entered Paul's eyes. He grabbed the man by the throat, shook him, and threw him to the ground. "If you don't detonate this piece of garbage, I will."

"No, stop!" The man lunged for Paul, and as they struggled, Paul knocked over the set, igniting a small spark. In spite of the wet and cold, the flicker became a deadly flame, crawling across the snow toward the street where the horse guard rumbled by with its prisoners.

Both men jumped to their feet and stared. Then the explosives man shoved what he could of his paraphernalia into his pockets and grabbed Paul's arm. "Run, man!" he said. "Get out of here!" He gave him a push and they took off at a dead run.

Before they could move more than a few meters, the white world around them exploded in a flash of smoke and snow, accompanied by the screams of men and horses. Paul swung around and began to run back toward the blast, but strong hands turned him and propelled him away.

It was Grisha, pulling him along as fast as he could through the blizzard. The heavy air weighed down the sounds of death, but it did not obliterate them. Paul knew he too would scream if they did not lose the noise behind them, and if he started, he was afraid he would never stop. A roaring rage pushed up from inside him, tearing at his soul, clawing at his heart.

Grisha was not surprised when Paul turned on him with wild eyes and the strength of a bear. "Where is she?" he roared. "What have you done with her?"

Grisha saw him coming for his throat and did the only

thing he could. He launched a swift blow to his friend's jaw and sent him sprawling in the snow, where he lay unmoving. Grisha knelt down and hoisted the tall, sturdy young man over his shoulder.

"I'm sorry, old friend," he said, "but there was no help for it." With Herculean effort, he trudged off into the snow, away from danger, his burden unbelievably heavy on his back.

"You've forced me to violence again, Tekanin," he panted. "Is there really no alternative?"

"What great problem occupies your mind today, my dear?" Heinrich had to stand directly in front of Katarina before she noticed him.

"Oh!" she exclaimed. "You startled me."

"Yes, it looks that way." He smiled as he pulled up a chair to join her by the library fireplace. "Is it something you might share with your father?"

Katya played with the lace on her cuff as she answered. "Well, with the war going on and all the turmoil in our country, I think our workers need encouragement and trust. They need to feel we are one with them and not over them." She looked to her father to see if he understood her meaning.

"Do you mean you feel we should deepen friendships that we may need later on?"

She saw he meant to test her ideas and took no offense at his deliberate misinterpretation. "Absolutely not. I mean no selfishness by it. I only think that if we really believe that all people are created equal, then we must live it out."

Heinrich encouraged her with a slight nod. "And how do you propose we do that, child?"

"Well, I'm not sure exactly, but I think we need to do something. . . . What is it, Father?"

He stroked his beard and spoke gently. "You can't stop the tide of war, Katie. I know you'd like to bring peace to the world, but even your sweet spirit is not capable of that."

"I know that, Papa. But I can bring peace to my little corner. We are only responsible for what we can do." Her green eyes implored him to understand.

"Yes, my dear, you are correct. We each have the responsibility of living at peace with others as much as we are able. I suppose with time and age, we become more cynical as to whether our contribution actually makes a difference."

"Well, Papa, I need to try. "

In the two months since the medical corps had been paralleling the front, Johann, Philipp, and the rest of the men had experienced many horrors. Most often, the medics' job was to try to make the dying comfortable, which was almost impossible without sufficient morphine.

Patching up the wounded wasn't much easier, since Johann knew he was only preparing them to return to the bloody fighting.

"I would hate to expose anyone to this carnage," he said to Philipp, "but sometimes I wish Katya were here." The two men had wearily pulled off their boots and were lying on makeshift bunks for a much-needed break.

Exhaustion nagged at Johann's brain. "Katya would be such a comfort to these men. She's so calm and capable in crises." He turned his head to look at Philipp. "I miss her strength," he continued, then chuckled. "She's embarrassed about her large hands and feet, but she's a strongly built woman. We could benefit from her strength here, both physical and spiritual."

He turned away and pulled the scratchy blanket up to his

chin, completely missing the knowing look on Philipp's face. In another minute, both men were sound asleep.

Johann jerked upright on his cot, his heart pounding and blood racing. Philipp was pulling on his boots.

"We have to move out," Philipp said, as he ran out the tent door. "The German army is almost here." Johann tugged on his own boots and jogged after him, his mind clicking into emergency mode.

Large wagons were already being drawn up for the wounded. The medics went to work immediately, moving the men most likely to survive. Their orders were to take the healthiest first. The weakest wouldn't even be aware of the situation, but the others tore Johann's heart—those missing limbs or burning with fever of infection.

"Medic!" called a soldier weakly, from the far corner of the post-op tent. "Medic, what's going on?"

Johann slowed his pace and tried to shield his heart from the pain. "Routine, soldier," he replied, avoiding the desperation in the fevered face. "I'll be back as soon as I can."

He ran to the next tent to begin the transfer. He could hear the boom and roar of cannon fire and smell smoke as the enemy loomed ever nearer. He and the others lifted and carried, trip after weary trip, until the wagons were piled to twice their capacity.

"Medic!" screamed the soldier in post-op. "Please take me too. Don't leave me at the mercy of the Germans."

"Move out!" shouted the commanding officer, as the wagons began to roll. "All medical personnel board your wagons."

"Medic!" the man screamed again. Johann stood at the foot of his mat, then found himself wrapping the man's emaciated form in his blanket and lifting him in his arms.

Another medic jogged by and slid to a stop beside him. "What are you doing, man?" he cried. "You know we're not supposed to bring the . . . " Johann's scalding look stemmed the flow of words, and he turned and ran toward the wagons.

Johann turned as well, his burden light in his arms. As he approached the last wagon, the man he carried suddenly stiffened and convulsed, then went limp. With tears streaming down his cheeks, Johann gently laid the dead man beside the tent and covered his face. "You're luckier than the rest of us," he whispered, as he stood to his feet. "Your battles are over."

He removed his glasses and wiped his eyes, then turned and sprinted toward the commando wagon as it pulled away from the site. Others had taken down the sleep and mess tents, as well as one of the hospital shelters. The dead and dying were left in the questionable dignity of the other shelter as they awaited their enemies.

Johann clapped his hands over his ears to shut out the screams and cries of the deserted, and rocked with the movement of the cart. His eyes wandered over the faces around him, searching for Philipp, but he was not there.

"Where's Wieler?" he asked sharply.

"Ain't here," answered Neumann, his eyes revealing the fear he tried so desperately to hide. Johann grabbed him by the shoulder and shook him. "I said, where is he?"

"Calm down, man," answered Neumann, shaking with the shock of the situation. "He grabbed a place on the last wagon, said he had to care for the wounded." He wrenched away from Johann and slumped into an exhausted stupor.

Johann put his head in his hands and prayed for the doomed men left behind at the temporary camp and for the wounded who would suffer abominably with the move. He prayed for Philipp as he sacrificed his strength, for his own sanity, and even for Isaac Neumann, whose bravado was crumbling.

Katarina stared out her bedroom window, pen in hand, her diary open before her. Winter had retreated gracefully to make way for exuberant spring, her favorite time of year. But this spring was unlike any she could recall. Even the year Mama died, she had had hope—there had been gradual recovery through the wisdom, love, and comfort of friends and family.

This spring of 1916, Katya had a hard time mustering up her usual optimism. It was partly the devastating war, she knew, but it was also her unnamed dread of an even greater devastation close to home. The abundant blooms and greenery in the park failed to inspire her to expect goodness, as it had in the past.

Katarina tapped her pen on the desk and wondered at her fears. Were they silly, groundless notions? No, she knew enough of world affairs and Russian politics to realize that her country was far from stable. She knew the Great War was still ravaging Europe, destroying millions in its wake.

So were her fears prophetic then? A kind of spiritual warning to prepare her for the evil descending unrelentingly on her and her people? She shuddered and stood to pace the room.

It was similar to what she had felt four years ago at the sinking of the *Titanic* in the frigid Atlantic. She vividly recalled the photographs in the newspapers and her reaction to them. All the finery, class and luxury meant nothing as people were swallowed by the monster sea.

We all hide behind some form of security, she thought now. *We play at living, pretending all is well, denying the waves of reality crashing on the deck of our fragile lives.*

She returned to her desk and began to write. *One day we find ourselves unprepared, calamity stealing every vestige of the life we knew. We discover that the things we clung to for security are no security at all, but weights that would pull us down to the depths. We must be willing to jump into the arms of our Savior, trusting him to bring us safely to shore.*

What are my sources of security? Who do I trust? Katya asked herself these questions and forced herself to answer. God. Papa. Home. Freedom from hunger and immediate danger. *What if I had no papa?* Her eyes glistened with unshed tears as she considered this. *Oh, God, I've already lost one parent. How could I bear losing Papa?* But even as the pain tightened around her heart, she knew she could survive, if she had to.

Home. Succoth. Katya knew she was blessed to be surrounded by such beauty and serenity. She did not take it for granted, but she did admit Succoth held a large piece of her heart. Could she carry on without its sanctuary?

My hope is in you, Lord, she wrote, *and in the power of your might. In you alone I find peace and dwell safely. In you I put my trust.* She believed these words. They would be enough for her. But the feelings of fear hovered, and she must keep fighting to come through. God would stand by her through every battle. Her true haven was not of this world. She had a home in heaven as sure as the lilacs bloomed beyond her window.

"Thank you, Lord," she prayed. "I decide to trust only in you. Please be my strength in weakness." She was amazed anew at the peace that flooded her soul as she laid her burden at Jesus' feet.

"Papa," Katarina ventured at supper that evening, "I think we should make a visit to Molotschna."

"Yes, yes!" chorused Anna and Kolya together. Heinrich stared at his daughter, his spoon halfway between his bowl and his mouth. He swallowed the hot, peppery borscht and wiped his mouth on his napkin. "What brings this up?" he asked. "Where is the Katarina who cannot exist away from her beloved Succoth?"

"I miss Mika and Oma and the Reimers. Who knows how often we'll be able to travel if the war continues?" Katya smiled self-consciously, then lifted her chin. "We cannot rely on material things to give us our security," she said. "As a minister once said, 'Only two things are eternal—God and people, so we do not trust in earthly things.' " She took another spoon of borscht and then spread butter on her thick slice of brown bread. "I think Oma would welcome a visit, don't you?"

"Yes, Papa, please take us to Alexanderkrone." Nicholas' eyes sparkled with anticipation at seeing his friends again.

Heinrich continued to study Katarina between bites of his supper. He smiled and murmured, "You can never understand them."

"What was that, Papa?" asked Katarina.

"I understand you've been doing some deep thinking," he answered. "I can sense the strength in you."

"Not my strength, but God's. I have no wish to live in fear."

"Let me think about your request for a bit." The younger children groaned, but Katya smiled as if it were already arranged.

It's uncanny how a woman can read your mind, thought Heinrich.

They left Succoth for the Molotschna the following week, after working ahead on studies and attending to the duties of the estate lands. Heinrich had been busy that spring, overseeing crop selection and rotation and supervising his large herd of cattle and the new horses he had shipped in from Orenburg. He also had to consider the general maintenance of the mansion and park, as well as Succoth chapel across the stream. He had spent many hours at the huge oak desk in his study, poring over papers and finances.

"Katya," he had said one day, "you need to know these things. If something should happen to me, you need know how this estate is run." He had followed this up with many hours of instruction, sometimes completely confusing to Katarina, sometimes fascinating.

"You also need to know where things are kept," he told her, then hesitated for a moment. "Ever since your mother died, I've felt an urgency to protect the records and financial statements. I don't want you to worry, just be prepared."

It was these conversations that had moved Katarina to consider her security. Heinrich had showed her the place where he kept the most important papers. At dusk, the two of them walked through the park and over the footbridge to the church. The first stars were glimmering in the darkening sky when Katarina began to climb the church steps.

But Heinrich took her arm and led her to the tomb where her mother's remains were buried. She looked at him in shock. He smiled slightly and shrugged his shoulders. "She wouldn't mind," he said, soothingly. "She's not here anyway." He walked around the outside of the burial place and returned to the front. Then, with a quick motion, he took hold of the door and pulled it toward him.

Katya gasped, much as Mary and Martha must have done at the tomb of their dear departed brother Lazarus. But this case was different. No enshrouded figure emerged to shock the watchers.

Heinrich stooped and entered the crypt, then lighted a candle that lay on a ledge just inside the door. The quivering flame illuminated the tiny space as Katarina, trembling, took hold of her father's coat and ducked inside after him.

Heinrich looked back, the candlelight revealing deep lines in his face. "Come, my dear," he said. "It's all right." Obediently, fearfully trusting, she took a deep breath of stale air, then wished she hadn't. On a large, stone shelf at the back of the tomb rested her mother's coffin, a richly burnished teak that was still handsome beneath several years of dust and cobwebs.

It was only a step away, but to Katya, her mother's casket seemed as unreachable and distant as if it sat in an immense cathedral. Her father's arm came around her shoulders and he hugged her close.

"It's really alright, Katie. She is not here. She is risen, just as he said she would be." His paraphrased words from the Bible penetrated her fear, and gradually she stopped shaking. She blinked her eyes to clear them and noticed something on the lid of the coffin. Heinrich followed her gaze and answered her unasked question.

"Rose petals," he said. "I bring them along each time I come. Would you do the honors this time?"

He handed her a little box and held the candle high. She lifted the lid of the little box and the fragrance of roses filled the space, reviving memories of her mother's love. A tear spilled over and rolled slowly down to Katya's chin as she took a handful of the velvety smooth petals and let them fall onto the casket.

"I miss you, Mama," she whispered, "but I know you're not here. We're managing fine and will come to you as soon as we are sent for." She sniffed and the tear from her chin fell onto the coffin to mix with the roses.

Heinrich crouched down and reached beneath the heavy casket, pulling out a long, thin box. He opened the clasp and lifted the lid, revealing a sheaf of papers.

"These, Katie, are the important papers, should you require them. They are proofs of our land ownership, receipts for taxes paid, certificates of births, marriages, and deaths. There are some large-denomination ruble notes, too, if you and the children should ever be in desperate straits. The Russian people are too superstitious to enter a tomb, so these are safe here."

"But I don't intend on leaving Succoth, especially without you."

"Katie, we must be realistic. I cannot read the future, but I feel strongly that great change is in store for us. Please pay attention." He reached into his coat pocket for the papers the two of them had recently completed and added them to the box. "All up to date. Keep it so, and should you be forced to leave, take what you can of these papers with you."

Heinrich looked at her stricken face and lifted her chin so their eyes met. "My darling daughter," he said with deep pain in his eyes. "If there were any way to spare you from this, you know I would. But I believe you will need to be wise and strong for us all, and so I will do my best to prepare you. Do you understand?"

Time stood still as they looked at each other. "Pray for me, Papa," she whispered. They replaced the box of papers beneath Mama's coffin and turned to leave. As Heinrich blew out the candle, bright stars winked placidly from a navy-blue sky, promising to keep this secret with all the others they had seen under the moon.

Heinrich closed the door firmly and carefully readjusted the pebbles in front of it. "Now you know why I've never allowed you to plant flowers here," he said with a wry smile. "Sometimes," he said soberly, "I think we should all have gone to America with Liesbet's brother George in the '80s. Then we wouldn't have to face all this turmoil."

"Oh, no, Papa," answered Katya. "We've experienced so much joy here."

Chapter 21

We're so glad you came," said Cornelia Reimer, folding Katya in her warm embrace. "We've missed you so much since January, and spring is such a lovely time for a visit—so beautiful everywhere."

Later, over a cup of peppermint tea, Mrs. Reimer asked Katya candidly, "You were so insistent in January about staying at Succoth. What made you change your mind?"

Katarina smiled. "I didn't change my mind. I needed to be home then to get us settled again. It seemed our family was fragmenting, and we needed to pull together. Even now, I didn't need a change of place, but to renew relationships."

She looked evenly at her older friend and said, "Papa and I feel that times are changing drastically, and we wanted to see you and Oma again. And Mika, of course. We got on very well at Christmas, and I miss her."

"Well," said Nellie in a distracted tone, "you begin to sound like Abram. He's so convinced bad times are coming that he is making all kinds of plans—what if this and what if that. It frightens me."

Katya grimaced. "I know. I don't like it either. These things may never come to pass, but it's so much better to be prepared and honest than to pretend all is well when it isn't."

"What do you mean, 'all isn't well?'"

The dismal atmosphere dissolved as Mika sailed into the room, beautiful and fragrant as a garden. Katarina gave a squeal of delight and jumped up to meet her.

After a warm hug, they stepped back to look at each other. "You look marvelous, as always," stated Katya and was surprised that the statement came from her heart. "I've missed you. The old house seems so empty without your grace and elegance."

"Careful with the compliments!" laughed Maria. "You'll make me more vain than I already am. Besides, dear sister, the true grace is yours, not mine. I've missed your gentle nature."

Cornelia sat quietly on the sofa, enjoying the interaction between the sisters. "It is so blessed to live in harmony," she commented when they turned to her. "You are most welcome to be at home here for as long as you please. Abram and I are honored."

Katarina smiled warmly and sat beside her. "Thank you for your hospitality," she said. "But we won't stay so long this time—a month at the most. The children need to get back to studies and routine, and Papa needs to oversee the fields and animals."

"Well, then," returned Mika, "we shall have to fit everything into a month. There's a wedding on Saturday . . ."

Katya smiled contentedly as Mika laid out the summer schedule. Yes, coming to Alexanderkrone was an excellent idea.

The Allied retreat had been an extended one, as the Germans pressed their advantage through Austria-Hungary and advanced deep into Russian soil. Eventually, the Forstei decided to move the wounded all the way back to the colonies. Johann Sudermann was one chosen to accompany the wagons.

They journeyed as far as the western border of the Molotschna settlement and there requested aid from their brethren. Out of duty or willingness to be of service, the people of Lichtenau, Fishau, and neighboring Mennonite villages opened their homes and their larders to the strangers.

Johann stayed with the Harder family in Fishau. Their five children ranged in age from ten to eighteen, all girls but the youngest. The Harders also kept four wounded men in their comfortable home.

Johann's orders, which he gladly obeyed, were to settle the men comfortably, then take a week off to rest. It didn't take long to settle the men, as Mrs. Harder and her brood of offspring plumped pillows and simmered homemade chicken soup.

With a promise to return in a week, Johann borrowed a horse and set out for Kleefeld to see his family. His heart longed for Succoth and his adopted family, but he knew time would not permit such a trip.

The eldest Harder girl reminded him of Katarina, and he was seized with a longing to see her. He guessed he needed a listening ear, and Katya was the best listener he knew.

He wouldn't have dreamed of intruding on Mika's life with horrific details of his recent experiences, but Katya was different, stronger. She wouldn't want him to carry the pain alone. How blessed he was to have such a friend.

His horse clip-clopped onto the main street of Kleefeld and turned toward the east. The telegram should have reached Johann's family yesterday to announce his coming. He had entertained the idea of arriving unannounced but dismissed it. Either way there would be some unpleasantness. It was better to prepare for it.

"Hans! Hans is home!" One of his sisters shouted the news, and soon all were clustered around him, shy but obviously glad of his presence.

"Come inside now," ordered his mother in the absence of her husband. "We must begin to put some meat back on those bones. So little time. Ah, he's so skinny. And pale. Poor boy." She muttered and murmured as she clattered pots and pans. Soon Johann sat at the long kitchen table with hot soup and rolls before him, then fresh apple-peach pie and strong coffee with thick cream.

The children stared at Johann as he ate, anticipating the stories he would tell of his adventures, but as yet he stayed with small talk.

"So how have you all been? Marichen, how many kinds of flowers did you and Mama plant this spring?" The flowers were many, the watermelons growing fast, school was over for the summer, and the boys were helping Father with the haying.

"What's new in the colonies?" asked Johann.

"Oh, lots of things," answered one of his sisters. "Old Mrs. Fisher finally died, and your Susannah married Gerhard Warkentin at Christmas. Jacob Neustaedter broke his leg bad falling off his horse. While his leg heals, his Oma is teaching him to knit."

They burst into fits of laughter at the thought, and Johann wondered how Nicholai would adapt to something like that. He smiled and shook his head. Not well, he decided.

"Oh, and your people from the Crimea are visiting in Alexanderkrone again." Marichen filled him in.

"They're here now?" he asked, his mouth going dry.

"Yah."

He finished his lunch mechanically and thanked his mother. "I think I'll rest awhile now, if I may."

"Of course, son. You rest. I'll start on supper." Beaming, she turned back to her pots and pans. *It's so easy to give someone joy,* he thought with a smile.

The next afternoon, Johann informed his mother he was riding over to Alexanderkrone to see the Hildebrandts. "I need to check up on my charges, Nicholai and Anna," he said.

The ride was short, only a few minutes. He was most thankful for the borrowed horse. His father had made it perfectly clear the night before that he could use some help on the farm, but at the very least, Johann should know better than to expect use of one of the farm horses. "Gadding about who knows where, and then he comes home to borrow my horses."

"Now, Heinz," Johann's mother had interrupted, "he's been working in the medical corps, not gadding about. And he already has a horse. Look at the boy, how skinny he is."

Mr. Sudermann had mumbled something and tromped noisily out to the barn. Johann wondered how one dealt with difficult people like his father. He considered himself more or less reasonable and agreeable, but his father never failed to bring out the worst in him. It would be a continuing struggle, he decided.

Alexanderkrone bustled with summer activity. The weather was comfortable, not yet hot, and women and children hoed and pulled weeds in the gardens, raked yards, and whitewashed fences. The atmosphere was pleasant and appealing. *So different from where I've been lately*, thought Johann. *A world away. Which is the reality?* he wondered, then realized they both were. *But realities change as we do, and each day must be taken as a gift.*

Johann thought of Philipp Wieler and wondered how he was faring. He had also been ordered to get a week's rest. How would his friend ever be able to leave his beloved Agnetha, once he saw her again?

He reigned in his mount at the Reimer residence and stepped down, tying the horse at the short hitching post. He pushed open the front gate and approached the house, then decided to peek around the side of the building to see if anyone was in the garden.

A figure knelt there, and he knew it was Katya, her unruly

curls tossed by the breeze, a sheen of perspiration on her face. Sensing someone near, she looked up against the sun, pushing her hair back with earth-stained hands.

She did not recognize Johann immediately. She stood, blinking, and wiped her hands on her apron as she walked toward him. Then suddenly she stopped. Her hands flew to her dirt-smudged face, and she uttered a strangled cry.

Johann broke into a grin and moved toward her. Without a word he took her in his arms and hugged her, long and hard. She hugged him back, and a weight seemed to roll off his shoulders, replaced by inexpressible comfort and contentment.

Finally she stepped back and looked at him, afraid to speak in case it might break the spell and he would be gone again. Her tentativeness made him smile, and he reached out to wipe the smudge from her face.

"Hello," he said. "They ordered me to take a week off, and I just found out you were here. I couldn't stay away." His own words amazed him as he looked at his dear friend. She hadn't changed, not really, except perhaps for a new strength in her eyes, in her manner. Self-consciously she pushed at her hair, attempting unsuccessfully to tame it.

"Don't do that," Johann said softly. "I like it that way."

He could tell she was beginning to come apart at the surprise of it all, and she had said nothing. Then she blinked twice, took a deep breath, and smiled. "Johann," she said in a tender voice, "it is so good to see you. I can't believe you're here. I . . . we've missed you so much. How are you?"

Concern showed on her face as she took in his thin frame and pale complexion. He smiled again and took her hand in his. "I'm fine now, Katya." He grew sober. "I've been to hell and back, but now it seems I've been granted a glimpse of heaven."

They turned to walk through the orchard, the smell of lilies and the sweet scent of roses drifting along with them. "Was it so terrible?" she asked, her face serious.

"Yes," he answered simply. "It was. So many men died. And they were the lucky ones. The ones we saved had to go back into the fight, but the ones maimed and torn, they really have no place to go." He couldn't tell her about the screaming, pleading soldiers left at the mercy of the approaching enemy. He couldn't put that into words even in his own mind.

Katya squeezed his hand. "Let it go for now, Johann," she said. "You do what you must each day. Now you are here, and you must let your soul heal so you have the strength to return. But if you ever need to speak about it, I will listen. I'm strong, usually."

He smiled and rubbed her hand with his thumb. "I know. Your face kept me going in many trials."

His words flustered her. These feelings were so hard to decipher. What kind of friendship was this between them? How should she respond? What did God expect of her?

"Katya," he said, reading her mind, "relax. Times are so hard right now. Let's not try to second-guess each other. Let's just support one another as best we can. Now, tell me what's been happening at home."

He always had a way of putting her at ease, and Katya's subsequent words were a salve to his parched soul.

The week slipped by like an hour, and soon it was time to leave. Johann had spent his week mostly at the Reimers', walking and talking with Katya, in deep discussions with Heinrich, and in wonderfully free games of tag and ball with the children. He and Mika managed to avoid each other for the most part, but they were able to be quite civil when necessary. Johann kept the Forestry Service at the back of his mind, so as not to spoil the present. But time would have its way.

"Tomorrow you go," stated Katarina. "Are you ready?"

"No," he grimaced. "Never ready for that."

"They need you," she said simply. "The men, and Philipp, and even Isaac Neumann. It's not wasted time, any of it. It's all part of God's plan for you. I'm just so thankful we could spend this week together. It's been a great encouragement to me."

"Oh, Katya." He took her hand, as had become his habit. "You don't know what it's meant to me—knowing that you know where I've been and where I must return, that you're praying for me, that you're keeping your family going."

She smiled. "We each have tremendous responsibilities. Remember to pray for strength each day. And please give my regards to Mr. Wieler. I would like to meet him someday."

They stood in the garden now, where they had met one week ago.

"Please be careful," she said.

"I will. And you."

She nodded, unable to say more.

He was about to turn and leave when he came to a decision, an understanding of which he had been only partly conscious before. "Katarina," he said, "you have come to mean a great deal to me. There's no one anywhere in this world who means as much to me as you."

She blushed and looked down, twisting her hands together. He lifted her chin. "Look at me, Katie. I've been slow and stupid about it, but I'm finally beginning to realize what you are to me. I'm not sure of it all yet, but I just wanted you to know. In the best and the worst situations I've experienced, your face comes to my mind, your gentle strength keeps me going. I will come back, God willing, and we will continue on from here. Agreed?"

"Agreed." It was a mere whisper, but they both heard it clearly in their hearts. They shared an embrace, and Johann walked away and mounted his horse. He rode off down the main street, then turned at the edge of town and waved.

Katya stood watching, waving back. Finally, he wheeled his horse and galloped off to Fishau to regroup his charges.

Paul Gregorovich woke slowly, in a painful haze. It was late morning, judging by the full summer sun beating in the windows of his attic room.

He was mildly surprised to find himself at home. Grisha must have brought him here, again. Headaches and a queasy stomach were becoming the norm for Paul. Ever since the disaster on Nevsky, he had sunk lower and lower into the pit of despair. He no longer remembered or cared what had happened the night before or with whom he had celebrated. His life had become an unending nightmare, and he didn't have the strength to awaken.

Gradually, as the fog in his mind cleared, he became aware of Grisha sitting at the tiny table, his head in his hands. Grisha—the only one who had stuck by him in this downward spiral. Why the man cared at all was beyond him. He only knew that without Grisha he would be dead.

Grisha lifted his head to meet Paul's groggy gaze. He sighed. "It's another day, Tekanin. Get up and wash your face. I've scrounged up some dry bread for you. We need to talk."

Paul winced at the sound of Grisha's voice. His head felt like an overripe pumpkin ready to burst, and each tiny sound produced shock waves that threatened to speed the process.

Groaning, he rolled onto his side and forced himself to a sitting position. "Grisha," he whispered, trying not to move his lips. "Go home. I just want to die here alone."

Grisha rose from the spindle-backed chair and stood beside the bed. "Get up," he said quietly but firmly. Paul did so, unsteadily at first, then gradually gaining control. As he steadied, his temper grew worse. He cursed as he splashed his face, cold water dribbling down his collar.

"What do you want? Why don't you just leave me?"

"Because you need me, and I won't let you give up. Here's some bread. Now come sit at the table and listen to me."

With surly obedience, Paul moved to the table and slumped into the other chair. He pushed the bread away with disgust. "Speak," he said.

A grin hovered around Grisha's mouth, but it died before it reached his eyes. His loyalty to Paul had melted into pity, and lately a sense of futility had begun to seep in as well. He fought against the futility, partly because he was a tremendously loyal person and partly because caring for Paul filled his own loneliness. How could he say these things to a hungover, destitute man?

"Paul," he began, trying to speak rationally, "you have been going downhill ever since Vera's death, and I think it's time you came to terms with it. You can't keep . . ."

"Stop!" shouted Paul, then held his head with both hands to keep it from exploding. More quietly he said, "You will not mention her name again."

Grisha stood and moved to Paul's side, then knelt on one knee and put his hand on his shoulder. "I *will* mention it," he insisted. "Vera is dead. You didn't mean for it to happen, but it did. They would have killed her anyway if we hadn't created a . . . diversion. You need to accept what has happened and deal with it."

"How?" Tekanin was coming apart. "She trusted me and I killed her. How do I deal with that? Just give me a drink, would you?"

"No. No more drinks and no more denial. What's done is done. Now we move on." Grisha stood, then sat down in his chair again.

"We? Why do you insist on hovering over me like a nursemaid? I don't need you."

"We need each other. I care about you."

At this admission, Paul stared darkly at him.

"It's an honest, brotherly caring," Grisha stated instantly as he read Paul's thoughts, "not some perversion of Petersburg society. I'm not Prince Yusopov. Give me some credit, will you?"

Paul looked away. "I still think you should let me be. Better for both of us. I'll drink myself into oblivion, and you'll never need to know what happened to me in the end."

"Your solution," answered Grisha, "is not mine." He paused a minute to collect his thoughts, then spoke again. "I had a brother," he said softly, "a couple of years younger than I. He was tall, like you, and good-looking. He knew it, too, and it went to his head. Got involved with a nasty crowd and was knifed in some back lane, probably for some thoughtless comment or action.

"I knew he was in trouble or at least heading for it," Grisha's face was tense with pain, "but I did nothing." He looked over at Paul. "It was his business, you know—his life. So I let him die, and I've never forgiven myself.

"That's why I joined the leftists. I needed something to distract me, something to believe in and put my whole soul into. You reminded me so much of Sergei—it was almost as if I'd been given another chance."

He smiled slightly at Paul, then sobered. "I won't let it happen again. Like a captain and his ship, we sink or float, but either way, we do it together. Do you understand me, Paul Gregorovich?"

Paul had sobered enough to listen. Presently he spoke. "How . . . how does one commit himself totally to a cause without allowing his feelings to intervene?"

"Lenin's objectives demand complete selflessness and devotion to the whole. The parts are not considered separately. You know that."

"But it's not humanly possible," argued Paul. "None of us is capable of detaching so entirely from his feelings."

"Some are. They're the dangerous ones. I think even Lenin himself could not totally disengage his feelings, but at his inspiration others would. There are a few I'm beginning to know, and they frighten me to the core."

"Djugashvili?"

"Yes. Stalin. Our 'man of steel.' "

"So what do we do? We seem to have lost our anchor."

Grisha smiled at Paul's acceptance of the plural "we." "Would you agree our nation is in a grave situation?"

"Absolutely," said Paul, looking directly at his friend. "Nicholas is an incompetent fool, and the empress a dangerously superstitious and frightened woman. And that devil Rasputin has her completely under his filthy thumb. If ever there was a vile creature, it is he. Loathsome and disgusting. What do women see in him?"

"I don't know," Grisha said, "except that society women are often so bored and neglected they grasp at any man who notices them. And Father Grigory is generous with himself. No," he continued, "I rather think he has a mesmerizing power."

"That's a great and formidable power to have. Where does it come from?"

Grisha stared at him. "It's black, that's for sure. Dark and evil. The only good thing about it is that he's almost single-handedly destroying the tsar's government. Makes for a much easier revolution."

"Yes, everyone's sick to death of Nicholas' futile attempts to pull it all together. He never will. So," he said again, eyeing Grisha across the small table, "what do we do?"

"Well, I'm not certain yet. It's only begun to form in my head. But we must find our own way to speed the downfall of the tsar. To redistribute the wealth of the aristocracy."

"Take from the rich and give to the poor," smirked Tekanin. "A Russian Robin Hood. I could wear skirts and be lovely maid Marion. I've fooled them before."

They both chuckled, remembering his close call and quick thinking at the Astoria. "You're too clumsy, and definitely not as good-looking as you think," answered Grisha. Their laughter faded, but Paul's face retained some of its lightness.

He cleared his throat and said, "Thank you, my friend. Now that my headache is clearing, I don't really want to die. It helps to know you too have experienced the devastation of losing someone because of your own pride and foolhardiness."

Grisha grimaced at the judgment, but he rejoiced that his revelation had helped his friend. "Then we will look out for each other and for some way to further cripple the present administration."

Paul had something else on his mind, Grisha could tell. "What is it, Paul Gregorovich?"

Paul rose to pace the room, then stopped finally before Grisha. "There's something I need to do," he said at last. "For . . . Vera. Will you show me where she is?"

Grisha stood and clapped a hand on Paul's shoulder. "Come, my friend. There's a flower shop on the way. Here," he added, "wear this hat and coat and stoop a little. You always were too striking to be out in public."

Johann met Philipp again at Schwarzwald, where he moved three of his four soldiers after their week of convalescence. These three would be sent back to the front; the fourth had not regained his strength sufficiently.

On his return, Johann was surprised to find he had been assigned a position right at the camp. New trainees would take his place at the front for a time, while he and Philipp and others would continue to care for the men at Schwarzwald.

Philipp was less than happy about the arrangement. "We already know what to do at the front," he said, "so why don't they let us do it? Why throw more innocent young men into that gruesome situation?"

"You *want* to go back?" Johann asked incredulously. "I was just thinking we were lucky to stay."

"I'm prepared to go back. I've requested it."

"Do you think you can handle the intensity? You look tired since you returned."

"That's just it," Philipp explained. "You let go to relax, and all your strength seeps away. We need to keep struggling. After all, the soldiers don't get a break. They don't stop fighting and dying."

Johann searched his friend's face. "Come walk with me," he invited. "I need to stretch my legs after the train ride."

They walked without speaking as far as the river and stood in the shelter of the water poplars. Johann asked, "What happened at home? Is Agnetha all right?"

"Yes, she's fine. Wonderful, actually." His eyes shone at the thought of his wife.

"So why are you so restless? Was it leaving that bothered you?"

Philipp did not speak for a few moments. Then he locked eyes with Johann, begging for understanding as he spoke. "It was the finality of it. I will carry her look and feel to my grave."

"Of course you will. But you make it sound imminent."

Philipp heaved a sigh and looked away. "That's because it is," he answered. "I won't see her again in this life."

"What? Why? Is she ill? You could have stayed back with her . . ."

Wieler held up his hand to stop the flow of words. "There's

nothing at all wrong with Agnetha or with me, for that matter," he said. "But I will not return to her."

"Why? How do you know?"

"It's in here," he said, tapping his chest. "I just know. My life will be brief. I haven't fully come to terms with it yet."

Johann stared at him with his mouth open, wanting to dispute what he heard but unable to do it. He didn't want to believe Philipp, but he had experienced his sixth sense before, his knowing when it was time to pack up and when it was better to stay. The man walked closely with God and seemed to be able to hear him when others couldn't.

"Tell me about it," Johann said finally. They walked and talked for a couple of hours before heading back to camp. Tomorrow they might be separated, and neither wanted to leave anything unsaid.

"I must speak with the commanding officer," Philipp said finally.

"I'll go with you."

"That's kind, but you don't need to."

"Well, I doubt he'll allow me to put in my own request for field duty if I don't talk with him personally."

"Your own request . . . Johann, you don't need to do that."

"Yes, I do," he said, tapping his chest. "I know it in here."

Chapter 22

I feel as you do," said Oma Peters to Heinrich and Katya as the three shared tea beneath the shady oaks at Ruekenau Home for the Aged. "I believe hard times are coming, persecutions and wars. Perhaps Christ will return for us soon, who knows, but either way, we must be strong for the coming storm."

The tea soothed Katarina's nerves. It was peaceful in the June sunshine, surrounded by trees and shrubs, the scent of roses, and the twitter of birds. Wagons rumbled slowly along Main Street, west to the general store or east to the windmill. The scene didn't lend itself to discussion of persecution and war, but reality had a way of shaking up the imagination.

"Have you heard from George at all?" Heinrich asked his mother-in-law. "Has he truly relocated to Canada?"

"Yah. To Saskatchewan." Oma struggled to pronounce the strange Indian word. "He says it's flat grassland with few trees, but many possibilities. That man is more adventurous than I ever thought. Used to be such a shy little one, but I suppose still waters run deep, don't they, dear?" She smiled at Katarina and patted her hand. "You're our strong, quiet one. Thank the Lord for you. "

"Oma, it frightens me when people say that—first Papa, then Mika, then Johann, and now you. What if I can't live up to it? I'm just as human and fearful as anyone else."

"Perhaps you are," answered her father, "but you don't let it consume you. You meet it face to face, and with God's help, you carry on. God gives you enough strength for each day."

They sipped tea as the sun began its slow descent to the west. "George says Saskatchewan is not as beautiful as South Russia, but it has a deep, hidden beauty, thousands of dessiatines—he calls them *acres*—of land to homestead, and freedom to live as one pleases. Perhaps you should consider going there yourselves," she said, looking first at Heinrich, then at Katarina. "If things continue to decline here, Canada may be your chance at freedom and peace."

"We'd never leave Russia, Oma," Katya said immediately, surprise in her voice. "But if we did, we would most certainly take you with us."

The old lady shook her head and chuckled. "You'd have to knock me out and tie me up," she said. "I'll not leave here anymore, but you might consider it. You have many years before you."

"Well, for the time being, we are free and I think we should start back to Reimers' for supper." Heinrich stood and planted a kiss on top of the old woman's kerchiefed head. "We will stop by again before we leave."

Mrs. Peters rose spryly and wrapped Katya in a hug. "You think about my words," she encouraged. "I've learned a thing or two in my life. Thank you for coming."

They walked toward the buggy and were about to climb in when Oma called after them. "Give my regards to Peter when you see him and to that nice young couple that looks after him. God bless you."

She watched as they drove away, headed southward to Alexanderkrone.

"Peter Hildebrandt," called Susannah softly as she entered the common room. She spotted him at the window overlooking the grounds, spellbound by the gardener and his work in the flowerbeds.

"Mama. Flowers," he said, as Susannah stood beside him. He was taller than she by a head and thin, but his face had filled out since coming to Bethany, and his eyes no longer harbored that wild look.

"Did your mama like flowers, Peter dear?" She put a hand lovingly on his shoulder and looked into his eyes.

"Mama. Flowers," he repeated, and turned to lean his curly dark head on her shoulder. His arms remained stiffly by his sides, but he continued to rest his head.

Susannah patted his back and he lifted his head, but he did not look at her. His eyes saw another, one who smelled of lilac water and cut roses, one who cradled his confused head and quieted his overactive limbs. "Hush, my darling," he heard in the deep recesses of his mind. "God and Mama will take care of you. Hush now." And then she would sing the songs of her childhood, the German playsongs that his siblings supplied actions for, the haunting Russian melodies of his neighbors, and the deeply touching hymns of faith.

He could see her and smell her now, with the fragrance of flowers drifting in the windows and comforting arms around him. He lifted his head and began to hum a tune dislodged from the many impressions in his cluttered memory.

Walking, sunshine, flowers, Mama. Warm breeze, soft hands, Mama. So tired. Always Mama.

Susannah guided him outside, settled him in the shade, and watched as he slept in the lounge chair beneath the oaks. The breeze rippled his dark curls. His long lashes brushed pale cheeks, and he held tightly to her hand. *Where are his thoughts?* she wondered. *Is he at peace?* "Dear God, grant him peace."

Gerhard approached from the administration building, an orderly by his side. Susannah released herself gently from

Peter's grasp and rose to make room for the orderly. "Let him sleep until suppertime," she whispered.

She looked up at Gerhard as they started back to the building. "The Hildebrandts have arrived," he informed her. "I told Yuri to have them wait in my office. What do you think?"

Susannah remained quiet as she considered. "I think we should reunite them," she said. "Peter has settled so well, and he doesn't mind any of the staff anymore. I think it would be a good plan. What do you think?"

Gerhard ran a hand over his hair and smiled at his young wife. "I think you're right, my angel," he answered. "Who knows how soon they'll get back here again?"

"The war?"

Gerhard grimaced. "War and rumors of war. No one knows what tomorrow may bring." He grabbed her hand and laced his fingers with hers.

"Gerhard!" she whispered. "We are on duty."

He held her hand more tightly and smiled. "Yes," he said with a smile, "and we mustn't let any false rumors spread about our happiness or lack of it. We're to be an example of marital bliss, difficult as that may be!"

Suse smiled with pleasure. "God has blessed us richly," she said softly as she gazed up at her husband.

Gerhard opened the waiting room door and stepped aside for Susannah to enter. Heinrich rose from his chair and Katarina also rose with shy excitement.

"Katya!" Susannah embraced her warmly, and Katya's shyness melted away as they smiled and exchanged greetings.

"Mr. Hildebrandt." Gerhard nodded and shook hands firmly with the older man. "So good to see you here again. And how are you children?" he asked of Anna and Nicholai. He greeted Katarina as Susannah shook hands with Heinrich, then turned at a glimpse of color to his right.

Mika moved from the window where she had been standing almost behind them and approached. Gerhard tried not to stare. She was indeed beautiful. A wave of dislike passed through Susannah's mind, but she dismissed it immediately, smiled, and stepped forward to take Mika's hand.

"You must be Maria. It's so good to meet you. Katarina has told me about you."

Gerhard also smiled and bowed slightly.

The warmth that had put Katarina at ease seemed to have the opposite effect on Maria. She smiled and nodded, but seemed somewhat nervous, even beneath her proper manners.

"I hope you had a pleasant ride," said Gerhard. "Peter just fell asleep in the garden, but he will be ready for supper in a few minutes and you are welcome to share it with him."

"Do you think that would be wise?" Katarina voiced the concern of all of them.

"We've discussed it," answered Gerhard, "and we feel it would be good to try it." He looked to Susannah for her confirmation.

She smiled at him. "Peter's been doing quite well lately," she said. "He eats well and usually appears calm. He enjoys the gardens, especially the flowers. And we look almost daily at the picture album you sent, Katya. He knows all of you."

"Which of us is his favorite?" asked Anna, looking at Katya as if to say it would be her.

Katya colored. "Anna, we don't have favorites in our family. We love each other equally, although in different ways."

Susannah smiled. "Actually," she said, "he does favor one picture, but it's not of any of you."

"It's Mama." It was Mika's voice, and at this moment her poise seemed about to crumble. She spoke in a near whisper. "Peter will be missing Mama most of all."

Heinrich stepped forward to wrap a comforting arm around Mika, then lifted his eyes to Gerhard "We would be most pleased to share supper with our Peter. Would you join us as well?"

"Of course," answered Gerhard. "This is a special reunion, and we would be honored to share it with you."

"I'll show you ladies where to freshen up," said Susannah, "and then we'll meet the men in the dining room." She looked over at Gerhard. "Could we move a couple of tables together in the far corner for our group?"

He bowed and smiled at her. "Your every wish is my command." Susannah and Katya grinned, Anna giggled, and even Maria managed a smile. Kolya simply rolled his eyes and followed the men from the room.

"He's so charming," said Katya after the men had gone. "You're a happy girl, I think."

"Oh, yes," Susannah agreed, "although we do have our disagreements. I'm quite convinced of my opinions and so is he, so we have some grand debates." She laughed. "I wouldn't trade it for the world."

"Nor should you," answered Katya. "The world isn't in very good condition these days. Anyway, I'm so happy for you."

Susannah turned to Mika. "Are you still staying with your relatives in Alexanderkrone?"

"Yes. Well, we're not actually related. They're just friends of our parents."

"And how are you enjoying it?"

"Oh, very much." Mika warmed to the subject. "We have lots of outings and things to do. Not like at Succoth." She glanced at her older sister. "That's why Katya goes and I stay: people."

Katya wrinkled her nose at Mika. "Yes," she agreed. "She seeks them and I hide from them."

They laughed as they walked along the hallway. After a few minutes the group met again at the door to the dining hall.

Residents of various degrees of mental disturbance were being led into the large sunlit room. Some could find their own seats and wait until their food was served. Others could not.

One young woman bounced and sang in a hoarse voice while her nurse held her firmly by the arm. Another, an older woman with frizzled white hair, seemed unaware of anything. She shuffled along after her companion, her eyes never leaving the floor, her hands hanging limp and useless. The Hildebrandt family struggled to accept what they saw and heard. It was, to them, a strange and sad place, no matter how clean and orderly.

"Let's take our place over in that corner." Gerhard ushered in the Hildebrandts, and they took their seats. Their laughter had been replaced by anxiety. They kept looking back to the doorway, anticipating the arrival of Peter.

When he came, it was as if the rest of the room did not exist. Heinrich and his children had seated themselves around the table in the same order they sat at home, with a place open for Peter beside Katya. Gerhard and Susannah sat at the end with an extra chair beside them.

When the boy was ushered in, he made his way to the chair beside Katya and sat down quietly, then bowed his head as he would at home. Heinrich, his heart in his throat, said the grace, then looked up at his oldest son. Blinking back tears, he spoke.

"Good evening, Peter. Did you have a pleasant day?" Not expecting an answer, he reached for his knife to butter a slice of bread.

"Mama. Flowers."

All eyes riveted on the boy who began to eat the bread Katya gave him. Then he pushed back his chair, grasped his bread in his hand, and moved stiffly to where Susannah sat with Gerhard. He lowered himself into the chair, turned to Susannah and rested his forehead on her shoulder.

Everyone watched in amazement as Peter, in his own way, transferred his loyalties from his family to his caregivers. Susannah's eyes betrayed her embarrassment at the switch, but they all knew it was Peter who had chosen. For a time, the meal was quiet and no one ate much, not even Nicholai.

Peter himself finally lightened the serious mood. "Peter dear," he said, when Anna asked shyly if he had any friends at Bethany Home. And his favorite food seemed to be "Mama's flowers."

He relaxed as the rest of the group did, and the mealtime became a unique reunion for all the Hildebrandts. Looking around her, Katya began to see not sadness and strangeness, but the deep love and commitment of the healthy who took care of those who could not care for themselves.

Later, walking back to the buggy, Katya fell into step beside Susannah. "I was so happy to hear about your marriage to Gerhard," said Katya. "You two look so happy together."

Susannah's smile widened, dimpling her round face. Her cheeks colored slightly as she spoke. "It's absolutely wonderful, Katya—so much more than I thought it would be. Gerhard and I are partners, friends. It gives life such joy and purpose."

She paused and then took Katarina's hand. "I wish the same for you, my friend. To be loved and cherished is the greatest gift in the world, next to faith in God. Have there been any changes in your relationship with Johann?"

The two young women lagged behind the rest. Gerhard was talking to Heinrich as Maria settled into the buggy beside Anna and Nicholai.

Katarina's hands flew to her warm cheeks. "Umm, I think possibly," she said quietly.

"Possibly? For you to say that, it must be something. Tell me, please."

"Well, he came to see me a couple of weeks ago, when he was on leave. He's in the Forstei, you know—he's been at the front lines on medical duty. He didn't know we were in Alexanderkrone until his sister happened to mention it. I'm so glad he found out or we might have missed each other altogether. He only had a week."

"And . . ."

"Well, we talked and . . . and held hands."

"So, what did you talk about?"

Katya sighed and smiled. "Mostly about his work and about our families, and then . . ." She looked over at Susannah, a head shorter than she, even with the golden braids crowning her head.

"Katya! You're baiting me."

They both giggled, and Mika stared at them from her seat in the wagon. "All right then," Katya continued. "He said I was more important to him than anyone else in this world and that he couldn't stay away when he heard I was there. He said he was discovering deep feelings for me, and I can't believe such a plain, big girl like me could make anyone feel that way."

She stopped, out of breath, and Susannah grinned at her. Katya could tell her friend was fighting the urge to squeal or jump up and down.

"First of all, Katya dear, you are not plain and big. You are strong and lovely, with a personality and character to capture a heart that's true. And second, if Hans said that to you, he meant it. It's more than I ever heard from him!"

Suddenly Gerhard was at her elbow, wearing a straight face that didn't match the twinkle in his eyes. "I really must apologize for my wife, Miss Hildebrandt. She has a way of keeping people longer than they intend. I hope it hasn't inconvenienced you."

Susannah gave her husband a sharp jab with her elbow, but he paid no mind. "Shall I escort you to your carriage?" he asked Katya.

"Not before we have a hug," insisted Susannah, reaching for Katarina. "I'll still be praying for you," she whispered. "God will work it out."

"What are you promising now, my love?" asked Gerhard in a mocking whisper. This set them both laughing again, and at last Katya was forced to pull away and climb up with her family.

"You two surely are chummy," commented Mika.

"Allow me," replied Katarina. "It's my first taste of it and I like it."

Mika's eyes softened as she looked at her sister, and she smiled. "You deserve it."

They turned to wave as the horses pulled them away from Bethany Home.

Chapter 23

"The isolation is going to kill us in this war," Grisha stated as he, Paul and several other young people sat at a table at the back of Piotr's Pub. "Last year the Allies tried to get through the Dardanelles and failed. Maybe their lust for control of Constantinople was greater than their incentive to establish contact with Russia, but no matter what, they failed."

"Yes, the Turks sent them scrambling like whipped dogs. Now we've been stymied from the north."

"How so?" asked a student they called Sasha.

"England was sending their Secretary of War—Kitchener, I believe his name was, to Petrograd and on to the front to discuss military and financial matters with the tsar, God bless his soul."

"Ha, ha!" laughed Paul. "Bless the tsar with the plague." The whole company laughed and banged on the table.

"So, anyway," continued Grisha, "their ship never made Archangel. Torpedoed by German U-boats, no doubt. The vessel was lost off the Orkney Islands on June 5."

Paul's angry laughter subsided. "So there's no one left to talk any sense into Nicholas. We're doomed, my friends, if we don't do something."

"Do what? Anyone who tries anything is shot or hung or blown to bits." Sasha missed the intense pain that tightened Paul's face.

"We must unite!" shouted Paul, rallying. "We can have an impact."

Grisha was beside him immediately, speaking with a calm urgency. "And we must organize quietly before we ignite the flame, my friend. We ally ourselves with the Bolsheviks and add our strength and determination to theirs. That is our present path."

"And are we Bolsheviks?" asked Paul in a hoarse whisper. He wore the look of a confused child, the look that overtook him every time he was reminded of Vera Guseyva.

Grisha smiled a tight smile. "We are chameleons, Paul Gregorovich."

Paul's eyes cleared as he puffed on a cheap cigarette. "Chameleons," he said, and coughed.

"And what's happening at the front?" asked Sasha, confused by the exchange.

Grisha filled in the details. "Apparently our General Brusilov and the Allies surprised Austria with a huge offensive on the Somme. Took two hundred thousand Austrian prisoners, the poor scoundrels. So Romania, trusting in our exalted leader, joined the Allies."

"That's good news for us," Sasha said.

"It *was*. Now Germany's taken over Romania. Romanian oil and wheat will be a great asset to the German war machine."

Paul had picked up these details at *PRAVDA*, still printing in spite of Cossack raids and Stalin's frequent Siberian consignments. There were always students ready and willing to become involved in the cause of the people, and *PRAVDA* could always use them.

"Oh, but we have new hope in Russia's eventual victory," continued Paul, his words tinged with sarcasm.

"Do tell," said Sasha, ready for a bit of relief.

"It's an apple," replied Tekanin. "Yes, an apple. It seems our holy friend Grigory Rasputin, the mad monk, has blessed an apple, and Alexandra herself has sent it to Nicholas at the front, begging him with all urgency to consume it."

"Yes, my friends," said Grisha with bitter humor, "now is our salvation at hand."

"I've heard," said Sasha conspiratorially, leaning forward, "that there may be a palace revolt in the wings. Apparently, one of the generals is at the root of the plans."

"It's Krymov," said Grisha. "Wants Nicholas to abdicate, not in favor of his son, but to his brother Michael."

"Fat lot of good that will do," said Paul angrily. "We need to get free of the whole works of those Romanovs. They've had more than three hundred years to learn how to rule this land, and they haven't yet learned how to do it. One more dictator isn't going to help anyone."

Sasha, his eyes wide, asked, "Do you think they'll oust the tsar? Russia without a Romanov is a strange concept."

"Strange and wonderful," put in one of the students.

"Well," said Grisha, "if Nicky doesn't get off his high horse and listen to the people, he's going to be in more trouble at home than at the front. Some of his more fearless relatives are begging him to consider what the populace is saying. And more than one foreign diplomat has advised the same."

"He's a weak leader," said Paul angrily. "With the help of his superstitious wife and that lecherous beast, Rasputin, he'll have us all begging for mercy from the Germans."

"Actually," said Grisha, his face tense, "we may not need to bother waiting for a palace revolt or for the tsar to bring about his own downfall. We've had word from the Big Man. He and Trotsky are in Austria or Switzerland, or somewhere thereabouts, and plan to return home as soon as they can cross the border. The Germans aren't overly willing to assist them in getting back into Russia."

"Well," said Paul, "Lenin had better find a way. The unrest among the proletariat is becoming unbearable. Some of the factory workers go back three generations in the same dirty, noisy building. It's where they work and sleep and eat, when food is available. It's where they've been born and where they will die, in the clanking darkness with no hope of relief."

Passionately he spilled out descriptions of the lives of these poor, forgotten creatures. These were Vera's people, Sasha's family, Grisha's relatives, and vicariously his as well.

"The workers won't hold back much longer."

Paul had kept a close eye on the situation, still passing on as much information and as many opinions as *PRAVDA* would accept. "Now that they've seen a glimpse of hope in Lenin's promises, the urgency for change builds daily."

"We're always hungry," said Sasha, "as if the others weren't aware. There's bread, you know," he said, "in the bakeries. It sits in the windows, but we can't buy it because we have no money."

He looked older than his seventeen years, and Grisha was pained at the sight. As the group broke up to go their separate ways, he tossed a coin to the bartender and covertly slipped another into Sasha's pocket.

"For the little ones," he murmured at Sasha's wide-eyed stare. It was Grisha's last coin. He and Paul would do without supper tonight. Perhaps a nip of vodka would ease the ache. At least Sasha's brother and sisters would be able to bite into a crust of black bread. The picture brought him solace.

Bread was also scarce at the camp where Johann and Philipp were stationed. The week of rest now seemed to Johann a dream. Had he really gone home, seen Katya, and said the words he thought he'd said? Now as he sat drinking weak tea and gnawing on a hard biscuit, they came back to him as clear as the September sun. "I've been slow and stupid . . . but I'm beginning to realize what you mean to me."

What does *she mean to me?* he asked himself. *What do I*

feel for her? He began a list in his mind: friend, confidante, the one I think of first in joy or in sorrow, a shelter in the storm . . ."

How he missed her presence, which he had taken so for granted back at Succoth. Back then, almost a year ago now, he'd still been enamored with Maria. What had she given him? False dreams, empty hopes. He had given her loyalty, adoration, attention, and always she had expected more. He was embarrassed that he had been so overwhelmed by outward beauty.

All the while Katarina had remained in the background, content, it seemed, to accept what friendship he offered and to return it without reservation. He realized now how much she had cared, how much she still cared, waiting so patiently and hoping for him to see it for himself.

Yes, he'd been slow and stupid. Even little Anna had seen it as plain as day. Katarina open-handedly offered her loyalty and her strength, and, quite assuredly, her love.

Did he love her like that? Philipp would laugh at his foolishness. Philipp said it was written all over his face when he spoke of her. Perhaps it was love itself he could not fully define. He thought of the apostle Paul's words: "Love is patient, kind, selfless, protective. It is trusting, hopeful, and determined."

Love is action, he decided, *not some vague fluttering in your chest, but action based on a decision.* If he decided to admit to loving Katarina Hildebrandt, could he be patient and kind to her? There was little doubt there; she demanded so little, and the less demanded, the more generous the giver. He trusted her completely, found hope and strength in her, and would most certainly protect her with his life.

"I love her," he murmured to himself. Philipp Wieler ducked into the tent at that moment and stopped still at the look on his friend's face. "I love Katya," Johann said aloud.

To his surprise, Philipp tipped back his head and laughed.

"I know. My sincere congratulations. Too bad you can't tell her."

"Perhaps I could send a telegram, just *'Dear K: I love you. J.'* "

Philipp grinned. "That would definitely give the village of Alexanderkrone something to talk about, and then old Mrs. Wuest would hobble out to Lichtfelde and tell them and they would, of course, make sure your people in Kleefeld knew, and then . . . "

"Stop, stop!" Johann was laughing now too, momentarily forgetting the violence and suffering around him. "Perhaps you have a point there. I'll have to wait to tell her in person."

They both sobered. "It won't be so long," Philipp encouraged. "Perhaps this year you will be able to go home for Christmas."

"Thank you, my friend. One can always hope. Now I must get back to work and you must rest awhile." Johann looked at Philipp with a trained eye. "You need to rest or you'll be ill. You know the danger of dysentery and typhus when the body's run down."

"Don't worry about me."

"Someone needs to. Can't do without you."

The men locked eyes for a moment before Johann stooped to leave the tent. He definitely worried about Philipp Wieler.

The summer days in the colonies had flown by, just like the storks as they flapped their way back to Egypt or Ethiopia or whatever warm climate called them away each autumn. Katarina was glad to be home. Days at the Reimers' had been lovely, as were the visits to Oma and even a shopping trip to Neu-Halbstadt. She and Mika had wandered through the shops and even tried on ready-made dresses. Mika purchased a chic little derby-style hat of deep maroon silk, with pure white plumes adorning one side. It showed off her glossy dark hair to great advantage. Katarina tried on a lovely straw hat with deep green ribbon encircling the crown and cascading over the brim at the back, but in spite of Mika's urging, she decided against the purchase.

"You know I'll never wear it, Maria. I prefer to be bareheaded until the weather's cold enough to wear a fur cap. Except when I'm riding Sunny, and I doubt she would appreciate the quality of this hat."

Mika had rolled her eyes, but she knew her sister was right. So today, back home at Succoth, Katya tied a kerchief peasant-style over her hair and walked briskly out to the stables. It had been much too long since she'd gone riding.

Freedom. Freedom to ride against the wind, to go where she pleased, to gallop through valleys and up hills, without having to speak to a soul.

Life had fallen into a routine again, but today was different. Papa had gone to Karassan to visit the banker, and Anna and Nicholai had gone with him.

"Are you sure you don't want to ride along?" Papa had asked. She was sure. She seldom felt lonely. Besides, it gave her space to think. She rode Sunny past the large grove of trees where the gypsies sometimes camped and dismounted. Tying her horse to a sturdy maple, she wandered off a short distance and lay down on the drying grass. The wild rye cushioned her head as she stared up at the sky, its serene blue shot through with an almost imperceptible brassiness and mottled by a random assortment of wispy clouds.

She let her thoughts drift with the clouds, but always they went back to Johann. Where was he now? Was he safe? Would God allow him to return to her, and would they actually continue where they'd left off? She had gone over this matter dozens of times since that week in July when Johann had come to see her. She vacillated between elation at his promise, substantiated by Susannah's claim that he was as good as his word, and doubt that he'd really meant what he said. Perhaps he remembered his words and wished he could recall them. Perhaps he would return to his home in Kleefeld and forget he'd ever seen Succoth or Katarina Hildebrandt.

According to the latest reports, the war against Germany and Austria-Hungary was not going well. It was almost impossible to send or receive mail regularly, especially when writing to anyone near the front lines. And she had no idea if Johann had access to a telegraph. Besides, what would he type? "I'm alive, as yet. We are losing the war; just wanted you to know." *No,* she thought, and sighed heavily. She must wait until he contacted her by telegraph or in person. But sometimes the wait was excruciating.

As September faded into October, activity in the gardens and park increased. Katarina loved to be involved. "The watermelon crop is excellent this year," said Heinrich as they sat together on the veranda enjoying the evening breeze. "Cook will be making a lot of syrup and pickles."

Katya smiled. "Did you stop in at the summer kitchen when you came back from Karassan?"

"Of course," he said. "Bustling like a beehive. I was surprised you weren't there. "

"I was for a while, but I decided to take Sunny for a gallop. The air is so fresh."

Heinrich smiled, but his eyes held a hint of a shadow. "Don't ride too far alone, Katie."

She looked at him skeptically. "Why not? Whatever could happen?"

"Oh, gypsies, travelers, you never know," he said evasively.

"I am safe with the gypsies—I think you know that," she said, without looking at him. "And who travels out where I ride?"

Heinrich tugged at his beard while he drummed a staccato pattern on the wooden arm of his chair. He looked over at her and then looked away again into space, somewhere she couldn't see.

"Do you remember when Maria and her friends were accosted by robbers in the colonies?"

"Of course. Why, has something else happened to her?" Katya sat forward now, hands on the arms of her chair, staring at Heinrich.

"No, no. Nothing like that. It's just that reports of robberies have increased of late, not so much here in the Crimea as up in the Molotschna. You need to at least tell me when and where you're going so I can keep track of you. War and unrest cause people to do things they might not normally consider. We're all aware that there is no love lost for us by the Russian peasants. In fact, they may well take out their revenge on anyone who is of German heritage or who has prospered. We fall into both categories, and I must warn you to be alert. You tend to overlook the bad in people, and that can be dangerous in times like these."

"I take it there is still unrest in the cities as well?"

"Oh, yes," her father answered. "I believe it will continue to worsen because absolutely nothing is being done about it. People continue to starve. Many have been turned out of their homes and winter approaches."

Katarina sat silent, leaning her head back in her chair, eyes half closed. "I understand your fears for me and I will do as you say," she agreed. "But I think it's time to do a little bridge-mending."

"What do you mean?"

"Our workers need to know we're on their side. I suggest we help them at the annual hog-butchering bee. Make a celebration of it."

"It already is a celebration without us."

"I know, but we could contribute some food, some hands."

"You mean buy the people's allegiance?"

"Papa, we've been through this before. We can't change the war or the internal problems, but we can help to build trust here, at Succoth. After all, we are all equal in God's sight. Would it hurt to go the extra mile?"

Heinrich sighed and then smiled at her. "We can try," he said, and she smiled her satisfaction.

The last Tuesday of October, the 27th, Katarina took Nicholai and Anna, dressed in ordinary peasant clothing, to the far side of the barns. There the Russian employees lived in a tiny gathering of cottages nestled in the shade of poplars and willows.

Although these people seemed to enjoy the shade of the huge old trees, they did nothing to further adorn their yards or gardens. These were purely functional. Katya wondered if they worked too hard on the farm, leaving no time or energy for their own lives. She needed to talk to Papa about that.

Today the courtyard in front of the houses was bustling with activity. Long tables had been set up in a nearby shed, and a coal stove glowed with heat. Outside in the yard, a huge black cauldron filled with water hung over an open fire. Katya took Anna with her into the shed while Kolya ran off with some boys to watch the men catch the pigs.

In short order, a couple of shots rang out, and Anna covered her ears with her hands and hid her face in Katya's skirts. The women working in the shed laughed and teased her. "It wasn't a pet of yours, child, was it?"

Eventually Anna let go of Katya to investigate some of the little girls' games going on in the yard. Katya moved over to the tables to help set up the sausage machine, tubs, and large kettle for cooking cracklings. The women laid out knives sharpened the night before and scrubbed all the surfaces to be used for cutting and wrapping. Papa had brought several large rolls of butcher paper home from Karassan, and this too was readied for when the real work began.

"Come! Come see!" called the boys, as the hogs were brought over from the barn on a cart. By a series of pulleys, the men raised each of the three animals so they hung well above the ground. They lowered them into the cauldron for scalding and then scraped them. As the first pig was gutted, scrubbed, and laid out on the table, the men began cutting chops, ribs, and hams, and the women started grinding meat for sausage and headcheese. Katarina found a place at one of the grinders and kept the handle turning until she thought her arm would come unhinged at the shoulder.

At first the other women treated her with deference, but once they realized she was there to work, they included her in their conversation.

Eventually, Katarina moved on to a farther table and helped an elderly woman wash out intestines to be used as sausage casings. The thin, skinned casings were soaked and washed repeatedly in hot, soapy water and then rinsed until they were pronounced pure. It was a difficult job because the casings tore easily, making them useless. Katarina tried her best with varying results until the old woman explained the trick of it to her.

"It's all in the lightness of the fingers," she said. "Old Nadia does this every year and now can do it as she sleeps!" Nadia patted Katya's hand. "Just a few more, maybe ten years, you can do like Nadia."

The old woman's toothless grin warmed Katya's heart and gave her courage to continue. "I want to learn," she said.

Nadia kept working. "Why you help?" she asked. "You get fingers all wrinkled and greasy skirts. Why you here?"

Katya continued to work too, glancing often at Nadia's nimble old fingers. "We eat this meat too. I thought I would like to help prepare it."

"You help or no, you still eat meat."

Katarina smiled. "I know. But it isn't fair. Why should I eat if I don't help?"

This time the old woman's hands grew still, resting in the bowl of warm water. "You come here is good," she said after a bit, "work together, touch souls. But you will always live there." She nodded toward the mansion, just visible through the trees. "And I always live here. Die here. So it is."

Katya didn't know what to say.

Nadia seemed to sense her discomfort and added, "You are good girl. I see you come with herbs when we are sick. Now you here. You do this from good heart."

"I only want to help. We are all created equal in God's sight. I'm no better because I live there." She tossed her head in the direction of the big house.

"My child," Nadia said, resuming her work as she spoke, "too many bad people in this world, too many years of hate. One kind girl cannot make all the bad stop. You see?" She looked at Katarina as she asked the question, then looked out the door of the shed and said quietly, "But God knows."

"Oh, yes," Katya agreed. "God loves us all and does not forget your plight. Is it very hard for you to live here? Do you have enough to live comfortably?"

"Yes, yes," chuckled the old woman. "We have enough. Your father is fair man. Now," she said more cheerfully, "I go rest. You come walk with me to my house. Come."

Katya wondered why the woman had asked for her company, but she realized, as they stood, that Nadia walked very poorly. Katya supported her as well as she could, and they headed for the cottages across the noisy, busy yard.

Nadia directed her to the house on the end, the smallest one. As they entered the door Katarina could see it was fairly neat, with everything in place—much different from some of the cottages she had entered to tend illnesses.

They walked over to the bed, and Katya helped Nadia remove her lace-up boots and crawl into her narrow bed. She covered the old woman with a tattered quilt and smoothed her hair. "I'll let you rest now, and I must get back to work. There's a lot to do. Thank you for teaching me."

The old woman smiled her toothless smile and held Katya's hand. "You help, maybe people remember."

Katya nodded and left the house, shutting the door softly behind her. It was all she could do.

Back at the shed, she fell into the pattern of work again, this time kneading spices into the sausage mixture. Before long the sun was high overhead, signaling time for the noon meal.

The women had cooked a huge batch of beet soup and that, along with fresh-baked black bread, took care of everyone's hunger. The men took time off to relax while the women cleaned up after dinner.

Katya had just returned from one of the cottages, where she had carried the clean plates, when laughter at the side of the shed caught her attention. It was an unnerving sound, not humorous or joking.

She immediately changed her course, but it was too late. They had spotted her. Several younger men sat on the ground beside the shed, leaning against it and passing a bottle between them.

"Well, there she is now," said one, "honoring us with her royal presence."

A chill crawled up Katarina's spine, but she kept walking, trying to ignore the taunts.

"Hey, you rich woman!" another yelled after her. "Come here and sit with us. Hah! She thinks she is too good for us. Go get her, Ivan."

Katya's eyes grew round with fear. She picked up her skirts and ran for the front of the shed, right into wiry old Misha, the man who took care of Sunny and the other horses.

Stepping back, her eyes still large with fright, she could only stare and stutter an apology. A moment later, one of the men who had taunted her came around the corner into the shed, bottle in hand.

Misha spoke sharply, halting the man in his tracks. "Take your filthy bottle and go. No more to bother this young lady. Go!"

The man went, but not before sending Katarina a black look filled with a meaning she tried not to decipher. Misha apologized for the unpleasantness and offered to see her home if she wished. She shook her head. "Thank you, but I am home," she said, "and there is much to do here."

Katya managed to get through the afternoon with the help of some women whose children she had treated at one time or another. She was physically and emotionally exhausted by the time she and her brother and sister trudged home at day's end.

Anna had stayed within sight playing with the girls, under the watchful eye of one of the older girls. Kolya had seen what happened to Katya and was rather subdued. He attempted to comfort her.

"It's all right, Katie. The boys weren't friendly to me either until I beat them at arm wrestling, and then they were better."

Heinrich eyed Katarina sharply at supper, but he did not press the matter, allowing Anna and Nicholai to carry the conversation. Nicholai seemed to catch the look, but for some reason he kept quiet about the incident, which suited Katya fine. She would talk to her father later.

Later turned out to be immediately following supper. "Katya, I need to talk with you in my office," he said, and she knew better than to ask why.

"Sit," he said, when they had closed the door. "Now tell me. I see pain written all over your face, and I want to know about it."

She sighed as she sat in the soft leather chair beside the desk. "It was mostly all right, Papa. I had a wonderful visit with Nadia while we cleaned casings, and the other women treated me decently. It was just . . ."

"Just what? I want the whole story."

"The younger men," she admitted. "They were drinking at noon—you know the people like to celebrate when they get together—and, well, they just teased me."

"What did they say?" He didn't want to hurt her, but he had to know what had happened.

"They called me 'rich woman' and said I thought I was too good for them. I . . . I didn't go when they called me."

She looked down, waiting for her father's anger on her behalf. But he was silent. When she looked up at him, there were unshed tears in his eyes. He reached across the desk and took her hands while he composed himself.

"My little angel," he began in a choked voice. "How I wish you could live in a perfect world with your loving, trusting heart. You don't deserve to face rejection and hurtful words. You've never uttered them to anyone else.

"I feel so powerless, not just to protect you from what you experienced today, but from what may come tomorrow. I just read the papers we managed to get from up north, and the country is disintegrating. There's violence and hate on every page of the papers.

"And then I see you trying to right it all with your smile. I cheer you on because you believe in your cause, but it can't succeed this time. Everything's gone too far."

Katya listened, her heart tight within her. She had been chasing a dream, hoping to change the world single-handedly. What had happened today, along with her father's gleanings from the papers, completely deflated her hopes.

She met Heinrich's eyes with a hollow look. "If I can't make a difference here at home, what purpose do I serve? I thought that was my mission, what God wanted me to do. What now?"

Heinrich couldn't speak for God, but he tried to help sort it out from his perspective. "Nothing we do or learn is ever wasted," he began. "Whether God wanted you there today or not is beyond me, although I'm tremendously grateful that he protected you from bodily harm. Perhaps God wanted to teach you something about human nature. We cannot change everyone."

"Which brings me back to my question: What am I meant to do now? I feel so lost and without purpose."

"You misjudge yourself, my dear. To your family, you are sunshine in the day and the moon by night. You are a mother to Anna and Nicholai and a great friend and comfort to me. You have no idea how you bless us all. The servants love you, and you yourself mentioned Nadia and Misha."

She smiled slightly, soaking up the encouragement like a dry sponge.

Heinrich continued. "I've noticed the change in your relationship with Maria, and I credit much of that to you. I also happen to know a certain young Mr. Sudermann thinks most highly of you."

She looked at him and felt her cheeks grow hot. "He told you that?" she asked in a hoarse whisper, her eyes wide with hope and disbelief.

"I am not at liberty to divulge my conversations with the young man in question," he answered, a twinkle in his eye and a twitch in his moustache. "But I would go so far as to say you definitely made a profound impression on him and have given him reason to return as soon as he possibly can."

Sobering, he said, "Katarina, you may not always see the purpose in your daily life, but be assured that you fill a very large place in your family's lives. Others may not understand, no matter what you say or do, but we who know you need no convincing.

"You are a sturdy, sweet-smelling flower planted here at Succoth. Bloom where you are, and if God should transplant you, he will supply the necessary nurture for you to bloom somewhere else."

They sat in silence for some minutes, lost in their own musings. At length, Katarina rose and walked over to her father's chair. Stooping, she kissed his cheek and wrapped her arms around his broad shoulders.

"Thank you, Papa," she whispered. "You're the most wonderful father and friend I could ever have. I love you."

Heinrich chuckled contentedly. "And I love you, child. Never stop believing in your own worth, and always wait on God. He will never forsake you."

Chapter 24

 Snow fell early that winter of 1916 in the colonies of south Russia. The plums, peaches, and apples had been dried and packed away; flower stems clipped and seeds saved; the grain threshed, bagged, and stored safely in attics and granaries. Even an early winter could not take these hard-working people by surprise.

But the early, fine dusting of white powder from the sky seemed an omen, a sign that nothing was sure anymore. One could not depend on things being the way they had always been.

Maria Hildebrandt frowned and turned her back on the scene outside the large kitchen window. "We were to have a fall picnic today. Now what shall we do? Sit at home?"

Nellie Reimer glanced over at Abram and raised her eyebrows. She dreaded Maria's anger, which seemed to pop up more often and unexpectedly than it had in the past. Unrest had reached its long fingers into the colonies. No one felt safe anymore. Change was in the air, and not for the better. The Russian people communicated a strong distrust for anyone foreign, and especially the German people, and there were frequent cases of theft and injustice on both sides.

Abram sighed, shook out the paper he'd been reading, and laid it aside. "Come and sit, Nellie, Maria. We should talk."

Cornelia sat in a kitchen chair by the table, her eyes still on Mika. "Come, sit by me, child," she said softly.

Mika stiffened. "I'd prefer to go to my room. I have letters to write."

"And so you shall, when we have spoken." Abram's words were kind but firm, and the girl recognized his serious tone.

When she had taken a place at the table, Abram began. "My dear ones, our lives and the lives of those around us in the villages and on the estates are being invaded by a silent and stealthy enemy. This enemy is fear. It sneaks into our thoughts, affects our actions, and robs us of peace. This should not be."

Mika tensed, but remained silent. It was Nellie who spoke. "Abram," she said, her hands clasping and unclasping, "is it really so serious? We live our lives as we always have."

"My dear, you are well aware of what happened to Maria and Aaron and their friends. And I told you how David Steffen and his brother were robbed in broad daylight. Women fear for their children if they run off too far to play. There is reason to be concerned." Abram sighed. "But the problem, I believe, is not so much the danger as fear itself. We must make a choice as to how we respond."

He looked at Maria, sitting stiff and straight in her chair, her lovely face framed by carefully coifed dark hair. "Your fear, Mika, shows in your angry outbursts. We cannot change the weather for your picnic today, but I don't believe that's really what's bothering you."

Marie's dark eyes flashed at being so humiliated. Abram noticed, but continued, "I believe you're afraid of the future and of anything in the present that you can't control."

Cornelia fidgeted nervously and tried to convey silently that her husband should back away from this confrontation. Maria was too angry to speak. She raised her fine chin and glared at Abram. But his gentle nature revealed a foundation of steel as he leaned forward and met her glaring eyes. "Now you aim your anger at me," he went on, "but I am not the reason for it either. The fear goes deeper, to your own heart.

"There's only one way to deal with fear, and that is to put

our trust in something or someone stronger than our circumstances. God knows our fears and the real reasons for them. He also cares and remains in control. We must trust the Lord in all of this."

He reached out a hand to Maria, but she pulled hers away and stood, knocking her chair over backward. She was shaking as she finally spoke. "Trust the Lord?" Sarcasm edged her sharp words. "Why would I trust him? God allowed my brother Peter to be born an idiot, and then he took away our mother. My world is falling apart in stages, and I'm supposed to trust God. Well, I can't. I don't believe God is in control."

She was crying now and could hardly get the words out. "I don't know if I believe anything anymore." She fled from the kitchen to her bedroom, slamming the door with a fierceness that matched her fears.

Cornelia started to rise, but Abram covered her hands with his and shook his head. "Let her be, my love. She needs time to think about what we have said."

Nellie wasn't convinced. "Perhaps you shouldn't have been so direct. You've wounded her."

"That's the only way anyone can get through to her, by directness. I said these things because I love her." He looked across the table at his wife. "Someone had to say them. She's so afraid already, and times are worsening. She won't be able to get through it if she doesn't face up to it."

"Perhaps you're right, Abram. "Perhaps you're right."

"It's worse than before, isn't it?" Johann sat on a rough woolen blanket in his corner of the torn tent. Philipp lay quietly next to him, on another piece of dirty blanket. He didn't answer Johann's question because the answer was obvious.

"We used to have barracks and decent tents," continued

Johann. "Now all we have are torn pieces of tarp secured to trees. Our blankets warm the wounded, leaving us only rags, and our food shipments are picked over by the time they get here, if they arrive at all."

Philipp remained quiet, so Johann kept his further thoughts to himself. The worst enemy in the camps now was not the cold or the lack of shelter, food, and clean water, but the result of them: disease. The ravages of war and lack of sanitation had promoted the spread of the deadly typhoid virus.

In Johann and Philipp's camp, lice promoted typhus, another dreaded disease. In spite of cooler weather, the vermin invaded every tent, every makeshift hospital ward, hiding in the seams of clothing and the folds of blankets, spreading the disease. A dark, purplish rash accompanied the severe headache and high fever.

So far, Johann and Philipp remained free of the typhus. Each night, or whenever they had a few moments, they rid themselves of vermin. But Johann worried about Philipp. The man gave himself so totally to the nursing of wounded that he had no energy left for himself. He went without sleep for days and offered his meager rations to those who needed extra nutrition.

"You must take care of yourself," Johann gently reminded his friend. "If you contract typhus or dysentery, you will be of no use to the patients."

"I do God's will, and he cares for me," was Philipp's answer. He would not allow any more discussion on the matter, so there was little Johann could do.

The men in camp had been through a terrible night—a train full of human wreckage delivered at nightfall, with only a handful still alive at dawn. Philipp almost collapsed on the way to their tent as the sun spread its warming rays over the horizon. He'd only reached his blanket with Johann's help.

In the dimness, Johann failed to notice the telltale rash, but once the sun rose, it showed up clearly. Philipp attempted to rise later, but his strength was gone. The doctor, a tall, thick-set man of about forty years, took one look at him and confirmed the worst: spotted fever. Typhus.

Johann ran for water and started to bathe Philipp's face. "Philipp! Philipp, you must fight this thing. Think of Agnetha!" The sick man's eyes rolled back, and he breathed shallowly, with his mouth open. He remained in a stupor for at least an hour while Johann tried to cool his burning skin and encourage him.

Just as he began to despair of getting a response, Philipp's eyes focused, and he stared around him. Throwing off his blanket, he sat up and began to speak excitedly, his words garbled and slurred. There was sheer panic in his eyes.

It took a moment for Johann to react. Then he grasped his friend's shoulders and eased him back to the ground. The delirium was more unsettling than the stupor had been.

The doctor returned, and between them they moved the sick man to the typhus isolation tent, where he was surrounded by at least six other typhus cases. Johann didn't want to leave him alone. He knew what was coming, the intense headaches with alternating delirium and stupor. He had seen it all too many times. To know this was to be Philipp's fate nearly drove him mad.

"He has a wife, Lord," he scolded in muttered words. "She needs him. Why not take me? Who would miss me?" He thought then of Katya. She would survive without him. She was strong. But in the same thought, he couldn't quite give up his hope of seeing her again. Perhaps that was it: Philipp believed he would die in the service. Johann had no such prophetic foresight. He would fight to survive.

"You! Get out now. This is isolation." The orderly assigned to the tent snarled as Johann knelt at Philipp's side.

"I need to care for him. Please."

"I will see to him. You can't stay here and then rejoin the others. It's like a leper camp, you know. Death reigns here."

"Just let me talk to him a moment more."

"No. Now get away from here."

Johann backed off. He would wait. He'd come back and see Philipp when the orderly was out. He must talk to him, just in case . . .

His chance came later that day. The man in charge of the typhus cases sat wearily sipping weak tea just outside the tent. Johann slipped around the back and in through a large tear in the canvas.

Sickening smells and heart-rending moans assailed his senses as his eyes adjusted to the dimness. Each moaning form resembled the others, except for a few that were thrashing about. He dared not touch anyone or anything for fear of spreading the disease, but his eyes found Philipp and he moved toward him.

Wieler's small form had become so emaciated that he was almost unrecognizable. His large eyes were glazed over, staring at nothing, his cheeks so sunken it appeared he had no teeth in his mouth.

"Philipp," whispered Johann, as he bent over his friend. "Philipp, it's me." The eyes continued to stare, then cleared and focused. Slowly, Philipp moved his head to one side and met Johann's eyes.

"Philipp. I'll bring you my tea and biscuits. You need strength to recover from this."

Philipp's eyes closed, and he shook his head slowly from side to side. Johann stopped speaking and waited in dread. Philipp moistened his lips with his tongue and tried to speak. A moan escaped him before he could command his voice to speak.

"I love . . . Agnetha . . . always." He paused for breath. "Hans. Brother. Help her . . ." He could say no more and lapsed into fevered silence.

Sweat poured off Johann's face as he edged closer. "Help her?"

The slightest smile appeared on the sick man's face as Johann said the words he had waited to hear. Just as softly as it came, the smile faded and the eyes glazed again. Stunned and hurting, Johann stared at the still form.

"Hey, you! I told you you're not allowed in here!" The voice of the typhus medic shocked Johann into reality, and he slipped out the back of the tent.

Stumbling blindly away from the "death tent," he broke through the trees surrounding the camp. The November air was cool and crisp; trees stretched out bare limbs like so many scrawny frozen corpses. Johann kept walking, trying to forget Philipp's face, with its wide eyes and gaping mouth. But the image kept coming back, like a slow-motion film he had seen once in Prischib. In the darkness, the trees were grotesque wooden ghosts grabbing for him, ready to wrap him in their terror and consume him.

Sobbing and shaking with shock and fear, Johann fought his way through the woods and emerged onto open prairie. In his surprise to be free, he tripped and sprawled face down in the dry, wild grass. He tried to rise, but the effort was too great. "Let me die here," he whispered, "I can't get through this without Philipp. Just let me die."

On the edge of no-man's-land in the middle of the Great War, Johann gave himself up to his fate. "I can't go another step," he murmured, cushioning his head on his hands. "I don't care anymore." And he slept there, in a patch of moonlight.

"Johann. Johann."

He tried to turn away from the sound, but the voice was insistent. Finally, he raised his head to see who called him. *Maybe it's Philipp,* he thought, then remembered how his friend had looked in the typhus tent. No, this was a man with medium build and curly red hair, crouched beside him and gently shaking his shoulder.

"Johann, get up now. We must take shelter in the trees."

Maybe this is a dream, he thought as he pulled himself groggily to his feet. The stranger took his arm and led him back. The trees didn't look at all ghostly now, but sheltering, covering, secure. Just within the boundary of the woods, the stranger stopped and motioned for Johann to sit.

"Here." The man offered him a mug of hot tea. "Have some. And my biscuits."

When Johann started to refuse, the man pressed him. "I have connections," he said. "My needs are all supplied."

Johann ate and discovered the biscuits were moist and fresh, not like the pieces of petrified dough he received most days. The tea held a hint of sweetness, like honey, soothing, calming, strengthening. Johann glanced over at the stranger and asked, between bites, "Who are you? I don't recall seeing you before."

The stranger smiled. "Oh, I'm in the same camp as you, but my job keeps me mostly behind the scenes. You may call me Joel."

Narrowing his eyes, Johann tried to remember if he'd seen this fellow before, but he came up blank. Before he could speak his thoughts, his companion spoke.

"This last while has been hard on you. Don't give up. You'll make it through. Many people rely on you."

Johann shook his head and looked at his feet. "No. I can't go on. I'm spent. Without Philipp I don't even want to try . . ." He covered his face with his hand to hide the fresh tears. Again he felt the comforting hand on his shoulder.

Gradually, his emotions eased, and Johann leaned back against a tree. He pulled off his glasses and rubbed them clean with the corner of his shirt. The cool November air awakened his senses, and his companion buoyed up his spirits.

"How can you be so positive? You're involved in the same war as I, and we're dying by dozens." Johann looked at Joel and waited for his reply.

"Oh, we're in the same war, definitely. Sometimes it seems beyond hope, but the end is in the hands of One who knows all and sees all. Remember, Hans?"

Johann smiled slightly and nodded. "I know, but I didn't remember for a while."

"When you're with God, you're never alone."

"That's what I thought, but Philipp is dying, may be dead now, and I can't even see him. Once he's gone I'll be alone. So often I've thanked God for bringing Wieler and me together, for his encouragement and patience with me."

"Mmm." Joel nodded, looking up through the branches to the stars beyond. "And who have you encouraged?"

Johann turned to stare at this stranger, indignant that he would cause him guilt at such a time of pain. Joel returned his stare, and finally Johann looked away.

"All right. I've used up all the help and haven't passed it on. Just trying to survive."

"As are all the others in this camp. Someone there needs your words just like you needed Philipp's."

"Is he gone then?" Johann's question was spoken so softly, the words seemed to linger in the air.

Joel smiled and answered, "You needn't worry about Philipp Wieler."

"You mean he's better? He'll recover?"

Joel shook his head slowly and gazed into Johann's eyes. "He is no longer your responsibility, friend. Now you must go on and fulfill your calling."

With that, Joel stood and stretched. "Time to be going back." He pointed Johann in the direction of the camp and followed him.

A new energy seeped into Johann's veins, born of hope, of

purpose, and of destiny. He spoke over his shoulder to his companion. "It's good we met, Joel. We will need each other in the days ahead." Shaking his head he said, "I honestly can't recall seeing you in camp."

"Don't put your trust in men, but in God," Joel said, ignoring Johann's last remark. "He has planned all your days and will give you everything you need."

"Thanks, Joel. You're heaven sent."

The lanterns of the medical camp shone dimly through the branches, welcoming them back. "I suppose I'd better get back to work or I'll be in trouble," Johann said. He glanced behind, but his friend was nowhere to be seen.

"What . . . Joel? Where did you . . ?" A chill ran up Johann's spine as he looked into the blackness. There was no one anywhere near, and why would Joel just leave without bidding him farewell? *Perhaps it was all a dream,* thought Johann, fingering the cup in his hand. The cup! It was Joel's cup. Just an ordinary tin one, but Johann had not taken it with him when he stumbled away from camp. Joel had given it to him. Joel was God's messenger. He shook his head in wonder, then lifted his chin and strode off with renewed energy to resume his duties.

Katarina's duties had multiplied over the past couple of months. Some were her own choice, such as visiting with Misha out in the stables. But other duties just appeared.

Last week, for example, old Nadia had come down with a fever, and insisted that Katya tend to her. "I am old, and my pleasures are few," the lady had said. "You, Katarina Hildebrandt, are one of them."

Katya took the praise with joy but also some caution. She had felt defeated after the butchering bee, and it had taken a toll on her confidence.

"Be patient," her father told her. "You are only one. You can't do it all."

"But I am one, Papa."

Katya and Heinrich had spent many hours pouring over Succoth records and documents, discussing business. Things that had never held interest for Katarina now filled her mind.

"You know, Papa," she said one day as they sat in the library, "Mika would be so much quicker at this than I am."

"Perhaps," he said, looking at her fondly, "but you are here and she is not. That is one reason. The other is that where she uses her head, you use your heart. Succoth is a matter of the heart for us, isn't it?"

Katarina smiled. "Yes." She looked at the fire in the large, stone grate, then back to her father. "I have a question," she said.

"Ask it."

"Would it be possible for me to meet the priest in Karassan, the one who receives your donations?"

"Why would you want to meet him?"

She shrugged her shoulders. "It would complement my knowledge of Succoth." She looked at him for his answer. "What do you think?"

"Hmmm." His eyes twinkled. "How about a buggy ride to Karassan this afternoon? You can even stop at Mr. Janzen's bookstore and see if he has any new arrivals for you to read."

Katarina grinned and jumped up to place a kiss on her father's cheek. "I'll go get ready."

As soon as Cook finished serving lunch, Heinrich and Katarina drove northwest for the ten-verst ride to Karassan. The air was cool now, with autumn drawing to a close and winter breathing down its neck. Katarina didn't completely understand her wish to meet the Russian Orthodox priest who had agreed to be a liaison between the giver and the needy. Perhaps he would react toward her as her Russian neighbors had, with suppressed hatred. On the other hand, he could be an ally.

As their buggy rolled down Main Street, friends and acquaintances waved and called greetings. Heinrich stopped near the library, and he and Katya got out. After tying the horse, they walked past the library and rounded a corner to meet the road leading west to Salgir Kiyat. On the far side of the street, partially surrounded by tall, bare trees, stood a small cathedral. It was elaborately built of limestone and brick, complete with a distinctive onion-shaped dome, but it was in deteriorating condition. As they entered the vestry door, Katarina noticed the ornate carving that followed the line of the roof.

It was dim inside the church, lit only by candles and rays of sunlight that filtered through the stained glass. Sorrowful paintings of a dying Christ hung along the walls, interspersed with aged and fraying tapestries that depicted judgment day. Worn gold gleamed faintly from the frame on a depiction of the virgin and child. A lone figure, robed in a dark cassock and crowned by an elaborate headpiece, knelt before an altar on a raised platform. He seemed not to sense their presence.

Heinrich and Katarina waited respectfully in the holy hush. The church seemed so different from their brightly lit, austere church building, yet strangely familiar. After some time, the priest stood, crossed himself, and rearranged several icons on the table beside the altar. He turned to meet the intruders, for that was how Katya felt, barging into this holy place to satisfy her curiosity.

The priest advanced toward them. Katya looked to her father to see if they should meet him halfway, but he stopped her with a hand on her arm. No one spoke. The man passed them in silence and motioned them into a small room. He turned to pull the door closed behind them, then locked eyes with Heinrich and broke into a warm smile. Clasping each other's shoulders, the two men chuckled and exchanged greetings in Russian.

Heinrich turned to Katarina, put his arm around her, and said, "This is my daughter, Katarina. She knows as much about Succoth as I do, perhaps more. Katarina, meet Father Serge Ivanovich, Russian Orthodox priest for Karassan."

Father Serge met her eyes, then bowed his head in greeting. "Welcome to Karassan," he said. Turning back to Heinrich, he asked, "What brings you here, friend? The usual or some new benevolence?" His words were sincere but carried a subtle hint of sarcastic humor, as if to say, "How may we honor your giving today?"

Katarina caught the nuance and gave a tiny smile, which the priest did not miss. It seemed to spur him on. "Come, sit. Your philanthropy must weary you."

Chuckling, Heinrich seated himself in one straight-back chair and Katya sat in another. Father Serge faced them from behind his battered desk and smiled. "God is good. Let us thank him." He held his hands over their heads and murmured a litany of thanksgiving that made Katarina's soul tingle. "One Lord, one Spirit . . ." echoed in her mind as the priest sat down and began to converse with her father.

The men spoke of the weather, the crops, markets, and world affairs. Katya listened intently, fascinated by the easy exchange between two men from such diverse worlds. Perhaps not as diverse as she had thought.

"Katarina wished to witness this part of Succoth affairs," said Heinrich. "She has been learning much."

"And is she duly impressed with her father's charity?" The man addressed Heinrich but looked at Katarina. She returned his look without her usual shyness. The man was really quite young for his position—in his early thirties, perhaps—with a transparent nature. She liked him, as much as one can like a stranger. His eyes still questioned her.

She answered him evenly. "It is not my father's charity that impresses me, but his response to the blessings God has given. We consider it a matter of stewardship."

With a pleased smile, the father again nodded, this time in approval. "You've done well, Heinrich Davidovitch." Then to Katarina he said, "Integrity is one of the greatest virtues a man or woman can have. Commitment to God is another. Hold fast to these, Miss Hildebrandt, and you will weather any storm. And if I can ever be of assistance to you, do not hesitate to ask."

Katarina treasured the young priest's openness and sincerity. He obviously possessed the qualities he had just described.

Heinrich and Father Serge completed their simple transaction and stood in farewell. "God keep you and your family," said the priest, his hand on the heavy gold cross that hung from a chain around his neck.

"And you."

The men shook hands. Father Serge bowed to Katarina, and father and daughter walked out of the church into the early winter sun.

"He loves the Lord," said Katya, as they walked briskly back to Main Street.

"I believe so. Does that surprise you?"

She smiled. "I never cease to be surprised by God."

Another blizzard bombarded the capital, forcing the people indoors. "Blasted weather isn't fit for man or beast," lamented Paul Gregorovich, rubbing his hands together to warm them over the woodstove. Several other men, mostly young, muttered their agreement.

Grisha, however, merely smiled and shook his head. "Paul Gregorovich, you pathetic southerner. Where's your mettle, your steel?"

He continued to grin, and Paul swore. "I'll tell you something. I don't intend to stay here forever. There has to be action south of here, and when there is, I'll be there."

The small, dim room gradually warmed from the fire and the number of bodies. As the temperature improved, so did the temperament of the gathering. The men began bantering about everything from the weather to their jobs or studies.

Grisha, the most composed of the group, sat quietly watching the young men. He slouched in his chair, tipped onto its back legs. His hat was pulled down on his forehead, his eyes shadowed, but any student of human nature could sense the fire burning in those eyes.

Let them calm their nerves, he told himself, *and then we'll talk.* The older man continued to watch as his acquaintances joked. It was survival, he knew, this feigned lightheartedness. *When the world does not go our way, we pretend; we change the rules. Self-deception—the age-old-escape.*

"My friends," he began, then waited until their attention focused on him. "We have assembled to discuss the political situation and our part in the greater scheme of things.

"Kamenev has been in touch." Here he glanced at Paul and noted the disdain on his face. "Orders are to keep our 'incidents' small and scattered. We are to confuse and distract the tsar's men, to keep them wondering what will happen next. We are the instigators.

"Meanwhile, Kerensky will be addressing the Duma, pleading for a government run by the people to meet their needs."

"Alexander Kerensky is not a revolutionary," Paul argued angrily. "He's a social democrat, a *menshevik*. If we wait for him, we'll die of old age before anything changes."

Grisha raised a hand to silence him. "Tekanin, Kerensky may well be our concert ticket."

"And what Kerensky doesn't know . . ." began one of the

men, " . . . may well hurt him," finished Paul. Looking over at Grisha, he continued, "We use all the advantages gained by Kerensky's party to fuel our own train. And then, when Lenin arrives to help us, we go for the throat.

"Hmmm." Paul thought out loud. "So our little disturbances and petty thievery will further stir up the populace against Nicholas, pressurize our cause, so to speak, so that when Lenin returns, all he has to do is pull the pin and chaos explodes."

"Yes, basically," commented Grisha dryly. "But there is also the matter of hunger and cold. Once robbing and looting begin, there will be no stopping it. People are dying for lack of bread."

One in the group added, "You can only walk past a bakery for so long and not take something—its window crammed full of fresh rolls and loaves, a yeasty aroma floating out the door. When I think of all the hungry children and the elderly . . ." He didn't finish, the picture was so strong in his mind, with names matching starving faces.

Paul smacked his palm with his fist. "This process is too slow. How many will die before we get results?"

"Many will die, whether we act now or later." Grisha eyed him squarely, willing him to be calm. *Since when did that bother you?* he thought. "But we will remain in control of ourselves until the time our plans can accomplish the goals we seek. We will wait." He challenged Tekanin with his look, and Paul met his stare evenly. "In the end we shall see what we shall see."

The others seemed not to notice the friction between their ringleaders. Or perhaps they knew loyalty ran deeper than differences of opinion. They went on to other news.

"Rumor has it," said Mikhail Karakozov, "that the tsar's extended family is begging him to listen to the Duma."

Dmitri Soloviev shared his opinions on that bit of rumor. "Best thing anyone could do for the tsar . . ."

"If one *wanted* to do anything for him," interjected Paul.

Laughter followed, but Soloviev was determined to speak his mind. "Best thing anybody could do would be to get rid of Rasputin."

"Slay the dragon!"

"Save the country from complete and utter degradation."

"Prince Yusopov hates him mightily," said Soloviev.

"I thought Felix rather liked men."

"Better than women." Raucous laughter scattered across the room until Grisha interrupted with a word of caution. "Keep out of that one, boys. I have a feeling the mad monk will soon be writing his own death certificate."

It happened sooner than even Grisha would have guessed. He and Paul sat talking late one December evening. The moon shone brightly in the brittle midnight, a peaceful setting, if one had heat. About 12:30, they were startled by a loud pounding at the door. Paul leaped up and cracked open the door.

"Dmitri!" he cried, opening the door fully and allowing the young man to stumble into the apartment. "What on earth . . . you look like you've seen a ghost!"

Dmitri Soloviev stood with one hand on the table, panting, his eyes wide and terrified. "He wouldn't die," he gasped. "The beast wouldn't die."

Grisha stood beside him now, patting his shoulder and offering him a stiff drink. "Calm yourself, Dmitri, calm yourself. Drink this and take a few deep breaths. Then we'll hear all about it."

Paul shut the door. They all sat down, and Dmitri began again. "They tried everything, and he just kept going."

"Dmitri, where were you?" asked Paul, trying to get to the heart of the matter.

The young student looked at Paul uncomprehendingly.

Paul repeated his question with uncharacteristic patience. "Where were you tonight?"

Soloviev blinked and swallowed, then answered in a trembling voice, almost a whisper. "Moika Palace."

"Prince Felix Yusopov's residence?"

Soloviev nodded.

"And what were you doing there?"

His silence betrayed his guilt. Finally he answered. "Helping."

"Helping Felix?"

Dmitri nodded again.

"Helping him do what?"

Soloviev looked directly into Paul's eyes. "Helping him kill Grigory Rasputin, the mad monk, the beast." He stood abruptly, and Grisha moved between him and the door.

Soloviev began to talk, raking his hands through his hair. "It was supposed to be so easy, a bit of arsenic in the cakes and maybe some in the vodka. I was only there as a backup, you know. Just a standby. I wasn't going to dirty my hands at all."

"What did Felix do?"

Dmitri sat, took another drink, and wiped his lips with the back of his hand. "He . . . he had a little party, just a few other men, some music on the gramophone, some opium, and . . . Father Grigory. The priest doesn't care what goes on as long as it entertains him."

Grisha and Paul looked at each other and took their chairs again. Soloviev continued. "So Yusopov had these little cakes made and laced them with arsenic. One should have been enough to slow an ox, but Rasputin asked for more, said he like them. Smiled and thanked Felix.

"Meanwhile, Felix was beginning to sweat. He got up and poured Rasputin another drink, with a killer dose of the poison. He . . . he was shaking so bad when he handed him the drink, I thought he'd spill it all."

"Where were you while all this was going on?" asked Paul, incredulous.

Soloviev waved a hand in the air as if it didn't matter. "Behind a curtain. There for the show. So Rasputin threw back the vodka and slumped there on the couch, eyes glazed, staring at the ceiling. Then he shook his head as if to clear it and tried to get up. I think he knew then, because he gave Yusopov such a confused and betrayed look. He couldn't get up and just toppled onto the couch." Soloviev stopped and gave his head a shake too, bringing himself back to the present.

"So he was finally dead then?"

"No!" Dmitri shouted the word at Paul. "We thought he was. We went over to carry him out and then he seemed to come out of it. He kept mumbling about deceit and treachery and fighting us off. So Felix ran upstairs for a gun—we were in the basement, you know—and he ran back, aimed the gun at Rasputin's heart." Dmitri stood and took aim, his shaking finger pointing at a figure only he could see. "And he pulled the trigger." Dmitri fired his imaginary pistol and stood with his eyes tight shut. Grisha reached out and eased the young man back into his chair.

"Shot him through the heart at close range. The priest gasped, fell to the floor, and lay still. Felix emptied a few more bullets into him to make sure, and we left him in the middle of the floor while we ran to get ropes to drag him out. He's a big man, you know." Soloviev's eyes now filled with horror. "When we returned, he wasn't there!"

"What!" Even Grisha was spooked by now, his usual calm demeanor shattered. "What is he, some kind of demon, that he could just disappear?"

"Oh, he didn't disappear," answered Dmitri. He shuddered as he remembered the rest. "He had, in our short absence, dragged himself up the stairs and out into the courtyard. We saw the trail of blood and followed it."

Dmitri looked at Grisha. "It was supposed to be so quick and neat: poison him, throw him into the river, and be rid of him and all his evil influence. But there was blood everywhere, and the job still wasn't done.

"We found him in the courtyard, heading for the gate, crawling and dragging himself with those huge, beefy hands. We . . . we . . ." He stopped and covered his face with both hands, sobbing and choking. "We clubbed him and beat him. Tied him up like an animal, put his body in a sack, and threw him into the Neva."

Grisha put a hand on the young man's shoulder. "It's over now, Dmitri. He's dead, gone."

Dmitri looked up at Grisha, his eyes panicked, his face wet with tears. "But will he stay dead? Will he come for me? He saw me, you know. He knows who I am."

Paul was sweating and shaking as he considered the grisly murder. Perhaps violence did still bother him. Perhaps that was a good sign. Or at least Grisha would say so.

"It will take some time to come to terms with this, Dmitri," said Grisha. "You can stay here with us tonight or as long as you need to. And don't tell anyone else of this. The less said, the better."

"If people knew you had a hand in getting rid of Rasputin, they'd probably make you a hero," said Paul. "Maybe even a saint."

Dmitri shook his head and drew a rasping breath. "I'm a murderer. I'm an accomplice to a violent crime. I'll burn forever for this."

Paul looked over at Grisha, but in his mind's eye, he saw Johann Sudermann instead. His friend was telling him to be careful of his revolutionary involvement. He was warning him of his choices, warning and always looking back at him with love and an outstretched hand.

Chapter 25

Johann reached out his hand to steady his companion. A group of a dozen men staggered along a snowy stretch of road just east of the Dnieper, the last stretch between them and the Molotschna colony.

Some would have considered this a stroke of luck, being able to return home, and in one piece, but Johann had ceased to categorize his life by luck or circumstance. It was simply life—good and bad together, sometimes bad and worse. Not much could be called good in this war experience.

His life continued to twist and turn in directions he'd never anticipated. He could hardly believe Philipp was gone. He had died the day the stranger came to Johann, the ministering angel, as he had come to think of him. And while he grieved deeply, there was also a sense of rightness that Philipp Wieler could go "home" ahead of the rest of them. He had walked so closely with God.

They had exchanged no last words when Johann returned to the typhus tent, but then Philipp's speech had always been like last words: true, straight, encouraging. He deserved his rest if anyone did.

Johann glanced back at Isaac Neumann, whose one good arm clutched the stump that was left of his other arm. The war zone had almost overtaken their medical camp the day after Philipp's death, and Isaac, slowed by fever and exhaustion, had been hit by shrapnel from a German shell. In shock, he had run along with the wagons. Eventually, someone had pulled him aboard and left him to lie in the bed of the wagon, unconscious. It was many hours before someone attended to his needs, and his arm was past saving.

Johann shuddered as he remembered the amputation and Neumann's blind strength as he fought against him. With their morphine gone, there had been no anesthesia but unconsciousness or death.

He pulled his shoulders back and walked over to Isaac. "Won't be long now, friend. The sun is sinking. We'll build a warm fire and sleep right through till morning."

Neumann grunted and kept struggling along. The war had robbed him of his spirit, but he still retained amazing physical strength. Johann handed him a canteen and helped him drink. Some of the icy water dribbled down his chin, but what he did swallow helped considerably.

They'd been on the road for ten days now, this motley group of retired medical servicemen. Most were injured like Neumann, or like Kliewer, who was missing his toes on one foot and needed a cane for balance. A few had sustained wounds unnoticeable unless you looked into their eyes and saw the emptiness, vagueness, and absence of purpose there.

Johann was surprised and then afraid when his commander ordered him to gather these men and accompany them home. "What if I lose one or they just wander off?"

"Do your best. They're no good to us here in the shape they're in. I certainly don't have time to baby-sit them."

Johann shifted from one foot to the other. "May I ask why I've been chosen, sir?"

The commander tipped back his canvas chair and stared hard at him. "I'm not sure, Sudermann. It's just how it came out. We needed someone we could trust and who had served his time. You fit the bill. I thought we needed you here more, but it was the suggestion of my superior. You're headed home, so don't question it."

Returning his chair to all four legs, he added, "Your replacements arrive at noon tomorrow. Be gone by first light."

"Yes, sir." Johann saluted and turned to walk out of the tent. He was halted by the commander's voice. "God help you."

Johann glanced back, but the man was busy now with his paperwork and did not look up. Johann wondered what he had meant. Was the chance of getting back home so slim or did he really wish him well?

"Sir," he asked, "how will I know how to lead them?"

The officer gave him a level look, pen poised in the air above his documents. "He who has learned to obey will know how to command."

After a moment's hesitation, Johann ducked outside into the cold December afternoon and strode off in the direction of the supply wagon. If those were all the directives he'd receive, he would do his best to scrounge enough basic supplies to keep his crew alive until they reached their destination.

Now, thinking back, he was thankful he had hunted up so many blankets, canteens, and matches. Rations were meager, but a couple of times the group had happened upon small villages or gypsy bands staked out for the winter. In each case, food, water, and shelter had been offered freely.

They passed many soldiers on the way. Some were heading in a westerly direction to join the fray, but most faced east. Devastation was carved into their faces, and their clothes hung in tatters. They dragged along empty guns, not to shoot with, but to use as clubs or bayonets or simply walking sticks. They were forgotten souls wandering the cold, dry steppes, many more dead than alive.

Johann tried to keep up his unit's morale with encouraging words and goals—walk so far and then rest, so far and then eat. He had to watch his group closely, so rations did not disappear. Sometimes he wondered if Joel, his ministering angel, refilled the sacks of crispbread from time to time. It still hadn't run out.

"Another two days and we should reach Lichtenau." Johann had pored over his map last night and figured out how long it would take them at their present pace. As he said that, a rumbling sound made him look over his shoulder. A wagon approached, pulled by two heavy horses. The driver, a dark-haired man with a black moustache, drew back on the reins. Johann acknowledged him with a wave. Walking up to the horses, he patted one on the neck admiringly. "Fine beasts you have here."

"Best around." The man rubbed his hands together. "You are needing rides?"

Johann tried to read the man's eyes, but they were hidden in the shade of his hat. It was hard to trust these days. Sensing Johann's caution, the man said, "I trade you transportation for company and news. You tell me what you know and I give you ride."

"You've got a deal." Johann was too exhausted to consider long. "Come on, men, jump on. We're riding home in style." A few whooped with joy, others merely shuffled up to the wagon and pulled themselves aboard. Johann helped those who needed it and counted heads again. All were present. He was surprised they had made it this far.

"Mild weather for December," commented the driver when Johann climbed up beside him. "Most time it snow by now."

"Yes. I'm grateful we didn't meet with any blizzards or we'd probably all be dead."

"How far you go?"

"Molotschna. The men are from several villages. I have to make sure they get home. "

The man glared at him darkly. "Germans."

"Russians," Johann replied. "These men have sacrificed much for Russia."

The man snapped the reins. "A German is a German."

"Why did you pick us up if you feel that way?"

The man glanced at him through narrowed eyes but said nothing. Johann felt a strange uneasiness. He turned to check on his men. They were sleeping, most of them, a few staring vacantly at the passing countryside.

"Where are you from?" asked Johann cautiously, thankful for each mile they rode, willing to suffer the driver's disdain for the sake of his men.

"Galai Polye. A *Russian* town."

Johann felt more and more uncomfortable with the man, but he tried to be patient. They talked of the war and Russia's political upheaval. In several hours they arrived at Lichtenau, near the station where Johann had boarded the train over two years ago. The driver pulled the horses to a stop and waited for the men to climb out. Their eyes began to shine again with the light of hope as they looked around and recognized familiar landmarks. Home had been a distant memory for so long that it had seemed a dream.

"Thank you for the ride, on behalf of my men," Johann said, reaching up to shake the driver's hand. "I have nothing but these blankets and canteens, but they're yours to use or give away or sell. Good-bye," he said in local Russian dialect.

The man nodded and shook Johann's hand. "What is the name?"

"Sudermann. Johann Sudermann."

"Machno," he returned. "Nestor Machno."

Suddenly, the man slapped the reins sharply and horses and wagon careened away north to Lindenau. There he would cross the bridge to the Russian settlements west of the Molotschnaya River.

Johann jumped back and looked around to see if there was a reason for his sudden departure. A constable was headed his way. He stopped and asked, "Who was that driver?"

"He said his name was Machno. Never met him before, but he gave us a ride into town. We're on our way back from the Forstei."

"Machno!" The constable cursed and snarled the name. "Stay away from the likes of him. He's supposed to be in prison."

"What did he do?"

"He's a thief, a rebel, a vicious man without conscience, that's what."

"I just gave him our blankets and canteens."

The constable stared at Johann and shook his head. "Probably a good thing you did. He would've taken them anyway and maybe hurt someone in the process. But I'll never catch him. He can hide behind a fence post, and you won't find him. He's an arrogant fool. One day we'll stop him."

Johann nodded and turned to gather his men.

It took two days to deliver everyone to their doors. Wives and mothers insisted that Johann come in for coffee and zweibach or to stay till the next day. The food was wonderful and the peace blessed, but he longed for Katya and Succoth. Besides, he had another mission to accomplish before heading south.

"Agnetha. Help Agnetha." He could hear Philipp's slurred words in his mind. She lived in Grossweide, a village on the far eastern side of the colony, and Johann planned to deliver all his men and stop at his parents' house before going to her.

Mother Sudermann was overjoyed to see her oldest son. "You've come home. Are you on leave? When must you go back? Are you hurt?" Her words, which had at times irritated him, now caressed like a warm summer breeze. How long was it since anyone had fussed over him? Well, there had been Joel, but angel or no angel, he didn't have a mother's touch!

So Johann relaxed and spent a week with his family. He knew he should get to Grossweide soon, but there was no telling when he'd be back this way and family was important. He avoided his father when he could and bit his tongue when he couldn't. No use starting an argument.

But the day before Johann planned to leave, his father confronted him. "Why are you running off again? It breaks your mother's heart every time, you know. Ungrateful lout."

Since when have you cared about my mother's heart? Johann thought. *And now I'm a lout. I should've brought my commanding officer along to put in a good word for me.*

Instead he said, "I'm going to Succoth because they need me there. And I need them. It's my place now."

"You've probably got some girl there, that's what. Pulling you away from your home. What kind of a girl would do that?"

Johann bristled at this negative reference to Katya. What right did his father have to criticize her? He was ready to speak his mind, to get it all out in the open, when his father turned sharply away and stood with his arms crossed. Something about his stance told Johann there was more to this tirade than normal bad temper.

His father was hurting. He had never allowed himself much emotion except anger and frustration, and he didn't know how else to express himself. The realization hit Johann like a fist in his stomach and he didn't know how to respond.

Finally he spoke. "Father, I know you don't understand my reasons—sometimes I don't understand them myself. But I feel Succoth is where God wants me to be. The Hildebrandts have had a hard time. Their family is gradually getting smaller and smaller.

"And, yes, I do have a girl there. To this point, we've only been friends." He ran a hand through his hair and chuckled. "She cared for me, but I was such a dunce I didn't even know it. Anyway, I know it now, and I plan to ask her to marry me. After all, I can't live at home all my life." His father had turned partway back, and Johann could see his profile, his bushy eyebrows working up and down as he tried to gain control of himself.

"You're right about something," he growled. "Wouldn't want you here all your life eating up our hard-earned food."

Johann was silent a moment. Then he began to laugh. He laughed until the tears came and he had to remove his glasses to wipe them away. His father jerked his head up and glared, then his own shoulders began to shake. Johann put one hand on his father's back, and they laughed together.

The laughter was as cleansing as the tears, and Johann thanked God for this unexpected breakthrough. "You may be a bear to get along with, Father, but I love you anyway." A muffled grunt was the only answer he received, but it was enough.

Braced by the ever-so-slight progress with his father, Johann put aside his pride and mounted his horse to ride to the Reimers' in Alexanderkrone. He appreciated Abram and Cornelia, but Maria Hildebrandt's presence never failed to fluster him. He felt like a fool every time he saw her, and he beat himself mentally for ever falling for her.

He gave himself a shake as he set out, cantering his horse over the bridge. No need to carry this to his grave. It was time to leave the past behind and embrace the future. God had saved him from hell and from the war. After paying his regards in Alexanderkrone and carrying on any greeting they had for their family in Crimea, his mission was to find Agnetha. Then he would get down to Succoth as fast as possible—back home, to Katya.

How he'd dreamed of her as he trudged eastward from the front to the colonies, as he and his troop lay shivering beneath cold starlight. When he'd thought himself in love with Mika, he'd seen her face, her beauty, but with Katya it was more. When he thought of Katya, he smiled. She was friendship, shared joys and sorrows, and compassion. When he was with her, he felt at home. Together they could face any trouble. Sometimes he forgot that he still needed to tell her all the things he'd realized since he discovered he loved her back at camp.

He trotted his horse past the west windmill of Alexanderkrone and turned up the street to the fifth house from the school. He wished he would find Katarina out back in the garden as he had in the summer, but the garden was picked and cleaned, and Katya was back at Succoth where she belonged. He dismounted, tied his horse, and stepped up to the door. Perhaps Mika would be gone somewhere, and he wouldn't have to face her. He chided himself. He had been praying about his hurt and humiliation, and now he must rely on God's promised resources and grow up.

The door opened at his knock, and he looked into the flashing dark eyes of Maria herself. She was unable to hide her surprise, but her natural poise soon took over. Johann used the moment to practice his own poise.

"Maria, how nice to see you. How have you been?"

She smiled politely then and opened the door wider for him. "I'm very well, thank you. When did you return from the Forstei?"

"Just three days ago, actually. I have a few errands to do here and then I'm going back to Succoth. Thought I might be able to carry greetings from you and the Reimers."

"Of course. Come into the parlor. I'll call Mr. and Mrs. Reimer and make us all some tea."

Johann smiled to himself as he sat down on a comfortable chair in the parlor. God had come through for him. "The vision of Eden" no longer held his heart in her hands. The peace felt good indeed.

Katarina bustled down the hallway with pine boughs in her arms, determined to make this Christmas merry. So what if it was only Papa, Nicholai, Anna, and herself. They would include all the house workers and even have a feast for the Russian laborers. Cook was not overjoyed at the prospect, but Katya had encouraged her that *Pozdyestvo Krislovo* was a special occasion for them too. She still needed to think of all the details. Where was Mika when she needed her?

"Anna," she called as she walked. "Anna!"

"I'm here, Katie." The little voice echoed from the front parlor where the family had set up a tall, thickly branched evergreen tree and decorated it with thin white candles. Katarina smiled as she caught sight of a bright yellow dress showing through the boughs.

"Where can Anna be?" she wondered aloud. "I'm sure I heard her voice in here." She heard giggles coming from the tree. "I know. I'll just follow the giggles."

Laying aside the evergreen boughs, Katya crept closer and closer to Anna's hiding place. She pounced. Anna screeched, and Katya wrapped her arms around her. They tickled and screeched until both were tired, then sat laughing on the Turkish rug, surrounded by the scent of pine and cinnamon.

Anna leaned against Katarina, her arms around her older sister's neck. "I love you, Katie." She looked up at her. "I wish I had a mama."

Katarina caught her breath and gave Anna a squeeze. "Dear little sister, I do my best, but I'm not Mama."

"Oh, I know that. You're wonderful, but I wish I had someone to call Mama. I don't remember our mama very much, but I miss her."

Katarina rocked the little girl back and forth. "Me too,"

she whispered. "Anya." She looked into the girl's eyes. "Anya, I promise to care for you as long as you need me. I promise. Things don't always happen the way we want them to, but we must make the best of them."

"God knows about us, doesn't he?" Anna's blue eyes searched her sister's. Katya reached out to tuck a strand of fine, blonde hair behind the little girl's ear.

"Yes, God knows, liebchen. He's taking good care of our mama, and someday when we get to heaven, we'll all be together again."

"Peter too?"

"Peter too."

"And Mr. Sudermann?"

Katya smiled. "Yes. He'll be there."

"I hope Mika comes too."

A lump formed in Katya's throat as she pulled Anna close. "God will look after our family. We must trust in God. Can you do that?"

"I think so."

"Good. Now come help me decorate the mantel with these boughs. Our guests will soon be here."

"I'm looking for Agnetha Wieler." Johann stood at the counter of the general store in Grossweide. It was a cheery place, with the smell of spices and dried apples, fresh bolts of bright cotton fabric, and dusty sacks of flour. Jars of hard stick candy lined the counter at children's eye level.

The hawk-nosed proprietress measured him shrewdly with her eyes. "She lives down at the end of Main Street, past the landowners' houses. There are eight landless cottages there. Hers is the last one on the north side of the street."

"Thank you." He turned to walk out.

"I imagine it will be a watchman's cottage soon." Johann turned back at her words. "Don't know how she gets food enough for herself, never mind a baby on the way."

Johann stared. "A baby?"

The woman seemed pleased that her information elicited such a response. "Oh, yes. That strange husband of hers makes a rare appearance and then leaves, never to be heard from again. Strange character. Too other-worldly for my taste."

Johann' s expression hardened. "Philipp Wieler was one of my dearest friends. He literally gave his life for others. Perhaps you should check out your stories before you spread them."

The woman raised her eyebrows in indignation, but Johann didn't give her a chance to respond. Besides, he had to get to Agnetha's before the wildfire gossip did. He could just imagine the story this woman could concoct about a young man riding into the village to see Sister Wieler. Mounting his horse, he took off at a canter.

Pulling up outside the cottage, he dismounted and wrapped the reins around the hitching post. He removed his hat, walked up to the door and knocked. A small woman opened the door almost immediately. Her general appearance was not unusual, but her face had an angelic quality that took his breath away.

She smiled slightly and motioned him in. "Welcome, Mr. Sudermann. I'm so pleased to meet you, but your presence tells me that my Philipp is gone home." Her lip quivered a little as she said the last words.

Johann stood dumbfounded. How did she know . . ? But then, who else would she expect? She walked away, turned her back to him, and gazed out the window. They stood in this way for several minutes, Johann turning his hat in his hands nervously, Agnetha as still as death.

Then she took a deep breath and turned to him. "I'm sorry. I knew in my heart the exact time when he left us, but now it's confirmed. Please have a chair while I make some coffee. You can tell me how it was."

Johann sat down. "How did you find me?" asked Agnetha.

"I stopped at the general store."

"Ahh. Then you know all there is to know about me and more."

"I told her to mind her own business."

She laughed, a light musical sound. "A common mistake."

Johann looked at her questioningly. "It only fuels her fire," she explained.

Agnetha took the chair opposite Johann and looked at him expectantly. He squirmed. "Just tell me," she said. "I'm a brave girl, and if you hide anything, I'll only imagine it worse than it was."

He grimaced and cleared his throat. "Typhus," he said.

She nodded, looking at her hands, sliding her wedding band round and round on her finger. "There were . . . there were lice everywhere. I've only just gotten rid of my own infestation. We did our best to stay clean, you know, but once the vermin attack, they're everywhere.

"Philipp might have made it if he'd taken care of himself, Mrs. Wieler, but he never quit. Always working, comforting, doing anything that needed doing. I tried to tell him to take his rest," Johann's voice cracked, "but he wouldn't listen. 'God will care for me,' he said."

Agnetha nodded, tears brimming in her eyes. She wiped them away and looked again at Johann, waiting for the rest.

"One morning he had no strength to rise and that's when I noticed the dark rash on his face. The doctor confirmed it immediately. Then they took him away to the typhus tent." Johann stood and took his turn at the window. He couldn't bear the pain in Agnetha's eyes.

"They wouldn't let anyone in there, but I sneaked in the back one time, and we exchanged a few words."

"What did he say?" Her voice was barely audible.

Johann tried in vain to swallow the lump in his throat. "He said he loved you always, and then he said, 'Help Agnetha.' "

There was silence in the cottage for some time as each re-lived memories of Philipp. At length, Johann turned back to Agnetha. "I know life is difficult for you here."

"There are many kind souls who help provide for my needs," she interrupted. "They're not all like Lydia at the general store."

"Yes. Well I have a suggestion, an idea. Something for you to consider."

"Go on."

"I'm from Kleefeld, but I've been teaching at an estate down in the Crimea. It has become home to me and that's where I'm headed." He glanced at her and searched his mind for the right words. "I propose that you accompany me to Succoth. The Hildebrandt family is warm and accepting, and they certainly have extra room."

He said these last words in a rush and then stood waiting for her response. Again she was quiet for some time before she spoke. "Exactly what are you proposing, Mr. Sudermann? What did my Philipp ask of you?"

The realization of what she was thinking hit Johann all at once, and his face turned red. Stammering he said, "No, no. Not that. I have . . . Katya and I . . . we're, I mean I am planning to marry Katarina Hildebrandt. But I haven't asked her yet. But I intend to . . . as soon as we get to Succoth."

Agnetha smiled through her tears at his stumbling explanation, and he felt like a fool. "I'm so relieved," she said, "because I don't intend to marry anyone, at least not for a very long time. My Philipp was one in a million, and my heart belongs to him."

"Yes, he was one in a million," replied Johann, relief spreading through him. "I admired him greatly and learned much from him."

"Would you allow me some time now to think and pray?"

"Of course."

"Thank you. If you come back tomorrow afternoon, I will have an answer for you."

"Fine. I'll find a place to stay and return tomorrow. Good-bye then."

"I'm sorry I can't offer you shelter, but I wouldn't want Lydia to carry that news around. Besides, I imagine you've seen worse than a livery stable for lodging."

Johann nodded. He left the house, exhaustion and memories swirling inside him until he felt he would collapse. A nice heap of clean straw would feel like heaven tonight.

When he returned the next afternoon, Agnetha met him at the door. "Come in, friend," she said. "I've almost finished packing. We never did get our coffee yesterday, so I made some now." She poured him a cup and sat down with him at the table.

"I don't imagine I'll need any household effects, so I've sold them to pay for my train ticket. The Ewert brothers had offered to buy, should I ever decide to leave here, so I talked to them this morning. I made enough money from the sale to buy a ticket for you as well. Providential, isn't it?"

Johann stared at her, amazed. He had expected tears, indecision, and second thoughts. But this small woman was most extraordinary. In the space of twenty-four hours, she had accepted and adapted to a whole new way of life.

"I see I've surprised you." She smiled at his raised eyebrows. "I may be weak, but God is mighty. He has given me peace to accompany you to Succoth. It reminds me of Abraham, leaving his homeland to go to unknown places. God blessed him with a refuge, and I see no reason to doubt he'll do the same for me. Just drink your coffee while I pack the last of my things. We can hitch a buggy ride up to Chernigovka and catch the east-west train this evening."

She got up from her chair and disappeared into her bedroom. Johann heard a faint humming as she moved about, opening and closing drawers, snapping hinges.

After a few minutes she reappeared, her face serene. "I'm ready to go, Mr. Sudermann. If you don't mind riding out to the livery again to tell them, it would be helpful."

He moved toward the door and then stopped. "Mrs. Wieler, I have a concern." He tried to keep his eyes on her face. "Are you up to such a trip?"

"Don't you worry about me," she said, a hand on her middle. "Babies are not as fragile as some people think. Besides, God promised me this one would be mine to keep."

Smiling, Johann left to call for the buggy and returned shortly. Agnetha had few possessions—one small trunk of clothing, a box of personal items and mementos, and a worn valise in which she carried her Bible.

As they were leaving, another buggy approached and drew up beside them. A red-faced woman extricated her stout body from her buggy and puffed over to Agnetha. Reaching up, she drew her into a firm embrace.

"Agnetha Wieler, I shall miss you. You are an angel in disguise. May God bless you in your life. As soon as I heard you were leaving, I told my Herman, I said, 'She'll need some roasted zweibach and some dried fruit. It's a long way to the Crimea.' So I just waddled over here, hoping to catch you in time."

She reached over to her buggy and yanked a sack out of the back. "Here you go, dearie, and a jar of cold coffee to go with it." She stepped back, content that she had done her part.

"Thank you so much, Sister Louisa." Agnetha kissed the little woman on her round red cheek. "You are a servant. May God reward you."

Johann helped Agnetha into the buggy and took his place

beside the driver. Her few belongings were crammed in with the Chernigovka deliveries. Johann tipped his hat to Herman's Louisa and Agnetha waved. She smiled as the woman struggled back into the buggy, but never once looked back to her own little cottage. Johann knew, because he kept his eye on her. The words "Help Agnetha" still echoed in his mind.

Chapter 26

Autumn leaves had long ago fallen and been gathered and burned, but the air remained comfortably warm. After an early frost and light snow, temperatures had mellowed, and the sun returned. Katarina breathed in the crisp, clean air and smiled. Such a day! Usually she didn't go riding this late, but her heart grew restless and she knew she had to go.

"Stay on the main road and do not ride far, child," Misha warned as he saddled Sunny. "Strangers I have seen lately."

"Strangers?"

He sighed and met her eye. "Soldiers. Deserters. They come on their way home. Some desperate men there are among them." He tightened the cinch and pulled Sunny's forelock over the bridle strap, stroking her small head. "I do not like for you to go out alone," he muttered.

"Misha . . ."

"Is not safe . . . I will come." With that, he unsaddled the horse and began to hitch her up to the light buggy. At first Katarina was angry, but she softened as she realized how much the old man had come to care for her. Their friendship had deepened over the past months, and she respected him too much to insist on her own way. But she really believed he was overreacting.

"How's Nadia?" asked Katya, as the buggy bounced along the road past the church.

"Better," Misha answered, his grip tight on the reins. "Lot of rheumatism, so says her daughter."

"Hmm. I should drop by again soon. Bring her some more of my herb tea."

Misha handed her the reins. "You are good girl, Katarina Hildebrandt, maybe angel. But you must take care. There are some that have no conscience. They would hurt you without a thought. You understand?"

She glanced at him and smiled at the concern lining his face. "Yes, dear Misha. I will take care, and I will try to believe what you say about the dangerous people." Her smile faded, and sadness clouded her eloquent green eyes. "Why must we live in fear?"

"Because people are hungry, cold, and afraid. Fear breeds more fear and anger and violence. It is the natural way of men."

"Perhaps we women could do better."

"Very likely, child, but this is a man's world and so will always be."

All at once he took the reins from Katarina and pulled the buggy up short. "Time for to go home, Sunny," he said in a calm voice. A strange tenseness filled his slight form and transferred to Katya beside him and to the horse at the end of the leathers.

"What is it?" asked Katya, as Sunny began to toss her head and prance. "What happened?"

Misha snapped the reins on Sunny's rump, and the horse and cart turned a half circle to return to Succoth. "Men," he said quietly. "In bushes by side of road." He glanced warily behind him and kept Sunny going at a good pace.

As they rounded the curve near the churchyard, a lone tramp stepped out from the shelter of the trees. He stood in the middle of the road and held up a hand for them to stop. There was no way around him but through the stream or the cemetery, so Misha pulled back on the reins and brought Sunny to a snorting halt. The pony shied away from the stranger, dressed in rags, with pieces of cloth wrapped around his feet for warmth.

"Go about your business," ordered Misha angrily, shooing the man away as he would a pestering fly. But the man took hold of Sunny's bridle and held her still.

"I just want something to fill my stomach, and I'll be on my way." The man looked old, his eyes sunken and dark, his cheekbones jutting out over hollow cheeks. His skin was leathery and dirty, and his smell drifted to Katarina as she sat unmoving in the buggy.

"Nothing here for you," insisted Misha. "Away with you."

"But Misha," whispered Katarina, "we must feed him. We have so much, and he will die if we don't"

"Yes, and every stray this side of Black Sea will find us and beg for same."

The stranger stepped closer. "You should listen to the lady," he said to Misha, his eyes flashing to Katya as he spoke.

Katarina sat up straight and looked directly at the speaker. "If you will follow us up to the big house, you will be fed and clothed . . . and washed," she added. She turned a deaf ear to Misha's indignant mutterings. "Please drive me to the house, Misha, so I may inform Cook of our guest."

With a frustrated exclamation, he obeyed, nearly knocking the stranger over in the process. The man followed slowly, trudging behind, oblivious to the dust rising up behind the buggy.

"You have no sense, girl." Misha shook his head over and over, mixing his scolding with Russian words Katya was thankful she didn't understand. "I warn you, but you not listen. How I can protect you, then? Ah!"

"I'm sorry, Misha, but I must do this. God will protect. We are only to obey."

At the house, she jumped lightly from the cart and ran up

the veranda steps and down the hallway while Misha returned the cart and horse to the barn. Sunny's ears pivoted back and forth nervously at the tongue-lashing she received in Katya's stead.

Katarina reappeared on the veranda within minutes, just as the stranger dragged himself over and sat on the bottom step. She carried a tray to him and set it beside him. "Here's hot tea and buttered bread. Supper is almost ready, and I will bring you some."

The man stuffed the bread into his mouth, butter glistening on his filthy fingers, then stopped mid-chew and stared at her. After a few moments he resumed eating, with somewhat more grace than he had begun.

After eating and drinking everything offered him, he wiped his mouth with the back of his hand. Nodding to Katarina he said, "I thank you, Miss. May I wait here for supper?"

Katya rose. "Come with me, please." She led him along the front of the mansion and around the side to the kitchen door. The man hesitated, but Katya motioned for him to follow. They entered the house, and she pointed to a small room near the door where Fyodor sulkily filled a washtub with warm water. Handing the tramp a square of soap and a large towel, Katarina said, "Bathe yourself and then put on those clothes. They will be much warmer than what you're wearing. Fyodor will wait outside the door until you're done."

Leaving the poor man in considerable shock, she withdrew and stepped into the kitchen. The sharp words flying there stopped in the air as she entered. "Our guest will be ready for supper shortly," she said to Cook. "He will eat here in the kitchen, and I will join him. And," she said, looking from face to face, "he will be treated with respect." Her gentle voice carried an unusual firmness, and silence followed her out the door.

"Hmph," said Cook, after Katarina's departure. "Only for

Katya would I do this. Even Heinrich Hildebrandt himself would have a hard time persuading me. But," she continued, "she has asked us, and we will do it."

The staff prepared and served supper to the bewildered but clean man as if he were the tsar's brother, and Katya sat across from him at the little round table in the windowed alcove. "I'm sorry I can only serve you soup and fresh bread, but I think if you ate too much, you would be ill. A cup of peppermint tea afterward will soothe your stomach." She noticed the stranger was much younger than she had first thought, possibly in his mid-thirties. His gauntness added years to his appearance.

"Thank you, Miss. I have never been treated this way before." He ate more soup, then looked up at her again. "Why do you do this? You don't know me."

She smiled self-consciously and tucked her hair behind her ears. She spoke softly, and he strained to hear. "I have a dear friend who is somewhere near the fighting. I hope that someone will help him if he is in need. Besides, God blesses so that we may give. It is my duty and my joy to share what God has given us."

Shaking his head, the man blinked away sudden tears and smiled across the table. "Thank you. You've given me much more than food." He paused. "My name is Steffan Dobrovsky. I'm trying to get back to Ogus Tobe, but they wouldn't let me ride the train looking like I did. I left a wife and family there, but I don't know if they will still be surviving. Pray for me, sister."

"I will. I am Katarina Hildebrandt—you may call me Katya, and I believe God is greater than all the sorrow and violence in this world."

Later on, after the family had finished supper in the dining room, Heinrich called Katarina into his office. The room welcomed them, with its blazing fire and soft leather chairs.

"So," he said, as they sat down. "I hear you've been up to your usual behavior while I was away at the neighbor's this afternoon."

"Papa, he was starving and cold and so dirty."

"Which one?"

"Which . . . pardon me?"

"There are seven men sleeping around the woodstove in the watchman's hut. All washed, fed, and clothed. While you were out visiting Nadia, more men came, and Cook and her forces felt compelled, for your sake, to take them in. I do believe you've started something bigger than you'd anticipated."

Katya's hands went to her cheeks, now red and hot. "Oh, my. I didn't know . . . They must be the others we saw past the church . . . "

"Yes, they must. I wonder how many more will hear the word."

For several moments Katya sat still and silent, then raised her eyes to her father. "Isn't it wonderful? They are in need, and we can help them. We have so much, Papa. Surely Christ would not have us turn them away. Perhaps it is for a time like this that God has put us here."

Heinrich sat back, stretched his long legs toward the fire, and folded his hands on his stomach. "Ah, Lord, how can I argue with this daughter you have given me? It would be like fighting against you. Only protect us, Father, and give us courage and compassion to match our assignment."

"Yes, Lord. Thank you," echoed Katya, as tears slipped down her freckled cheeks and onto her colorful shawl. "Isn't it strange how joy sometimes hurts?"

When Katarina looked out of her window the next morning, a light snow was falling. Large, lazy flakes drifted softly down, carried on winsome air currents, to rest on bough and branch. "So liltingly lovely," she penned in the journal Johann had given her almost two years ago.

She pulled the quilt snugly around her as she sat on the rocker before the fire. "I wonder if the men will move on today or stay for more rest," she wrote. "It's only two days until Christmas, so some of them will no doubt try to get home in time. God, please take care of Johann at the front."

Putting aside her journal and pen, she rose and folded the blue-green quilt at the foot of her bed. Dressing quickly, she hurried down to the kitchen, determined to help Cook and her staff in gratitude for all they had done in her name the day before.

The big, bright kitchen smelled of yeast and anise seed. Katya inhaled deeply as she entered. "Good morning, everyone," she said. "I want to thank you all for what you did for those cold and starving men yesterday."

"We just did what our Katya would do," said Cook. "But I will need more help in here if they keep coming in bunches. So dirty and worn out they all are."

Katya smiled at the stout woman, swathed in her large white apron. "You are a prize," she said and gave her a hug. "Now what can I do?"

"Well, to begin, you can place the Pfeffernuesse on the pans as Hilda cuts them. I have bread to bake—lots of it. Hilda, put the vegetables in the soup now. Hurry, so it can simmer longer."

Katarina made herself comfortable on a wooden chair by the large worktable and carefully placed the small round bits of spicy cookie dough on the metal oven pans. "Two for the pan, one for the taster . . . "

"You'd best watch yourself, child," said Cook with a warning smile, "or you'll have one bad stomachache." Katie remembered.

About nine in the morning, between forming bread loaves and mixing cookie dough, Cook whipped up an enormous pot of oatmeal porridge for the "uninvited guests," as she called them.

A table had been set up in the wide hall just outside the kitchen, and here the seven men assembled for their morning meal. They looked proper in their clean clothes, with hair combed and a good night's sleep behind them.

Katya stepped into the hall to meet them, shy but in control, determined to see through what she had begun.

The men got to their feet as she approached. Their self-appointed spokesman, Steffan Dobrovsky, nodded to her and cleared his throat. "Miss Hildebrandt, we all here thank you for helping us. We do not know how to ever repay your kindness. Some of us must move on, but Mikhail and Boris, they stay to work for their food and shelter, if you could use them." He pointed to two men in the group, one young, very tall, and thin, the other middle-aged with sparse hair circling his shiny, bald head.

"I'll speak to my father about Mikhail and Boris," she said. "And you are all welcome. Perhaps someday my family and I will be in need, and someone will come to our aid. God bless you all." She retreated to the kitchen and the Pfeffernuesse, while the men gratefully consumed the porridge and cream, dried fruit, buttered bread, and steaming coffee.

Just before noon, Katarina took a walk to stretch her legs and enjoy the winter air. Wrapped in the thick shawl her own dear Oma had knitted, she walked the length of the veranda and out onto the steps, lifting her face up to the snow that caressed her with numbing little kisses.

Her eyes followed the path as it wound through the park, past fruit and flower trees and rose gardens, now bare of foliage. She frowned slightly as she noticed something on the path, as far along as she could see. Something, no some*one,* was walking down Magnolia Lane. As the dark outline came nearer, she could identify two people, on foot.

"Oh, dear," she sighed. "What will Papa say? Well, I'd best go tell Cook to add a bit of water to the soup to feed two more weary wanderers."

She began to walk back along the veranda, but her shawl caught on the railing. As she turned to free it, she glanced once again at the approaching pair. With a gasp, her hands flew to her face and she stood staring. At the same moment, the larger of the two figures seemed to spot her and stopped still. His companion, who now appeared to be a warmly dressed woman, looked up at him. She seemed to listen as he said a few words, then nodded.

The man set down the case he carried and began to walk, then run toward the house. Katya, her eyes blurred by tears, ran down the steps to meet him as if she had wings.

"Katya!" he called as he ran, almost tripping in the gathering snow.

She couldn't answer for sobbing, but in a moment he had folded her into his embrace. Time ceased to exist as they stood holding each other close. Finally he released her and scanned her face. There was no need to ask how it was between them. The truth was in their eyes.

"Oh, Johann, I can't stop crying," she sobbed, holding tightly to his coat. "You're here. You're safe." She reached out to touch his weary, bearded face.

"Katarina Hildebrandt," he said, his voice trembling but earnest, "I love you now and always. I pledge to love and care for you all my days. Please, my dear Katya, will you be my wife?"

Her tears now began afresh, her sobs shaking her strong frame to the core. She nodded her head vigorously, then buried her face in his coat. Gradually, the shuddering sobs faded and calm returned. As if emerging from a dream, she drew away and looked up into Johann's gray-blue eyes. His glasses, smudged and tear-stained, magnified the love shining out of them.

"You always were a woman of few words." He smiled at her. "I still need a reply to my request."

Taking a deep breath, she smiled back, her plain face radiantly transformed into beauty. "Oh, yes, Johann, I will be your wife. I will love and honor you as long as we both shall live."

Throwing his arms around her, he swung her in a circle until they both nearly collapsed with laughter.

"Careful, Johann," she gasped. "You'll hurt your back."

"I'm too happy to hurt. Where's your father? Let's go tell him."

"Excuse me." A small voice interrupted them as Johann's companion tapped him on the shoulder. "I'm sorry to intrude on this heart-warming event, but would there be some facilities available, and perhaps a cup of hot tea?"

Johann slapped his hand on his thigh. "I'm sorry! I forgot about you." Turning to Katya he said, "Katie, this is Agnetha Wieler, Philipp's wife. Agnetha, this is Katarina Hildebrandt, my soon-to-be wife."

Agnetha was again forgotten as Johann gazed into the green eyes of his best friend. Katya smiled warmly and turned to embrace Agnetha. "I'm so pleased to finally meet you. Is Philipp still at the front?"

Agnetha shook her head slightly. "Philipp is dead—I am his widow. Johann kindly located me and insisted that I accompany him here. I need not stay long."

Katarina's emotions were high, her face flaming, her eyes expressing all the joy and sorrow she felt at this moment. "I'm so sorry to hear about Philipp. Johann told me he was a true saint, completely devoted to Jesus. May God comfort you.

"Please know that Succoth is your home permanently or for as long as you should wish. We want to share God's blessings."

"Thank you, Katarina. And my congratulations to both of you."

"Come inside, Agnetha. Johann will bring your bag." She turned to him questioningly. "How did you get here? You couldn't have walked all the way."

"We walked and we walked. Only my love for you kept me going. And my companion's encouragement."

Agnetha made a face. "We took a train to Dzhankoi, hitched a buggy ride to the estate, and walked the lane. My trunk is at the road where they let us off."

Katarina grinned. "Johann can hitch up a buggy and retrieve it for you while we go inside." She reached out and patted his cheek, her eyes twinkling.

Bemused, Johann shook his head. "I will do whatever you ask, my dear, and then I desperately need a man-to-man talk with your father."

Laughing, Katarina led Agnetha up the steps. Johann started walking back to where he had dropped the valise. He kicked at the snow, feeling like a boy again, then reached down and picked up a fistful of the white stuff. It wasn't quite as sticky as it should be but . . .

Turning quickly, he whipped the snowball through the air toward the house. At that moment, the front doors opened and Heinrich stepped out. The wet wad met him on the chin, and two pairs of eyes darted back and forth from Johann to Heinrich.

Taking in the young people's shocked expressions, Heinrich could scarcely suppress his laughter. His voice boomed, "As soon as you come inside, son, you and I will have a long talk."

"This year, *Weinachten* came early," said Anna, rolling a long, golden ringlet around her small finger. "I have my teacher back and a new brother. And he won't always tease me like Kolya does."

"Then I'll just have to tease for both of us," said Nicholai, tossing a cushion at her.

"Don't throw pillows near the fire," scolded Katya.

"And don't hit this beautiful tree," added Agnetha, gazing up at the glowing candles. "I can't remember the last time I've felt so warm and comfortable and loved. It's so good to be part of this family."

"You're welcome to be part of us, daughter, and that goes as well for your young one when he arrives," said Heinrich. "Our home has been too sparsely inhabited over the past couple of years. Now we have a new baby to look forward to and a wedding."

Johann and Katarina stood together watching the scene. Joy and peace surrounded everyone in the room. They each knew that whatever the future might bring, this day was special. They would always remember this gathering on the pages of their minds, etched in their memories. "This is the day that the Lord hath made. Let us rejoice and be glad in it."

Notes

Scripture in this book is taken from the King James Version and New International Version of the Bible.

Sentence pronounced upon Dirk Willems (p. 14) from "Dirk Willems: A Heart Undivided" by Paul Toews, *Profiles of Mennonite Faith,* Vol. 1, p. 2, www.fresno.edu/hc/dirk.htm. Historical Commission of the General Conference of Mennonite Brethren Churches: 1997.

"Song of the bridal wreath" (p. 20) from *Mennonite Foods & Folkways from South Russia*, Vol. 2, by Norma Jost Voth, p. 148. Good Books, Intercourse, Pa.: 1991.

The Author

Janice L. Dick lives with her husband, Wayne, on a grain farm in central Saskatchewan. She is a member of Philadelphia Mennonite Brethren Church and works as a distributor for Living Books, Inc. Russian history has intrigued Janice since her high school days. Her parents were born in Russia, and her husband's family has roots there. *Calm Before the Storm* is based on her years of interest and research. It is her first novel.